THE OF THE BRITISH VAMPIRE

THE FOURTH STORY OF HIS MAJESTY'S OFFICE OF THE WITCHFINDER GENERAL

PROTECTING THE PUBLIC FROM THE UNNATURAL SINCE 1645

Also by Simon Kewin

Stories of HM Office of the Witchfinder General

The Eye Collectors

The Seven Succubi

Head Full of Dark

THE ORDER OF THE BRITISH VAMPIRE

THE FOURTH STORY OF HIS MAJESTY'S OFFICE OF THE WITCHFINDER GENERAL

PROTECTING THE PUBLIC FROM THE UNNATURAL SINCE 1645

SIMON KEWIN

Elsewhen Press

The Order of the British Vampire
First published in Great Britain by Elsewhen Press, 2025
An imprint of Alnpete Limited

Copyright © Simon Kewin, 2025. All rights reserved
The right of Simon Kewin to be identified as the author of this work has been asserted in accordance with sections 77 and 78 of the Copyright, Designs and Patents Act 1988. No part of this publication may be reproduced, scanned, stored in a retrieval system or transmitted in any form, or by any means (electronic, mechanical, telepathic, magical, or otherwise) without the prior written permission of the copyright owner. No part of this book may be used or reproduced in any manner for the purpose of training artificial intelligence technologies or systems. In accordance with Article 4(3) of the Digital Single Market Directive 2019/790, Elsewhen Press expressly reserves this work from the text and data mining exception.

Quotes are included from: *Beowulf*, (tr) John Lesslie Hall, Boston: D.C. Heath and Company, 1892; *Dracula*, Bram Stoker, London, Archibald Constable and Company 1897; *The History of the Kings of Britain*, Geoffrey of Monmouth, 1138, (tr) Sebastian Evans, 1904; *The Mabinogion*, from the translation by Lady Charlotte Guest, London: Longman, Brown, Green and Longmans, 1848; *Le Morte d'Arthur*, Sir Thomas Malory, c. 1469, London: William Caxton, 1485, from the modern rendering edited by Pollard, A. W., New York: Macmillan, 1903; *Vikram and the Vampire*, Richard Burton, London: Longmans, Green and Co., 1870. Quotes from personal journals and documents in the internal archives of His Majesty's Office of the Witchfinder General that are no longer, or have never been, in the public domain, are used with permission.

Elsewhen Press, PO Box 757, Dartford, Kent DA2 7TQ
www.elsewhen.press

British Library Cataloguing in Publication Data.
A catalogue record for this book is available from the British Library.

ISBN 978-1-915304-82-7 Print edition
ISBN 978-1-915304-92-6 eBook edition

Condition of Sale
This book is sold subject to the condition that it shall not, by way of trade or otherwise, be lent, re-sold, hired out or otherwise circulated in any form of binding or cover other than that in which it is published and without a similar condition including this condition being imposed on the subsequent purchaser.

This book is copyright under the Berne Convention.
Elsewhen Press & Planet-Clock Design are trademarks of Alnpete Limited

Designed and formatted by Elsewhen Press

This book is a work of fiction. All names, characters, organisations, places, and events are either a product of the author's fertile imagination or are used fictitiously. Any resemblance to actual events, forests, cities, magical cults, or people (living, dead, undead or in Oblivion) is purely coincidental.

Bentley is a trademark of Bentley Motors Limited; Lexus is a trademark of Toyota Jidosha Kabushiki Kaisha (aka Toyota Motor Corporation); Mercedes is a trademark of Mercedes-Benz Group AG; Mini is a trademark of Bayerische Motoren Werke Aktiengesellschaft; Wikipedia is a trademark of Wikimedia Foundation, Inc. Use of trademarks has not been authorised, sponsored, or otherwise approved by the trademark owners.

Nihil obstat: Dorothy Aphrodite Coldwater
Imprimatur: Campbell Percy Hardknott-Lewis KCB DL,
　　　　　　　Witchfinder General

CONTENTS

1 – The Brief Afterlife of Nigel Digbeth 1
2 – Warlock 15
3 – Witchfinder General 27
4 – Scratching Sounds in the Darkness 39
5 – The Sound of Silent Houses 55
6 – A Family of Demon Hunters 69
7 – Next Level 87
8 – Descending to the Depths 99
9 – De Magicae Mortis 107
10 – Weapons for the Despatch of Demons 117
11 – Atmospheric Disturbances 127
12 – The House on Cathedral Road 145
13 – The Stationery and Office Paper Select Committee 159
14 – The Rules of Invitation and Banishment .. 171
15 – An Unholy Trinity 185
16 – The Brief History of William Bone 197
17 – Earthworks 205
18 – Hooded in Black 221
19 – A Final Act of Slaughter 227
20 – The Deeper Woods 241
21 – A Bone to Pick 251
22 – Life and Death 263
23 – An Ancient Vampire 275

For Brian Fotheringham

1 – The Brief Afterlife of Nigel Digbeth

> There seemed a strange stillness over everything. But as I listened, I heard as if from down below in the valley the howling of many wolves. The Count's eyes gleamed, and he said.
> "Listen to them, the children of the night. What music they make!" Seeing, I suppose, some expression in my face strange to him, he added, "Ah, sir, you dwellers in the city cannot enter into the feelings of the hunter."
> – Bram Stoker, *Dracula*, 1897

Grey. The universe was an endless, lifeless grey; no heat to it, no light. No sensation of any sort. Time did not pass.

Then, moment by moment, it did. To Digbeth, it felt like he was emerging from the unlit depths of some cold ocean, infinitely deep. He had no idea where he was or what had happened. How he had got there. Some hard surface was beneath the bones of his back. Oddly, he felt no pain, no discomfort. He was used to hangovers, to forcing himself to function despite drinking himself to oblivion the night before. This was ... different. He'd been *really* out of it for one thing. Had he been ill? In some accident? He must have fallen into deep unconsciousness, for God knew how long.

He surfaced. The impression of light came to his eyes through his eyelids. His body felt oddly light and strong, as it hadn't for a long time.

Memories returned to him in flashes and glimpses.

Yes.

He'd been instructed to finally break his cover and lure

the Shahzan boy into a trap, show him how weak he was before meeting his end. It hadn't worked out like that. That bastard Shahzan had *powers*. Dark magical powers. How hadn't he spotted that? The devious little bastard.

Digbeth relived the final moments on Lindisfarne: the flaring red heat blasting from Shahzan's hand, the fury of it knocking Digbeth backwards. The raging heat burning his flesh, consuming him.

Killing him.

There was no way he could have survived such an attack. Yet, here he was, his sluggish thoughts picking up speed. Then he understood what had happened, and a thrill like a golden light surged through him. Yes. That had to be it. Oh, he had longed for this, worked towards it, desired it with every ounce of his being. Earl Grey had promised it to him in return for his devotion. Earl Grey that, Digbeth knew, was no more than an underling himself. An interlocuter. Digbeth had pieced together the clues and hints over many years. Earl Grey was one more servant of the ultimate power: the Warlock himself. The ancient vampire who lay at the heart of so much that happened in transmundane Britain.

Ascension. This was what he'd craved for so long. Elevation to the hallowed ranks of the undying, to the immortal aristocracy. Power would be his. Freedom from pain and fear would be his. He would never have to fawn and scrape to any mortal again. He knew what they said about him: *Poor old Digbeth* and *Useless Digbeth, he was once so good at his job*. It hadn't taken him long to see that he had no future working for Hardknott-Lewis, that he risked his life repeatedly for no reward other than his pitiful pay packet. Now he'd have his revenge on all of them, the stupid weak sheep who filled the Office of the Witchfinder General.

And Shahzan would be the first.

He opened his eyes. He was no longer in the chamber on Lindisfarne, that was clear. He was in a house, grand and rich. Red and gold tapestries adorned the walls, torches in candelabras making the fantastical beasts depicted – dragons and unicorns – lurch and leap. There was no sound of the sea. He found his hearing was astonishingly acute. He could hear the hissing of each individual flame. Somewhere in a roof space up above him, a tiny creature scratched and scraped at a plank of wood, gnawing a hole in it. Far, far below him – many layers of wood and stone between them – he sensed a large mass of individuals. He felt the confusion and fear clouding their minds, picking it up like a radio tuned to a distant station. A wild wind howled in the distance, making the stones of the building moan and boom. Birds croaked and cried from the air. The leaves of lashing trees were a whispered roar. Yet more distant, he could hear the snuffling and baying of … were they hounds?

Somewhere nearer by, making no sound, another individual was sitting and waiting for him. Three or four floors above him. Digbeth was being summoned, he knew it with an absolute certainty even though there had been no word spoken. The call was impossible to resist. He rose to his feet, and the motion was … effortless. No muscles complained, no joints ached. He felt young again, strong. Stronger than he ever had before. He felt fucking *glorious*. The stupid stories that people believed had vampirism down as a curse, a taint. It was the very opposite of that: a rare and precious gift, carefully bestowed upon the chosen few.

He glanced back at the stone sepulchre he'd lain upon. This was where it had been done. This was where the Warlock had brought him back to repay him for his sacrifice and devotion. A stain, deep brown, marred the surface. His blood. He laughed at the sight of it. He didn't need it. There would be plenty more to be drained from others. He was *free* now.

Digbeth – or the thing that had been Digbeth – couldn't hear the breathing of the individual that waited for him. Of course. Nor, he noticed then, could he hear himself breathe. His heart didn't pump, his lungs had no need to labour. Stolen lifeforce flowed through his veins instead, lifeforce carried by stolen blood. The realisation sent more joy fizzing through him. It was true. He was unliving. He was complete.

Delighting in his lithe step, the way he seemed to float across the ground, he passed through a carved wooden doorway to a round chamber, the floor a mosaic depiction of some battlefield, cowering people being slaughtered by armoured soldiers. An elaborate oak staircase led upwards. It creaked beneath his feet as he climbed. The wind whistled through the window frames, fell back to a low moan. After four flights, he crossed a polished wooden floor to enter a library. The other individual sat there in a leather armchair, studying a book while he sipped from a silver goblet. The light was dim, but this apparently didn't stop the other from reading. A grand stone fireplace, carved like the high altar in some cathedral, was next to him, but the fire was unlit. Digbeth realised only then that he felt no cold, despite the rime of frost visible on the windows.

The figure looked up at him. An old man, his skin pale, his head hairless. If it were anyone else, Digbeth might have suspected he was afflicted by some terrible condition, some cancer leaching the life from him. But the other's eyes were sharp as thorns, sharp as metal spikes. Digbeth could feel the power coiling off the sitting entity.

The figure spoke through his thin, bloodless lips. "Finally, you have returned to the world."

His voice was little more than a whisper. Was there a hint of accusation in it, as if Digbeth had taken his time to waken? He nodded but knew it was best not to speak. In truth, he would know *some* fear in this new life of his. Figures such as this could snuff out his existence should they choose to – until he acquired enough power of his own. For now, at least, he could take out any resentment, any frustration, upon the common herd. There weren't many who would have power over him. And, who knew, one distant day, as events unfolded, it might be *him* sitting there in that chair, watching some other underling creep in.

The other nodded, as if Digbeth had done the right thing, thought the right thoughts.

"Do you know who I am?" the other asked.

"You are the Warlock," Digbeth said.

The figure scowled at that, moved his hand as if swatting aside an annoying thought.

"My real name, though. My title. Do you know who I am?"

Digbeth found, those eyes impaling him, that he could not lie. Not that it made much difference: *Warlock* was the only name he knew.

"I do not."

"You have been a faithful servant of the Office of the Witchfinder General for so long. Surely you must know something about me? Am I so … insignificant?"

Still that gaze pinned him to the air. He could speak only the truth. And he *had* searched, scoured the archives and case notes on MORIARTY, looking for some clue – but he had never found anything. No one in the Office, with the possible exception of Earl Grey, the Witchfinder General, knew the true name or the whereabouts of the Warlock.

Digbeth shook his head. "I know nothing."

"Yet you recognize me."

"You have returned me to this world. Who else could you be?"

The Warlock nodded, satisfied with something.

"You were accompanying Shahzan?"

"I was instructed to go with him, persuade him to follow a dangerous road. I did as I was told, but then…"

"Then he killed you. Did you truly have no idea of his powers?"

"None, no. The Witchfinder General said nothing."

"Your Earl Grey is dead."

That sent a bolt of shock through Digbeth. Earl Grey had been his protector. His shield.

"May I ask how?"

"Shahzan, of course. Once he'd dealt with you, he went for Earl Grey."

Digbeth tried to make sense of that. How was the boy

capable of such things? And, did the Warlock blame him for leaving Earl Grey, his pawn, vulnerable?

"Forgive me, I had no idea the boy had such power."

Another swat of the hand, little more than a flick of the fingers. "He is capable of much, that one. I assume you know where he lives? Where he goes, whom he sees?"

The Warlock's questions troubled Digbeth more and more. He had passed everything he knew about Danesh Shahzan onto Earl Grey: where he lived, who he met. Much of it was already available to the Witchfinder General via the case notes, of course, but there were incidental details that were never recorded. Friendly asides, hints, social visits. All of these had been dutifully relayed to Earl Grey. Didn't the Warlock know all this? The worm of doubt squirming through Digbeth was this: had Earl Grey kept information from the Warlock? Was it possible, as Digbeth had sometimes suspected, that Earl Grey had been using him in some private battle with the Warlock? Was this, his appearance now in front of the Warlock, an act of punishment?

He calmed himself. Of course not. If the Warlock suspected Digbeth of being Earl Grey's man, faithful only to him, he would never have brought Digbeth back to life. He was perfectly safe.

"I do," he said. "I can tell you everything."

"Do you know the whereabouts of his abode?"

"His flat? Yes. Details like that are obviously kept very secret, but I know where he lives."

"Tell me all you know."

When Digbeth had finished relaying all of the details he could recall, the Warlock said, "And, his acquaintances? Those he," – the Warlock spoke the words as if they tasted unpleasant in his mouth – "cares for?"

"His mother, of course," Digbeth replied. He gave the Warlock the address of her house in London. "Then there was the police officer I mentioned, Detective Inspector Nikola Zubrasky. But she's only a contact, I think. A friend, nothing more. There is, however, one other significant person."

"Who?"

"Shahzan has kept her a secret, made no mention of her in the official record. Reading between the lines, piecing together things I've overheard, I believe she may be a user. A magic-wielder. An acquaintance from the other side that Shahzan has formed an attachment to."

"Can you be sure of this?"

"He gives things away if you watch him carefully. Facial expressions, hushed phone conversations. Then there was the book, delivered to him in mysterious circumstances."

"What book?"

"A copy of *The Picture of Dorian Gray*. He leafed through it repeatedly, searching for something, fascinated. It was obviously significant. Anyone could see from his face that there was a … fondness there."

"And does he prefer females to males?"

"He does."

"Who gave the book to him?"

"I don't know for sure, but I looked at it when he left it in his desk. Someone had written *Borderlands Reading Group* in it. A woman's hand, I'm sure of it. Later, Danesh also made a secret visit to an address in Cardiff taking a Grafton Projector without authorization. He recorded no details of any of it in his logs. I found nothing when I went there, but I was eventually able to find a name associated with the house."

"What was the name?"

"Sally Spender."

"Were you familiar with this name?"

"Earl Grey was."

The Warlock nodded, his eyes narrowing slightly as he considered this information. It was new to him, Digbeth was sure. Earl Grey hadn't passed it along. Digbeth's previous alarm faded. The Warlock would surely value him now.

"What else do you know about Shahzan? Tell me everything, however unimportant it may seem."

Again, the iron compulsion in his mind. He could only tell the truth. "I've told you everything I know."

"What do you know of his brother?"

"So far as I know, he has no brother. He is an only child."

The Warlock held his gaze for a moment, as if he were shining a bright light into every dark corner of Digbeth's mind. After long moments of this, he appeared to be satisfied.

He nodded almost imperceptibly. "I have asked you many questions. Are there any you would ask of me?"

Digbeth nearly spoke, then hesitated. Was this another test? A way of discovering what he, Digbeth, really knew and didn't know?

"Will you tell me your true name?"

The Warlock's voice took on a lower note, a hiss to it. "Why do you wish to know that?"

Not a question he should have asked. He changed the subject: "Is it true you control everything? Everything taking place in the supernatural underworld, I mean."

"Not all of it, alas, but a great deal of it. Much that takes place in the more mundane walks of life as well, though. A lot of what your governments do only makes sense when you know they are acting in the interests of a small vampiric cabal."

"Is it true you control English Wizardry?"

"That is the common belief in the Office?"

"It is one theory."

"Well. An unimportant one, now. English Wizardry have been taken off the board. But, yes. English Wizardry were one of the blades that I wielded. They were a façade; useful idiots, fervently believing all that *true English magic* nonsense. They happily got their hands dirty so I didn't have to. When I needed to eliminate an enemy, I needed only to whisper some cant about a threat to the *Old Ways* and they jumped."

"Are you even from here? Originally, I mean?"

The Warlock seemed amused at the question. "Here? What is *here*?"

"England. Britain."

"Ah. Well, I wasn't born on these particular islands, if

that's what you mean. Borders and countries come and go. But, after years of travelling in former days, I have certainly come to regard these domains as my home. Surely centuries of living here have naturalized me now?"

For some reason, the ancient vampire seemed to be happy to reminisce about his origins. Digbeth wondered about that. Did vampires like him get lonely? Or was he providing Digbeth with the knowledge he would need for his new existence?

"May I ask why are you are here?" Digbeth asked. "In this country, I mean."

"You may ask."

The response threw Digbeth for a moment. "Uh, thank you. Tell me, why are you here?"

"Ultimately, habit, I suppose. I've run this land for so long that I've become rather used to it. It's a sort of game. The world changes and I like to see how I can adapt. I do it rather well, I have to say. Whatever happens, I remain quietly in charge."

"You came here to invade? Originally."

"Ah, no. The truth of that might amuse you."

"Will you tell me?"

"We came for the climate. Poor old damp and cloudy Britain: it suits us. Despite what the stories say, we can venture out in daylight; we don't turn to dust or any of that nonsense, but direct sunlight is ... bothersome. Draining. We prefer to avoid it. Living here, well, it's so rarely a problem is it? Cloudy, rainy Britain; it's paradise."

"And is the Office another of your puppets?"

"Earl Grey was mine. The question is how many of the other Witchfinders can be trusted."

"I am yours, too," The thing that had been Digbeth said. "You have my word on it."

"The promises of a vampire are not to be trusted, but it is good that you say that."

The Warlock set his goblet and book down. In a single fluid motion, as if he were being pulled by strings, he stood.

"Come," he said. "There is another I would like you to meet."

He crossed to a tall set of windows that were, Digbeth now saw, a pair of doors. The Warlock pulled them open. Air streamed past him, billowing the flowing robes he wore. He stepped outside onto a balcony. Digbeth followed. A green landscape lay all around, a sea of trees beneath an iron sky. Somewhere in the distance, the smell of salt and seaweed clear to Digbeth's nose, lay the sea. He picked out the hungry bayings of hounds again, louder now. At the foot of the wall, across a stone driveway, a figure waited at the edge of the trees. Large black dogs milled backwards and forwards around them, excitement visible in the set of their limbs. The figure held them back – barely – by their straining leashes.

Quietly, from beside him, the Warlock said, "We will go down. Jump, now."

Briefly, Digbeth tried to resist. The hard stone of the ground was three flights below. What was left of the human in him recoiled in horror at the thought. The fall would kill him, fracture his skeleton into fragments, burst organs. At the same time, he could not resist the Warlock's words. There were tones in them, harmonics, that seemed to hook directly into Digbeth's motor functions.

"Jump, now," the Warlock repeated, his voice deep with power, "We must join our wild hunt."

Despite himself, Digbeth found himself climbing onto the stone balustrade of the balcony. The gusting wind made him wobble for a moment, his legs shaking. So far as he knew, vampires could not fly, could not turn themselves into bats – or any other creature – as the stories claimed. Their magical power lay largely in the way they bent the minds of animals and humans – they didn't see the distinction – to their own. He could not resist the Warlock's instructions. Was this it, then, after all? This was his punishment for failing? Perhaps to repeat his death plunge over and over until he was finally broken?

With one helpless look back, Digbeth stepped into the air.

He flailed. The ground was suddenly huge around him, throwing itself at him. He struck it hard, legs first, thumping into the hard stones. He crumpled, fell in a heap ... but there was no pain. He did not die. He climbed to his knees and then to his feet and found, the vestiges of his human brain registering astonishment, that he could stand and walk with ease. That he was utterly unharmed.

The power of the vampire lay also in its indestructibility.

The Warlock landed more gracefully beside him, touching down as if he had only stepped from a low stair. He carried a silver-capped cane of some black wood in his hand. He clearly didn't need it for support, but as he walked, he limped slightly, leaning on the cane. It was clearly all for show: any injury a vampire received would heal almost immediately.

"Follow," he said.

The dogs were not dogs, Digbeth saw. Or not normal dogs. They were huge and night-black and their eyes were red as fire, red as blood. Something like the *Cŵn Annwn* he'd seen more than once in Wales. Those creatures could be spectral, ghosting through solid objects, but these beasts were definitely solid, creatures of flesh and blood. And, judging by their fanged mouths, the way they snarled and snapped, the growls deep in their throats, they were also hungry.

The other figure – Digbeth found he knew it was also a vampire – dipped his head very slightly to the Warlock. This vampire appeared to be younger than the Warlock, and was not dressed in the clothes that Digbeth might have expected. There were no capes or black leather. Instead, he was kitted out like a country squire – or, actually, like a city man visiting the country and adopting the uniform they thought they were supposed to wear. There was a lot of green tweed. It made the ghastly pallor of his face only more striking. The younger vampire was studying him intently; Digbeth could feel his mind worming around in his own.

"Here is our friend from the Office of the Witchfinder General," the Warlock said. "Witchfinder Digbeth. He has come to take part in our hunt today."

The other didn't speak – instead, opening his mouth, baring his teeth as if anticipating a delicious meal. Behind, Digbeth now noticed, deep in the shadows beneath the trees, perhaps a hundred yards away, there were other figures. He could smell that they were humans, and he could also smell the fear coming off them. His eyesight, growing keener all the time, picked them out. They were naked and shivering, three women and two men. They were secured to a tree to prevent them from fleeing. From the lines of the bones in their faces and arms, their bare feet, it was clear they were in poor shape, malnourished, shivering from cold and fear. They clutched at each other with twig fingers for comfort or reassurance.

They were the quarry for the hunt.

The Warlock spoke, indicating the vampire holding the leashes of the hounds. "Tell me, Witchfinder Digbeth, do you know who this is?"

Digbeth stared into the other set of cold eyes. Again, he knew he could not lie.

"No. So far as I know, he is unknown to the Office."

The new vampire finally spoke. "You truly know nothing of us?"

"The Office knows about a figure called the Warlock, and it knows about a cabal of powerful vampires that are responsible for much taking place in Britain. The Order of the British Vampire. But the Office is in the dark, lacking any useful detail. They don't know who you are and they don't know where you might be found."

"Perhaps you were not told the details of all the things your superiors know?"

"They trusted me completely. I read the records and logs very carefully, and I've talked to people. They've wasted a lot of effort trying to track you down over the years, and I know they have failed."

"And this Shahzan boy?"

"He is also ignorant. He knows nothing more."

There was, Digbeth thought, the very slightest relaxation in the frame of the younger vampire. Whatever this creature's name was, he showed no fear, looked utterly powerful, but he had been worried on some level.

"Very well," said the Warlock, "let us proceed with the hunt. We can talk once we have had our fun."

The hounds, sensing that things were finally moving, strained and howled, pulling the younger vampire forwards. A human, Digbeth thought, would have been dragged to the ground. The three vampires padded softly between the trees towards the waiting humans. The creatures knew what was coming, knew what was in store for them. They shivered and whined like the apes they were, reduced to mere animals in their terror. One fell to their knees and begged to be freed, begged for someone else to be hunted in their place. The Warlock paid the creature no attention. Another of the humans, features twisted into fear and fury, took a step nearer the Warlock and spat into his face.

The Warlock turned his head slowly to consider this creature. His voice remained quiet.

"Tell me, do you know the cliché about being hunted? That you don't have to run faster than the hunter, just faster than someone else being pursued?"

The human looked baffled. He indicated that he understood with a hesitant nod.

"Excellent," said the Warlock. "The others will be delighted." With a rapid, practised motion, he struck the human's left thigh with his cane, snapping the leg in two like a twig. The crack of the bone and the shriek of agony were loud in the hushed woods. The human collapsed, writhing in agony, his shattered leg at a bad angle. Blood pumped onto the leaf mould, his bone visible through his skin.

The Warlock turned away. He picked up the strong ropes that held the humans to the tree. With another quick motion, he tore the ropes apart as if they were nothing more than threads of cotton. He let the ends loose by slowly unfolding his fingers.

"Run, now," he said to the naked humans. "Those of you who can, at least. Run or crawl. You have a few minutes before the hunt comes for you. Give us some sport. Put up a fight, at least."

The humans needed no further bidding. One of the women kicked and punched one of the standing men, hoping to slow him down and increase her chances of escaping. The man with the shattered thigh attempted to crawl on his belly, pull himself along by his hands. It barely mattered; they surely had no chance of outrunning the black hounds or the vampires. They fled as best they could, scattering in random directions. Digbeth watched them go with a mounting hunger in his stomach. These would be his first. His first act of revenge for every wrong done to him.

The Warlock's voice was quiet behind him. "You, too, Witchfinder Digbeth. You should also run."

Digbeth's mind wheeled as he tried to understand the Warlock's words. "But … but I'm one of you! I'm hunter, not prey. I have told you everything, given you everything!"

"You have told us what we needed to know," the Warlock said. "Yes. We know for sure the depth of the Office's ignorance now. You have fulfilled your purpose. Now, flee. You at least will give us good sport today. Fight us."

"But…"

The younger vampire spoke. "Run, now. Put the humans between us and you, at least. It will buy you a few more minutes."

Digbeth saw the hunger in the faces of the two vampires as they watched him. This time, he didn't need their mind-control powers to force his limbs into action.

Turning, he ran.

2 – Warlock

> Vampirism is a trait that is passed on from individual to individual, although this is not a simple matter of being bitten in the manner often seen in films and books. The decision to bestow the gift (or the taint, depending on your perspective), is never taken lightly: typically, it is given to the chosen successor of a family line, or to some other revered clan member. This demonstrates a fundamental point: in the British Isles, vampirism is strongly associated with the aristocracy. It is used in the same way that wealth, privilege and deference are used, namely to maintain the social distance between the aristocracy and the commoners. Vampires are almost exclusively wealthy and titled, from families able to trace their roots back over many, many centuries.
> – Dr Miriam Seacastle, *Red Dragon, a Bestiary of Modern Britain*, 1999

An hour after the ending of the hunt, Sir Jacob Charnel – the Warlock – gazed down from a high window in the Eastern Tower of his castle. His mind was cold fury. Below, Tremaine's black Bentley swept away through the gatehouse in a spray of gravel. Charnel glowered at that, too; he would have to have one of the thralls rake the courtyard smooth later. He would make Tremaine pay for that small slight as well as for everything else.

In a moment, the underling vampire's car was gone, leaving Charnel alone with his household. Tremaine's invitation had been revoked. Formally and permanently revoked. Lord Tremaine would not be returning; it was time to draw a veil over his three hundred years of existence. Time to scatter his seared and blackened dust to the winds of Albion. In normal times, Charnel would have allowed Tremaine to survive – for a time. The thrill of the hunt, the final bloodied showdown with a powerful quarry, the particular heady tang of vampire blood: these could be a rare pleasure, even after so long. But these were not normal times. The destruction of the Witchfinder, Digbeth, would have to suffice for now. The gathering and the hunt had been useful, reassuring him that the Office were woefully ignorant while also confirming his opinions of Tremaine. Charnel faced too many threats that he'd thought he was forever immune from. He faced a very real fight for his existence, and he did not need mosquitos like Tremaine buzzing around sucking a pinprick of his blood.

It didn't matter that Tremaine was little more than a messenger, racing north once again to hurl his pathetic accusations that he, Charnel, had lost control of events. The underling had taken far too much pleasure in his telling: he'd looked almost gleeful as he explained in unnecessary detail the betrayals – and then the destruction – of Earl Grey. What mattered was that Grey had paid the price for his deceptions. The fact that Shahzan had been the one to kill him was troubling, but it altered little in the end. Individuals and their petty concerns came and went.

For now, Lord Tremaine would have to die. And lashing out in some bloody, brutal way: it could be an excellent way of relieving frustration, of allowing the mind to find calm and focus. This was Charnel's happy place. In time, some new, young vampire – *young* was relative – would be elevated to his inner cabal of three advisors, appointed to the grouping currently known as the Order of the British Vampire. And then, in time, after the present difficulties were over, his long unlife could return to normal and the world could continue to shape itself to his needs and his whims.

A storm off the North Sea rattled his windows, hissing icy air at him through the gaps in the mullion. Charnel relished the chill in it, the cold of ice floes and the deep rolling fathoms washing through him. Such weather suited him; it chimed with his emotions. He obviously felt no discomfort from the cold, and his house was perhaps at its finest when frost sparkled on the *inside* of the mediaeval stained-glass windows and the breath billowed from the cattle he fed off when he came for them. The weather had been like this the day he and his two companions arrived, long, long ago. They'd come on foot rather than across the waters, crossing Doggerland from the greater landmass and then striking north into the wilds to find a secure and shadowy place to settle. In later years, the humans had told tales of how he had sailed across the sea like some storm-wracked carrion bird. It hadn't been like that at all, but the legend was … gratifying. It felt like it should be true, even if the humans at the time had seen his kind as vermin, repellent.

He put his hands to the stones of the castle – the building was old, but he clearly remembered the first foundations of the inner keep being laid – and, with a concentrated magical effort, set about reweaving the powerful wards that he kept wrapped around his home. Revoking or refusing the *Invitation* was enough to keep many of his ilk out, but not all of them, not if they acted in concert. And there were other dangers in the world apart from his fellow vampires. The spells he ran through the very grain of the old stones would be enough to repel just about any intruder or attacker who might seek to destroy him – be they vampiric, demonic, ghostly, fae, or a mere human with powerful sorcery. If some truly fearsome entity came for him, a power the wards couldn't withstand, the hexes would at least give him warning and time to prepare.

It took him thirty minutes to complete the incantations. The effect was … draining, even for one such as him. His house was large. He would have to refresh himself soon, drink deep of three, four, five of his dungeon herd. He would be weak for a few hours, but then he would be strong again. He would always be strong again.

Then he would strike, remove Tremaine from the board before moving onto the other threats he faced. The Office of the Witchfinder General might be in pieces now, castrated and broken, but there were people connected to it he still needed to be wary of. It had been the same in the days of Queen Victoria, when Isaac Shackleton was Lord High Witchfinder. Many in his charge were weak and corrupted, but one or two – including Shackleton himself – had been dangerous. So it was in the current day. Hardknott-Lewis was a clear threat, but Shahzan was another. The boy was growing in power all the time, and now it was clear: he was not the weak, mewling irrelevance that Earl Grey had claimed. Most likely, Earl Grey had intended to keep Shahzan's mounting powers a secret, hoping to turn them against Charnel at some point. Once Shahzan fully understood his inheritance, his abilities, he would be formidable. That made him a significant threat, one that needed to be stopped. And if there were *two* Shahzan practitioners in the world, and if they worked together – well, that wasn't to be considered. That had to be stopped before it could happen.

Partly, also, Charnel had kept this one of the Shahzans alive so that the boy could come fully into his powers. Charnel needed to discover his true abilities, rip the facts from him one way or another. Charnel still did not fully understand the abilities that the Shahzan practitioners had brought with them, how they'd proved to be such a threat. The timing of his intervention was a delicate balance to strike: wait long enough for the boy to learn, but not so long that he became too powerful.

Now was the time to act.

And at least he knew where to find Shahzan – and those he cared for. The Office did a very good job of protecting its operatives, hiding them with all the tricks that technology and magic could provide, keeping them out of all public records. Earl Grey had that information, of course, but he'd always insisted it would look too obvious if he broke the rules and revealed Office secrets. All a part of his game, an attempt to keep Shahzan in reserve as a weapon. It didn't matter. It had never mattered. Charnel had already put out the word to track down the Shahzan boy, bring him to the castle, and now he could whisper to his underlings where, precisely, Shahzan might be found.

It occurred to Charnel then that he must go and check the grave bell he kept in one of the chambers in the east wing. He would surely hear its doleful ringing if it sounded – but still, it did no harm to check. He had to be completely certain that only *one* Shahzan was on the board.

Then there was Arthur Stonewall and his ragtag coterie of renegade practitioners. Charnel would preserve some special death for the betrayer, *The Destroyer*, but he had no idea where Stonewall was hiding. It was somewhere annoyingly beyond the bounds of Charnel's gaze. Sometimes he hoped that Stonewall was dead, or lost in some distant realm, but Charnel knew in his icy heart that wasn't true. Stonewall was biding his time, preparing, choosing his moment to strike. He was powerful enough in his own way, and his knowledge of the arcane arts was unsurpassed among humans. The important thing when faced with such a threat was to attack first. Distract the enemy with one hand while the other swept unexpectedly to cut the enemy off at the knees. Charnel hadn't survived all these centuries without doing precisely that. Sometimes, *literally* that. This Sally Spender that Witchfinder Digbeth had mentioned: unless he was mistaken, she was one of Stonewall's coterie. She might be the weak link in his enemy's defences, a way to finally track him down. And Shahzan might be the way to get to her, too.

This work of weaving his wards complete, and deep in thought, Charnel descended the spiralling stone stairs of the tower to stand before a particularly heavy set of iron doors, locked with more powerful magics – as well as three top-of-the-range mechanical locks for which only he had the key. He released all of them now and opened the door. Musty, still air breathed up at him from below. The staircase to the crypt, cut into the hard stone, stretched before him. With a wave of his hand, he sparked the torches set around the underground chamber into life. Their yellow and red flames sent flickering shadows licking up the stairs. Electric lights would have been very much more convenient, and he didn't, in truth, need any light, being perfectly capable of seeing in darkness, but he was a traditionalist at heart. He liked the effect of the guttering torches, the whip of their flames and the smell of the burning oil.

He descended the long flight of steps down to the round vault that lay beneath his hill-top castle. It was completely separate from the cellars where he kept his community of blood donors and financial wizards. The crypt was far older; he'd added it in the fifteenth century, an age when it was so much easier to find cheap, reliable labourers and masons to complete such work – workers about whom others wouldn't ask awkward questions when they disappeared afterwards. Paper trails and bureaucracy could be such a bore, another aspect of the modern world he found irksome. Nearly fifty men had worked on the crypt, and once their labours were complete, he'd personally slaughtered each and every one of them, draining them of their blood and their life force. The crypt, truly, had been their life's work.

Now, he was the only person in existence who knew about the presence of the *sanctum sanctorum* – unless you counted the single other vampire who was a permanent resident in the castle.

Magor had been by his side when the three of them had come to this land: himself, Valian and Magor. Of the two buck vampires, he, Charnel, was slightly older, but the two had been a match in their skill with vampiric magic, their ability to beguile and control the humans they fed off. Magor, ultimately, had also proved too much of a threat to Charnel. He'd had to go. But, killing – permanently, irrevocably killing – so ancient and powerful a vampire as he was a difficult thing to do. Not impossible, but difficult. In the films and books that the humans loved to devour, the process was ridiculously easy: a useful myth that he was happy to allow to continue. Sunlight, a spike of wood, some religious symbol. Laughable.

The truth was, ancient vampires faded away to bones if they weren't fed, but they didn't expire. They simply ... remained, littering the tombs of ancient country houses, no doubt fuelling all the stories people loved to read, the supposed fear of daylight and all the rest of it. Properly despatching a vampire such as Magor required strong magic. Strong, distasteful magic. In the end, Charnel had let Magor survive, keeping him skewered and broken in the crypt where no one could come for him and there was no hope of rescue.

Charnel was honest enough with himself to admit, also, that the thought of permanently destroying Magor had left him feeling oddly, well, the word was probably *lonely*. Was that what the humans called it? Vampires such as he had no time for emotion, for empathy, and he didn't really understand what the words meant, but the fact remained that Magor was the only connection Charnel had left with the ancient world that had spawned both of them. In the end, he hadn't been able to bring himself to work the spells to shatter and destroy the ancient vampire and instead had kept him locked away down here, always on the point of death but clinging to existence by the sheer brute stubbornness of his own willpower.

Magor had been down there for a hundred years. Every now and then, Charnel brought him round, allowed him to rise towards something like full consciousness so they could exchange a few words. The experience was never very satisfactory. Magor was generally more concerned with venting his frustrations than he was with discussing the good old days.

The similarities of the little arrangement to the Office's Oblivion amused Charnel – and also troubled him. It was supposedly impossible to escape either prison, but the release of Evangelina Mormont (admittedly under his direction) had proved this wasn't the case. Another reason he really should set aside his own ridiculous sentimentality and finally destroy the ancient vampire he kept clinging to unlife within his crypt. There truly were few in the land who could be a threat to him in single combat – but a fully reanimated Magor was one of them.

The husk of the ancient vampire lay on a stone altar in the centre of the round room. There wasn't much left of him. To anyone else's eyes, he appeared to be little more than a mummified shell, his parchment skin stretched across the hard edges of his bones, his mouth gaping wide in a permanent, silent scream. Anyone thinking that would be wrong. Embedded in Magor's chest was *Norskrang*, the yew spike ensorcelled with its grim sorcerous power. Charnel had stolen this artefact from the shaman who had crafted it and bewitched it, deep in the dawn of the world. It was, perhaps, the only weapon capable of slaying one such as Magor if the right incantations were used and the right actions taken. Charnel didn't know how many sacrifices had been expended to weave Norskrang's magic into it, but it was many. In truth, he found such witch-magic distasteful, but it had its uses. The urge to destroy the object – fearsomely dangerous to him as it was – had always been strong, but Charnel had resisted, seeing a day when he might need to use Norskrang on a rival. Thinking even as they had walked into this land, Norskrang hidden in a leather pouch, that one day he might need to use it upon Magor and Valian. And so it had turned out. It was Norskrang that had kept Magor pinned helplessly to his stone altar all this time, alive but not alive, dead but not dead.

Using a pair of intricately-carved iron tongs – and a set of heavy, furnaceman's leather gloves so that there was no risk of the spike coming into contact with his own skin – Charnel set about working the shard of ancient wood free from the heart of Magor's desiccated remains. The artefact resisted him; it loved its victim, burrowing into him like some cadaver worm, drinking and drinking at his life.

But Charnel knew the incantations needed to control the actions of Norskrang. He had wrung the words from the shaman upon pain of death – and then, when he had them straight, had inflicted that very pain of death upon the shaman. No one else in the wide world knew the wording of the spells woven into the spike. No one else but he would ever be able to wield the object.

There was a leathery squelching noise. With a grunt of effort, he worked Norskrang out of Magor's body. There was the faintest sigh from the shard of ancient wood as he pulled it clear. Charnel held it at arm's length, the iron of the tongs and the leather gloves between it and his flesh. He studied it for a moment: an unimpressive spike of yew, twisted and worn. He could feel the hot malice burning through it. The familiar dull ache in his leg flared up sharply. It was the only wound he had ever received that hadn't healed up immediately. The fact had had a sobering effect upon him over the past few decades. The artefact that had inflicted his wound was not this one, and had been destroyed, but it was something similar to Norskrang; a weaker cousin that must have shared many of the same incantations. The gash in his leg felt the burn of them. Charnel put the pangs of pain – such an unusual, unfamiliar sensation – out of his mind.

After a few moments, the sinews of the ancient vampire upon the dais began to twitch and stretch. Magor's muscles worked even as the faintest flush of colour returned to his flesh. He would be hopelessly weak, left without sustenance all this time, the life within him a trickle, but he was still a danger. He would grow stronger with each moment. Charnel wouldn't give him long.

Magor's lips moved. His voice was a dry rasp. "Release me, friend. I will leave this land; you have my word. The world is wide. We need not continue this little disagreement."

Charnel moved his face so that he was in Magor's vision. The lustre of malice was already returning to the ancient vampire's eyes.

"We both know the word of a vampire means nothing, Magor. You would slay me in a moment if you could. Even if you couldn't, you would devote your existence to trying."

The faintest smile seemed to flicker across Magor's

face, but he didn't respond. They both knew Charnel's words were true. The torches wavered in unison as some gust of cold air swirled around. Charnel set about working the incantations he needed. In his mind's eye, Norskrang was a spike of pain, purple-black smoke coiling off it. He wouldn't give Magor long. His old friend would have the dignity of understanding it was the end, but nothing more. Charnel needed the Norskrang Artefact to despatch Tremaine – and any other vampires who stood with him.

It was time to finally set sentimentality aside.

Magor, perhaps seeing something in Charnel's eyes, understood. "Where is Valian?" he said. "Has she not come to witness my final departure?"

He had never told Magor of Valian's fate. He wasn't completely sure why. They'd both loved the female, in the hungered, lustful way of their kind, and news of her destruction would be a bitter blow to Magor. Still, he had refrained from telling him. Perhaps it was because Magor would know how cruel a blow it must have been to Charnel, too. Magor might enjoy knowing Charnel had lost his eternal love.

"I am going to destroy you, now," Charnel said. "You cannot be allowed to live. I should never have granted you this stay of execution."

"You are weak," said Magor. "I would never have given you even this." His voice was a croak, a whisper from the grave, but it was becoming clearer with every passing moment. Charnel had never quite been able to shake the worry that Magor knew something of Norskrang's incantations, too. There had been some talk of words set down upon a parchment by that long-dead shaman, although Charnel had never been able to get to the bottom of it.

"I will miss you," said Charnel. "The modern world: it is a strange and confusing place at times. I shall miss our little reminiscences."

"Do what you have to do," said Magor. "We both know your time is short. A few more minutes and I shall ... arise."

Magor was perfectly correct. Summoning the stolen magical essence from deep within him, he uttered syllables – harsh and spiky even to his ears – that worked the incantations required on the Norskrang artefact. He thrust the yew spike back into Magor's chest.

The wind whipped through the stone vault again as he laboured. The torches guttered gratifyingly. There was a moment when Charnel feared he had miscalculated, that Magor was not going to succumb. That, somehow, his fellow-vampire *had* worked ancient incantations of his own to turn the destructive force of the artefact onto Charnel. Then Magor gasped, and a line of some yellow liquid seeped from the side of his mouth. The light in his ancient eyes faded, and his bones crumbled to a tiny mountain range of dust.

At its centre, untouched, lay Norskrang. Charnel picked the grim object up with the tongs once more, studying it with fascination while making very sure it didn't touch him. He dropped it into a casket and locked it, then placed that casket into a larger chest and locked that, too. It could stay there untouched.

For now.

Back upstairs, alone in the house apart from his servants and the penned creatures he fed off, he paused in thought for a moment. His boots echoed on the hard stones of his castle as he strode into the east wing. The slight pause and clack of his stride; the pain in his leg was still troubling him.

The grave bell hung from the vaulted ceiling of its chamber. The rope led from it over a pulley, across the ceiling – and then faded into purple mist as it passed into the other realm. The bell was silent, unmoving in the still air. That threat at least remained unaltered. To be doubly sure, Charnel bent to listen to the twisted little demon statuette that stood upon a plinth next to the bell. The bell wasn't only a bell, just as the rope – with its thread of silver woven through it – wasn't only a rope. The contraption worked both ways.

The statuette was still working, still whispering its

endless stream of muttered syllables into the bell. Faintly, he could also hear the whispers coming back the other way: the possessing spirit occupying that distant body was continuing to carry out the instructions it had been bound to. Charnel had picked up the statuette many centuries ago, taking it from a Summoner living in a remote tower somewhere in Assyria. The magician had used the artefact to keep the demons he brought through the veils bound to this world. Charnel had killed the Summoner but kept the object, thinking he might find a use for it one day. As he had.

Satisfied, he reclimbed the stairs of the eastern tower. It wasn't simply because he appreciated the looming perspective it gave him on the world; the more annoying truth was that it was only there that he had a reliable phone signal. Really, what was the point of effectively running the country if one couldn't even arrange decent coverage? He could have resorted to all manner of magical communication, manifesting in the presence of the person he needed to speak to, or making his disembodied voice speak from the shadows of some distant room. That was all rather showy, needlessly melodramatic. A simple phone call was easier.

He had other weapons beside Norskrang. Many other weapons. He may have put word out that Shahzan was a foe, but he'd decided it was time to set a very specific underling on the boy's trail. A particularly effective and reliable hunting dog.

The one he needed to speak to picked up immediately when Charnel dialled his number. Of course.

"I have instructions for you, Bone," said Charnel. "Come to me. Your Invitation is renewed. I have my knives ready."

Rather than the intelligible words of language, the sound on the other end was little more than a breathing sound. There was the rumble of a bestial growl to it, too.

The snarl of the hunting animal.

3 – Witchfinder General

> Woe unto the Red Dragon, for his extermination draweth nigh; and his caverns shall be occupied of the White Dragon.
> – Geoffrey of Monmouth, *The History of the Kings of Britain*, 1138

Those that remained of the Welsh Office of the Witchfinder General gathered at Hardknott-Lewis's home in the hills inland from Cardiff. The house was gratifyingly similar to the grand manor I'd imagined for him, although smaller in scale and I'd seen no sign of a butler or any of the domestic staff I'd assumed. But there was a sweeping gravel drive outside, and there was wisteria creeping across the impressive Georgian façade. The interior was hushed and comfortable, all leather seats and wooden panels, tiled stone floors and full book shelves. A globe depicting the world as it used to be stood on a table next to the hatstand. The lack of modern paraphernalia made for an interior that might not have changed for a hundred years.

There were six of us, a ragtag assortment, all that was left of the Office of the Witchfinder General in Wales: myself, the Crow, Kerrigan, Olwen and McLeland. Lady Coldwater, the Librarian who wasn't, strictly speaking, a member of the group was also there, glowering in the background. She'd studied the titles on Hardknott-Lewis's shelves before grunting her acceptance and sitting down. The Crow himself had made tea and coffee – all served, I was gratified to see, in the finest bone China cups, decorated with a stylized design of daffodils. There were also biscuits: plain, no-nonsense digestives, not a hint of anything frivolous such as chocolate in sight.

We sat in silence. I sipped my coffee, thinking about how few of us there were left. Seeing us all together in the same room for once only emphasised the fact. One by one, the Office was crumbling – or being dismantled. There'd been no new recruits since me and Olwen. Rain spattered against the sash window as if someone were out there hurling gravel.

The Crow, standing, cleared his throat and thanked us for coming. His voice was low, but carried to every corner of the hushed room.

"The position of the Office of the Witchfinder General is now somewhat precarious, as you might have guessed. The treachery of Earl Grey, not to mention his killing by one of our own, has inevitably sent rumbles of discontent through the corridors of Whitehall. Or at least, those parts of it that are aware of us."

Kerrigan spoke, his voice a growl. In his defiance, he sounded a lot more Welsh than he usually did. "They should be pleased we did our bloody job. That Danesh did his job, removing a dangerous threat."

The Crow held up his hand to stop Kerrigan. "Absolutely. I made that very point to the Stationery and Office Paper Select Committee just yesterday. Events at Earl Grey's house in London should be seen as a sign of our strength, not our weakness. Alas, many do not regard the situation in quite this way. The Office of the Witchfinder General is a considerable burden on the public purse, and there are those who would like to see cuts being made. Savage cuts. Such are the days we live in. There is even talk of outsourcing our efforts to some private company of *ghost hunters*, who would be paid a certain amount for each revenant despatched and so forth."

"My God," said Kerrigan.

"Well, yes," Hardknott-Lewis replied. "One certainly shudders at the thought."

Lady Coldwater snorted. "Do they want us to be *less* effective, then? Do we need to let a few more horrors slip through the net in order to get the respect we deserve?"

"It does sometimes seems that way," said the Crow. He looked uncharacteristically deflated. Almost, defeated. "With an outsourced agency, the financial incentive to have *more* spectres and ghosts and the like manifesting rather than fewer are obvious. The work we do to prevent incursions from happening is obviously vital; I do not need to tell any of you that. I had to explain this to the committee at length: the threat posed by the Warlock; the demons and the revenants; the full gamut of transmundane threats."

"The books in the libraries need to be guarded as well," Lady Coldwater said. "I should be there now, watching over them. Then there are people like Gilroy, locked away in the basement. Who's looking out for them?"

"Again, I made these points," said the Crow.

"Wait," I said, still catching up. "The *Stationery and Office Paper Select Committee*. What exactly is that?"

Hardknott-Lewis raised a single eyebrow, a gesture that represented considerable amusement in him. "Although we have a direct link to the Prime Minister via 13 Downing Street, our day-to-day operations are controlled by a committee that oversees everything we do. It meets rarely. It is populated by a few MPs and Lords who are in the know."

"But, *Stationery and Office Paper*?"

"Obviously they could not call it the Magical Defence Select Committee or some such. The group was given a deliberately dull name in order to keep it from public attention."

"Is the Archbishop of Canterbury involved in this?" I asked. "You said the Office often disagrees with the archbishops."

"The Archbishop of Canterbury is on the committee, yes."

"Was what you said to them enough?" Kerrigan asked. "Did it persuade them, or are we here because the Office has been shut down?"

The Crow sat back in his chair and formed a gothic arch with his splayed fingers. "The situation is, as they would put it, under review. After some disagreement, it has been decided to allow the Office to continue with its day-to-day operations for now, given the pressing nature of the dangers we face. Longer term, well, I have no idea."

"Have you been in touch with the other regions?" McLeland asked. He was a generation older than Kerrigan, closer in age to the Crow or Lady Coldwater. He'd always been the quiet one of the group, spending most of this time reading old books and making copious handwritten notes, venturing out into the field only when he had to. I'd put that down to indifference at first, even laziness – but I'd since learned it was nothing of the sort. He was an extremely effective operative. He'd stayed alive for as long as he had because of the careful planning he carried out.

"Informally," said the Crow. "That is another point you need to be aware of. The five surviving Keyholders – England still hasn't identified a replacement for Mason – agreed last night to the importance of having a Witchfinder General in place, someone to act as the Office's sole representative. Circumventing all the normal processes, we elected myself to the position by a margin of 4 to 1."

"The one being you?" I ventured.

The Crow inclined his head in assent.

"Who's Wales then?" Kerrigan asked. "Once Earl Grey became Witchfinder General he handed over England to Mason Greentree. That's how it works."

"Indeed so," said the Crow. "That would be the normal situation. I think it is up to us, to the five of you, to decide on that. I can combine both roles for now, or one of you can step up to become Lord High Witchfinder of All Wales."

Another snort came from the Librarian. "Somehow I suspect that doesn't include me."

"We live in strange times," the Crow responded. "I have gathered you here because one of us needs to be in charge of the Welsh office. There is, simply, no one else."

There was a silence as we glanced at one another, no doubt mentally imagining ourselves and then each other as the Welsh Witchfinder. All my talk of improving the Office's diversity and dragging it into the modern world: here was a chance to do something about it. But I could immediately see I was going to fail. I didn't want the role, that was completely clear. I was on a very different career path. Olwen, surely, was too young and the Lady wasn't even Office. It came down to one of the older hands: McLeland or Kerrigan. Another white guy. But I knew either could handle it.

A look passed between the two of them. They'd worked it out, too. Perhaps they'd each worked it out a long time ago.

It was Kerrigan who spoke. "I propose you stay in position, Lord Witchfinder. Combine both roles. We're in enough chaos as it is, and we need your steadying hand." He looked at McLeland, a questioning eyebrow raised.

"Agreed," McLeland said. "Once things settle down, if they ever settle down, the Keyholders can review the situation."

Olwen, to my left, nodded her assent. Three votes; the decision was made. Assuming we were a democracy, now, I nodded my agreement as well. I had no idea where I stood with the Office, how things were going to turn out – but I knew I didn't want either Kerrigan or McLeland to have to grapple with my ... compromised situation.

At the back of the room, Lady Coldwater shrugged.

"Very well," said the Crow. "Thank you for your vote of confidence. I shall attempt to continue for now. I will obviously be somewhat distracted, and I beg your indulgence on that front. We are, of course, always short-staffed, and the situation is worse since the loss of Digbeth. All we can do is pull together. I see no other way forwards. Please, return to your normal duties and we will continue to fight the good fight. Between us, I am sure, we will prevail. Because, what else can we do?"

We nodded and mumbled our acceptance and, one-by-one, rose to leave. As I was heading for the door, the

Crow placed a gentle hand on my arm, threw a glance at me, and I understood that he wanted to have a conversation in private.

He stood by the window, his back to me, while the others drove away. The headlights of their cars splayed across the ceiling and faded. It was suddenly very quiet in his remote house. It occurred to me that, so far as I knew, I was alone with him.

A game of chess had been set up on a round table in one corner of the room, the playing pieces of some finely carved and polished stone. One chair was next to it, as if the Crow sat there alone to consider his next move. I wondered who he was playing against. Black appeared to be losing badly: the king had only a few pawns left to defend him. I couldn't see any winning move.

I picked out a framed photograph set upon the polished iron mantlepiece. I hadn't noticed it before, but I suddenly couldn't take my eyes off it. The way it had been set: it had a central position in the room, the chairs arranged around it as they might a television in a normal house. A couple of brass candlesticks stood on either side of the picture, in an almost shrine-like arrangement. The photograph depicted a man and a woman, with a young boy standing between them, hair combed into a ruler-straight side-parting, his expression sombre. The man, unmistakably, was a young Hardknott-Lewis, standing erect and proud, his intent gaze drilling out of the frame. I didn't know the woman.

The Crow had turned and had seen where I was looking. He looked suddenly older, I thought, more troubled than I ever remembered seeing him. His rallying cry to the troops had been for show. A leader doing what had to be done, nothing more. His voice was even more hushed in the quiet room as he spoke.

"She was a Witchfinder, too," he said. "Welsh office, although we lived in mid-Wales then, high up in the hills. We didn't need anyone else. We met in the Office as acolytes."

"Can I ask what happened to her?"

"She died in the attack that all-but killed Gregory. She died protecting him, I have no doubt. I wasn't there, you see. I tried to get to them when word came through of what was taking place, but I was too late. Always, too late. When I reached them, she was gone, and Gregory was, well, he had one foot in this world and one in the grave. The curse was consuming him as I watched, like a black fire burning his flesh. Like a line of marching ants crawling through him. All I could do was to freeze him with holdfasts and beg the Witchfinder of the time, Rhys Griffith, to place him into Oblivion while I attempted to unravel the curses that had been used. Rhys agreed when perhaps he should not have done, but in all the years since, I have never able to find a way to save Gregory. I..."

He stopped talking, looked down at the ground as he attempted to recover himself.

I'd had no idea. Some of the older hands in the office must have known, but none had ever talked about it. And, the parallels between Hardknott-Lewis's fate and my own were hard to miss. Again, I thought, this had to explain his indulgent attitude towards me. Incongruously, the flirting landlady of the pub we'd visited on the day I'd opened up the (supposed) grave of Owain Williams came to mind. She clearly knew and admired the Crow, and had called him by his first name, but I'd detected a certain polite coldness from him in response. My guess was that he'd simply turned his back on that part of his life with the death of his wife. Closed the book and put it back on the shelf. Moral absolutes: such a response would be typical of him.

"Who attacked your family?" I asked. "Was it the Warlock or one of his minions?"

"I do not think so, no. Although, who knows what associations and connections exist between those we face? But I believe it was a lone Welsh spellworker I was pursuing. A death wizard; a black-hearted man called Cornog. At the time I was trying and failing to tackle the continuing situation at Caerlech, which had recently come to light. I mentioned to you that I had had some dealings with the Owain Williams entity; my theory at the time was that Williams and Cornog were one and the same person. That is still a possibility. I was never able to track Cornog down."

The Crow's absolute abhorrence of magic use seemed suddenly a little more understandable. I wondered how he felt about me as I became more and more of a spellworker, right there in front of him. He knew, of course. It was an unspoken understanding between us. We shared some sort of fate with our family backgrounds, but he had to see me as the enemy, too. A little twist of alarm wriggled through my mind. He was the Witchfinder General, now. He had absolute power when it came to administering magus law. No one was going to question him if he identified and despatched an illegal magic user. No one would stop him if he ordered I take up a position in Oblivion next to my twin brother.

A shudder went through the Crow's frame, and he seemed to sag a little more. Was he thinking similar thoughts to me? He glanced up, some amusement sparkling in his eye, some irony, then he looked away.

"Come," he said. "Please, sit. Let us discuss your situation. Given the situation with Az, and of course your own ... nature, you might be forgiven for celebrating the likely destruction of the Office of the Witchfinder General."

Once I might have found this notion an alarming one. Later on, I might have welcomed it. In truth, I hadn't recently given the idea much thought.

"If we can work together to track down and destroy the Warlock, and to rescue Az," I said, "then I'm happy to continue to work with you."

The Crow looked like he wanted to say more but did not. He nodded his acceptance of the situation. What would happen afterwards – assuming there was an afterwards – remained unclear. It would have to do for now.

"Very well," said the Crow. "I hoped that would be

your answer. Firstly, as to your family, you will recall our discussion immediately after the death of Earl Grey. I said at the time that only the Witchfinder General could sanction informing a lay person of the existence of Oblivion. Now that I hold that office, you should know that I consent to telling your mother. She deserves to know the truth. It will be hard for her, but she is, I believe, not wholly ignorant of the existence of the supernatural threats we face. I leave it to you to decide how to handle the situation, but my approval is there."

"And the removal of Az?" I said. "You can sanction that, too, can't you?"

He nodded. "I can, and I do, but we must be careful. We simply do not know what the effect on your brother would be if he were returned to life. He may be, like Gregory, mid-way through breathing his last breath. This is the main reason why I wanted to talk to you. I would like you to pursue the Warlock, partly because that being remains a dire threat, but also because we might be able to learn more about the facts surrounding the attack on your family and how to safely return your twin to the waking world. We don't even know the entity's true identity and its exact nature, let alone where its lair is. Our colleagues in England and Scotland have scoured Lindisfarne but have found no useful trace. From everything you have reported, my assumption is that the vampiric entity known as the Warlock supplied the magic that Earl Grey used to attack your family, or at least had some hand in it. Earl Grey said he was supposed to despatch both you and your brother all those years ago because the Warlock was – and presumably still is – afraid of you. We need to understand why. Earl Grey also claimed that he allowed you to live because he wished to use you as a weapon against the Warlock. I suspect the Warlock has been doing the opposite, holding you in reserve as a bulwark against potential Earl Grey treachery. A test. I believe the Warlock will come for you now. He will throw everything at you. I understand that Az is your primary concern here, naturally, but if you do have some power over the Warlock then, I am sorry, we cannot afford to waste that potential."

Both Earl Grey and the Warlock had used me as a playing piece in their games. Now the Crow was doing the same. I was tempted to hurl the fact back at him, but instead I looked him in the eye and nodded. He understood my distaste; I saw it in him.

"It will be hard for you to delve into these matters, I know," he said. "I will of course give you all the help I can."

"I want to see Az," I said. "You obviously have the ability to go to Oblivion without succumbing to its effects."

The Crow nodded. "There are ways to make the journey in relative safety. Certain devices to stave off the life-sapping effects of the place. We will start there. I will make the arrangements. Please, give me a day or two."

"Thank you."

"May I make a suggestion? I would advise you not to stay at your usual address. Given the betrayal of both Digbeth and Earl Grey, I think we can be sure that our enemy now knows where you live. We still have a few safe houses. No need to tell me which you are using, but please, move to one of them for a time."

I nodded. He had a good point. I already had a possible location in mind. The more troubling thought was that if he couldn't track me down, the Warlock might try to get to me via my friends and loved ones. I had to assume the enemy would know where they lived now, too. I wasn't very close to many people outside work – but I needed to do everything I could to keep the few I did care about safe.

These troubling anxieties churning through me, my gaze returned to the game of chess.

"Which are you, black or white?"

An amused look came into his eye.

"Given your private nickname for me, I would have thought you could have worked that out."

That threw me. Once, the revelation would have filled

me with horror. Now, it was one more thing that didn't seem to matter much anymore.

"You know I call you the Crow?"

"Naturally. I take it as a compliment. Very intelligent birds. Very resourceful. I am simply pleased that you did not choose to name me after some unnatural entity."

"How long have you known?"

"Oh, some time."

I studied the board once more. It really was not a strong position for black.

"Who is playing white?" I asked.

"No one. The Warlock, I suppose, but I don't communicate with that thing, obviously. This is more of a thought experiment. The game helps me to concentrate when I am faced with some particularly troublesome foe."

"White has a lot of pieces still in play."

"Regrettably, yes."

A thought occurred to me. "The Warlock … are we sure it is vampiric in nature. Not some similar entity, a wight for instance?"

"Quirk, especially, is sure. He has pursued this foe for a long time."

"I need to speak to him again, find out what he knows."

The Crow nodded. "An excellent place to start. At the risk of repeating former mistakes, I can tell you that I trust Quirk utterly."

"And black … the pawns are us? That's how you see us?"

He waved that away with a sad little smile.

"Not at all. It's merely a way of gauging our strengths against those we face."

"The endgame doesn't look good."

"No, well. One hopes for a checkmate move that our opponent fails to see coming."

He lost himself in contemplation of the game on the chessboard, doubtless seeing subtleties that I wasn't privy too, standing there staring down and looking more like an actual crow than I could ever remember. It had to be a quiet life, a lonely life, just him in this big old house.

As I was leaving, I said, "Oh, and congratulations on your promotion. You've followed Emrys Robinson to become a Witchfinder General from Wales after all."

There was no elation in him at my words as he stood holding his front door open. "Thank you. But it is a Pyrrhic victory, I rather suspect. I have become the leader of something that probably will not exist for very much longer. In all likelihood, I will be the last Witchfinder General, and that is hardly a great claim to fame. I can only attempt to do what I can to protect people in the time available."

Outside, a ragged sky was scattered with tatters of grey cloud and patches of bright blue. Wales had conspired to be sunny *and* raining heavily at the same time. Somewhere, there'd be a rainbow. From the sanctuary of the Mini, I glimpsed the Crow staring out of his window again, his hands clasped behind his back as he peered down.

I glanced up again in my rear-view mirror as I swept away, but he was gone.

4 – Scratching Sounds in the Darkness

> 'Neath the cloudy cliffs came from the moor then
> Grendel going, God's anger bare he.
> The monster intended some one of earthmen
> In the hall-building grand to entrap and make way with
>
> – original unknown, trans. Lesslie Hall,
> *Beowulf*, 1892

Charnel watched from his tower as the dark-coated individual strode out of the banks of grey trees. Misty rain drizzled down. The figure paused only momentarily at the front door, as if overcoming some invisible obstacle, then reached out a hand to pound upon the ancient wood. A thrall would admit the visitor soon enough. It was time to carry out the procedure. Charnel crossed the room and stepped down the stone staircase that wound through this tower, descending to the basement room that was set out for the operation. The stone slab, the array of sharp knives and needles, the little pot of purple liquid. All was ready. Charnel took a small glass vial of blood from its place on a wooden rack and pulled out the cork. He smelled it, letting its aroma bring back all the memories of events two decades previously.

Yes, there could be no doubt whose sample this was. His palette was extremely finely tuned. A low snarl rumbled involuntarily from his throat at the scent.

Charnel tipped the blood into the ink and stirred the mixture with a needle-fine blade. All was ready. He stepped around the slab, trailing his fingers over it. Again, the only illumination in the room was provided by the torches set into the walls. A human surgeon might have needed stronger lighting to perform such a delicate operation. They might have preferred antiseptic conditions, too, but that also wasn't going to be needed.

The door thrall appeared, a creeping, bent human wearing rags. The creature shivered in the freezing air, its skin blue, and there was a helpless look of horror in its eyes. Charnel waved the thrall away with a flick of his hand. The visitor, William Bone, emerged from the shadows behind, ducking his powerful frame beneath the doorway to stand in the room.

Anyone else might have felt intimidated by the appearance of the vampire. He was tall and grim-faced. Unusually, for one of their kind, his features were scarred and pocked. His ankle-length black leather overcoat exaggerated rather than concealed his powerful build. He moved with a feline fluidity to stand before the familiar slab. The stone he had lain upon many times over the centuries. The rugged skin of his face, neck and hands – indeed, Charnel knew, his whole body – was a canvas of tattoos. The shifting flames made them flick and leap. There were hundreds of them now, each carved into Bone's flesh by Charnel's knife. Names. Faces. Often, only a symbol representing the victim Bone had to pursue: a bishop's mitre, a sheaf of papers, the door of some particular house, a book, a family crest. Even, in one case, a crown. Each representing a victim that Bone had pursued. Pursued, always, to the grave.

Bone was ... inevitable.

And now there would be a new tattoo. Bone's expression remained an empty scowl. Without needing to be told, the huge vampire removed his ankle-length leather coat and his shirt, then lay face down on the stone slab. There were still gaps to be filled upon his back. Charnel, saying nothing, set to work, taking up his sharpest knife and pressing it into Bone's flesh.

In the past, he had taken time over his artistry, spent long hours with a needle creating an accurate portrait or drawing a name in the finest calligraphy. A certain beauty could be found in the working of this spell. He was in too much of a hurry now, though. The simple initials would suffice. *DS*. The symbol itself wasn't the essential part of the invocation; it was the ink that mattered, the purple dye admixed with a drop of blood from the target. Injecting it would be enough to impel Bone – he was little more than a thrall in this regard – to hunt down his quarry, carry out his next act of slaughter. These were the terms upon which Bone had been ascended, so very long ago now. Bone had been a capable and resourceful foe, vicious, and Charnel had seen the potential of bringing him back once he was defeated, binding the man to his will. Bone had proved very useful over the years.

He lay completely still while Charnel worked, not flinching. Charnel knew he would be feeling every cut and every prick of the knife.

"This will be my last hunt for you," Bone said, his voice muffled. "I have killed so many over the centuries. I have earned my freedom."

Bone knew what he was, knew what he had been. Charnel hadn't spared him that little horror in his new existence. The mortal William Bone would have despised what Charnel had turned him into and made him do. His tame avenging angel. One found one's amusements where one could.

"You have no freedom and you never will. You know this, my friend. There will always be new enemies I need to have removed, and you are so very good at the task."

"I will run out of flesh for your knife eventually. What then, vampire?"

"There is room on the canvas, yet. Vampire. There is your face. The soles of your feet. Your genitals. Then, when you are purple head-to-toe, I can simply start again with ink of another colour."

"Put your blood into me. Set me upon your trail. Give me a fair fight."

The words were quietly spoken, whispered like a guilty secret.

Charnel chuckled. This wasn't the first time he had

heard that particular demand. "Oh, I think not. I'm sure I could defeat you even if you were much more powerful than you are, even if you were compelled to destroy me, but the fact remains that you are far too useful to waste."

Bone's only response was a grunt. Charnel took a fine needle and drew up some of the ink. He began to work, injecting the blood mixture beneath Bone's flesh, drawing the lines. After a few moments, despite himself, Bone lifted his head, sniffing out his prey.

"This one is far away, not on this world. I cannot reach him."

"Search deeper," Charnel replied as he worked. "There is another; a blood twin. That is your prey. Search hard and you will find him."

Bone snuffled the air again, this side and that, as if the scent of his new victim were drifting by on the air.

Kerrigan plonked himself beside me as I sat at my desk. I'd just returned from visiting my flat to clear out the few essentials I'd need for a trip to London to visit my mother – and then for a stay in a safe house once I was back in Cardiff. I'd dropped into the office for an hour to sort out travel arrangements. Instead of doing that, I'd found myself staring at my screen, my churning thoughts elsewhere, so much so that I didn't notice him for a moment.

"Laddo," he said. "Sorry to bother."

He placed a cup of coffee on my desk. Not the murky puddle water our ever-optimistic office machine produces; he'd been out to buy the proper stuff for everyone. The smell was rich and nutty, drawing me inexorably back into the present moment.

Did I mention that I love Kerrigan?

I'd picked out a wariness to his voice these past few days, though. He was Office through and through, and the existential threat to the organisation that I'd triggered by exposing and then despatching Earl Grey must have shaken his world view. Maybe I was imagining it, but was there a look in his eye, something guarded, that suggested either that he blamed me – or even that he knew or had guessed at the truth about me?

Whatever the truth of it, Kerrigan couldn't help himself worrying about his surviving colleagues. He was what he was: our mother hen. Terrifying to behold in his shaggy wild man way, but loyal to a fault and utterly dependable. In other times, with the Crow elevated, he'd have been the one I'd have wanted to see as the Lord High Witchfinder of All Wales.

He asked his question hesitantly, as if fearing what the response might be. "So, what are you working on at the moment? Need any input?" He'd seen Hardknott-Lewis holding me back for a private word. He knew something was going on.

"Honestly?" I said. "I'm spiralling a bit. Trying to get my head round things."

He nodded his shaggy head. "Processing, right. I get that. Same for bloody all of us, I'm not going to lie. There are shouts that need answering. You know how it is; the restless dead refuse to lie down."

I knew him well enough to see that he wasn't just trying to get work out of me. He was trying to help me, give me something to focus on. A distraction. And he probably had something there. But honestly, my passionate desire for protecting the good people of Wales from the unnatural and the ineffable was burning low. I figured they'd probably survive a week or two without us watching over them.

Probably.

On the other hand, there *was* the problem of my burgeoning magical prowess, as illuminated by my immersion in Stonewall's woodland pool. I could feel the power of it twisting through my bones, rushing through my veins. It was *me*, I knew, but I also knew it could destroy me. Burn me up, drain me to a husk. I hadn't dared use my powers to attack Earl Grey, resorting instead to punching him *really* hard when it came to it. I knew that wasn't always going to work. It certainly wasn't going to work if – when – I came into contact with the Warlock. I needed to hone my skills, discover what I was capable of.

For that, I needed the help of Sally and her coterie, and any other user I could trust. I needed all the help I could get. So maybe Kerrigan was right if for a different reason: a nice little Office job tackling a gibbering revenant or some possessed statue was maybe just what I needed. I could practise all I wanted, employ my illegal powers in a live-fire situation, and no one needed to know anything about it.

"Tell me what we've got facing us," I said.

Kerrigan leaned back in his chair, which creaked like the door of some abandoned castle slowly opening to reveal its hidden darknesses. He grinned. This was more within his comfort zone. He scratched at his bushy beard while he spoke.

"There's a lot on. Things are getting hairy out there; we're seeing a lot of hostile activity. I don't know, it almost feels coordinated."

"The word has got round that we're weakened," I suggested. But I also wondered if this was some deliberate act by the Warlock. The loosening of binds on those under his control to overwhelm us.

Kerrigan leaned back up near me, as if to utter some dark secret. "I even heard a whisper that The Shuttered Lantern is up and running again."

"That can't be true," I replied. "Things can't be that bad."

The Shuttered Lantern: a semi-mythical underground tavern where, according to the stories, the denizens of the demi-monde had once gathered in something like safety. The undead, creatures from other dimensions, human users, the fae, the undefinable – all were welcome, no questions asked. The place had thrived in the 60s and early 70s, tolerated, and Office operatives at the time had used the place to gather intel, get the whisper from beneath the streets. Then the Office had turned more authoritarian and had raided the place repeatedly, shutting it down. It hadn't existed in my life time. I wasn't entirely sure I believed any of the stories about the place. If it was operating again

– if there was even the suggestion that it might operate again – it was a sign of the times for sure.

Kerrigan shrugged. "Maybe. Maybe not. Our control is slipping, no doubt about it. We're seeing the full range of supernatural bastards out there. Take your pick, basically, isn't it?"

"Anything particularly dangerous?"

He threw me a calculating glance at that, like he worried I was on some sort of death wish.

"It's all particularly dangerous. We've got a nasty Code 11 at a suburban house that was converted from a village school building ten years back. Owners say faces keep appearing overnight, drawn onto the walls. Like, red and black lines, soaking through the plaster, images of people in pain or screaming in fury. *Like old photographs*, they say. Apparently they move, too. Not as you look at them, but if you wash them off or paint over them, they're there again the following day, eyes open a little wider, snarl a bit nastier, that sort of thing."

It sounded disturbing – but probably harmless. Low level haunting.

"Anything else?"

Kerrigan pulled out his phone and swiped through items in some *Malign Evil To-Do List* app. "Group of drinkers reported being pursued by a hooded figure down Chippy Lane in the early hours of Sunday. Probably pissed-up, right? Let's see: black cats, grey ladies, black dogs, yada yada. Oh, a report of scratching sounds heard in the darkness beneath Cardiff Castle."

"So, rats or something."

"Not sure. They baited traps but got nothing. And the sounds are coming from behind solid stone walls or beneath the floor. Somewhere there can't be anything to do any scratching, I'm told."

"Hardly sounds urgent. Probably pipes heating up or something."

"Sure, yeah, that'll be it. Ah, here's one that has *Danesh Shahzan* written all over it."

"Go on."

"It was passed onto us from the regulars. Several recent reports of graves being disturbed in churchyards across the city centre. They gave it to us because they thought it might be a coordinated Code 19 attack."

Code 19: zombie or other revenant activity. The truth is, people disturb graves for all sorts of reasons, some of which it doesn't bear thinking about. *Actual* cases of bodysnatching are rare, but they do happen. In my experience, the main question in such cases is: where did the digging start: from above or below? You generally hope for the former, but even that can be the prelude to some dark rite or amateur attempt at reanimation – or else it's some malign creature snuffling out carrion. Or a dog.

"Any sign of bodies being removed? Or ... removing themselves?" I asked.

"Details aren't clear, seems like the regulars took one look at it and decided to hand everything over to us. That's why we need our top guy on the case."

"But they weren't available so you're asking me?"

The weak attempt at humour seemed to cheer Kerrigan up a little. "We all have to make sacrifices. Not literally, obviously. Will you pursue it?"

The case might be just what I needed. If it was revenant activity, it might give me some good practice. I doubted vampires were involved – their tastes tended to be much more refined – but you never knew. It might give me a lead on the Warlock.

I thought, also, of the cyhyraeth I'd encountered in the rune-infested warehouse on the bay: the vicious wraith-like entity of flesh and bone summoned by Owain Williams – or whatever Owain Williams now was – to destroy his descendant, Hywel Williams. He and I had defeated the entity, but perhaps this was another attempt by the man's malign ancestor. Owain's efforts with the runes had threatened the entire city, and that was the last thing we needed. I was, as one more item on my own Big List of Things To Do, supposed to be tracking Hywel down, bringing him in for his own protection. I'd put little effort into that: he was good at hiding and, more to the point, I wasn't at all clear how much protection the Office could currently provide. But, you never knew. I might be able to kill two birds with one stone. Or maybe even three.

"Any harbinger activity?" I asked. "Any suggestion the activity is portending someone's death?"

"There's no known correlation, but it's always a possibility, right?"

"I…"

I was about to reply when a strange shudder ran through my bones, as if I'd heard a sharply discordant sound or tasted something vile. An unpleasant sensation, distressing. There was something else to it, too. I knew the tug of magical activity now, the sickly flicker of it in my belly, the shadow across my vision. There was sorcery going on, and there was a malicious edge to it. A sense of uncaring, vicious brutality. I heard ragged screams, caught impressions of animals leaping at me, pointed teeth vicious. Something like one of my old attacks, except I knew this was very definitely coming from outside, not my own head.

I half-stood and, alarmed, looked around to find the source. Adrenaline surged through me as I readied myself to fight whatever was coming for me.

Kerrigan laid a hand on my arm. The confusion on his face told me he hadn't felt the intrusion, hadn't heard anything.

"What is it? What's going on?"

"There's something…" I started. Then I remembered who Kerrigan was, and who I was. The sensation of being watched, of something cruel leaping at me, intending to rip out my throat, abruptly vanished. The sense of threat was gone, dissipating as rapidly as it had come. I sank back to my chair. "I thought … sorry, I thought I heard something."

The concern was clear in Kerrigan's gaze. "You look like someone just walked over your grave, laddo. Maybe you should head home, take the day off. You've been through a lot."

"I'm fine," I said. "It's nothing. I'll take the Code 19; I need to get back out there."

I could see Kerrigan didn't like it, but he also couldn't deny the reality of the Office's situation.

"Only if you're sure."

"I presume we don't have the numbers right now to enforce the *two operatives* rule?" I asked.

"We don't. You're on your own."

Excellent. Just what I needed.

"I'll look into it," I said. "Give me what you've got."

Charnel watched as Bone snarled, baring his teeth. His eyes were narrowed, as if focussed on some prey half-glimpsed through the trees.

"I see him," Bone said. "I hear him."

"The one in this world?"

"In this world."

Charnel hadn't known for sure that the twin's blood – kept in reserve for many years in case the reassurances of Earl Grey proved to be unreliable – would suffice.

"Excellent," said Charnel. "Hunt him down. Bring him here to me. Alive is better, but it makes no difference in the end. Once I have finished marking you, go. And, be assured that your right to return here is revoked unless you have the Shahzan boy with you."

The animal growl came again. "I understand. Finish your work, vampire and let me leave."

Two pairs of eyes studied Bone as he left the castle and dropped into a loping run across the gravel and into the shadows of the forest. One set belonged to Charnel, watching the weapon he had unsheathed from behind the red and blue panes of his lead-lined window. Once Bone was beyond the boundaries, Charnel set about reworking the terms of the invitation that had allowed Bone to briefly enter. The new terms were more complicated, but they would be as strong as iron bars once he had them in place. The small danger of Bone's resentment averted, Charnel returned to his library and his goblet of fresh blood and his plans for the future of the country.

The other pair of eyes were rounder, wider. A barn owl,

perched high in one of the oaks, invisible against the dark of the woods and making no sound, watched the figure prowl away from the castle. A wary silence descended upon the forest at Bone's passing, all rustling and scratching stilled. The creatures of the forest were oblivious to his nature, but knew well the smell and the actions of the predator.

After a few moments, the ghost-white owl took to the sky, drifting between the boughs on silent wings, heading in a different direction. Into the deep and secluded woods in the forest's heart.

When Kerrigan was gone, I sipped at the coffee and tried to form an intelligible plan from the maelstrom of thoughts swirling in my brain. The sensation that something was pursuing me, sniffing me out, had given me fresh purpose to act.

My mental to-do list went something like this:
- Explain truth about Az to mother
- Return Az to the world
- Track down Warlock – speak to Quirk?
- Magical skills – pursue bodysnatching(?) case
- Sally

The last item brought all manner of delightful sensations – also anxieties – into my mind. I needed to see Sally again. The thought of her smile lit up my darkest thoughts. The last time we'd talked, she'd been little more than a magically-animated charcoal drawing on a canvas. It was hardly the basis for a satisfying physical relationship. I needed her help, sure – and maybe she needed mine given that the Warlock would be pursuing her – but my main concern was a heady mix of romantic desire and lust. I could admit this to myself at least. Also, she was maybe the only person I could be completely open with. The Librarian knew a lot about me, but it was Sally I needed to talk to. For many reasons.

Despite all that – because I had no actual way to contact her – it was DI Zubrasky that I tracked down first.

She was a friend – I was pretty sure I could call her that – and her name was on the grave disturbance referral note as one of the investigating officers. I'd also promised to get back in touch with her once I'd returned from my trips around the isles, and I'd utterly failed to do so. I felt bad about that.

For once, I tried to follow the proper protocols to get in touch with her, navigating the labyrinthine *Heddlu* phone menu armed only with my case number. Eventually, I got through to DI Evans, the officer who'd been there the first time I entered the Cardiff warehouse, and he told me where I could find Zubrasky. Rather than tackling all the really serious and heavy stuff hanging over me, I stood and left to pay the DI a visit.

Sometimes, when it's all on top of you, it's better to do just something, anything, than nothing at all.

I watched the unfolding police operation leaning against the bonnet of my car. I liked to think it made me look cool, like a cop in some movie. The fact that my car is a battered Mini in need of a wash, and that the sky was sliding to the ground in a fine drizzle, probably combined to reduce the effect.

DI Zubrasky noticed me, but carried on with her work, taking notes as she interviewed a man with a cut forehead standing outside a shop. I couldn't work out if he was a culprit or a victim. Maybe he was both. The police have their own grey areas. The window behind her was badly cracked as if something heavy had smashed into it. Maybe it was the forehead. A yellow plastic ribbon had been set up on stands around the scene to keep the public out. A police van had been parked at a jaunty angle into the street, giving the officers the chance to do their work in some sort of peace.

Eventually, Zubrasky slipped her device into one of her many body armour pockets, handed the man over to a uniformed officer, then headed over to see me, ducking under the yellow tape in a very practised way.

"Danesh," she said. "You're back in Cardiff. The last

time we spoke you were heading off to the Isle of Wight as I recall."

"Isle of Man. Yeah, I've actually been back for a while."

She scowled very slightly at that. "You didn't think I might be worrying about you? You said you were heading into danger. I believe *significant threats* was the term you used. You managed to apprehend your suspect, then?"

I nodded, glancing around to be absolutely sure no one who wasn't *in the know* could overhear us.

"Apprehend is maybe not the right word. *Neutralize* might be better."

She nodded. I could see in the depths of her green eyes that she fully understood what I meant, but decided it was best not to push me any further. I could see, also, that some of the sparkle was back in those eyes. The last time we'd spoken, she'd been down, deflated, some of her fight gone. She'd told me all about it. Maybe she was simply in work mode, but it looked to me like she'd come through it.

"The word on the street is that you spooks are in some kind of trouble," she went on.

Spooks. Proper police officers like Zubrasky and Evans sometimes refer to Office operatives as spooks, no doubt enjoying the hilarious wordplay. We, however, never use the word to talk about ourselves – although I had learned that prior generations of Office operatives had used the term to describe their counterparts in the Mystical Council. The word at least made more sense for them: they were a secretive organization of state agents who *were* mystical and magical in nature.

"Oh?" I asked. "Which street is that?"

"You know what I mean. Is it true?"

I nodded. I wished I smoked, because this would have been a cool moment to flick the butt away, let out a sigh of smoke. "Yeah, you could say that. I mean, we're functioning, but maybe not for much longer."

"You said your days in the Office were numbered anyway."

"That's also still very likely."

"So, what do we do when we face something outside of our ... realm?"

"I wish I knew. For now, we're just getting on with things as best we can."

"Is that why you're here? This grave disturbance case?"

I glanced around again, just to be absolutely sure. The man with the cut forehead was being placed into the back of a police car, an officer's hand on the top of his head to stop him further injuring himself, presumably.

"Partly that, yes, but partly also to tell you to be careful."

She looked amused. "Oh, I'm always careful. Is there a specific threat?"

"Hard to be sure. There are ... *powers* who have become a very clear threat to me, and it's possible they'll use my known contacts to track me down or to apply pressure. I'm sorry, I didn't mean to drag you into this; I'm sure you have plenty of other dangers to be dealing with."

She put a hand on my arm and considered me with her green eyes. She mainly looked amused.

"I'm not an innocent member of the public. We all signed up for this."

"You may not have signed up for what's coming after me. Hoodlums with knives or guns are one thing, screaming horrors from other dimensions are another."

Her eyes very definitely sparkled. How did she do that? "Is that what it is? Screaming horrors from another dimension?"

"It might be. It's hard to be sure what is going to be thrown at me. There might be ... vampires."

Rather than dismissing my words as any normal, sane person would, she gave them full consideration.

She nodded. "I'll be careful."

"Thank you. If you see anything weird – like, out of the ordinary weird – get in touch with me, okay?"

"Sure."

"And, I think you should also assume there are

evildoers out there who know your home address, who will come for you. I'm sorry."

Again, that suggestion seemed to amuse Zubrasky rather than worry her. Now the look in her eye was playful. "They may know my address, but they may not know where I'm actually living right now."

"Oh?" I said. "I thought you'd sworn off women *and* men."

"Yeah, well. That didn't work out well at all."

"Someone new?"

"You remember the woman I was with, that I said I'd lost? Turns out I know nothing. We, well, got back together."

I could see it in her now. It was like she was quietly glowing from within.

"Excellent," I said. "And, ah, nobody official knows her address?"

Zubrasky shook her head. "Nobody at all. If anyone – or anything – comes looking for me, I doubt they're going to find me."

"It still might be worth moving somewhere else for a time. The two of you, I mean. I don't want to be responsible for any harm done to you or your partner."

"I'll think about it."

"Perfect," I said. "Hopefully the situation will resolve itself before too long, but it could get seriously nasty for a time."

"The threat is that significant?"

"We're talking end-of-game boss fight stuff."

"Shit. Are you prepared for that?"

"Guess we'll find out. I hope so."

"Anything we can do – anything I can do – just say, yeah?"

"Thanks." I meant it, too. She and I had come on a journey since I was little more than the Office contact tapping her for information.

"And the mysterious Sally?" she asked. "Did you get anywhere with her?"

I sighed. "I wish I knew; I really do. Do you have time

for a coffee and a handover on the bodysnatcher case? Perhaps you can give me some womanly advice while we're at it."

She smiled in amusement at something.

"Let's do it," she said.

5 – The Sound of Silent Houses

> The victim passed to us by Sister Dorothy Aphrodite Coldwater of the Cardiff Chapter continues to thrive under our care. We believe we have now completely unravelled the hexes that fuddled her thoughts for so many years. She will never be fully healed, and may suffer moments of confusion or memory-loss for the rest of her life, but she is now identifiably herself to talk to. As her natural brain patterns continue to assert themselves, she will recall more and more of her past – and should also start to look forward to the new possibilities that open up for her future.
> – Sister Jane Livingstone, *Minutes of the Gravesend Chapter of the Pale Sisterhood*, 2023

Bone watched from the dark interior of his anonymous black Lexus. The residential street of the London suburb was quiet. Lines of expensive cars were parked beneath a canopy of overhanging tree branches, the first buds emerging from their skeletal branches. Lights were coming on inside the houses, squares of white and pastel tessellating along the two rows of properties. He glanced up into his rear-view mirror, caught a glimpse of his scarred and pocked face, his glowering expression. He looked away.

He knew there was one human inside the address that Charnel had given him. He hadn't seen her; she hadn't left or arrived, but he knew. He no longer noticed how heightened his perceptions were compared to those of a human. He could hear her shuffling around in there: the clinks of cups and saucers, the rustle of papers. The thumping pump of her heart. The sighs. She was very definitely alone. His first plan had been to drive to Cardiff. Find Shahzan, disable him, bind him, then drive him north to his fate with Charnel. The quicker he could complete the hunt, the sooner he could return to his lair to anaesthetize away his teeming thoughts on what it was he had become and the terrible things he'd done. At least his vampire constitution allowed him to drown himself in whatever intoxicants and distractions he could get his hands on – the hardest of drugs, the deepest of self-inflicted cuts – and not die from the effects upon his body. In life, he had shunned all such immorality, save for the sip of Communion wine. Now he was debased. This was another part of Charnel's punishment upon him.

Then this plan had presented itself to him. *Gain intelligence. Learn about your prey.* And she was much nearer to his lair than the Shahzan boy was. Instead of an immediate attack, he would do what he preferred to do on any hunt: circle and stalk. He told himself this was simply the correct tactical approach. He knew, deep down, that it was displacement behaviour, that he was putting off having to commit another atrocity.

The pain of his latest cutting was still sharp in the flesh of his back, but he could easily ignore it, switch it off. It was unimportant. It was the itch that irked him: not just creeping across his skin, but running deeper. The itch was in his blood, in his guts, his mind, compelling him forwards.

He knew he could not resist it. Oh, he had tried, long and often. He had pushed his mind into deep unconsciousness. He had bound his body up with the strongest chains. He had thrown himself from tall buildings and jumped into flames.

Always he emerged or broke free to commit another crime, and there was nothing he could do about it. Biding his time, gathering information, creeping towards his quarry – these things satisfied the itch for a time, but that wouldn't last. The compulsion was growing in his brain like an electrical storm. Soon there would be another act of brutality by his hand, another stain on his ruined soul. He was Charnel's weapon, Charnel's tool.

Perhaps because of his own turmoil, he tried to give those he despatched quick deaths, save them from as much torment as he could. They hadn't thanked him, of course, but it made him extract a morsel of satisfaction from what he did.

What he longed for was revenge on his tormentor. Slaying Charnel, reducing him to dust, would free Bone and all the others in thrall to the Warlock. He knew such a thing was impossible: Charnel was too careful, too powerful. There was no one in the land strong enough to defeat him.

Understanding this, Bone longed mainly for release, his own end. He had lived too long. Again, he knew Charnel would never give him what he wanted. Bone was immensely strong himself, probably indestructibly so, but in this one thing his will was not his own. He had to drink blood in order to continue to exist. Had to pick out vulnerable, lonely people and slaughter them, cut into their flesh to drink from them. The cruelty and the odd intimacy of it. Other vampires supposedly enjoyed feeding, relished the hunt. He did not. Whether this was some shred of his former self lingering within him, or a part of the way that the Warlock was punishing him, he didn't know.

A low rumble of self-loathing growled in his throat. It was an unpleasant habit that had come upon him at some point in the previous hundred years or so. A sign of his descent into barbarism.

Time to act.

He moved, briefly checking his mirrors once again for anyone watching, then sliding out of the car in one fluid motion to stand on the pavement. He had a good idea of the layout of the house, a map built up in his mind both from the movements of the female human, but also from the patchwork perceptions of the moths and spiders and mice that he had tapped into. It was a simple enough trick. He had tried to read directly from the female's mind, but that had proved oddly difficult. There was some protection or corruption in her, turning her thoughts to a language he couldn't read. She had no magical power, though. She was just a human. He would have no trouble subduing her.

If he couldn't siphon what he needed from her mind, she could certainly be persuaded to tell him everything he needed to know. Addresses, insights, contact details, names. The sorts of things only a mother would know. He only hoped that he didn't have to apply too much pressure to persuade her to talk. Too much torment. On the other hand, he had learned there was an art to the hunt. No, art was the wrong word. A *logic*. Cruelty brought to bear in the right place could flush out a quarry, make them react. He could incapacitate this human female by tying her up if he could not control her mind – but he could also fracture her limbs to stop her moving and to make her more pliable. He knew how to do that without actually causing death. It was another mercy no one was ever grateful for.

Keeping to the shadows that were his home, Bone slipped up the side of the house, flitting past lit windows and slipping around the black shapes of wheelie-bins. Empty plant pots lay strewn around at ankle-height, easy to trip over, send clattering, but he picked them out easily. His first plan had been to enter through the back door, but there was a small balcony overlooking the garden on the floor above. Those doors would be locked, too, but the room inside was dark, and he liked the idea of appearing unexpectedly from above to surprise his prey. He would suffer as he crossed the threshold, uninvited as he was. Any vampire endured agonies if they attempted to push themselves through when they were barred. For many, such torment was too much – but he welcomed it, as if it were penance he was paying. It was possible the strength to accomplish this feat was something Charnel had instilled in him, his assassin, all those years ago. The effort would diminish him for a day, but he would remain potent enough for what was needed.

He jumped to the balcony, vaulting effortlessly over the balustrade to land with complete silence. It was an act that would have seemed impossible to the mortal William Bone. No new sounds stirred from within the house; he heard no alarms or gasps. The balcony doors were locked, but by the simple act of holding one in place and pulling sharply on the other, he fractured the three steel bolts connecting the doors to gain access. The woman would be alert to him now, the sharp cracks of his attack on the door loud. She would be concerned, confused. How could there be such a sound from above? That moment of uncertainty would give him time to act, sweep downstairs to incapacitate her and begin his inquisition.

Hating himself, ignoring the mounting agonies, Bone pushed over the threshold and stepped into the room.

I reached my childhood home late that evening. For once, the trains from Cardiff to Paddington and then across London whisked me without delay or difficulty to Dulwich. So that was weird. As I walked along familiar childhood streets, I could see lights blazing through the patterned scarlet curtains that had been a fixture of the family home for as long as I could remember. My mother was there. I wasn't sure if she was expecting me: I'd texted once I'd reached London so as not to give her time to spend hours and hours cooking for me, but I'd received no reply.

I gave up trying to find the right words to explain to her that Az was still alive. I should have told her sooner; I should have told her the moment I found out. Of course, I should. And it wasn't that I was waiting for permission from the Crow. Partly, I thought, I was trying to work out how I felt about the revelation. And partly, I hadn't wanted to raise her hopes that she might see her boy again when she might not. We still didn't know the truth about his status, but I'd decided I couldn't wait any longer. Being honest with myself, I'd also been delaying telling her everything out of straightforward cowardice. It was going to be a tricky conversation – not just because of the hope I would give her when there might be none, but also because of all that the truth of the matter implied: my nature, my work, Az's nature, our family's nature, Earl Grey and the Warlock, the threats to us all.

Enough time had passed since I'd lived at the house that I felt like I should ring the bell before going inside. I resisted the impulse; my mother would be scornful of such formality. I pushed open the outer door and twisted the familiar brass handle on the inner. Smells of wood polish and spicy food came to me. Good signs: she was taking more and more care of herself and the house. On the shoe rack, in the hallway, the wellington boots I'd worn at school were still lined up ready for me. The sight filled me with an odd mixture of emotions.

I shouted into the house that it was only me. No response came. Heating pipes ticked from beneath the floorboards somewhere. Other than that, the house was silent.

A sliver of alarm slithered through me. I'd expected the onrush of her delighted hug at my appearance. I slipped off my shoes and shrugged off my coat, my boyhood programming intact, then stepped inside, senses suddenly on high alert. I called out again, trying to sound light and breezy. What came back to me wasn't a response – but the unmistakable echo of discharged magic twisting in my guts. Something had happened recently in the house. The taste of it was unsettling, unfamiliar.

I peered around the corner of the sitting room, the dining room, the kitchen. Everything was in its place, the house looking better than it had for years, objects in their logical places, all the usual clutter of a life present. A half-finished mug of tea on the coffee table. Bills and letters open on the kitchen table. Newspapers and magazines and a single bowl drying on the rack. Everything normal except for the absence of my mother.

The single, slight *thump* of sound from the next floor up.

This time, as I crept upwards, peering around the corners of the stairwell, I didn't call out. Cold air blew down onto my face. A window was open somewhere. I climbed past the array of family photographs decorating the stairs: holiday and formal shots of the four of us. The three of us. The two. I tried not to think about where *that* countdown was leading. I drew my gun and dialled up the anti-vampire round with a flick of my thumb. At the same time, I readied my own magical powers, focussing on the ever-present swirl of power coiling away within me. I'd wanted practice, the chance to use my abilities, but not like this, not like this.

I peeped into the bedrooms. All were empty of people. People or … other entities. Everything was as it should be. The attic ladder was folded down in the spare room, my mother presumably tidying things away. That was normal enough these days. Then, in her bedroom, the one overlooking the back garden, I saw that one side of the French doors was wide open, blinds swaying in the breeze from outside, flicking like a striking snake. The noise I'd heard was them banging against the wall. A pot plant on a stand had been knocked over, a smudge of soil on the carpet.

Alarm rang through me. My mother might open the doors on a hot summer's day, but not at night and not at this time of year. What had happened here? The sense of a magical discharge grew stronger, becoming a stench in my nose. I crept towards the balcony. I could see someone had ripped the doors open, shearing the bolts with enormous force, something a human would need machinery to achieve.

I pushed the broken door open with my foot and, swatting the flailing blind aside, stepped onto the little balcony.

There was no one there. A few dim stars blazed down through the orange glow of the suburban sky. This was where the magical discharge had happened: some unleashing of a potent spell, some hex to inflict harm. To kill.

I peered over the balcony, down to the ground, flicking on the light built into my gun, fully expecting to see the huddled form of my mother down there on the hard stones of the patio.

Nothing, there was nothing. What was going on here?

Another sound, from higher up in the house. The noise of something heavy scraping across the floor above.

The attic.

We'd never been allowed up there as boys, the lack of floorboards making it unsafe, but I knew my mother stored all the usual boxes and bags and crates up there. It occurred to me it was odd that I'd never helped her. She always fobbed me off, told me there was no need for me to go to the trouble.

Moving as silently as I could manage, I ascended. There was light up there, the sound of something rustling. Peering over the lip of the hatch, I caught a glimpse of an unexpectedly large attic room, the spaces under the eaves lined with shelves that looked to be full of boxes, papers and random objects that my glance couldn't immediately make sense of. At the far end of the room, a pool of light illuminated a desk, the shape of someone bending over it, their back to me. They appeared to be rummaging through the papers in a box.

I climbed the last few steps. The room in the roof was not what I'd expected: it was well-appointed; there were floorboards and there was warmth. It looked very well-used. The sight threw me for a moment. This was not the freezing, cobweb-bedecked storage space I'd been told about. There were secrets here, family mysteries. I hadn't lived at home for a while, but this loft had clearly been in use for a long time. I had no time to ponder what was going on. Keeping my weapon trained on the crouched figure, I crept forwards.

Then I saw who this was. A curious mixture of relief and confusion washed through me. I lowered my gun. My mother was standing there. There was no mark upon her, no sign of an attack. She looked completely well, completely calm. She was lifting something out of one of the boxes, holding it with delicate reverence to the light. It was, I saw, a crude toy house fashioned from bits of card and coloured paper and drawn doors and windows. I had never seen it before. She held it up to the light studying it from all angles and made a little noise that sounded like satisfaction.

I took another step, and the creak of a floorboard gave me away. She turned sharply towards me, alarm melting into pleasure when she saw me.

"Danesh! This is a surprise." She never mistook me for Az these days. I was grateful for that. "You should have said you were coming." She didn't look alarmed in the least. She looked as she always did: delighted to see me.

"What's going on?" I asked. "Are you okay?"

She looked baffled for a moment. "I'm completely fine."

"The balcony door downstairs. What happened? Someone used a great deal of force to break it down. Were we burgled?"

"Oh! Did it blow open? It'll be fine once I get someone to fix the lock."

"Mother! What happened?"

"It's nothing. Someone tried to break in."

"When was this?"

"Oh, I don't know. Half an hour ago?"

She was being weirdly dismissive of the whole situation.

"*Half an hour*? Who was it? What do you mean *tried* to break in. They clearly did break in."

"No, no. They didn't get inside."

That made no sense. The feeling of mysteries being kept from me grew a little. I tried a different approach.

"Did you phone the police?"

"No, no."

"Why not?"

She set the delicate toy house down and considered me.

"You know why, love. The police wouldn't be any help against the thing that tried to get in here, would they?"

"The ... thing?"

"What would you say? Supernatural entity? Monster? It was a vampire, I think. Something of that sort, anyway. I'm no expert."

This conversation was not going as I'd expected. Not at all.

"You … know about such things?"

She smiled the smile of any parent amused by their child's cuteness. So far as I knew, her side of the family had no magical powers at all – but she had been married to my father and had known Bi Bi, my grandfather. I knew, also, that she had some idea of what I did for a living, even though she was supposed to be an innocent civilian. In best British fashion, we'd handled that situation by not talking about it. Sure, she'd have picked up a few hints about things, but mentioning *a vampire* seemed like a very concrete – and probably accurate – piece of knowledge. She'd never said or hinted at any such knowledge over the years since Az, but maybe that was simply one more thing that had been confused out of her by the curse.

She stepped forwards to hug me close, amused by my confusion. This was the precise opposite of our usual situation. Then she held me at arms' length to look into my eyes. A puzzled look came into her eyes.

"Something's wrong. What is it?"

"You just admitted to me that something like a vampire tried to get inside your house. Tried to attack you. What do you think is wrong?"

She shook her head. "It's not that. There's something else. I see it in you; you're worried about it. Sad. What's happened?"

Mothers. There's no hiding things from them. It had been a damn sight easier to keep things secret when her mind was fuddled.

"Tell me if we're in any immediate danger," I said. "Tell me if this vampire is going to return."

"I doubt it very much. The wards are still potent. I checked."

I needed to find out what she meant by that, too.

"Let's go downstairs and make a cup of tea," I said. "There are obviously things we both need to explain."

THE ORDER OF THE BRITISH VAMPIRE

The owl, feathers as white as old bones, settled on the branch of another oak tree. It swayed for a few moments, peering all around, its bird nature still dominant, the human within it taking a few seconds to find control. Find a voice.

Once she was herself again, Sally spoke with her mind to the man she had traversed the woods to visit. She had to force the owl whose body she had borrowed to remain on the branch of that particular tree. On some level, the owl was aware of its nature, and its urge to move on from it was strong.

"There can be no doubt," she said. "The Wolf has been set on his trail. It won't be long, now."

The man's voice was faint when it came, his mind – normally so sparkling bright – a place of grey shadows. Words took moments to form.

"We can't be sure … that the wolf is pursuing Danesh."

"Who else would it be? The master knows what is coming and is preparing his defences, unleashing his dogs. It may already be too late."

"We are doing … all we can."

"We don't have long. When will this great magic of yours be complete?"

"It is never complete. You know this. It simply becomes more potent. The longer it is worked."

"We need to give Danesh the weapon now. It far exceeds anything he may craft for himself."

"Not yet. He is still learning. He has come a long way but … a little more time."

"If he dies battling Bone then we are lost. There is no one else who can defeat the Warlock. The chance may not come again for a thousand years."

Stonewall didn't respond for long moments. It was like that these days. Again and again, she thought he was gone, finally succumbing to the rigours of his ordeal. He couldn't take much more of what he was doing to himself.

Finally he responded, a faint hint of amusement in his voice. How could he find levity in this situation?

"There is more to this than destroying our enemy. You desire Danesh."

"We are asking too much of him, putting him at too great a risk."

"We are asking nothing of him. He chooses his own path. He can't escape who he is."

"We could help him more."

"We are helping him. We will help him soon."

"When?"

"Six more days now, I think. Six, and then I can rest. Six and the weapon will finally be ready. Come find me then. The acorns I gave you will allow you access in human form. They open the ways. Walk the paths and find me, you and the boy."

"You said they were to summon you to the outside world. In case of need, for me or Danesh."

"They do that too – although, given my current situation, that time may be past now. Matters have come to a head quicker than I imagined."

She hesitated. She had always followed his bidding in the past.

"You can't survive another six days of this."

"I have no choice."

"Danesh may not survive that long. either. He is not ready for what is to come. He will blunder into the trap and won't walk out again."

"You underestimate him."

"And you think he is his grandfather. I told you; he isn't ready."

"This will help him become ready. He must face it on his own. Grow. This is what we agreed. I think he may surprise us yet."

"And if it kills him?"

"Then he would never have succeeded anyway. I understand it is a terrible sacrifice."

That he, of all people, in his current position, should talk about *sacrifice* finally stilled her. Logically, he was right. She might be able to defeat Bone, the Warlock's wolf, but she could never destroy the Warlock himself.

Only Danesh could do that. Only Danesh when he was ready.

Only Danesh if he lived long enough.

"It is hard to do nothing," she said. "To simply watch."

"I know. I am sorry," Stonewall said, his voice a whisper in the mist. "It is a hard lesson that everyone who loves, learns. Sometimes you have to let go. And you: you must fly now, little bird. Fly before I succumb to temptation and draw upon you as I have all these others. Watch and wait, then bring him here in six days. If he lives. That is all we can do."

Sally wanted to say more, but there was nothing more to say. All she was doing was weakening him further by distracting him. She let the nature of the owl form she'd borrowed take over, gladly receding from her human turmoil for a time.

She took wing, drifting silently away from the great oak and towards the endless woods, and then to the outside world where her own body was waiting.

6 – A Family of Demon Hunters

> Having taken his sword, the Raja fearlessly climbed the tree, and ordering his son to stand away from below, clutched the Vampire's hair with one hand, and with the other struck such a blow of the sword, that the bough was cut and the thing fell heavily upon the ground. Immediately on falling it gnashed its teeth and began to utter a loud wailing cry like the screams of an infant in pain. Vikram having heard the sound of its lamentations, was pleased, and began to say to himself, "This devil must be alive." Then nimbly sliding down the trunk, he made a captive of the body, and asked "Who art thou?"
>
> – Richard Burton, *Vikram and the Vampire*, 1870

My mother listened in silence, sipping at her tea, as I told her everything. Exactly what I did for a living in the Office. Lady Coldwater and the Sisters. My complicated relationship with Hardknott-Lewis. My doubts and difficulties over my nature. A brief summary of my experiences: the battles I'd fought as an operative but also the extracurricular stuff: Sally and Stonewall and strange things happening in strange woods.

I was avoiding the main point, circling. Delicious smells of some curry dish she had bubbling away on the hob filled the room. My mother nodded but said nothing, waiting for me to get to it. Occasionally she winced as I mentioned some dire threat I'd faced. Animated statues. Angry spirits. Then I got to it: the betrayal of Earl Grey. The Warlock.

Az.

She gasped as I told her that my twin brother was still alive — if that was the right word — and had been frozen away in a magical Oblivion ever since his supposed death. Whatever she'd been expecting, it wasn't that. She sat open-mouthed. It took her a few seconds to process what I was saying.

"Azad?" she managed finally. "Your brother is still alive?"

A distant look of delight lit up her features. This was her greatest desire, her deepest wound. It was also impossible news, a thing she'd never dared hope for. I could see her struggling to contain the hope burning through her. She was aware on some level of the delusions that had beset her over the years, and she couldn't be sure, even now, that this was real.

I set down my mug of tea, kneeled beside her and held her close. The reassurance of close physical contact. Also, just then, I needed it, too. I had missed my brother in ways I couldn't spell out, and this wound in our family, this terrible truth we circled around and tried to live with: it was painful to confront full on, even if the news was positive.

"He's magically frozen as he was on that day," I managed. "He may well be suffering the effects of some malign curse or killing spell. Right now, if we were to pull him out, it might finish him off. The magic might complete its work. We don't know. But, yes, at this moment he is still alive. And the man who attacked him in the woods, Earl Grey, the shadowy figure with the long coat and the demon eyes, has paid the price for what he did. He is dead."

I let her go to consider her. Her mouth worked a few times as she made sense of things.

"If you cure Az, remove the curse — just like the Pale Sisters removed the curse from me — then you can bring him out, save him? Tell me you can do that."

"We hope so. We need to tread carefully, obviously, but there's a chance. We will obviously do everything we can."

"I want to see him."

"The place where he is; it's dangerous. I've been there a few times and barely survived. It might not be good for you."

"I want to see him, Danesh."

Of course she did. I did, too. "I'll see what I can work out. If we can't get him out quickly then we'll find a way to take you in there."

Another thought occurred to her. "You said he was frozen as he was on that day. That means that he's…"

"He's still an eight-year-old boy, yes. He's my twin but he's eight."

"He'll be so confused. Us being suddenly twenty years older. The world as it is now."

She was starting to race ahead, starting to believe. I'd done something similar myself. It would be a rocky road. But, if we got him out, I knew he'd be enfolded in love. He'd be given all the help it was possible to give: emotional, medical, magical. Whether it would be enough, whether he'd be unscathed, happy, it was impossible to know. We could only try.

Another thought struck me, a bittersweet one. In the fight that was to come, there was a very good chance I wasn't going to survive. I obviously hadn't spelled this out to my mother. For her to lose both her boys: that could finish her off. But if we got Az out, at least it meant she'd have one son left, whatever happened. Just a different one.

Before her illness – in my memory at least – my mother was always a practical woman. Faced with difficulties and setbacks, she rolled her sleeves up and did *something*, fixed what she could fix. Before the curse, she was strong. Maybe as the mother of two young boys, living a complicated life facing dangers she had little control over, that was what she had to be. I could see that back in her now, that fight. It was like the opposite of having her life drained away by some vampire.

"This Warlock," she said as she wrapped her mind around everything, "you're saying he's the one responsible for everything? For nearly killing Az and giving your Earl Grey his orders? You're saying he's still out there?"

I nodded. "And it was most likely one of his minions who tried to break in here tonight. Perhaps it was even the Warlock himself, although he prefers to stay in the shadows as much as possible. It's him I'm pursuing. He needs to pay for what he's done to us. And for many, many other things."

I thought she was going to tell me to be careful, not take unnecessary risks. Instead, she did what she must have done many times, with her husband and with me. She did what I guessed all parents had to do all the time, despite their private fears: trust their children.

"I think I can help you."

I sat back to consider her. The little tatty paper house was on the table between us. She'd carried it carefully down from the attic. There was a quiet look on her face that said she'd fight anyone and anything that dared to threaten her or her family.

"How?" I asked. "Your side of the family doesn't have any sort of magic use in it, as far as I know."

She nodded and picked up the delicate model house, turning with her fingertips to study.

"True, yes. There were witches in the north of England and I've sometimes wondered if I have a connection there; that this partly explains why your father and I were attracted to each other. But, you're right. So far as I know I have no special abilities beyond the normal *mother* superpowers. By the sound of it, I may only have survived because I'm no threat to this Warlock. But that doesn't mean I haven't learned a lot."

"From Dad?"

"And his father. You know this was your grandparents' house before it became ours. This was Bi Bi's home, and it contains a lot of echoes of him. His secrets. There are things about this place I should have told you about a long time ago."

"You've been distracted. You haven't been yourself."

"Which, honestly, I'm beginning to think may have been deliberate on our enemy's part. I was also in denial about the dangers you're facing, I think. I haven't done a very good job of preparing you for your life as someone who can use magic. I haven't always known the right things to say. I know there's so much that I don't know."

"It must have been hard for you at times, raising children from a mixed magical/nonmagical background. Telling us the facts while trying to protect us at the same time."

"Your father ... at first, he was very reluctant to expose me to the supernatural world. He tried to protect me. Then, when we came to starting a family, he sat me down and, well, spelled everything out, the good and the bad. He was very modern about things like that; we had no secrets from each other. He was very clear that any children we might have could well have his family's abilities, and while that was wonderful, it could also be extremely dangerous. He wanted me to be very clear on the risks."

"The risks of you staying with him and having children."

"I loved him so much. There was never any question in my mind."

Her eyes were still on the model house with its glued-on strips of pink and orange paper. I could see there were words written upon it now, apparently random lines at odd angles here and there. Spell components, I presumed. The symbols looked like Sanskrit, but I couldn't be sure.

"And, these secrets you mentioned. This paper house is one of them?"

She nodded. "You and I have talked about clearing out this old place and me moving to Wales to be nearer to you. Now, after tonight, I'm not so sure that's a good idea. It would be lovely to be near you, of course it would, but this house ... it's a safe place. Your father and grandfather made sure of it. There are wards worked into the brickwork. Spells of protection woven through the joists. They laboured on them for years, adding to them, strengthening them. This tatty paper house is one of the totems Bi Bi used. It's a sort of avatar of the house itself. The way your dad explained it, it represents the house from a magical point of view. If any of the actual wards are breached, I may not know, but the gaps would show up on this model. Paper strips would fall away, holes would appear. Burn marks."

A childhood memory came to me: a day when some floorboards were being replaced in one of the bedrooms. I recalled seeing odd, intricate carvings in the joists, remembered running my fingers over the smooth shapes in the wood, intrigued. My guess was that there were similar spell components worked throughout the fabric of the family home. It was going to make selling the house – if it ever came to that – interesting.

"And the paper house is intact."

"It is."

"That's why your attacker couldn't get inside. That's how you know you're still safe."

"They were powerful sorcerers, your dad and your grandad. Very powerful. I think you have that, too. Az as well, for all I know."

I thought about my father and grandfather, the battles they must have fought, the risks they must have taken. In that moment, I wished more than anything that I could talk to them, my father especially. I had no memories of Bi Bi, but his presence in the family was a constant (a fond, emotional presence rather than a supernatural one). My mother always spoke warmly of both my father's parents. Bi Bi had died at the age of 64, when Az and I were nearly 2 years old. I had no recollection of him, but I did recall the phrase used by my parents in the years afterwards, whispered like a mantra: *he'd died young, far too young*. It hadn't made much sense to me at the time; 64 seemed impossibly ancient, but I think now that the repeated words were a reaction to the family's shock at his sudden death. My grandfather had been fit, had suffered no medical conditions worth mentioning. And then he stopped, was no longer there. *His* father had lived well into his nineties. I think now, also, that the words were a way of *not* saying something; of protecting Az and me from a grim truth understood by my mother and father: that my grandfather hadn't simply died.

That he'd been killed.

I thought about the picture Gilroy had shown me of Bi Bi: his tall, gangly frame, his tweed suit. His boyish face. Had he felt as unprepared and vulnerable then as I now did?

And then, of course, there was my father. Dead at the age of 40, the terrible pattern repeating, the spiral tightening. Nobody ever said *he'd* died too young, I think because the fact of his loss was too much. The fact was, the males in my family were dying younger and younger. It was not a trend I was keen to continue.

"I wonder what either of them would have made of me ending up in the Office."

She smiled a weak little smile at that. "Perhaps I should have stopped you going there, given everything. Perhaps it's been the best place for you, given you a way into that world. I don't know. At the time, I probably wasn't thinking very straight."

Maybe she was right. The Office, for all its flaws, had led me into a world where I belonged. I'd sort of *reversed* in, to be sure, but I'd got there.

"You're still not completely safe here," I said. "Not outside, maybe not even inside if they throw their full might at you."

"No one is ever completely safe. Everything in life is a risk. For now, I think it's probably better if I'm here. I don't think they're going to expend too much energy trying to get to me. Perhaps it would be better if you slept here, too. At least until you've destroyed this Warlock."

It was tempting. But, broken as the Office was, I still had my responsibilities there. Not so much to the Office, but to some of the things the Office did. In any case, I didn't think I'd be getting too much sleep over the days and weeks to come. And if I were here, the risk to my mother would surely be greater.

"I'll bear it in mind, I will," I said. "I need to tackle the Warlock situation, and I won't be able to do much if I hide away here. Same with sorting out Az."

She nodded. It worried her, but she accepted the truth of it.

I said, "So, you knew they were both active users? Dad and his father I mean."

"Oh yes."

I knew Bi Bi had been active in the Magical Council before that was disbanded. Obviously neither had had anything to do with the Office of the Witchfinder General.

"Were they working alone?"

"Alone or with like-minded friends. They were a sort of informal resistance to magical threats, trying to carry on the work that Bi Bi had been doing for the government."

"Do you know about the Magical Council?"

"Your dad told me something about it. He regretted its disbandment, said it was a terrible mistake. He would have been at home there."

My memories of my father were happy ones: his ready smile beneath his moustache; his laugh. His terrible skill with a football. He was a warm and loving family man, always there for me, always enjoying spending time with me. At the same time, he'd given me no introduction to the magical world that he and his father were part of. He had to have suspected I'd need instruction, guidance, but he'd given me nothing. A little burst of resentment at that ran through me.

I let it go; there was no point to it. After Az, he must have been terrified about losing me and had tried to keep me away from such things. My father must have known that Az had died because of the powers he had given his son. Now that I thought about it, that knowledge must have eaten my father up.

I wished I could sit down with him to talk about all this with him.

Instead I said, "The attic, all those books and boxes. That was Dad's?"

"And Bi Bi's before him. It's a whole treasure trove of texts and books and notes. There's generations of magical work up there, a lot of which Bi Bi brought with him from India. *Folk magic*, your dad used to call it, and I could tell from the way he said it that he was hugely respectful of it. He said that Bi Bi came from a family of demon hunters, experts in destroying creatures like the *vetala* and the *rakshasa*. I told you there are things I should have mentioned a long time ago. The magical knowledge contained up there is part of it. I was up there the other day thinking I needed to sort through it all. I don't know where to start. But, now that you're facing this Warlock and all the rest of it, I think *you* should. Who knows what you might find up there that's useful?"

I thought about Gilroy, and the mantras he'd mentioned that I was supposed to be practising. I sat back, my gaze rising upwards as if I could glimpse all the books in the attic. I desperately needed magical guidance, and all that was up there, waiting for me. Why hadn't it occurred to me to look? Time was short, now, and I could probably spend years up there learning the wisdom of my forebears – but my mother was right. There had to be useful knowledge in the attic for the fight that was to come.

"Mind if I stay a night or two to go through it all?" I asked. I didn't say that I also wanted to be around just in case another attack came. The only reply I got was my mother's frown of disapproval at my question. It said: *of course I could stay. I didn't need to ask. I never needed to ask. Idiot.*

I didn't get too much sleep over the next two days. Mostly, I sat in the attic poring over the notes and books and scribbled texts piled on the shelves up there. Occasionally, the wind picked up outside, making the roof-beams creak like the spars of a wooden sailing ship and sending jets of air hissing through tiny gaps between roof and walls. Despite that, the space was cozy, the warmth of the house rising through it, and it was comfortable. My father and grandfather had clearly spent a lot of time up there. The space felt ... lived in. Inhabited. It wasn't the heart of the house – that was the kitchen – but it felt like the heart of *something*. A world. An identity. The sounds of the outside were muffled and distant.

As I worked, my mother materialised occasionally to bring coffee and food, the two of us falling back into comfortable parent/child roles. I think we both enjoyed it. The coffee she made, I noted was good: strong, black, rich. When she'd laboured under the mind-hex all those years, she'd brought me tea or – even worse – weak, milky instant coffee. It was another good sign.

On one of these occasions, a thought occurred to my mother, and she stopped before descending the ladder. This was something she often did, to gaze fondly upon me, but this time she spoke.

"Do you think they've always known about this address? This Warlock. Or have they just learned about it now somehow?"

"I wish I knew," I said. It was a good question. I couldn't see how they might have found out about my mother, but the timing couldn't be a coincidence. The sense of a net closing in, a rope tightening about us, was hard to avoid.

Other than these occasional visits, I was on my own, lost in the demon-hunting world of the forebears on my father's side. We suffered no more attacks. A locksmith came to fix the shattered balcony door, but thankfully he didn't ask too many questions about how it had happened.

Bi Bi's filing system was confusing at first, but once I'd grasped that he was arranging his notes by what he called his *precepts* – the particular magical underpinning of the spell or rite involved – I began to make progress. A lot of the more recent entries were in English, but older items were written in different languages and using different alphabets. I could read Urdu and could pick my way through anything written in Sanskrit – but the Indian subcontinent had and has a lot of languages and scripts. I was going to struggle with most of them. Lady Coldwater might be able to help me with some of it, and if she couldn't, I guessed I might be able to enlist the help of the bookwyrm creature that roved the Librarian's books.

I made a mental note to talk to Lady Coldwater about moving the entire collection of magical texts into the care of the Pale Sisters. It became more and more obvious as I worked that there were some serious magical fireworks described in these old tomes and letters. In the wrong hands a lot of it could be seriously misused, and I was committing several magus law crimes simply by reading it. I was committing one serious offence by being in the same room as some of it. The writings had to be a part of the reason the house had been attacked; the sooner it was gone, the safer my mother would be.

On the second day of searching, I tracked down some of Bi Bi's journals of his time with the Mystical Council. Before I'd killed him, Peter Warder had told me there was no mention of my grandfather in the Office's *English Wizardry* archive – but now I discovered that there should have been a lot. Bi Bi mentioned numerous occasions upon which the Council and the Office co-operated to tackle some supernatural horror or a sect of magical fascists intent on unleashing their latest atrocity. There was clearly a grudging cooperation between these magical and non-magical arms of the British state, a fact that had been written out of our later accounts. The arrangement had all come to an end with the disbandment of the Council. My guess was that all mentions of Bi Bi – or any Shahzans – had been expunged from the Office archives, upon the orders of the Warlock.

I also found some interesting details of the activities of Bi Bi's father back in India in the early twentieth century. One particular account detailed his battle with a *rakshasa*, a demon-like entity that I was vaguely familiar with from childhood stories. From the accounts, it was hard not to see parallels between these creatures and the beings we would call vampires in the west: the fanged mouths, the fondness for human blood. The incredible physical strength. Very often, the terrible cruelty. Whether these were the same entities, or cousins, I wasn't enough of a cryptozoologist to know, despite the subject matter of my thesis, but it was interesting to read how Bi Bi had found that the skills and weapons our family had wielded in India had proved useful in Britain.

Again and again in the notes, the references to enchantments and incantations were frustratingly obscure. The name of a weapon or a ritual with no explanation of what they were. Many of the names of the moves and stances evoked a life and a time I would never know: *Horns of the Water Buffalo*; *Rearing Cobra*; *Soaring Kite*; *Leaping Tiger*. The most detailed account I found was another of my great-grandfather's battles, this one with committing a *vetala*, a voracious spirit capable of possession. He spelled out in some detail the steps and the mantras he employed while battling the entity with his physical weapons. His attack sounded almost like a ritual dance, movements and words in synchronization. He mentioned steps and poses and blows to be struck on certain syllables, but still the detail was lacking – frustratingly so. The assumption was that the reader would understand precisely what the various magical precepts were.

Lodged behind a pile of dog-eared manilla folders, I did find three blue hardback notebooks in a little pile on their own. Whether this was part of some elaborate filing system or the books were being concealed, I didn't know. Opening one – the familiar smell of dust and paper strong – I saw what I'd come to recognize as my grandfather's handwriting. His script was very formal, each letter beautifully formed in purple ink, even when he was jotting down some stray thought or recounting a terrifying battle he'd fought.

Leafing through the book, my eye hit upon one such battle. The word *Warlock* leapt out at me.

The date of the entry was 1949 – the year on the back of the photograph Gilroy had shown me. My grandfather would have been 17 or 18. Gilroy had said that picture was taken during celebrations at Chequers following the defeat of some malign foe – and also that the Council was derided and disbanded within a year of the event. Reading Bi Bi's account now, I wondered if this was the very event that had triggered the destruction of the Mystical Council.

> We cornered one of the devils in Westminster. It was out in the open during the hours of daylight, concealing itself within the folds of a thick London smog that rendered it impossible for anyone to see more than a few yards — anyone human, at least. We had good intelligence that not only was this the very leader of the beasts in this country, but also that it was intending to launch an attack upon a certain very prominent politician (there is no need to name him) who had not, presumably, seen fit to cooperate with the Vampire Lord's demands on some detail of national policy and was, therefore, now to be coerced into compliance.
>
> The politician in question was in the habit of walking along the Embankment near to the Palace of Westminster before attending a session of parliament, presumably in an effort to find clearer air near the water. The revenant, knowing this, chose the spot to spring its attack — but we, likewise, did the same.
>
> It was a grim battle, the creature monstrously strong and able to move with terrifying speed. At times, it seemed to be little more than a blur of black lines in the grey. The politician, at least, was saved, hurrying off into the fog for the Palace at

our shouts for him to flee. One of our number, Thagenham, was not so lucky. The vampire skewered him with its bare hand, lifting him high off the ground before hurling him into the Thames. Thagenham's screams made for an ugly sound as they disappeared into the fog. Another of our number, a fearless boy called Gilroy, made use of the moment to swing his ensorcelled blade at the vampire. The sword metal did little, weak and primitive as it was, but it at least struck its target, hacking a cruel gash out of the creature's side. The vampire healed almost immediately, a poisonous black smoke coming from it to reknit its flesh. But the creature's attention upon Thagenham and Gilroy at least gave me the briefest moment to make my own attack.

I had brought with me weapons of my own — including Vaknis, the twisted Neem tree spike that I had carried with me half way across the world. It was a fearsome weapon to one of this vampire's kind, the spells running through it a bane and an anathema. I had slain many such abominations with it over the years, both here in England and upon the Subcontinent — and I knew that my forebears had wielded it for centuries before me, devoting long hours to its refinement.

This was to be its last attack. I struck the Vampire Lord upon its leg, this limb being the nearest part of its body as I completed the ritual forms and movements required to magnify my attack. The weapon had a clear effect, making the creature howl in the most animal and unsettling manner imaginable.

> *The Warlock writhed as I held the weapon in its cursed flesh, and I felt the magic flowing from me as Vaknis drew upon my strength, pulling in more and more as it hungered to overcome the Warlock's defences.*
>
> *I hung on for as long as I could. The wooden spike was hot in my hand, black smoke coiling off it, but I refused to relent. The Warlock lashed and snapped at me, but the spike of wood pinned him into place so that he was unable to free himself.*
>
> *I will never know how close I came to destroying that foul creature that day. I persisted until it felt as though every drop of my being had been consumed by the magical battle. A dark fog filled my vision, one much grimmer and more profound than the standard London smog around us.*
>
> *With a cry of anguish, I relented and fell to the ground. Vaknis burned with a black flame and was utterly destroyed. The Warlock sprang free from its hold. He regarded me with a look of purest malice for a moment as if he intended to devour me there and then — and vanished in a blur into the fogs, his designs frustrated for the moment.*
>
> *It took me a day or two to fully recover from this encounter. I have no doubt that our reprieve from this abomination will only be temporary.*

I read the passage again and again, seeking some detail that might be useful to me. It wasn't the first mention I'd come across of the Vaknis artefact: this had been referenced several times, along with a speculation that other, yet more powerful such weapons might be found in the world. One was mentioned, supposedly the most fearsome of them all: the *Norskrang artefact*. So far as anyone knew, it was long-gone, long-destroyed, though no one seemed to be sure exactly *how* long.

Again and again, though, there were the unexplained references to words, movements, even states of mind, that Bi Bi had employed in his fights with the Warlock. They were generally Indian words rendered in English: the anti-vampire and anti-demon lore of our family. Stonewall might have learned some of them from my grandfather, as others might – but here, clearly, was an invaluable treasure-trove of powerful magics that I would need in my fight to come, if only I could decipher them.

I thought about the Warlock's clear antipathy to my family. Bi Bi's account explained some of it, but I saw that there was a lot more to it. The Warlock feared our knowledge, our skills, our histories. We were a threat to him. Which meant I urgently needed to acquire this knowledge myself.

Many hours later, my back cramping and my eyes feeling like they were full of sand, it was a simple step backwards that finally gave me what I needed. Looking around the attic space, searching for something that would explain what these various mantras and spells and movements might be, a board creaked beneath my heel and wobbled very slightly.

It was a small thing. But it was also a huge thing. Crouching, I traced the outline of the loose board showing through the rug. Underneath, it was clear that a small section of the floor had been sawed out to form a little hideaway. Levering it up with my fingernails, my heart galloping with sudden excitement, I shone in the light from my phone.

Another book. A hardback notebook the size of the red diary volumes, but this one was gold-edged, the cover a pattern of marbled swirls. There was no title upon it. Inside, there was more purple handwriting, even more formal than the diaries, the writing closer to calligraphy.

There were also finely-drawn diagrams depicting combat dance-steps as well as patterns of rune-like characters arrayed in circles and triangles. Elsewhere, there were sketches of the constellations – the Indian ones rather than the Western – as well as representations of the moon in its various phases. There were also depictions of weapons: straight and curved blades, wooden stakes with tiny runes etched upon them, hammers of the sort that might be used to strike bells.

At the top of each page, written in a curling, sculpted script, was the name of the *precept* the text and the diagrams were describing.

The spell.

I tried one in the quiet of the room, the simplest I could find, one that appeared to need no particular phase of the moon or time of the year to function. Bi Bi's title called it *The First Opening of the Way*, although whether this was his description or a traditional name, I had no way of knowing. I took it slowly, not wanting to summon some dire threat into our quiet house, unsure if that was even possible, but needing to know if the magical recipes in the book worked. If I could make them work.

I began to intone the words on the page. Reading them out loud, I found a rhythm to them, a resonance. The process of crafting magic was becoming easier and easier since my immersion in the cold pool in Stonewall's wood. My voice seemed to take on an extra timbre. At the same time, I felt the familiar flutter and rush of magic within my stomach. The swirling power of it mounted rapidly, and I glimpsed a shadow coalescing before me in the centre of the attic floor, a blue-purple tinge to it. Raising my hand – an action depicted on the page – I found I could seize hold of the shadow, move it from side-to-side, direct it. I knew that if I wanted to, I could use it, hurl it at some foe to engulf them, send them swirling into some other plane of existence. I'd seen similar things, of course. Our clothcutter knives achieved a similar effect as, I guessed, did Sesames.

The urge to use the magic I was forming, unleash it,

was powerful. It was compelling; maybe too much so. With an effort, I closed my eyes, lowered my hand to let the magic subside. After a few moments when it seemed to resist me, the patch of shadow faded.

I closed the book. It was real. It was also incomplete – or at least, it wasn't full. Maybe my grandfather had been working on it when he'd met his end. Maybe it was his life's work. In the end, I spent three nights at my boyhood home, cross-referencing every note and scrap of information about the magic that my family had wielded for so many centuries. I could have stayed longer: the attic was a treasure-trove. What was more, I felt cocooned, given the protections on the house. It was a luxurious feeling, but I knew it couldn't last. My enemies were out there, and they weren't going to take kindly to being thwarted.

I'd received a message from Zubrasky telling me she'd correlated a few more pieces of information on the bodysnatcher matter. It wasn't that which finally drew me away from London, though. It was a message from the Crow telling me he'd made arrangements for me to visit Az in Oblivion.

I explained everything I'd uncovered to my mother and left her with my solemn vows to look after myself and to do everything I could for my brother. Soon, Bi Bi's spell book in my bag, I was rattling westwards en route to Cardiff.

7 – Next Level

> Of weapons for the despatch of demons and other malevolent entities, much has been written – and much more, no doubt, lost as this or that practitioner dies taking their hard-won knowledge with them. My search for the *De Magicae Mortis* book continues. I have uncovered more references to it, including further suggestions that it contains instructions for the crafting of powerful antivampiric weapons such as my own *Vaknis* (the loss of which I still feel) and the fabled *Norskrang* artefact. Stonewall remains especially fascinated in this aspect of our fight, and spends much of his time scouring arcane libraries around the country in search of the tome – or of extracts from it. No doubt these are harsh magics, spells I would fear to employ myself, but Stonewall appears to have no such qualms.
>
> – Amoor Shahzan, *Private Diary*, 1953

I arrived back at the office that evening, my bag dropped beside me on the floor because I hadn't dared return to my flat. I needed to sort out somewhere to sleep, which I had a plan for. Before I got to that, I flicked through the latest items on MORIARTY looking for anything worth reading. It was the usual stream of sightings, rumours, false alarms, the occasional genuine case. Olwen, I noted in passing, was spending more and more time in the field. We were stretched far too thinly; the two-operative rule appeared to have been completely dropped, unless the shout was some very clear danger.

There were also some notes from Zubrasky, all her latest research entered onto the standard police system, which we had backdoor entry to. She'd been careful, hadn't used any Office terminology or made any mention of possible supernatural activity, but she'd woven in a few keywords that she knew our systems would pick up. *Graves. Disturbed remains. Unexplained.* She'd even slyly included the number 19 a couple of times (I must have mentioned to her that we'd tag the case a Code 19), in dates and counts and the like. She was teasing me.

She did mention that she wouldn't be pursuing the case any further – and also that she was out of town on a separate investigation for the next few weeks, which I took to mean she'd heeded my advice and, after further reflection, had taken herself and her partner off somewhere unspecified for a time. That was good. It meant we weren't going to get a chance for the handover in person, but she was one less person for me to worry about, and she had provided everything in the notes I might need.

She'd also drawn a plot of the reported cases overlaid onto the city centre. Most, but not all, coincided with active or historical burial grounds – to be expected in a disturbed graveyard case. I figured the outliers might be more interesting. Nearly all of them coincided with the site of an old building – although that might mean nothing. Long-established cities like Cardiff have old buildings and remains everywhere. If I squinted at the pattern in my best unscientific method, I could see a rough line to the sites, like a diagonal slash across the city centre.

I'd start by looking into a few of them tomorrow. It was an odd sensation to find myself hoping there was some revenant or ghoul behind the attacks, as I very much wanted to try out some of the moves and spells I'd been learning. I'd spent the train journey back from London surreptitiously studying Bi Bi's book, quietly mouthing a number of the precepts, feeling the magical tug within as each one worked their effect. Some of them were seriously heavyweight, gruelling magic, spells for which I needed to practice the movements in harmony with the words – a thing I'd decided probably wasn't socially acceptable on a train.

Now, I made my way down to the library. I'd decided to tell Lady Coldwater all about the cache of forbidden books at my childhood home – at some point. I'd become more and more worried about them sitting there, a potential target for any inquisitive or malevolent user. And, of course, I could help with their removal and cataloguing. But that wasn't the main reason for my visit: I had a more pressing need.

As on my previous visit, my pass still admitted me to the hallowed domain. I tried to ignore the notion that I was like a vampire with an invitation to enter a building. As before, I moved with deliberate noise – a heavy footfall – so that there was no possibility of the Lady thinking I was creeping into the library to commit some terrible crime like trying to borrow a book.

This time, I only got half-way to the centre before stopping. To my amazement, there was someone else down there, sitting with their back to me at one of the tables, quietly reading a book as if this was just a *library* library. A tall pile of tomes stood on the desk next to them, as if the Lady would just let you take as many as you wanted. It was a man, I thought, but not Hardknott-Lewis or Kerrigan or anyone that might be found down here. Now I did tread more warily, unclear what was going on. The xylophone floorboards did their work, alerting the Lady to my location and direction. She glanced up at me from the hexagonal desk at the centre of Level -1, then looked back down to her own book as if I were of no interest whatsoever.

I took this to mean that I was allowed to approach. I'd just about reached her when the sitting man turned to regard me.

Gilroy.

The sight stopped me mid-stride. How had he escaped his confinement from that other basement? And what the hell was he doing *here*? At the very least, I'd have expected him to flee to a week-long hedonistic bender, make the most of his freedom. Not come and read books.

"Danesh," he said. There was a definite sparkle of

amusement in his eye. I wondered which Gilroy this was: the foul-mouthed abrasive man who answered the door to his flat, or the learned, thoughtful person who sat alone behind the door, buried in his researches. His clothes, at least, were sharper than the baggy beigy things he usually wore.

"What are you doing here?" I asked.

"Reading books. Obviously."

"But ... how? Why?"

Lady Coldwater, seemingly able to move completely quietly despite the clicky clacky floor, appeared beside me.

"I let him out."

"You?"

"I needed to talk to him. We can't leave the poor soul languishing in there with the Office falling apart, can we? You may disapprove of him, but he's still a person. You'd probably forget he was there and let him starve."

Not entirely fair, but I let it pass.

"Does Hardknott-Lewis know about this?"

She shrugged, as if it was a matter of no consequence. "I haven't told him. Whether or not he *knows* is another matter. I suspect he has other things on his mind given the way things are going. The fact remains that Gilroy is here by my invitation. The question I have is, why are you here, Danesh?"

"I need a safe place to stay. The rooms where you hid Oliver Auchter during the *Eyes* investigation: I assume they're empty now?"

The Librarian considered me for several moments, her gaze intent. I felt like we trusted each other now; we'd come a long way. Clearly not enough for her to welcome me into her lair without a second thought.

"You're hiding from the Warlock and his minions?"

"It seems sensible. This is the safest place I know."

She snorted, as if I'd seriously underestimated the powers of my enemies.

"What about your mother?"

"We decided she's safest where she is for now."

"The wards protecting her house. The ones set up by your father and grandfather."

"You know about those?"

"Obviously. Otherwise, I wouldn't have been able to mention them just now. Are you saying you *weren't* aware of them?"

"Not until very recently."

She didn't look angry with me. She looked disappointed. "Very well, yes, you can stay. I can't guarantee you'll be safe. I can guarantee you won't be safe if you meddle with any of the books without me knowing."

It was as close to a fond and loving embrace as I was going to get. I thanked her.

Gilroy, watching the exchange with a grin on his face, said, "Well, well. We'll be neighbours, Danesh. You can come over for a boy's night in."

He hadn't really forgiven me falling for his boorish toxic male act. I told him I looked forward to it, then went to drop my bag in the plain little cell that I recalled from my former visit. It hadn't changed: there was a bed and a chair, a few tattered works of fiction on a shelf and a television screen that may or may not have worked screwed to the wall. The only decoration to brighten up the bare surfaces was the red rug on the floor.

There was no sign at all of any sort of machine or device for making a decent cup of coffee. The terrible sacrifices we had to make in the fight against evil.

I returned to find the Librarian and Gilroy deep in conversation. It still jarred to see them together, close neighbours as they'd been for so long a time. How long had this been going on? Had she been letting him out regularly when we weren't looking? There were the security cameras on his door, of course, but the Lady had no qualms with deploying magic so long as it was used for good. For all I knew, she'd been hexing the system for years to give Gilroy access to the library. Gilroy had insisted to me that he and Lady Coldwater rarely communicated, but maybe that was the story they'd agreed between them. His researches into the history of the Office and the Mystical Council: the two of them might have been working together on it for years.

The thought was a satisfying one. The Office had treated Gilroy terribly.

As I approached, they looked up to consider me. A look passed between them, the sort of silent communication that old friends and lovers employ. They appeared to have decided it was time to tell me something.

"Sit down, Danesh," the Librarian said. "There are things we need to tell you. And things you need to tell us."

I sat. Gilroy kicked off first. He was definitely the version I'd been introduced to inside his lair: polite, learned, thoughtful. I caught him glancing at Lady Coldwater occasionally, and I think I understood at least part of the reason he was being so restrained.

"Have you got close to the Warlock yet?" he asked. "Have you managed to work out where its lair is? You're obviously aware you need to seek it out and destroy it before it does the same to you?"

"I'm making some progress in preparing for the fight, but please, feel free to give me any help you can."

"Why do you think I'm here, spending my few-remaining days reading old books?"

He didn't look like he was on his last legs. It looked to me like he'd come back to life, but I didn't say so.

"Why *are* you here?" I asked. "I mean, if you can come and go freely, why haven't you simply walked away, disappeared?"

"Do I really have to explain that? I'm here for the same reason you are. Jail doors work both ways: they keep you in, but they also keep the world *out*."

"The Warlock will come for you, too."

"Of course. If that thing learns I'm walking the streets again, it'll track me down. That or send one if its minions on my trail. That's why I'm depending on you, boy."

"These books you mentioned: what are they? How can you help?"

"You reminded me of it yourself. That photo I showed you of your grandfather and the Mystical Council."

"There was a Gilroy there," I said, "fighting alongside my grandfather, according to Bi Bi's diary. But that can't have been you. You're not *that* old." The image of Owain Williams flashed through my mind at that point. "Wait. Unless that *was* you and you've worked some years-defying necromancy spell. Evangelina Mormont was the same; she didn't seem to age at all."

This time, the scowl on Gilroy's face was clearly no act. "*Necromancer*. That's all you lot think I am. Let me tell you, boy, that's a label you applied to me because I have some abilities communing with the recently-departed. It does not define who I am."

"Sorry," I said. "Please, tell me who was in the picture. It had to be a relative."

"My father. You've probably worked out that magic runs in families, like any hereditary condition. My father told me all about it, how he helped in the fight against an ancient and powerful vampire in the fogs of London. That was the Warlock, wasn't it?"

"Bi Bi thought so."

Gilroy nodded. "Did the account you read make mention of Vaknis? The wooden stake your grandfather used to harm the Warlock?"

"He said it was consumed by the attack. It simply wasn't powerful enough."

"That's what I thought. It's also the only example I know of someone being able to inflict any harm at all upon the vampire Lord. Which brings us to why I'm here in the library."

"There's a book?" I asked.

"Our ace investigator," he said. "Yes. My father told me that he recalled your grandfather and Arthur Stonewall discussing a tome of really powerful incantations, including those required to make artefacts like Vaknis. The rites and sacrifices needed to enchant anti-vampire weapons. Bi Bi didn't have a copy of the book, but he'd learned of its existence. Your grandfather knew how to wield such a weapon better than anyone, but he didn't know how to make one. Stonewall was extremely interested in finding out; he spent years trying to find a copy of the book."

"Did he succeed?"

"We don't know."

"Are you saying there's a copy of this book here?"

The Librarian spoke now, the familiar chill of warning in her voice she used whenever anyone dared to suggest referring to one of the items in her care.

"One of the books on Level -4 is called *De Magicae Mortis*. That's *Of Death Magic* if your Latin is as bad as I assume."

"I think I could have worked that out."

"Oh? And will you be able to read the entire book, too?"

"Probably not. Go on."

"The tome is mediaeval, hand-written. Beautifully illuminated in its own way – but not, I assume, by any sect of virtuous monks. It's under extreme protection, a very nasty book full of very nasty magic. From what we've worked out, this was the book your grandfather was talking about."

Level -4. I'd only been down as far as Level -3, on our visit to consult The Book of Shadows in the *head full of dark* case. That had been alarming enough, the destructive magic coiling off the tome filling my vision with dark clouds. The books on Level -4 had to be seriously malign. The library, I knew, only went to Level -5 – and it was said that the bottom level contained only a single, apocalyptic tome that I hoped I'd never have to open.

"If there's something useful in this book, though, we have to go and look at it," I said.

The Librarian was predictably scornful. "You can't just *go and look at it* like it's some pleasant little work of fantasy. The risks of even going near it are grave. Do I need to keep telling you this?"

"But you must have been down there. You must have put the book there, set up the wards and so on around it. You must, I don't know, go and check on it from time to time. Make sure it hasn't escaped its shackles or summoned a nest of demons or something."

She really didn't like to admit it. My words might be true, but my guess was she'd done all of that – and hadn't escaped unscathed from her experiences.

Another look passed between the Lady and Gilroy.

"We've been planning an expedition down there," Gilroy said. "It will be dangerous."

"We have to go, despite the risks," I said. "We can't afford not to. There's a danger to every course of action at this point."

Lady Coldwater's voice was quiet. She was seriously spooked by what we were about to attempt. That troubled me more than anything. Very little alarmed the Librarian.

"We will make the attempt," she said. "The three of us. I shall begin unwinding the wards, but we will have to seal the doors behind us when we go down there, in case things go badly. There's a chance we may end up trapped with entities that we can't allow out into the world. Do you understand?"

"I understand."

"Very well. Give me an hour or two, and I'll be ready."

I nodded to my two unlikely conspirators. We were, perhaps, the oddest party ever assembled to venture into a dungeon. The delay, though, gave me time to make my other descent, the one the Crow had set up for me.

"I'll be back soon."

Once again, the Lady appeared to know all about what had been happening to me.

"You're making your visit to Oblivion with Hardknott-Lewis now?"

"You know about that?"

Not replying, she hurried over to her desk. I threw a questioning glance at Gilroy, but he shrugged.

She returned holding a small brass device with a lens at one end, something like a small telescope. A pretty useless telescope, because you couldn't look through it.

"When you get to your brother, embed this in the ice above him. Lens down. Push it in as far as it will go."

"Did you know he was in there? Did you know all this time?"

"I found out very recently. I don't keep secrets for Campbell, or for anyone. I keep only my own secrets."

She handed me the object. It was surprisingly heavy, more to it than an empty tube. Something small rattled within it. I peered into the lens – and saw an eye staring back at me. It wasn't my eye. This one was green, and it scanned around constantly as if searching for something. It blinked. It was alive.

"What is it? Whose eye is this?"

"There's nothing evil about it, if that's what you're thinking. It's a *watchpiece*. We use them to protect and stand guard over things – and in order to study a location where it isn't safe to stay."

"*We* as in the Pale Sisters?"

"The eye in there came from one of us, freely donated when she died in order to carry on the fight."

"What will it do?"

"Your brother ... we need to find out what's going on with him. Is there a killing curse upon him like Hardknott-Lewis's boy? This will allow me to investigate. Not as good as being there, but I can work through the watchpiece. Your brother's thoughts will be sluggish, perhaps too slow to read, but I may be able to pick up something through the shadows. A memory of his last few moments, perhaps, some clue as to any curse or hex that was thrown at him. I'll also know if anyone attempts to disturb your brother's resting place."

"Who would do that?"

"I have no idea. Do you?"

"We need to pull him out of there," I said. "Return him to the world."

"I assume you explained everything to your mother?"

"I did."

"How did she take it?"

"I'd say she took it surprisingly well. Obviously, it's a lot to process. She wants to visit him."

The Lady nodded in satisfaction at that. The Pale Sisters had done a good job with my mother.

"I doubt she's ready for that journey yet. And removing

your brother from Oblivion won't be as simple as digging him out of the ice and carrying him here. There might be all manner of wards and incantations surrounding him. Traps and protections. I don't understand why he's even there. I believe Earl Grey was the one responsible for interring him?"

"With the Warlock in the background."

She nodded. "You did good, by the way. Killing Grey. You have my gratitude for that. But, whatever their reason for doing this, holding your brother, they would have taken care to protect themselves. Hopefully I can work out what they did, what magic is at work on your twin. I can't promise anything. You see this little dial on the watchpiece? Once the device is in place, the marker will move to the left. That means it's properly positioned. Make sure it's set up properly, or I won't be able to help."

A tiny brass triangular pointer sat in a slot on the top of the device. I could barely see it even in the well-lit library. I could only hope I could make it out in Oblivion. I slipped the watchpiece into my pocket, thanked her, and headed for the surface.

8 – Descending to the Depths

Undertook my monthly visit to Oblivion today. These things become more routine, but they do not become any easier. I removed the helmet from my suit for as long as I could bear it, wanting to have as little as possible between myself and my boy. I know that the distance between us remains unbridgeable. As ever, he looked so alive there in the ice, as if I had only to warm him up to bring him back to me. I talked to him for as long as I could manage to do so.

As I returned to the portal, I noted a new tomb dug into the ice. It is not the work of the Welsh Office; I can only assume one of the other regions has committed this fresh unfortunate to that terrible domain. The shocking thing was the age of the individual: a mere boy, seven or eight years old, younger even than Gregory. I cannot begin to imagine what crime this lad could have committed to warrant such a grim incarceration. I shall endeavour to find out, for surely there is more to this than meets the eye. Alas, my time was already running out on this visit, preventing me from carrying out further investigation.

– Campbell Hardknott-Lewis, Lord High Witchfinder of All Wales, *private journal*, 2013

The suit I needed for my journey to Oblivion stood quietly in a corner of the Office supply room.

In truth, it had always freaked me out a little bit. I'd have been okay if it had been folded away on a shelf or left in a heap in a corner. It was the fact that it *stood* there that did it, with its empty gaze and its faceless wooden mannikin for a skeleton. It was always hard to escape the delusion that the damn thing was watching me when I dropped in to, say, refresh my supply of Armitage Hobbles or to steal the Grafton Projector in an illicit attempt to make contact with Sally.

More than anything, the suit resembled an old-fashioned deep-sea diver's suit, the sort they used before they'd figured out how a diver could carry an oxygen supply on their back. The helmet was a solid brass sphere with three little windows in it, a big one at the front and smaller ones to each side. The front one opened up on an actual hinge if you unscrewed the catches. A snaking tube of thick rubber led out of the back of the helmet. As with the mundane design upon which the suit was based, this carried breathable air to the wearer – but the whole thing wasn't designed to keep the water out, nor to allow a descent into the depths of a mere ocean. Strong enchantments had been woven into its tough canvas, etched into its brass fittings. In Office parlance, it was an IDES: an *Inimical Dimension Exploration Suit*.

This was a suit built to allow the wearer to withstand the baleful environment of Oblivion.

It was also damned heavy. The boots were like bricks – which made no sense. Buoyancy wasn't a challenge in Oblivion. I guessed there were other dimensions where you might get swept away on currents of purest malice if you weren't careful. You didn't need to wear a suit to survive in Oblivion – I'd proved that, and I knew Hardknott-Lewis had made the journey unprotected on numerous occasions – but wearing it gave you more time to play with. This was how operatives had the time to inter forgotten souls in the deep ice of that distant realm. I threaded one arm through the coiled rubber hose and set out to carry the suit to the portal – which is to say, to the broom cupboard down the corridor. The temptation to wear the helmet as I strode down the corridor was irresistible, but, disappointingly, I didn't encounter anyone else.

Hardknott-Lewis was waiting for me at the portal. He'd

uttered the chthonic syllables – no doubt with distaste in his mouth – to open up the doorway. The little square room where mops and brushes and industrial-sized bottles of detergent were normally kept was now transformed. For one thing, the space was much larger, receding into an impossible distance. Then there was the swirling spiral of bruise-blue and ultra-violent purple where the far wall should be. I could hear the gateway whispering to me in my brain, tugging at me. Beckoning me.

The Crow was already in a suit, save for his gauntlets and helmet. He clearly had his own equipment; his suit looked decidedly cleaner and newer than the one I bore. It appeared to have been tailored to his exact size, whereas mine had apparently been sized for a prop forward in the Welsh rugby team. Which I was not. I wondered how many private excursions Hardknott-Lewis had made to Oblivion for a quiet word with his son over the years.

He nodded at me, then proceeded to help me into the suit, holding each leg so I could step into it, then pulling laces tight and zipping zips on my back to swaddle me as tightly as possible in the outfit. There were various pouches and pockets on the exterior of the suit. I slipped the Lady's watchpiece into one. The Crow noticed, but didn't say anything.

"How long will we have in there?" I asked as I worked my fingers into the gauntlets and screwed the brass cuffs into place to prevent any Oblivion air seeping in. The old metal squealed as I turned it, which didn't give me great confidence in how well the suit had been maintained.

"In theory, we would be unharmed after an hour," the Crow said, "but I would suggest we restrict ourselves to half that, to be on the safe side."

He took my rubber air tube and connected the other end to a nozzle in the wall, turning a brass wheel to lock it into place.

"This is just air?" I asked.

"Air and certain other additions mixed in to protect you."

More m/tech. I spared him the inquisition on how he justified this latest use of magic. Once he was happy that the air supply was functioning – I could hear the pump and hiss of it – he held up the helmet to place it over my head like he was going to crown me. I knew from my jape in the corridor that the damned thing was incredibly heavy, but that didn't appear to trouble Hardknott-Lewis, wire-strong as he was.

He placed it sideways on my shoulders, then gave it a quarter-turn to lock it into place. The world immediately dimmed as it receded behind the thick viewing glass. Reality warped. I sucked in air and tasted rubber and sweat and the definite tang of something sorcerous. I could see Hardknott-Lewis's lips moving as he said something, his features distorting through the old glass. No sound came through. Assuming he was asking if I could breathe, I nodded my head. The effort of doing so made my neck muscles creak sharply. I needed to try and keep my head upright. It seemed impossible that anyone could move around in a suit like this, let alone exert themselves carrying bodies and digging holes in the Oblivion permafrost.

The buzz and crackle of white noise sounded in my ear, then, and Hardknott-Lewis's voice began to speak to me. Clearly the suits had some sort of crude radio connection. I could see that he had his own helmet on now.

"Danesh? Can you hear me?"

"I can. Do radio connections work in Oblivion?"

"Surprisingly, they do. I have no idea why. There is a small battery pack on your back. So long as we stay near to each other we can communicate, but if we move more than twenty yards apart, we will lose contact. Hold one of your arms up in the air."

He clearly knew what he was doing; I did as he said for once. It was an effort in the bulky suit.

"Very good. This is a sign that means we have some sort of problem and need to return to our world. Two arms means *now*. Another good indication is to lie down on the ground and not move."

It took me a moment to realise this latter sentence was probably a joke.

"I'll try not to do either."

"Good. I shall leave the return portal in clear view so either of us can reach it if needed. Hopefully we will both return safely."

"Yeah," I said. "That would be ideal."

"Whatever you do, please don't wander off in the opposite direction. The Oblivion dimension is endless and does not conform to the geometries we would consider normal. If you lose sight of the portal, you may never find it again. For you it may never *exist* again."

The memory of Jamie Tavish flashed through my mind, the sight of his lifeless body lying on the ground seemingly a few steps away from the mirror-portal that had been opened up from his house in Tintern.

His resting place.

I gave a thumbs-up and clumped forwards, fighting the weight of the suit. My breathing was loud in my ears, the sound echoing off the brass sphere. I found I had to time my breaths with the puffs of air being pumped through the tube, then the exhaled air being sucked back out. The whole arrangement felt very unreliable.

Hardknott-Lewis reached the swirling purple-blue gateway first. Without looking back, he strode through. The air-tubes of his own suit now stopped in mid-air, but the portal didn't sever them. Again, I had no idea how that worked. Maybe physics stopped at the portal. I lifted my left foot and stepped into the wall. There was an odd sensation, a tingling in my bones, as I stood with one foot in our dimension and the other in Oblivion. Then I was completely through.

The landscape was becoming familiar to me now: the endless flat, grey plain of the frozen ground and the endless, flat grey plain of the sky. The only detail disrupting the endless tedium of it was the little forest of iron spikes that marked the Office's burial site. At least the suit appeared to be doing its job of protecting me: the life-devouring cold was reduced to a distant chill in my fingers and toes. My mind remained clear. Turning awkwardly and peering through the helmet's side window, I could see the purple-blue outline of the doorway back to our world.

I followed Hardknott-Lewis. Neither of us spoke as we skirted the patch of clear ice with the marker at its head that read *Gregory Hardknott-Lewis*. I could see him down there through ice that was like glass. A young lad lying as if simply asleep in his outdoor clothes, a red jumper and blue jeans – asleep, except for the fact that his eyes were wide open, staring out at us. The shiver that ran through me at the sight had nothing to do with the icy atmosphere of Oblivion.

My breath grew heavier in my ears, ragged, as we lumbered forwards, weaving around more plots, past the one I recognized as the sometime home of Evangelina Mormont, to reach the unmarked one I'd stumbled upon – quite literally – during my previous visit.

I wanted to kneel but wasn't at all sure I'd be able to stand up again. Hardknott-Lewis and I stood side-by-side, neither of us wanting to set foot on the ice directly over my brother. Az looked just as I remembered: his lips blue, his skin tinged with frost, but also weirdly alive as though he could just wake up. His flesh was full, his eyes also open. The ice of Oblivion wasn't like the ice of our world. It froze you in more profound ways than simply sucking cold out of you. It *stopped* you as you were.

I noticed something else, too, a detail I hadn't spotted on my previous visit, nearly dying as I'd been. From some angles it was invisible, but it became clear as I stepped sideways: a silvery cord leading out of the ice and upwards into the sky. Craning my heavy head as far back as I could, I saw that, someway above, the line stopped abruptly. Nothing held it there.

Hardknott-Lewis had seen where I was looking. "That has always been there. It must have been installed when your brother was interred. I assume it leads out of this dimension to some other."

Now I did drop heavily to my knees so I could get a

closer look. The delicate silvery line led into the ice. When it reached Az's forehead, it split into two, one line going into each of his ears.

"What the hell is it doing?"

The Crow's voice was fuzzy in my ears, coming at me between his breaths. "At first I thought it might be a grave bell."

I'd never heard of such a thing. "A grave bell?"

"People used to have them fitted when they were buried. In Victorian times, I mean. The idea was you could pull the rope and ring a bell. If you woke up to find you had been buried."

"My god."

"People were really worried about it for a time."

"Did they ever work? Did the bells get rung?"

"In truth, there are cases in the Office archives. This, though, it is different. There is obviously something magical to it given its location. And I cannot see how your brother could ever pull the rope."

"Why is it going into his ears?"

"That I don't know. I haven't dared intervene. I assume it is … whispering something to him."

"What's at the other end?"

"Regrettably, I have never been able to find that out, either. After you uncovered Earl Grey's treachery, I thought his quarters might lie at the other end. Our searches there have found nothing."

"So, perhaps the Warlock's lair."

"I would say that is most likely, yes. Of course, we do not know where that is, only that it is not in any of the locations we know about."

I peered back down at my brother. He looked peaceful at least. Confused, maybe, too, the hint of a frown on his perfect skin. I hoped that was simply how he'd been caught in the moment and that his life wasn't one drawn-out sensation of alarm. I pulled a heavy knife from my belt and began to hack out an indentation over Az's head, wide enough for the watchpiece. The ice was surprisingly easy to work. It also refused to behave in expected ways:

the shards I chipped out of the ice didn't lie around as they would have in the real world. They simply vanished, like a bad graphical effect in a computer game.

When I had a hole big enough, I plucked out the watchpiece and pressed it in so it was only a few centimetres from Az's face. Switching the damn thing on was the hardest part in my bulky gauntlets. I got it after only about seventeen attempts. Or I thought I did. The little pointer looked like it had moved, but I couldn't tell if the device was now active.

I felt Hardknott-Lewis's hand upon my shoulder. He knew what I was doing. He wasn't trying to stop me; he was offering me a hand to stand up. I rose to one knee and let him haul me to my feet.

He spoke, his voice quiet despite his closeness. "If we could get to the Warlock, we might know a lot more about the magic that has been worked here. The rope, the curse – all of it."

I could feel the first tendrils of cold slipping into my mind, now. The first dark thoughts of despair. What chance did I have to rescue Az? How could I ever hope to defeat the Warlock? I wanted to shout at the Crow that we could never defeat such an opponent. That the attempt was simply going to mean my death.

Instead I said, "We should go back."

"Of course. We can return as often as you like."

The Crow turned and began to trudge his way back to the portal. I hesitated for a moment, turning off the suit's radio so the Crow wouldn't hear, before speaking directly to my brother below me in the ice.

"I'm going to get you out of there, Az. I killed one of the people who did this to you, and now I'm going to destroy the other. Then we'll get you out of there, I promise, little brother."

Little brother. Az was born half an hour before I was. Technically he was, in fact, my big brother.

9 – De Magicae Mortis

> After much searching through the shelves of the accursed library we found, in a secret compartment triggered by the rotation of the statue of a most hideous imp, the single volume we had travelled to Cambridge to recover. The master of that manor, choosing his own death rather than to give up his secrets, proved to be of little use. No matter; the book became ours. A very cruel and vicious tome it undoubtedly is. The covering at first appeared to be some animal leather – vellum perhaps – but its yellow colour and familiar texture soon suggested to us that the binding was of human, not bovine, flesh. Once it is secured in our own care, we can rebind it and right at least that small wrong. What we cannot do is to right the horrors contained within. The impulse to burn the book was strong, but we had agreed not to, for who knows when and where knowledge of the cruel magics contained within might prove useful to us – or to those who come after us?
>
> – Sister Anna Dottery, *The Pale Sisterhood*, 1886

Back in the library, the Lady, Gilroy and I began our descent to the depths of the lower levels. As on my previous visit, we each carried an FTET – a Feynman's Thaumic Exposure Tube – to check our exposure to potentially harmful magical fields. I went with a standard-issue electrically-powered Office one, although both the Lady and Gilroy, I noticed, preferred an old-fashioned brass contraption. Lady Coldwater also disappeared for a moment behind her desk and returned with a pair of very shiny, and doubtlessly very sharp, katanas. I could see runes engraved upon them. She laid them gently on the desk while she shrugged her way into a leather harness, then slid the blades into an X across her back. They maybe ruined the line of her long floral dress slightly.

"You're expecting a swordfight?" I asked.

She shrugged. "Honestly? If it comes to that, we're not going to come back alive."

"Then why take them?"

"Habit, I suppose. I feel safer carrying them. I assume you have all your standard Office equipment?"

"I do."

She nodded at both of us in a *let's do this* way. She went first, unlocking each door with keys and biometrics and some sort of *unlock* spell judging by the pull of magic I felt each time. After each door, she waited for us to go past so she could secure it behind us.

Not talking, we wound down the spiral stairs to the smooth concrete walls of Level -2, oddly modern-looking in comparison to the rows of ancient and slightly twisted wooden bookshelves with their lines of chained tomes on Level -1. We passed the display case where the bookwyrm was devouring some new set of written ideas, some new world of concepts, the dazzling little illuminated dragon sniffing its way along the lines of cramped handwriting of some dusty tome with a green binding. Then we passed through the bank-vault blast-proof steel doors that protected the books down on Level -3 – or, more likely, protected the outside world from the books.

At the bottom of the spiral iron stairs, I stood for a moment in the more subdued lighting while my eyes adjusted, my ears picking out the background symphony of rustles and growls and snarls I recalled from my previous visit. It was emanating from the assembled books – or from entities trapped within their words. There were no bookcases here; each volume was kept in isolation within its own locked display case, a clear space around it. The fizzing sense of *potential* in the air was powerful, as if lightning was about to strike. I found myself wishing I was still wearing my Inimical Dimension Exploration Suit.

We hurried through, padding in a straight line along shadow-banked aisles, directly past the small volume bound in red leather that we'd come to interrogate on our previous visit. The *Book of Shadows*. Was it my impression or did it twitch as I walked by, like it was preparing to leap at me?

This time there were two sets of heavy steel doors, a small room between them like an airlock on a spaceship. We stood in that plain cell for a moment, locked doors ahead and behind, while the atmosphere or the pressure or something sorted itself out. Again, we didn't speak. The Lady had put her hand to a pad on the inner door, making a red light blink. There was a hiss of air from somewhere. Up above, in the ceiling, there was a metal grille, and I was reminded of the murder-holes castle defenders had once supposedly used to tip hot oil onto attackers. The good news was, no hot oil came gushing down onto us. After a moment, the red light went green, and we proceeded. Another spiral staircase, clanging loudly under our feet, deposited us upon Level -4.

Once again, the background lighting was subdued, but there were columns of blue light all across the space, like some sort of art installation. It took me a moment to understand what I was seeing. Mesh spheres the size of footballs were held in mid-air by chains attached to the ceiling and floor. The chains were heavy, the sort that might have been used to moor a ship. Within each sphere was a single book. Each was illuminated by a blue spot light shining from above, by which I could see that runic circles had been marked onto the floor around each anchor-point. Not drawn or painted – drawings could be rubbed out and paint could fade – these were etched into the concrete in hard lines. I knew enough of the forbidden alphabets by now to recognize powerful containment and forbidding spells.

The air was still but the spheres, I noted, were all moving, swaying and jerking.

The Lady spoke quietly beside me, explaining what we were seeing. "Those are pure iron spheres and chains. Not as strong as steel to us, but much worse for them. Between them, and the wards, most incursions will be contained, but obviously do not enter any of the runic circles. If you do, I am not going to follow you inside to save you."

"How do we get to *De Magicae Mortis* then?" I asked.

"We'll activate some extra defences that should temporarily suppress anything malign trying to break out."

"It's hard not to focus on the word *should* in that sentence."

The Lady considered me through her glasses as if trying to understand me.

She said, "Eventually, it all comes down to a matter of luck."

"That's not encouraging."

"Do you want to give up and go back upstairs? Because that's honestly the sensible thing to do."

I shook my head. We all knew we were going to make the attempt.

I followed the Lady warily, suddenly very conscious of where I was placing each foot. Strange how walking in a straight line becomes difficult if you start concentrating upon it. The first spheres we neared were clearly aware of us. They lashed around frantically, their chains squealing. One book – a bound pad of something that looked like papyrus – flew against its iron sphere like a trapped chicken desperately flapping its wings. Dark shapes flickered from the books as if the paragraphs were trying to tear themselves free. I saw the outlines of demonic creatures emerging, straining to escape, before collapsing back into the pages. A rising cacophony of howls and snarls filled the room.

"How do books become possessed like this anyway?" I asked. "They're just words on paper, right?" I was talking out of nervousness. I'd seen enough weird shit not to find this baffling. But the shrieks from the books were sending primal shivers of revulsion through my bones.

"People read the words, that's the problem," she said. "I told you, reading books is dangerous and should be avoided at all cost. Working the spells activates them, begins the process of summoning entities into our world. The problem is they can get … anchored to the summoning words. Half-manifested. Especially with repeated use. Often, in fact, it's the author that is the problem. They re-read what they've written, and without realising it they work the magic. Some of these books have the potential to cause huge harm."

As she spoke, a line of shadow, something like a long, bony arm, flew out of one of the volumes, reaching through the mesh towards us. It got so close that I found myself ducking. There was a howl of pain and fury from the book, and I glimpsed a red eye between its pages, glaring at me.

"Wouldn't it be better to burn them all?" I asked as I hurried past.

To my surprise, she didn't object to my heresy.

"Often, yes, that would be safest. But then someone comes knocking on my door, demanding to discover some detail of a spell or a rite for good reasons. Someone like you. Would we be any the safer if our enemies had these books and we didn't?"

We stopped at the circle that contained *De Magicae Mortis*. I didn't need to be a highly-trained expert in the arcane to know it was an evil book. The angry shadows lashing off it, like solar flares upon a black star, made that clear enough. The smell of corruption and sulphur and something like burning metal – pervasive in the room – became much stronger.

Not looking at the book, the Lady and Gilroy set about creating another circle, slightly outside the etched one in the concrete. They set a series of multicoloured crystals on the ground, spacing them out carefully, turning them so that certain facets pointed in certain directions.

"Tell me what you're doing," I said.

The Lady's reply was to tell me to ready my weapons. Gilroy, though, glancing up at me, was more helpful.

"We're going to create a purification cone. A space summoned creatures can't enter. Most summoned creatures. It won't last long though; they're damned hard to maintain. Between the Librarian and me, we'll have maybe a minute."

"I'll join in with the effort," I said.

The Lady made a noise that suggested she doubted I could do much. Gilroy, again, wasn't so dismissive.

"Think you can do that? They'll exploit any weakness in the circle, use you to break out."

"I can do it," I said. I'd come across spells along similar lines in Bi Bi's book – and I was learning that working magic was not, a lot of the time, a simple matter of components, of words and runes and artefacts; it was a matter of magical potential being harnessed and directed, using those components as something like scaffolding. I could follow the lead of the Lady and Gilroy, add my strength to theirs.

Once the crystals were in place, the Lady pulled a pair of gloves from a pocket. Instead of the usual white cotton ones librarians use for old and delicate books, these were thicker, almost like gauntlets, made from some heavy white material. A filigree of silver filaments ran through them, something like that woven into the IDES, I assumed. There were rubber tips on the fingers to help with turning pages.

"No one else is to touch the book," she said. "Understood?"

We both nodded. Neither of us needed telling. I didn't pull my gun or my clothcutter knife – but I touched each, reassuring myself that they were both there.

For a moment nothing happened. Then a face, its features twisted into purest malice, loomed out of the book before being snapped back into its pages. I felt the tug of magic in my gut, like a thrill of excitement and fear mixed together. The crystals began to glow. I could feel both the Lady and Gilroy streaming magical energy into them. Tentatively, wary of overwhelming the effort, I lent my strength to that effort. It was like joining in with a group of singers, of moderating your voice so that it harmonised – or at least wasn't discordant. With gratifying ease, I found the note. The magic swelled and the light from the crystals joined, then began to reach upwards forming a cone that reached into the runic circle to surround the book.

The light became too bright to look at with my open eyes. I felt the moment, like a shout of *now* in my head, as we completed the spell, tied it off. Once again, I worked the magic more or less instinctively. It felt like pieces falling into the right place in my mind. The light flared even brighter for a moment – pink and brown through my eyelids – then cooled slightly.

"Hurry now," the Lady said. "The things in this book will only be suppressed for a few moments."

I knew the magic had worked – no gurning forms leered out of the book now – but I still hesitated, letting the Lady and Gilroy cross the circle first. Nothing happened when they did so. I made a little show of glancing at my FTET – I was exposed, but not dangerously so – then stepped up to the book.

The Lady already had it open. I saw cramped handwriting, many sections annotated with scribbled sidenotes. There were diagrams of constellations, and what looked like maps, although the regions or countries were unfamiliar. There were many runes, some in lines, others in circles, and there were sketches of entities that were clearly demonic. One page depicted an oak tree, drawn in simple lines. It didn't have the seven stars arrayed above it, but the similarity to the drawing at the start of *The Old Ways* was striking. Bedfellowes might have lifted his design from this very book.

The Lady must have seen the surprise on my face.

"Very good. You have been paying attention. You recognize this."

"English Wizardry copied it," I said.

"Bedfellowes was a fool, completely misguided, completely out of his depth. But he did have access to powerful and genuine books when he cobbled together his nonsense – including *this* book, by the look of it."

The next page was a tightly-written mass of more handwritten text, barely any spaces between the words. It looked like Latin. The Lady scanned it, her lips moving as she picked out phrases. A frown of anger clouded her features. She turned the page to reveal another depiction of an oak tree. This one, though, was altered. Many tiny objects festooned its wide branches, hanging there like Christmas decorations.

I knew they were not Christmas decorations.

"I've seen this tree, too," I said.

The Lady looked up sharply at me. It was Gilroy that spoke, though. "In which book?"

"Not in any book. I mean, I've really seen a tree like this. In the woods"

"Which woods?"

"That's actually a hard question to answer. The woods. Stonewall was there. He led me there in his guise as the horned man. He'd gone full *Jack in the Green*."

The Lady didn't attempt to hide her disapproving frown. "You never told me about any of this."

"It was during my visit to the Isle of Man – or at least, I reached his woods from there, but I think I was somewhere else. Wherever these woods are, that's where he's been hiding."

"You're sure he had a tree like this?" Gilroy asked. "Festooned with all these dead woodland animals?"

It wasn't a vision I was likely to forget in a hurry. "He insisted he hadn't killed any of them – or at least that they'd been about to die when he found them. Mice, voles, squirrels. Birds like robins and blackbirds. Also, larger creatures, I don't know, ferrets and foxes and pine martens and even small deer."

The Lady was shaking her head. "So much power. So much death. I wonder if it will be enough. Did he give the tree a name?"

I thought back. "*Darach dubh*, he called it. The *black oak*, right? I think he also referred to it as *the winter tree*."

"Did he explain to you why he was doing this?"

"He refused to tell me anything. He said it was *a slow, deep incantation*. He talked about *deep roots* as I recall."

"Roots?"

I thought back to the scene. I'd assumed he meant figurative roots, magical roots. But there had been an actual root, too: an exposed section of wood like a toe the tree was dipping into the ground. The light that had flowed through the great oak – the light that had come from the unfortunate mouse or vole he'd tied to it – I'd assumed the light had simply passed down through that root into the ground for some reason. Now I wasn't so sure.

"You must be able to work out from this book what he was doing," I said.

Another glance passed between Gilroy and the Librarian. They both understood something I didn't. The Lady turned another page, read more text, nodding her head faintly as if the words were confirming her suspicions.

She was about to turn another leaf when the white light of the purification cone flickered noticeably. It returned, but it was definitely dimmer. I saw there was a depiction of a four-legged demon on the page, cruelty caught in the inked lines of its face. I saw the creature twitch and writhe, like it was trying to tear itself free of its bindings.

"Back outside the circle," the Lady said. "*Now*."

We needed no further prompting. The Lady slammed the book shut and we threw ourselves through the stuttering cone of light. A claw that was half-shadow and half-malice reached out at me, nearly catching my foot as I stumbled to relative safety. It hit the invisible wall of the runic circle like it was striking glass.

The cone of light failed completely. I found I was breathing heavily.

At the same time, ideas clicked together in my mind. Understanding. "You said my grandfather and Stonewall were interested in creating anti-vampire weapons. Artefacts like Vaknis. Is that what Stonewall is doing?"

The other books seemed riled by our actions, the snarls

and screams mounting in volume. It was like being inside the cage of a pack of riled chimpanzees.

"Leave the crystals," the Librarian said. "We're going."

She hurried from the book, leading us back to the door, glancing from side to side as she did so, as if expecting an ambush at any moment. We followed. The Librarian drew one of her swords, but she answered my question over her shoulder.

"Stonewall may have been working on his magic for a long time, each small death another sacrifice, another shot of stolen power. It's terrible sorcery. In the past, many innocents have been slaughtered to work it, whole populations sacrificed."

"He's creating another Vaknis?"

"So it would seem."

We reached the door – which, mercifully, opened. Once everything was sealed back up, we began to climb. I thought about Stonewall alone in his woods. I thought about the acorn he'd given me, the one he said the oak itself had dropped and that I could crush to summon him when I faced the Warlock. Did I want to do that? How could I know he'd be ready? If he was engaged in working this long, powerful magic, maybe I didn't want to distract him. I also knew I didn't want to face the Warlock while simply hoping that Stonewall was ready and willing to fight at my side.

I had a new item for my to-do list. Speaking mainly to myself, I said, "Okay. I need to talk to Stonewall again."

10 – Weapons for the Despatch of Demons

> Be aware that certain spellcrafted items make for very effective weapons in the fight against the foes that beset us. The humblest sliver of metal or wood may become a fearsome tool of destruction once the necessary spells and hexes are woven into it. Indeed, there are many of the more powerful classes of demons and the undying that can only be harmed by such artefacts: the more terrible the entity, the more powerful the magical weapon needed. Some of the more powerful of such artefacts are themselves grim and terrible objects, seething with magic that has been ingrained within them at terrible cost and sacrifice. Such is the price that must sometimes be paid to defend the living.
> – original unknown, trans. Amoor Shahzan, *Destroying the Vetala*, 1964

It was getting on for midnight by the time I finally reached the seclusion of my cell in the library. The bed was hard beneath my back as I lay in the darkness. I'd been afraid that Gilroy would insist on calling, but, mercifully, he left me in peace. I was exhausted; it had been a long day, but sleep wouldn't come. Thoughts about the Warlock, and Stonewall, and Sally and my mother swirled around in my mind.

Eventually, I gave up and took my grandfather's book out of my backpack. I ran through the precepts I'd already learned, spelling them out in my mind, visualising each without actually working it. It was already becoming a familiar routine. My mantras, I guessed. Gilroy would have been proud of me.

I wanted each spell to be instinctive if the time came to use them. Confronted by the Warlock or one of his minions, I was not going to be allowed to fumble around with a book; my demonic foe was not going to wait politely while I found the correct page and reminded myself of the syllables and movements I needed to perform. As I envisioned each spell, I felt its potency as the suggestion of a tug or a flaring of heat in my gut. I was getting better at understanding which was powerful and which I had more trouble with. One or two, still, I could not get to work at all. I wished I had my grandfather there to give me the precise syllables to speak, the exact motions to make. The written word could only convey so much. Gilroy hadn't been any help when I'd questioned him: he recalled my grandfather gesturing and intoning, but had no understanding of how the magic worked. I'd quizzed the Lady about it, too, and had received only a raised eyebrow in response.

One other item was defeating me: many of the precepts involved the use of artefacts – very often, weapons like the Vaknis that Gilroy had mentioned. These precepts I could do little with – but many of them were precisely the ones I needed to employ when it came to facing vampiric entities such as the Warlock. The talk of Stonewall and his tree in the woods had given me the idea that I could perhaps fashion *something* that might help me if it came to it. Anything I could produce in a short space of time was going to be weak, but it might be better than nothing. My grandfather's book did spell out a few basic cantrips for the creation of such artefacts. I assumed they were weak, low-level, given his interest in *De Magicae Mortis* – but I hoped they might be good enough for the creation of everyday weapons.

So far as I could tell from the text, any short spike into which the relevant incantations could be ingrained would suffice – but wood was easiest. Something to do with *the natural energy flowing through the mother tree* according to the book, but I suspected it was because wood was easier to carve runes into.

I had nothing that would suffice, though. Something as simple as a doorstop might do – but the sharper it was, the better. In the end, I left my lair to see if the Lady was still awake. Inevitably she was – did she ever sleep? – sitting in the pool of light at her desk while the rest of the library slumbered in darkness. I watched from a distance as she tore a page out of some book and set fire to it with a match, holding it for as long as she could bear in her fingers while it crisped and bent into ashes.

It wasn't the normal behaviour for a librarian.

I padded towards her, taking great care not to move silently. I could tell from the angle of her head as she worked that she was aware of me.

"Gilroy's gone?" I asked.

She didn't look up at me as her fingers ran down the next page of the tome she was working on. "Sleeps in his bed in his flat."

"I'd have thought he'd have preferred to be free of it?"

She shrugged. "Says it's comfortable, he's used to it. I suppose not having a locked door in the way makes all the difference."

I wanted to ask her why she was burning pages from a book, but I decided against it. Instead, I explained what I was looking for, then waited while she finished her page.

She looked up at me through her glasses, her eyes large. "Are you trying to make your own weapon to fight the Warlock, or is this for practice?"

"Both."

"I have one or two items that might suffice." She sounded reluctant. My guess was she was having trouble sharing her space, her world, with Gilroy and me. With anyone, really.

She stood, marking her page with a slip of red silk before closing the book. She swept the ashes of the burned pages – there was quite a pile, I saw – into a brass pot with a small brush. Then she led me across the library floor away from my room, leading me down the

Oneiromancy, Haruspicy and Divination aisle to a plain door marked *No Admittance – Staff Room*. I'd glimpsed it before and assumed it was some sort of storage space for books, but I saw that wasn't it at all once she led me inside.

It was, indeed, a staff room – but there was also a great range of other weaponry carefully arranged in racks around the walls. Swords curved and straight, daggers, throwing stars, maces, hammers, spears. Also shields, crossbows, batons, and an array of other devices for inflicting damage upon the human (and unhuman) form, weapons that I didn't have names for. There were a couple of pikes strung across the roof that were so long I couldn't even see how she'd managed to manoeuvre them down the stairs. I could tell from the background hum of energy in the room that many of the weapons were enchanted. There were also firearms, from discreet pistols up to rifles and shotguns, one with an enormously long barrel for shooting something really, really big. There were also much smaller racks holding bullets of many different sizes, as well as cartridges and quarrels and arrows – and, in a rack at knee-height on the far wall, a large collection of short wooden spikes.

She plucked five of them off the wall and handed them to me, blunt end first.

"Will these do?" she asked.

I took the first. It was some heavy wood, nearly black and carved to a sharp point. It was comfortable to hold and felt well-balanced to attack with. I felt the faintest tingle of magic coming off it, a distant *hunger* from the spike. The Librarian obviously made no attempt to hide her weapons as m/tech.

"They're enchanted," I said.

"Barely. They're the best I have. A friend of mine in Cwmbran, a Sister, carves them for me and imbues them with as much magic as she can. They're nothing like Vaknis, obviously, but they're good enough for weak vampiric entities. The newly arisen, those that haven't fed for a long time. In truth, a blow from one of these is more likely to piss a vampire off than to destroy it, in my experience."

I took all five. "Thank you."

"I'm here to serve," she said, with a look that suggested she believed the exact opposite.

Returning to my cell, I began to work with the weapons, holding them in the manner Bi Bi had spelled out, concealing them in one moment and then slashing and stabbing with them at another. I was struck, once again, how similar the actions were to the steps of a dance. There was a ritual to it, a formality. Whether this was an essential part of the magic or simply the means by which the magic had been passed down in the days before the written word, I had no way of knowing. Dutifully, I practised each routine, performing each spin and step and lunge over and over. When I got it right, I felt … *something*. It was magical in nature, I knew, but it wasn't like the burning energy that I occasionally unleashed. It felt like a *rightness* inside me; the sense of things slotting into their correct place. It allowed me to perfect my movements and my timings the more I practised.

The weapons themselves, though, were as weak as the Lady had said. A brief glow of destructive magic was all I got from wielding them. My grandfather had apparently been a master at brandishing such weapons, but it was clear from his 1953 writings that he hadn't known how to fashion or enhance them. He hadn't brought that knowledge with him from India. His later writings were a little more helpful. So far as I could tell, he'd never made use of a copy of *De Magicae Mortis*, but he had tracked down other sources that contained a few scraps on how spikes and daggers could be powered up. He'd set these down, transcribing runes into his book and detailing how they be strung together to form syllables, words. He also explained how *life force* could be infused into a spike – *such that, given enough spirit, enough blood, a weapon may become truly fearsome* – but he didn't spell out the rites required. Either he never found out, or he'd found the magic too distasteful.

I could at least try etching his runes into the Librarian's spikes. I sat on my bed and pulled out my clothcutter knife. It wasn't its intended purpose, but it would do. I had to work carefully, tracing out each rune in thin lines before cutting them properly into the wood. As I worked, I became slowly aware of a presence in the shadowy corner of the room, standing there behind me. I paid it no direct attention, aware of it but not turning to look at it, sensing somehow that to do so would dismiss it. It was too faint and weak for the light of close attention. It intrigued me. I knew it was watching me with hungry intent, but it wasn't moving. The presence was troubling – I half-suspected some malign side-effect of my trip down into the depths of the library – but some deeper voice in me told me I didn't need to be afraid. After a time, I grasped why, who this was.

I continued to work, scraping away slivers of wood with my knife, forming the required runes of the forbidden alphabets. Once or twice, I felt the thrill of power as I got something right. Too often, that didn't happen, and I knew I'd spoiled the sigil, formed a letter without the required resonance. Sometimes I could rectify the situation, mostly I could not. I ruined the first two spikes I worked on, turning them into nothing more than sharp slivers of wood with some scratches on them.

Then, on the third, I felt the gentle hand upon mine, enfolding mine, as the presence in the room took my fingers, showed me the right lines to carve.

His voice seemed to come from a long way away, but at the same time it was right beside my ear.

"Here. Like this, and like this. Don't cut all at once. Shave away a little at a time and you will find the right line as you go. Let your senses guide you, but follow the grain of the wood also. Work with the wood, not against it."

Still I didn't look up at him.

"How are you here? You died decades ago."

My grandfather – or the shade of my grandfather – ignored my question, continuing to direct my fingers.

After a few cuts, I tried again. "Are you real? Have I summoned you, or are you in my imagination?"

Finally, he replied. "Does it matter? Is there any difference, given who you are?"

"What does that mean?"

"You are in great need, and you are my grandson. We share a bond, a connection. We would have been close, I think."

"But you died."

"It's possible I left a few shreds lingering. For the right person to find."

"I visited your secret room, found your book."

"Ah, yes. That would be it. I left something of myself in those pages. An echo."

"You knew what was going to happen?"

"I suspected."

"The Warlock came for you, killed you."

"He did."

"Why did he stop there? Why did he let the rest of us live?"

That appeared to amuse Bi Bi. "Oh, I think I frightened him. Nothing had really threatened that monster for a long time, centuries and centuries, and then along comes this practitioner of folk magic from a distant land, wielding weapons and spells of unexpected potency, and I hurt him. Me, he killed out of spite or revenge. The rest of the family, I think, he kept alive so he could watch you, try and understand you."

"That's changed, though. Now, he's coming for me."

"You must have frightened him, too. He fears you are like me, or more powerful still."

"I wish I'd met you properly," I said. "I wish we'd both had you there to guide us, my brother and I."

"You had your father and your mother."

He clearly knew nothing of subsequent events. I chose not to tell him. He continued to move my fingers, gently manipulating them as if they were the knife. I relaxed and let him do it. But I felt the power thrilling through the spike as I worked the runes into it.

He said, "I remember you, even if you do not remember me. I would have stayed alive for you, if I could."

"I know."

"You have a good eye and a steady hand. The power runs deep in you. I'm not sure there's much I could have told you, in truth."

"Most of the time I barely know what I'm doing."

"I never did either. It sometimes seemed that the more I learned, the less I knew. It will come, with practice."

When the carving of the spike was done, he relaxed his grip and I ran my fingers along the ensorcelled shard of wood. I could feel the hungry energy coiling off it.

"This is like Vaknis?" I asked.

"No, no. I never found out how to create an artefact such as that. In truth, I never wanted to. The sacrifice of life required was too much."

I looked up at him, finally, this tall presence beside me. My grandfather smiled down at me, his hand on my shoulder. He was older than the lad in the photograph, his moustache and hair white. This was how he was on the day he died.

"The fight against the Warlock," I said. "I don't think I'm ready."

His grip tightened for a moment, a motion of reassurance. "I know. Perhaps no one is ever ready for such a battle. I wish more than anything that I could be there, that I could lead the attempt. You are capable of a great deal, my boy, but let me give you this advice: do not go alone. He came for me when I was alone and there was nothing I could do. That was why he destroyed the Council. You have friends and allies, I think. I see echoes of them in your mind. Work with them. Take the fight to him. Between you, perhaps you will be enough."

"One of them is Stonewall."

"Ah. So he is still around."

"Should I trust him?"

"Stonewall? You can trust him to be on your side, absolutely. He's a good man, perhaps a little … driven.

Obsessed, you might say. He certainly despises cruelty. You know, I once asked him whether he'd prefer to stop spending all his time trying to fight the forces of evil and settle down with a partner perhaps, enjoy the pleasures of life."

"What did he say?"

The ghost of a smile played on Bi Bi's features. "Oh, he didn't reply. He was too busy concentrating on the tome he'd discovered. That's Stonewall, I'm afraid. He's more prepared to do bad things to achieve good ends than I was, perhaps, but who's to say who is right in the end?"

I hoped I was more like my grandfather than Stonewall. But, right then, I had to be more Stonewall. I couldn't afford to settle down and enjoy life's pleasures. *One day*, I told myself. *One day*.

"Will you show me the steps?" I asked. "The movements as you wield these weapons? I cannot get them right."

He nodded and stepped back. I folded the red rug away, and we spent the next hour or more dancing, this shadow of my grandfather and I: he leading, me following, his arms and legs showing me how to time my movements, weigh my actions, when to hold off and went to feint and when to lunge. Slowly, moment by moment, the actions became more instinctive. In the end, he was barely touching me, and I knew I was performing the dance correctly.

There came a moment when I became aware that his touch was gone. I turned, and all that was left of him was an outline, a pencil scribble in the dark corner of the room, seeming to recede into some infinite distance that hadn't been there before.

"Stay," I said. "I have so many things I need to ask you."

"Ah, boy. I think my time is over. It was always a borrowed moment, nothing more."

"Will you come back?" I asked. "When I need you again?"

His wide smile was tinged with sorrow as he shook his

head. "I should have been there for you much more. I have done all I can, lingered all this time. I'm afraid there is no more."

"But..."

"I'm sorry, boy. I will say this: destroy this curse if you can, but I beg you, do not get yourself killed in the trying. Too many have died, me included. Better to flee than die, in the end. Better to live."

I was about to say more, ask more, but he was gone, and I was alone in the room once more.

I sat on the bed, the carved spike in my hand, watching and waiting, hoping for him to come back to me, but nothing more happened and the library was very quiet.

11 – Atmospheric Disturbances

> Terms like *ghost*, *ghast* and *wraith* cover a wide variety of incorporeal spirits. Some are the souls of the dead who linger in the physical realm out of confusion, love or anger at some perceived injustice. Others are entities that have never had physical form – e.g. those that dwell in the aether – but that manage to seep through the cracks between the worlds to trouble ours.
>
> There are many, many reports [of such activity] to be found in the literature. The majority of these, no doubt, are fallacious: the result of suggestible individuals reacting to odd or suggestive situations. Undeniably, however, there are many real and provable examples of what we might term *hauntings*.
>
> – Dr Miriam Seacastle, *Red Dragon, a Bestiary of Modern Britain*, 1999

The following morning, I left my lair in the library to walk into the centre of Cardiff. An invisible drizzle misted the air, slicking the pavements and roads into marred mirrors. I'd slept surprisingly well on the thin mattress in the library room. It was a peaceful place to rest, apart from the occasional papery *thump* as the Lady slammed some tome shut in her anger or disgust. My thoughts were elsewhere: I needed to pursue the bodysnatcher case – mainly to practise my magical arts but also, you know, to protect the Welsh public. I also figured that if I needed to track down Stonewall, it made for one more reason to speak to Sally. Stonewall had told me that Sally had visited him in the woods, more than once. She knew how to put the word out to him. Which was why English Wizardry had put so much effort into finding *her*.

The last time I'd seen her, though, she'd been nothing more than a magically-animated charcoal sketch on a canvas in the attic of her house on Cathedral Road. It was hardly a good basis for a satisfying romantic liaison. As distance relationships went, it was all kinds of distant. We'd worked closely enough on the eye collectors case, infiltrated Faebrook Folly together, but since her extradimensional struggles with Evangelina Mormont and the ensuing aging curse, she'd been elusive. Whether she was nursing her wounds or taking greater care to protect Stonewall, I had no idea. I'd assumed she was more or less indifferent to me – but that wasn't what Stonewall had said at all; he'd, well, painted a very different picture. In my happier moments, I liked to fantasize that Sally was as into me as I was into her – but that she was being wary, worried about my Office connections.

My hope was that would be changing now. My slaying of Earl Grey and the resulting weakening of the Office itself: that had to count for something. If it were all some cover story to gain her trust, it was pretty extreme. And Stonewall had trusted me. She surely had to, too.

The number she'd voodooed into my phone under the name *Goddess* had lately stopped being unobtainable, and once or twice someone had picked up when I rang. No one ever spoke and text messages were never replied to. I obviously couldn't be sure it was Sally on the other end, but I took it to mean that there was hope there. The only thing I could think of to try in order to reach her was to search her house again – I obviously doubted she'd be there – in the hope of uncovering another subtle trail. This was how we'd communicated in the past. Her flat, I'd discovered, *had* recently changed hands, the ownership passing to someone called Gwendoline Danvers. I'd thought this was perhaps another pseudonym Sally had adopted, sending me some subtle clue, and I'd wasted ten minutes of my life trying to form meaningful anagrams from the letters. Then I'd researched Gwendoline and found that she was a perfectly innocent and (more to the point) perfectly *real* person that was not on our books in any way. She was not Sally, but she was a GP living a perfectly respectable life.

The house, though: I figured she was holding onto that for a reason.

I'd head over that way now. The route across Bute Park and then Sophia Gardens on the other side of the Taff would allow me to take in a couple of the sites connected to the supposed bodysnatcher activity identified in Zubrasky's notes.

The first of these was in Cardiff Castle itself. I'd decided to add the vague *underground scratching sounds* report that Kerrigan had mentioned to the case. The location fitted in well enough with the rough line I'd imagined across the city centre – but I'd also dug up some old maps of the various tunnels criss-crossing beneath Cardiff and had found a faint but definitely *there* dotted line that ran from the castle to the ruins of the nearby Blackfriars Priory. It more or less coincided with my line. If I extended the plot further on, it took me to a church within the graveyard of which one of the grave robbing attacks had taken place. It all might be coincidence; it might be nothing at all. The map marking the tunnel was old itself – Victorian – and didn't look particularly official. The marked tunnel was hundreds of years older still; the unnamed Victorian cartographer had inscribed the word *Mediaeval* along it. Whether the drawer had read about it or imagined it or had actually traversed it, I had no way of knowing. I could at least take in both sites on my way to Cathedral Road to see for myself.

A tiny part of me wondered if this was all some subtle trail left by Sally so I could track her down. If it was, it was getting ridiculous. She needed to just pick up the damned phone and speak to me.

The castle grounds were open to the fee-paying public,

as they usually were, but my Office pass got me inside for free because the Crow used rooms at the top of the Black Tower as his private office/eyrie. The pass came in handy when summer outdoor concerts were held inside the walls of the castle too, I'm not going to lie.

Instead of taking the familiar stone steps up to Hardknott-Lewis's lair, I headed down into the dungeons: the tunnels and the oubliette beneath the tower where prisoners were once thrown into darkness to be forgotten. I had to hope they weren't still there. The light on my phone sent oversized shadows looming over my back. I found a set of steps that were worn into glassy smoothness by the passage of many feet. It was hushed below ground level, a watchful silence in the walls. Here and there, blooms of green algae coloured the stone walls. I had a map giving me the location where the sounds had been heard. The tunnels beneath the castle are extensive, with many relatively recent additions but some, I knew, dating back to the thirteenth century. There could be all manner of supernatural entity down there. The damp air chilled my face.

I eventually reached a locked iron door for which I had no key. It was tempting to work my *sesame* trick on it to spring it open, or even to blast the blockage aside with magic. The thought that something might be contained down there – the door was iron after all, even if it was a little rusted – dissuaded me. I was retracing my steps thinking that maybe the Crow could give me a key, when a light up ahead blinded me for a moment. Someone was coming down the corridor towards me.

My hand went to my revolver, my thumb resting on the round selection dial as I tried to figure out if this was a vampire or a demon or a ghost or a whatever. Cardiff was a muffled roar through the stone above me.

"Are we lost? I'm afraid you're not supposed to be down here."

The voice echoing down the stone corridor was reassuringly human. Male, older. The voice polite on the surface but not prepared to take any messing underneath.

The voice of someone used to dealing with the public, I figured.

I walked towards the light. "I'm here on official business," I said. It sounded pretty ridiculous even to me.

"And what official business would that be then?"

He was still coming towards me. Impossible to see if he was armed – or if he was actually human come to that – against the light of his torch.

"I have ID," I said. "Can I show it to you?" I prepared my usual speech of explaining who I was without actually explaining who I was. *Something something government department something.* I didn't need witty comments about my job title just then. I also didn't want to spook him and think I was drawing a weapon.

"ID?"

I took that to be approval. We were close now, within slashing distance. I pulled out my card and held it forward for him to see.

"I'm…" I began.

He cut me off. There was definitely a warmer edge to his voice as he spoke. "Ah, you're one of Campbell's team. Been waiting for someone to come and investigate."

Of course. He'd know the Crow. He appeared to be at least partly in the know, too.

"I … yes," I said. "I'm Danesh. Sorry it's taken so long to get to you."

"Sam," he said. He lowered his light so I could see his features by the glow from my phone. He was shaven-haired, mid-forties, slightly gone to seed. A man who'd maybe once been military and was now living a more relaxed life working at a local tourist attraction. His high-vis jacket was noticeably stretched over his belly.

"I know how it is," he said, and I wondered how much the Crow had told him about the Office's troubles. "I locked the door until you came to check it out. Don't want to take any chances, do we? I'll show you in now."

I walked ahead of him to the door. "Do you get many people down here?"

"Tourists," he said. "Come to look at the wartime air raid shelters. These older tunnels too."

"Was it you who reported these sounds?"

"I keep an eye on everything down here."

"You know all the tunnels."

"I should do."

"I've read there's an old one leading out to the ruins of Blackfriars."

He paused, staring to the ground as if he were activating his X-ray vision. "Never come across anything like that. Must be deeper than these passages if it's there."

"There's definitely no way down? Sealed-off steps or a well or something?"

He shook his head. "I'd know if there was. Is that where you think the sounds are coming from?"

"It's my working theory," I said, as if I'd spent many hours agonizing over the investigation.

The door yielded to his key. I expected the hinges to send their harsh squeal grating up my spine, but he'd obviously kept them well-oiled. The room was empty apart from some opaque plastic crates storing what appeared to be Christmas decorations. A couple of iron eyes were cemented into the stonework, as if prisoners had once been shackled down there. The stone-flagged floor sloped noticeably to one corner, where there was a small oval drain about the size of a cat flap. A little iron grille had been embedded into the masonry to cover it, three padlocks keeping it firmly sealed. The locks looked new, no rust on them at all.

"Do you have the keys for those locks?"

Sam shook his head. "Those are yours, not mine. Best ask Campbell."

He crossed to the corner and got to his knees with a grunt of discomfort. He put his ear to the drain and crouched unmoving for long moments.

"Can't hear nothing now," he said.

"What did it sound like?" I asked. My voice echoed hard and hollow in the enclosed stone space.

"There was a scratching sound, something being dragged along, then the muffled voices."

That was news. I hadn't heard anything about voices. "Could you make out any words?"

"Couldn't even tell what language it was."

"It was definitely from below?"

"Definitely."

"Any idea where this drain goes?"

"I assumed into the bedrock, but there may be a brook or something running down there. Do you reckon something's come upstream from the sea or some such? Could be all sorts down there."

He seemed to find the prospect exciting. He probably longed for a bit of excitement. I knelt beside Sam and put my ear to the iron grating. A faint but clear breath of icy air tickled my skin – which meant an air flow. Whatever the tunnel or waterway down there was, it opened out onto the surface somewhere. Distantly, maybe, I could hear the chortle of running water, faint against the boom of traffic on the streets above. There were no voices.

"Could you tell which way the sounds moved?" I asked.

Sam knelt up and nodded his head towards the stone wall. "Seemed to come right beneath this room and off up that way."

I was completely disorientated. "Which way is that?"

"North, more or less. What are you thinking? I've heard all the tales about the monsters that live in the tunnels beneath Cardiff."

"That doesn't trouble you, given your job?"

He grinned. "Nah. I'm sure you must have seen lots of things, right?"

"One or two. Do you mind if I set up a microphone and a recorder in here to monitor?"

"I was going to suggest exactly that."

I'd brought some equipment with me: nothing m/tech, just a standard device with a sensitive microphone that would record any sounds it picked up and that I could leave for a few days. We sometimes left one in supposedly haunted houses. We had good software to pick through background noise and hiss to look for patterns of speech and the like. I lowered the microphone down the drain for a metre or so – it was waterproof, but I wanted it to be in the air – then set the device to recording. I nodded to Sam, and we tiptoed out of the chamber, Sam locking the gate behind me.

"I'll come back in a day or two to see what it's picked up," I said. "Can you make sure no one goes near it until then?"

"Right you are." In the bright light of the courtyard outside, he looked like he was having the best time, imagining himself on the trail of some chthonic fiend threatening his castle. Which, maybe, he was.

"And if you hear or see anything else out of the ordinary, be sure to let me know, yes?"

"I will. Straight away."

"And please don't tackle anything unworldly. Leave anything like that to the experts. Just call it in and stay away."

"Right you are. Understood."

I left him walking the grounds of the castle, peering suspiciously into every corner as if he expected a demon or a ghoul to leap at him at any moment.

I think I'd made his day.

I crossed the little bridge where I'd once stopped to speak to Zubrasky as the eyes case kicked off. From there I turned left, following the tarmac path between rows of trees to cross the water for a second time. The flow came from the nearby Taff, I knew, filtered off long ago to form a moat for the castle. It certainly wasn't out of the question that the water had sought out underground fissures and cracks over time to slowly form a tunnel beneath the castle. I wondered briefly if there was some underground connection between the castle and our library underneath Alexandra Gardens, not too far away across North Road. I'd never heard any mention of such a connection. I had to assume that the Lady would have known all about it if there were such a tunnel.

There's little left of Blackfriars Priory now: a set of low stones marking the original outlines of walls and columns that lie under the ground, along with a small-scale model of how it might once have looked. There's also a vandalized plaque providing some history. The establishment's earliest origins lay in the thirteenth century, and it had survived until the sixteenth, the age when Henry VIII dissolved the monasteries in Britain.

When I'd spotted the ruins of the friary on the map, and looked at images of the friars with their long black robes, I'd inevitably conjured up images of some dark sect of summoners or devil-worshippers, cut off from the world and dabbling in the arcane, pursuing false gods. The literature had described that happening elsewhere, more than once: sects of passionate adherents devoting themselves to destructive and dangerous obsessions. There was probably an undercurrent of suppressed sexuality to such behaviour. To be fair, from what I could tell, that didn't appear to be the case here: the friars had lived simple, peaceful lives, doing all they could to help the communities around them. Admirable really – although personally I doubted I'd have got on with the vow of absolute poverty they'd taken.

There were also, I noted, some old grave marker stones to be found at the site. The reports in the case had made no mention of disturbance at the location, but its proximity to my line made the place worth investigating. Such a long and occasionally troubled history – the friary had been burned down at least once – might at least make it the focus for vengeful hauntings or some other paranormal activity.

The stones were very definitely undisturbed, though. Nothing had tried to lever them up from above and nothing had tried to heave them aside from below. I studied the picture I'd taken on my phone of the map with the supposed *Mediaeval* tunnel marked, but it was impossible to say with any accuracy where it might be in the ground. I stamped around a bit, optimistically hoping to hear echoing sounds beneath my boots, maybe even put my heel through into some suspicious hollow, but I got nothing. I did get a few dog walkers glancing at me with suspicion on their faces. Which was fair enough.

I took a few pictures of the site for my own records, then headed off in the direction of the local church where grave disturbance activity definitely had taken place.

As I knelt to study one of the graves around which – comically – the police had established one of their yellow tape cordons, the vicar emerged from a side-door of the church. I'd obviously come during some ceremony or practice, because she was wearing her full regalia. She tacked towards me like a galleon under full sail in the Cardiff wind.

"Hello. Are you a relative?" She managed to sound both sympathetic to my possible loss and, at the same time, wary of my motivations for being there.

I stood and showed her my credentials. The Office and the churches are often on the opposite side of things these days – but at least they tend to know who we are. That we *exist* in any case. I could tell from the slightest narrowing of her eyes that she was somewhere in the know. Or at least in the *vaguely aware*.

"I was expecting another visit from the police. This has all been very upsetting for the people coming here to visit their relatives, you know."

Yeah. I had some insight into how that must feel.

"Have you seen any other damage since this grave was disturbed?" I asked.

"The officer who came took a full statement."

"Please. I'd like to hear it from you. We tend to have a ... different focus on matters."

She sighed. The clergy of inner-city churches are pretty unflappable in my experience, but I could tell how much this was getting to her.

"Three graves were attacked, the ground dug up and some of the remains removed. We've never had anything like this before."

I studied the plot in front of me. Apart from the police tape, it looked normal, the soil replaced and smoothed down. The words carved onto the stone were hard to read, rubbed out by the weather and partially obliterated by coins of green lichen. I half-expected to see *Williams* mentioned, some relative of Owain, but instead it said *Osian Beddoe*, along with an inscription in Latin that was something to do with sleep, and then a date in the 1840s. That was good: there wouldn't be any grieving relatives traumatized by the attack. The name carved onto the stone meant nothing to me.

"From what I read, bones were dug up?" I asked.

"I'm afraid so. We reinterred him the day after. What was left of him."

"The police didn't ask you to wait?"

"They said it wasn't worth it, given the age of the burial."

I nodded. It was fair enough. It wasn't a victimless crime, but it wasn't far off. The police had plenty of living victims to worry about.

"What do you mean, *What was left of him*?"

She winced visibly, glanced to the sky as if receiving instructions or strength from on high. "The Crime Scene Investigator who attended said the skeleton wasn't complete. Bones were missing."

"Any way of knowing if they'd ever been there?"

"Well, no, but it's a troubling thought. Why would someone steal a few bones?"

Most likely, I thought, a component in a ritual. Either a summoning or some sort of act of revenge, a curse. I wondered if Osian Beddoe had ever made such powerful enemies that his descendants were still trying to get some payback.

I didn't mention this.

"Do you know which bones were missing?"

She clearly found this whole conversation distasteful. "A femur, I believe. Ribs."

"Do you mind if I take photographs?"

"If you think it will help."

I took shots of the grave from all angles. While I did so, I slipped my thaumometer out of my pocket and took a few readings. Maybe the pastor would think it was a light meter. I got the faintest flicker of a reading – which didn't surprise me at all. I'd already felt a faint flutter in my belly that told me magic had been worked at the site in recent days.

"Do you mind if I look at the other graves?"

I could see that she was reluctant. She wanted me away from there.

I said: "I can remove the police tape; let you get everything back to normal."

"Are you allowed to do that?"

"It'll be fine."

That placated her, and she nodded. I wound up the tape around Osian's grave, doing my best to treat the site with respect. Whoever he was, someone had probably loved him.

When I was done, she nodded in approval. "Follow me."

The two other graves were round the back of the church, invisible from the road. Once again, there was yellow tape, which, once again, I removed. There could be no doubt the attacks were similar: the magical traces were there. I took more pictures. The two victims were slightly older according to the headstones: William Cadwaladr had died in 1812 and Cadoc Lush in 1822. As with the first grave, the plots had been restored to something like their undisturbed state. Two undisturbed plots lay between them, their crosses canting over at alarming angles. One was a woman, Agnes Merryweather, who'd died *A Spinster* at the age of 32 in 1812. That was a bit judgemental, wasn't it? Next to her was a plot taken up by a couple: Albert Tonypandy who'd died in 1814 and then his *beloved wife* Blodwyn, who had lived on for thirty-two years after the death of her husband. A third of a century of mourning and widowhood in veiled black, or long years of quiet freedom and liberation? I'd never know.

"More bones were taken from these two graves?" I asked.

"We believe so."

"The same ones."

"Different ones."

"Was there anything visible on the ground around the plots? Footprints or the like?"

"The police would have checked for anything like that."

"They didn't record anything. I wondered if you'd noticed any detail that might be helpful."

She shook her head. "The ground is grass and gravel as you can see. People come and go all the time."

"And you've had no other disturbances? You've not seen anything else odd or inexplicable?"

"Oh, I see lots that's odd and inexplicable in this parish, but none of it's supernatural."

"I don't suppose there's CCTV footage?"

"Of a graveyard? Of course not. We respect people's privacy."

I considered the cemetery and the church, trying to imagine what might have happened there. Were these reports across the city connected, or was I just seeing connections where there weren't any? Was it possible I was putting off the fight against the Warlock?

I looked up at the roofline, where a line of grotesques and gargoyles leered down at me. I wondered if any were alive; if they were, they might be persuaded to pass on information in return for a peaceful life. I reached out with my mind, hoping to pick up a flicker of magical activity from one of them. I got nothing. They were either stone carvings or so deeply asleep that I doubted they would have noticed anything. My gaze fell to the stones in the wall of the church. There was something of interest there, though. Higher up, the stones were smaller, the lines fresh, but at ground level, they were larger and rougher. They looked like they'd been there a lot longer.

"When was the church built?" I asked.

"It's Victorian."

I crossed to look at the wall, touch the sandpapery stone with my fingers.

"On the site of an older building?"

"There's been a church here for centuries. The earlier one partially collapsed so a new one was erected on the foundations."

"Is there a crypt?"

"There is, but we don't use it much. It's a bit damp down there to be honest."

"Can I see?"

"Will it take long? Only, forgive me, I have a group of mothers coming in twenty minutes and choir practice after that. If the coffee and biscuits aren't ready, there'll be a riot."

She was joking. I was pretty sure she was joking.

"I'll be quick."

She led me inside the cool, echoing space of the church. I was struck, as I always was in such buildings, how hushed the building was, how peaceful it became. Something to do with thick walls. I followed her to a hidden corner to one side of the nave. There was a wooden door there, comically small. There *were* creatures that would fit through it perfectly, but most people I knew would have to duck. She unlocked it and flicked on the light. It was a small square room, red hymn books stacked on shelves and white robes hanging from pegs. In the middle of the wooden floor was a hatchway.

"Do you lock any of the doors?" I asked.

"We try not to. We try to provide a sanctuary and a quiet space for people at any time."

An iron ring was inset into the hatch. She levered the door up with this – the hinges groaning – then reached down to flick on a switch below floor level. I peered into the hole. I could see a step set of wooden stairs, then a flagged stone floor a few metres below me. The air coming out of the crypt was damp and musty.

"Do you mind if I go down?"

"Please, be my guest. I'll go and put the kettle on before the mothers arrive."

I climbed down to stand on the old stone floor, trying not to imagine someone slamming the hatchway shut and sealing me in down there. Things like that only happen in books and films, right? The single bulb hanging from a bare cable near the steps didn't illuminate much: a small copse of worn stone pillars, deep shadows around the edges of the space. Also, some stone sarcophagi around the edges of the walls. I slipped out my gun and dialled up *anti-vampire*, just in case, then crept towards the nearest one. I kept my magical senses on high alert, feeling the coiling power in my gut mounting but holding it in check, too. I was getting better at that. I had three rune-carved and ensorcelled stakes in my pocket where I could get at them quickly. If there was something down there, I was ready to practice my moves.

Again, my imagination raced on ahead of me, seeing the lid of one of the tombs thrown aside and the slumbering vampire within come lunging at me, jaws agape. That didn't happen. I reached the first stone tomb, an oddly little stone box with a peaked lid. There might have been words carved on it once but they were unreadable now. The tomb had been outside, open to the elements once. I touched its surface and nothing happened: no movement, no flare of magic. Lichen had crept over the join between lid and base; the tomb hadn't been opened for a long time.

Still, that didn't mean it was harmless. Nor that the others were the same. I rotated on the spot, checking for signs of movement from the other tombs. It was hard to be sure; the light from my phone and the single bulb sent deep shadows lurking behind the pillars, shadows that shifted as I moved.

I did catch a hint of something, though: colder air, damper air, breathing onto my face from the far corner of the crypt, where the deepest shadows were. I stepped that way. Above me, I could hear the rumble of steps on the wooden floor. The arriving mothers, I presumed. I wove around a couple of pillars – oddly worn, as if water had once rushed through the crypt – to find, in the far corner of the room, a low arched opening, barely ten centimetres high, with heavy iron bars cemented into the stones. They were rusted but completely solid when I pulled on them. They looked like they'd been there for a long time.

The wash of cold air was definitely coming through the little opening. I shone my light inside but could see only a rough slope of stones and packed soil, leading off too far for my light to reach. I put my ear to the bars and could hear, once again, the babble of running water. Some underground stream, perhaps even connected to the one under the castle. There was also – although I might have been imagining this – a moaning sound, rising and falling. If it was real, it might be something completely benign, a pipe resonating as water passed over it. From somewhere down there, with impressive dramatic timing, a single drop of water spattered to the floor, and then another after a few moments. It was hard not to imagine it as the ticking of some slow, inexorable clock.

I squatted on my haunches, considering. There was no way anything larger than a cat could squeeze through the bars – and a well-fed cat might have trouble. *Something* could have slithered up from down there, but it certainly wasn't anything human-sized. Maybe something with, I don't know, tentacles. There was a scattering of gritty dust on the floor around the opening, damp to the touch. Traces of soil? It was hard to be sure; it might be nothing more than generic old crypt dirt. Neither my thaumometer nor my innate senses picked up anything magical from it.

I set up another sound recording device next to the opening, and put a small motion-sensitive infra-red camera on a little tripod next to it, too. A brief circuit of the rest of the crypt revealed little more of interest: more seemingly inert tombs and a patch on the wall where someone had made some scratch marks but which I could pull no meaning from. The slabs beneath my feet were uneven, rising and falling like a petrified lake on a really windy day. I tried tapping each stone hoping to detect hollows, but the ground remained reassuringly solid.

I ascended to the living world, peeping round the door to catch the gaze of the vicar. She made some apologies to the gathered circle of women in the nave and came to see me.

"Thanks," I said. "I'll let myself out. I've left some recording equipment in the crypt if that's okay."

"You think something came up from down there?"

"As the police say, I'm excluding possibilities. Might be worth leaving something heavy on top of that hatch, though, or locking it shut if you can."

She didn't look in the least alarmed by the possibilities I was suggesting. I guessed the notion of demons living deep below the ground wasn't completely alien to her.

"I'll do as you suggest. I assume you'll be back soon?"

"I will." I gave her my phone number. "Please, let me know if you hear or see anything unnatural. Or if some detail occurs to you, however small. Other than that, I'll tell the regulars that we have everything under control and you won't need to keep anyone away from crime scenes or anything like that."

She looked relieved, a warm smile coming to her face for the first time.

"Thank you, Danesh. Now, if you'll excuse me, the mothers will be growing restless. And no one wants that."

She swept away, gown billowing. I wondered if she always floated around wearing her ecclesiastical garb. It seemed like a lot of washing as much as anything. I also wondered how she knew my name – but, of course, I'd shown her my card.

I took one last look around, trying to imagine if some subterranean horror had crept up through the crypt to reach the graveyard – or if the whole thing was nothing more than pissed-up kids causing trouble, dabbling in what they liked to imagine was black magic.

The gargoyles on top of the church walls watched me as I stood there, but although several had their mouths wide open, none of them deigned to comment in any kind of useful way.

12 – The House on Cathedral Road

> The exact nature of the *Invitation* can be both a boon and a curse to our noble and powerful vampiric masters. It is possible that the magic was originally worked into the bloodline by the first vampires themselves as a way of stopping them from slaughtering each other. The matter is not as straightforward as many believe – but then, there is much misunderstanding about the true nature of these noble and terrible entities. Put simply, a vampire may not enter a dwelling without being invited to do so by the dweller. If this invitation is revoked, the vampire may no longer cross the threshold. But, as it may be seen, there are many complications to this apparently simple injunction. What constitutes "a dwelling" and what "a dweller"? The terms are not always clear. Then there is the fact that the barrier does not *always* prevent a vampire from entering – it simply makes doing so a great deal harder. One or two remain powerful enough to enter even if they have been barred, although this always comes at a grim cost, and they will never make such a passage lightly.
> – Samuel Bedfellowes, *The Old Ways*, 1847

Bone knew a trap when he saw it. He could *smell* it. Had developed a sense for it over the years. The question thrumming through his mind was, who was this a trap for? Something about this building struck him as odd. He'd been badly burned by his attempt to enter the house in London. He wasn't going to make the same mistake.

There'd been no Invitation allowing him inside, luring him there. Nor had there been a revoked Invitation to bar his entry. The people in the London house had not appeared to know who and what he was – and then the vicious magical discharges had detonated as he crossed the threshold, and he'd been hurled away and down to the ground.

The physical harm was unimportant, and he was used to pain. He had already healed. It was the sense of wounded pride that troubled him, the fear that he wasn't in control. Because, if he could no longer serve his purpose as a reliable killer, what was he for? What reason would the Warlock – the despised Warlock – have for keeping him around? A release from his long torments would of course be highly desirable, but he had no confidence the Warlock would grant him that. An eternity of endless torment, without hope or reason or respite, was more the Warlock's style. The better to motivate whichever unfortunate became the next thralled assassin under the Warlock's control.

Bone had to stay alive and free – not that he was free – if he was ever going to find a way to destroy the Warlock. Which meant he had to do precisely what the Warlock wanted him to do.

For now.

He watched this new house for three or four hours from the safety of his car (a different car, in case anyone had noticed the one he'd used in London), debating with himself the best course to take. A watchful quiet filled the street, a quiet that brought with it a sense of foreboding. If this was a trap, was he the bait or the prey? He could sense his quarry drawing nearer all the time, and the house, undoubtedly, was the perfect place to spring an attack. He preferred, always, to work in the shadows, hide away what he was and what he did. But he knew he had to act now if he was going to act at all.

Leaving the car, he buttoned up his black leather coat and pulled his hoodie over his head. He hunched his shoulders – trying, as he knew he often did when outside, to conceal his height and bulk as much as possible. He didn't want people to notice him. They invariably did. His size and the tapestry of tattoos and scars covering his flesh inevitably alarmed people. He understood it. One advantage of being a vampire was that he couldn't look at his own reflection. Didn't have to see what he'd become every day.

He walked briskly, keeping to the shadowy side of the street to reach the house. He knew there was no one inside – no one he could sense at any rate, although there might be all manner of trap or summoned entity or explosive warding spell waiting for him. There was also the possibility that he was welcome inside. That this was the unseen hand of the Warlock at work, helping Bone to complete the work assigned to him.

He ignored the front door and the front windows. Too visible from the street. There would be cameras and neighbours catching a glimpse. He needed to get out of sight as quickly as possible. Most of the houses in the street formed continuous terraces, but this one was detached, standing alone with paths round each side leading to the rear. Darker, quieter, safer. He slipped round the back to a tree-shadowed yard where no one could see him. He placed his hand on the handle of the back door. It was locked, of course. That presented no difficulty. As in London, he could shear through the steel bolts with one pull. There might be alarms, but they didn't trouble him either. He could move quickly enough to smash the mechanism before it properly rang.

Still he hesitated, memories of the agonies inflicted by the London house burning through him. Sometimes it seemed like everyone was trying to hurt him.

With a grunt of frustration, he pulled on the handle, fracturing the steel bolts to open the door.

No magical attacks threw him backwards. He wasn't the prey; he was the trap.

He slipped inside to wait.

Cathedral Road was strangely quiet as I worked my way along it, finding myself in the lull between the tides of commuters and shoppers and the schoolchildren that washed regularly along it. I glanced into each parked car with suspicion as I walked, trying at the same time to detect if anyone was eyeing me from the high windows of the grand houses that lined the street. Nothing leapt out at me – figuratively or literally.

A single crow perched high in the black branches of one of the trees, an inky shape against the grey sky. It grated out its rough call again and again, and it was hard not to imagine the sound as a repeated threat.

I only ever seemed to visit the street when I was tracking down Sally. I'd first talked to her via magical vision in her flat on one side of the road, and then I'd used the borrowed Grafton Projector to discover the address she'd daubed on a canvas in the attic of the house on the *other* side of the road. The address that she'd written in the past and then painted over, assuming I would somehow work out what she'd done and peer back in time to uncover the message. Which, to be fair to her, I did do. Finally, in that same room, I'd conversed with her animated charcoal-sketch avatar.

Was it really too much to expect that I could ring her bell and she'd open the door?

It was. I tried it, but precisely nothing happened. So far as I could tell, the bell wasn't even ringing – or maybe it was ringing in some other, distant house where Sally was currently holed up. I obviously could have used my bag of m/tech tricks to open the door, but something in the feel of the house stopped me. In a way that I couldn't quite put my finger on, something didn't seem right about the place. A faint shiver shimmered down my spine as I touched the door and I tasted something bitter in my throat. I'd been ambushed in there before. What would happen if I simply barged my way in?

I was getting better at trusting my instincts, and my instincts said stepping inside might be a really bad idea.

I took a step back to consider. Blinds were drawn across the ground-floor windows but, by peering through the cracks, I could glimpse narrow vertical sections of the rooms inside. They were all empty. Not just of people and demons, but also furniture and carpets and paintings on the walls. Sally, it appeared, had left the building. Still the sense of foreboding filled me. I took note of it and set it to one side. I needed to know who or what was in there.

Round the back of the house, past the empty wheelie bins, I found that someone had forced their way inside the house, smashed the locks with apparent ease. I'd seen *that* done before. The vampire that had attacked my family home – that thing was *here*? Perhaps even the Warlock himself?

Another possibility occurred to me: Sally hadn't been in touch for the simple reason that the Warlock had her. Because she was being used as the bait in a trap set for me. Whether that was possible – whether the Warlock could overpower Sally, a powerful user in her own right – I didn't know. But I couldn't ignore the possibility. And, even if it meant walking into a trap, I knew I wasn't going to simply stroll away and leave her.

I drew my gun and pulled a wooden stake from the inside pocket of my jacket. My fingers found another small object there. Stonewall's acorn. I carried it with me at all times; it was good to know it was there if I needed it. How quickly would it summon him? I'd had the impression he would come immediately to my aid. *When you need it most, perhaps if you find yourself facing the Warlock, crush it beneath your heel and I will hear. And then, together, we can face our enemy.*

I clutched the acorn alongside the wooden stake.

The dance step moves of the *Rearing Cobra* attack ritual were there in my head and in my muscles, clear and ready. I pushed the door open. I placed a foot inside, stepping onto the terracotta stones flagging the kitchen floor, my senses reaching out into the shadows.

The kitchen, too, had been stripped of all its objects and utensils, all of the gleaming high-end clutter I'd seen before. There wasn't even anything so basic as a kettle for boiling water on the black marble worktops. I stepped through empty room after empty room. Everything was silent and empty. There was the faintest tang of fresh paint in the air. The brightly-coloured walls were gone, those bold purples and reds replaced by the inevitable inoffensive magnolia. This was what you did when you wanted to sell a house. When it was no longer home. Had she grown bored of it, or was it no longer safe for her? The bookcase where I'd once noted an edition of the *Mabinogion* and her copy of *The Picture of Dorian Gray* next to it was gone, leaving behind only a faint rectangle in the carpet. The ornamental sleeping cat was still there, holding down the flap of carpet that covered the hatch into the cellar, the rectangle of it clear as if something were trying to push its way up.

I hesitated. Should I delve into the cellar – where I'd once been attacked by the *Pestilential Presence* – or head upstairs? I had a growing sense of being watched. I couldn't decide if it was my own imagination getting the better of me. The house was so damn quiet. *Too*, as they say in the movies, *quiet*. More than once, I turned my head sharply, seeming to see a blur of movement in the corner of my vision, like a rush of shadows. There was never anything there. I could see nothing more solid and couldn't sense any kind of presence. I thought of the crow and its warning croaks. The fizzing in my gut told me there was something supernatural or magical going on in the house – but whether this was a present threat or the lingering echo of Sally, I couldn't tell. My fingers went again and again to the sharp point of the enchanted wooden stake I carried in my pocket.

I decided to leave the cellar to last and headed upstairs. More empty rooms greeted me – except for one of them. It had been her bedroom as far as I recalled, a large and airy room overlooking the street, the triple-glazed windows and, for all I know, strong magic keeping the siren wails and shouts of the city out. Light filtered in through gauzy blinds. The bed and furniture were gone. The spray of red flowers in the ornate iron fireplace was gone. The floor was expensive-looking wood, oak maybe, but there was a rug where the bed had been. The marks of the bed's feet impressed into it looked oddly like the hoofprints of a deer. There were also paintings around the walls. Twelve of them. I recognized Sally's hand; the way she had of conjuring up hills and valleys with a simple sweep of a line. It had to be significant that they'd been left there.

I caught a sound behind me, like the rush of wind. I spun on the spot but there was nothing. Again, it might have been inside my head. The house settled back into its watchful hush. I stepped into Sally's bedroom to study the pictures. There had to be some meaning to them, some clue.

I put my weapons away for a moment – the gun into its holster across my chest, the stake into the back pocket of my jeans – and walked clockwise around the room, taking a photo of each painting. They were all landscapes: steep-sided valleys, lone trees, the waters of a lake or pond, a copse of oaks, the curve of a winding river. A line of gently curving hills was in the background of each, topped by a grey-blue sky streaked with grey-white clouds. The pictures didn't join up, but I had the clear sense that they were a sequence, meant to be seen together in a particular order. None of them were signed.

Twelve of them. I thought of a clock face. Was that relevant? I couldn't work out why. Or maybe there were directions there, the twelve referring to the points on a compass rose. But that didn't make sense either: compasses generally defined 4, 8 or 16 headings, not 12.

I studied each for some hidden meaning, a letter hidden in the painted lines. Perhaps, as before, there was something beneath the paint, and I needed an X-ray machine or the Grafton Projector to reveal it. Somehow I doubted it; it wasn't like her to repeat a trick. And I liked to believe that any new message would be easier to spot.

After two complete circumnavigations of the room, I stopped in the middle, none the wiser. The spars of the house groaned as the wind picked up. I could make nothing of the paintings. Then I saw what it had to be: I was looking at the problem all wrong. The images were a distraction; she had to have placed a message on the back of each canvas.

I turned the nearest one over, expecting to see a letter there, the name of a place I had to go to. Or maybe a new phone number I had to call.

But there was only a blank square of canvas, no marks upon it at all. I leaned in closer, examining it minutely, when the voice spoke behind me.

"There is nothing here, Danesh Shahzan. She has gone and left no clues. There is only you and me."

I spun on the spot, bracing ready to leap into the first steps of my attack pattern. A huge figure stood framed in the doorway. In fact, not really *framed*: whoever it was had to duck to enter the room. I had the clear impression of them stepping from the shadows, as if they had been hiding in the darkness and watching me all this time.

A vampire, no doubt about it, but *vast*. His face was pocked and scarred, tattoos creeping up his neck and over his hands. He wore a black leather long coat, like some modern reboot of *Death*. No sign of a scythe, though. His expression was something between a snarl and a smile.

I talked while I slipped my phone back into my pocket and pulled out my revolver. "Who are you?" I said. "Are you the Warlock?"

An odd expression passed across the vampire's features at that: something between amusement and rage. He saw my weapons but didn't appear to be troubled by them.

"I've come to take you to him. Dead if necessary, but I can bring you in alive if you don't struggle and whine."

"What does he want from me?"

"To *end* you. But there are quick ways and there are slow ways for that to happen. Some of them very slow indeed."

Again, a discordant expression twisted the vampire's features for a moment. The creature looked almost troubled. I filed the fact away.

"It was you that attacked my family home in London."

"The Warlock gave me several addresses. This is one. Taking you there would have saved me a journey."

He seemed content to talk, as if happy to put off the moment when he went for me. What was that about? I glanced around the room, seeking something I could turn to my advantage, a way out. There was only the window and the doorway that he filled. I thought, briefly, about the rug. Why had she left it? Could there be some sort of hatch or portal beneath it? Maybe she simply didn't like it anymore.

"You know where he is," I said. "You know how to reach him."

"And soon you will, too, when I take you there. Do I have to kill you first?"

"I'd rather you didn't. I have a lot of things I need to do today."

He leapt at me then, the speed of his movement throwing me completely. He didn't seem to cross the intervening space between us. Either he moved at incredible speed, or he stepped into and out of some shadow realm. He was suddenly upon me, hurling me back against the wall. His hand iron-tight around my throat, he lifted me into the air so that I couldn't breathe, couldn't speak. I already felt the mounting panic of oxygen starvation in my tissues.

But I wasn't defenceless anymore. I pushed at his body with the flat palm of my empty hand, at the same time unleashing the storm of energy that coiled inside me. Once again, my control was better. I threw him off me, smashing him backwards against the far wall, but I cut the blast off before it burned out of control and did me any damage.

I landed on my toes, my hand still held out at him, the other holding my gun. He stood, preparing to throw himself at me again. Before he could, I fired, emptying the antivampire round into his chest. It hurt him, but not enough to drop him to the floor. He snarled his animal teeth at me. Before he could act, I pumped the remaining five rounds into him: Silver, Standard, Holdfast, Clothcutter, Anti-demon.

He walked into them, taking each shot in his body,

twitching but not stopping. The holdfast paused him for a few microseconds before he shrugged it off. Sluggish gouts of blood slugged from his wounds.

When he saw I had no more bullets to fire, he grinned. "Done? Shall I kill you now?"

I threw the gun aside, using the action to cover pulling out a wooden stake and the acorn from my pocket. I held the spike of wood in the *Snake who Hides its Fangs* position for the moment, point backwards down the line of my wrist.

This time, I caught the faintest tensing of his powerful muscles as he prepared to throw himself at me. He seemed to prefer the hands-on approach to murder. His movement was my mark. I lunged forwards at him, keeping low to knock him off balance, use his own momentum against him. At the same time, I twisted to spin into an attack, my hand with the spike still clenched into a fist. The first words of the *Rearing Cobra* attack spell played in my mind, each syllable coinciding with a movement, a step. I felt the power of it thrilling through me.

I smashed into his thighs mid-spin as he tried to adjust to my movement. It was like thumping into the bough of a tree, utterly hard and unmoveable. With a single, rapid movement of his knee, he caught me in the belly, rag dolling me backwards to thump heavily into the wall, sending one of the pictures crashing to the floor.

But I'd hit him. I pushed my way back up to my feet, then held out my hand, empty now, to show him. A moment of puzzlement passed across his features as he saw it. Then his hand went to the side of his own abdomen.

To the spot where my wooden spike was embedded deep in his flesh. The pain of it seemed to strike him only in that moment, the shock of his realisation. The syllables of the killing spell – the spell woven into the attack and unleashed as I struck, the spell learned from my grandfather's book and my grandfather's lips – echoed in my mind. I knew I had worked it well, waking the power of the wooden shard and the ancient magics.

The vampire made a noise somewhere between a snarl and a shriek. Something like black smoke coiled off the wound as he clutched at it. As he did so, a tiny round object spun and nodded to a halt on the floor between us. Stonewall's acorn; I must have dropped it during my lunge. No matter. In case I needed it, I pulled a second stake from my pocket, making no attempt to conceal it this time. If my first blow had slowed him, I could unleash a more powerful attack, one that gave me more seconds to spin it up to its full fury. He had no way of knowing how many stakes I had.

I watched, wary, ready, as the vampire grasped the first wooden spike with his hand. More smoke coiled off him as his hand burned with the antagonistic magic. He grunted from clear pain as he pulled the shard of wood from his own flesh, putting all his strength into it as if the stake were resisting him. He shook with the effort of it ... until he had it free. He dropped it to the floor. It smouldered there, smoking. He kicked it away with a black leather boot, smashing it to ashes.

"That was fucking vicious," he said. He was noticeably panting now. "I tried to be kind; I really did. I am going to have to kill you now."

He flashed across the room again, this time disappearing and reappearing before I could so much as flinch, crushing me hard against the wall, squeezing the breath from my body. I was barely ready for the attack; I saw I should have pressed my advantage while he was removing the first stake, hit him again while he was vulnerable. A valuable lesson – one I hoped I'd get the chance to learn from.

Again, his hands went to my throat to stop me breathing. His crushing grip was brutal; it felt like his fingers were gripping my spinal column. Again, I wasn't utterly vulnerable: I had the second stake held in the *Ox Horn* position, point forwards, low and slightly to the side. My vision began to fade, black blobs crowding the world out. I had to act. Flipping my grip, I jabbed it hard into his right side, a second blow symmetrical with the first. No time to enact the powering incantations or ritual steps, I had to shock him, get him off me.

Once again, the incantations worked into the stake hurt him. I could see it in his eyes. I could see, also, that suffering and agony were familiar to him, that he could ignore them. He squeezed tighter still, like he intended to rip my head clean off. I still had my hand on the stake. I pushed it into him, deeper and deeper, twisting it. I poured what magic I could muster into it: undisciplined, unformed power made of fear.

We held the position for a moment, each hurting the other, our agonies mounting, until with a snarl he stepped backwards, releasing my neck. Another step backwards, and another, while both his hands went to the second stake. He ripped it from his flesh in a spray of black smoke, burning blood. I smelled the bitter stench of it.

But he didn't go down. His constitution, his ability to repel and repair harm was incredible. But I'd learned my lesson. I'd already pulled out my third and final stake, holding it out in front of me, point-forwards, the *Spearhead*, showing him that he'd be impaled if he threw himself at me again. The words of the powering spell were hoarse in my bruised throat as I voiced them, but the effect was the same. Perhaps, in my desperation, the magic was even stronger. I stepped forwards, clumsily finding the steps and arm-movements required to work the *Rearing Cobra*, the most powerful attack I'd mastered. I put all my essence into it. I had to kill this monster now or I'd never do so.

He saw what I was doing, took another step backwards as he prepared his own attack. His eyes were pools of purest black now. He hated me. He feared me. He didn't understand who and what I was. I worked the false lunge into my steps, forwards and backwards to incite fear. He stepped backwards again. There was a gentle crunch as something was crushed beneath his boot.

The vampire lifted his boot. The smashed acorn lay on the wooden floor. The acorn from *darach dubh*. The irony of it was delicious; my attacker had summoned the mighty Stonewall to the fight. I would survive this. Between us, we would destroy this hulking, tattooed monster. We might even be able to wring the location of the Warlock's lair out of him. What would happen? Stonewall would appear in a blaze of light, unleashing arcane magic that would burn the vampire to black smoke? I glanced to the window and the door, waiting for him to appear. Perhaps he would even manifest from the wooden floor.

There was another pause when nothing at all happened. The wind moaned outside and I thought it had to be him, sweeping to my side.

Then the sound died away and there was only silence. I felt the coiling magic within me dwindle. I'd failed to keep my focus, chant the flow of syllables, dance the steps. My grandfather's book had said it: the key isn't the simple act of remembering; the key is not letting fear or panic break you. They key is staying true to your calling and your powers.

The vampire must have seen the look of alarm in my eyes. He saw his opportunity. He rushed at me for a third time, thundering into me, willingly impaling himself upon the stake I held forth. He appeared not to care. More of his flesh and blood burned into black smoke, the stench choking. He didn't let it stop him. This time he went for my eyes, pressing a thumb into each, pushing my head hard against the wall.

The agony of it was intense, sickening. Panic mounted. I lost all thought of working magic, of throwing my power at him. I let go of the stake and gripped his arms, desperately trying to pull his hands away from my face. His grip was too strong. The vampire snarled as the stake buried itself into his chest but he didn't relent.

I screamed for Stonewall, but still he didn't come. The vampire dropped his grip back to my throat. Now that I was incapacitated, he wanted to choke the life from me. The black blobs were covering all of my vision, now, the world receding.

I refused to give in and threw my last raw shreds of

magic at him. It was unfocused, uncontrolled, a scream of fear and rage. It staggered him back but not enough. Not nearly enough. He was too strong. Through my blurred vision I could see him grinning at me, considering me, angling his head as if deciding how best to destroy me.

Still Stonewall didn't come.

The vampire lunged at me again, clamping his great hands back around my throat. His grip was far too strong for me to release. There was no magic left inside me, nothing to fight with. The creature whispered into my ear as he worked, his quiet voice strangely intimate.

"I will carry your lifeless form to the Warlock, and you can be his next thrall, his next slave. His next plaything. Now, stop wriggling while I kill you."

I screamed one final time for Stonewall, but all that came out was a strangled gurgle.

Still Stonewall didn't come.

13 – The Stationery and Office Paper Select Committee

Our Order has never laboured under the yoke of any sort of constitution or rulebook. To do so would be an anathema to us all. We are not a democracy or a corporation or a society or a family. We are, at best, a loose association of individuals who act as one when it seems to us useful to do so – for instance, when agreeing on some detail of how the country is to be organized. This, by its nature, requires there to be an *inner circle* – as well as an individual who makes the final decisions. As with the wolf pack, there must be hierarchy if there is not to be constant fighting and destruction. There must be a pack leader. Although we consider ourselves to be free-thinkers, unshackled by rules such as those that control the human herd, the Order is a dictatorship, a tyranny. It is simply one that its members choose, out of their own self-interest, to accede to. Most of the time.
– Arnold Enderby Smithwick, *Annals of the Order of the British Vampire*, 1929

Jacob Charnel watched the mundane world slip by through the tinted windows of his chauffeured black Mercedes.

It wasn't an extravagant car; he preferred to remain anonymous on the few forays he made from his castle. It occurred to him that he had become much more reclusive of late, feeling the need to remain behind high walls and magical wards. Let people come to him so he could carefully control who he saw. It was a troubling realisation; he had seen something similar often enough in really old vampires. They became weary of the world, wary of it even, and withdrew. That way lay the long stupor of centuries spent lying in a crypt. He wanted no part of it. Once the current difficulties were resolved – the last of the dangers removed from the board – he would, he decided, become more active in the world. More *hands on*. This was his domain; he might as well enjoy ruling over it.

They were passing through the suburbs of London now, and he found himself fascinated by the lives the humans outside the vehicle windows lived. He slipped in and out of their minds as if leafing through the pages of a book, tasting their petty concerns and emotions: worry, joy, despair, satisfaction, dread. Most of them weren't feeling very much at all; they were simply *there*, walking the street, browsing in shops, sitting on buses, staring at nothing. They all seemed so very insignificant, yet they scurried around as if their lives were of the greatest importance; as if anything they did *mattered*.

The car slowed as the traffic ahead compressed in on itself, the road suddenly awash with red lights. A twist of frustration ran through Charnel. This was the modern age. He had no time for this. He had come south to attend to two important matters – a set of orders to be given and a murder to be carried out – and he wished to complete both without delay.

He glanced aside at the locked metal briefcase on the seat beside him, as if the object it contained might have worked itself free somehow. As if it were alive. He would be glad to be rid of it. He had held onto it for too long. He had this one more use for it, then he would destroy it back at the castle.

"Keep going," he said to the thrall driving the car. "Don't slow down. I will make a way through the traffic for us."

The driver nodded but didn't look back. He obviously

didn't glance at Charnel in the rear-view mirror. There would have been no point. Charnel reached out into the minds of the drivers of the vehicles up ahead, instructing this one or that one to veer out of the way, pull aside, clear a path for the Mercedes to come through. He had to work farther and farther ahead, onto crossing roads, slowing down approaching vehicles, or otherwise there would be no gaps he could force the nearer cars into.

He made several cars drive through red lights and one or two mount the pavement to make the necessary room. There were numerous scrapes and collisions. Some pedestrians had to scramble out of the way to avoid being struck. There were some screams, spikes of alarm stirring the humans from their meanderings. He always rather enjoyed the three-dimensional challenge of the traffic puzzle, the speed with which he had to leap from brain to brain to direct the humans. Some were more resistant than others, of course, forcing him to put more effort into the coercion. He was always strong enough. The only problems he had were in the small – but growing – number of cars that didn't have an active human driver. He couldn't control the mind of a self-driving vehicle. He made a mental note to issue instructions to the government so that such machines got out of his way automatically. In time, on a journey like this, he wouldn't have to exert any control at all; the traffic would simply part to let him through.

Truly, the modern age was a place of wonders.

His car, he knew, would register on the traffic cameras that were all across the city, but he wasn't concerned. Crimes and police investigations were trivial matters that applied to the humans of this land, not to him. He would be automatically immune, and any humans involved would automatically forget what they had seen. In his mind's eye, he could now see the route the car would take to reach Westminster, the ripples in the traffic on surrounding streets as he forced open a patch of clear road.

All was well. The Mercedes sped on, slowing down

only for corners, the lines of traffic miraculously opening up in front of it and closing behind it.

The politician he had come to meet was waiting for him in an oak-panelled room on the top floor of the Whitehall office. Charnel swept in. She was a junior minister, unimportant in the grand scheme of things, but she was also, Charnel knew, the only undecided member of the committee when it came to the question of the Office's future. She kept her expression neutral as she stood to greet him in her expensive suit and her immaculate make-up, but her mind was a confusing mess of emotions. Fear, alarm – naturally – but also a burning ambition and the hope that this situation might be turned to her advantage.

He could work with all of that. He sat without speaking and waved away her offer of a drink. The suggestion amused him, because her young neck was tempting, but there would be plenty of time for that later.

He let his gaze do its work upon her for a few moments, then spoke.

"I presume you know who I am?"

To give her her due, the response she gave was calm despite her inner turmoil. She would go far if she were allowed to.

"Off the record, naturally I am fully aware of your … unique position," she said. "On the record, you are, of course, no more than a trusted expert advisor to the Stationery and Office Paper Select Committee. One whose opinions we … value greatly."

She said exactly what she was supposed to say, leaving the little gap in the sentence to indicate that what she really meant was *obey*.

"Very good. I have some instructions for you."

Charnel felt the little thrill in her at that. He had come to *her*, of all the committee members. She was also wary, though. Her career was what mattered to her, the manoeuvrings she made to push herself ahead over the years, the sacrifices and compromises. He could have coerced her easily enough, told her the words to parrot, but in the long run it was easier to have humans like this on his side. In his debt.

"His Majesty's Office of the Witchfinder General," he said. "I think, given recent events, the corruption at its heart and its manifold failings in recent years, that it is time it was disbanded. Permanently. Do you agree?"

She sat back in her chair as if giving his views their due consideration. The blue brooch she wore on her lapel sparkled in the overhead lights.

She said, "It has done important work over the years and centuries, though. It may have let us down in recent years, but the threats that the realm faces are still there. Since the disbandment of the Mystical Council, the Office has played a key role in the delicate balance of powers upon which we all depend."

He had to admire her spirit. Most people would have nodded their acceptance of his orders. He liked her. He enjoyed the way she was playing the game.

"We can no longer trust them to protect us," he said. "If significant threats arise, there are, shall we say, *other* powers who can intervene."

"People such as yourself?" she asked quietly.

Charnel allowed himself a smile. "One is, of course, always willing to do one's patriotic duty."

Her eyes sparkled at that. It was a good line. Then she looked thoughtful, as if carefully weighing up pros and cons.

"There are, naturally, many calls upon the public purse. We could put the money we save into all manner of good uses. There must be, I don't know, hospitals and schools who would love the extra funding. But there are those on the committee who wish to see the Office continue, even have extra resources. The PM, I happen to know, is sympathetic to this view. He wants to see reform, but he likes the sense of control the current arrangement offers. The secret passageway between Number 10 and Number 13 in Downing Street."

"Just so," he said, waiting for her to catch up.

He saw the moment she got it. "You are suggesting that

you become the Witchfinder General? That the PM, whoever that is, comes to you to discuss anything ... relevant. Anything not for the ears of those not in the know."

He nodded his head slowly, enjoying the delicious irony of the idea.

"Is there anyone more knowledgeable about such matters? And the British state does so value its traditions and its unelected officers; its Lords and its monarchs, does it not? I think, on reflection, that I would fit right on. I could give the PM everything he or she wants, without the need for the rest of the Office of the Witchfinder General."

She frowned, either out of some unconcealed fear for how this might work out – or as part of the careful game she was playing. Yes. Her mention of *the PM* was not, of course, accidental. This was where her ambitions lay. This was what she was asking for in return.

He gave her his smile again, the faintest glimpse of his teeth. "You know, I hear there is a cabinet reshuffle taking place soon."

She couldn't stop her eyes going slightly wider. "I hadn't heard any whisper about that."

"No, well. I've just decided it," he said. "I can foresee several positions that a skilled politician such as yourself could advance to ... should your work on this committee be completed. The right people instructed to make the right choices, a few enthusiastic stories placed in the media and, really, anything is possible."

Now it was her turn to smile. He could feel the light glowing inside her mind. The hunger. Her ambitions: they were unlimited. She saw herself in the Order, too. She saw herself leading it, replacing him in time. He admired that. He had maintained his position for so long by using such people – and then destroying them before they became too powerful.

She said, "I think, on reflection, that the Office of the Witchfinder General has, indeed, become an anachronism. It's too self-absorbed, too expensive.

Poorly suited to the modern age. Yes. Time for it to be swept away. Time to bring in an expert in matters supernatural."

Charnel stood. Her conclusion was inevitable but still gratifying. This was but one more step in his slow dismantlement of the arms of the British state that stood in his way. The Council, and now the Office.

"Very well. We will talk again. I'm sure we will discover that there are many areas of policy in which our priorities ... align, yes? Areas where my advice will be needed."

There was, perhaps, the slightest hint of alarm in her features at that, but she masked it well enough. She knew the price she was paying. She paid it without giving it a second thought.

"Of course," she said. "You know how to find me."

"Yes," he said. "I do indeed."

That task completed, Charnel left Whitehall for the Thames. He had to pass through several layers of security – human and technological – but none restricted him in any way. If any doors did refuse to open to him, he could, of course, simply smash them down, just as he could easily eliminate any person standing in his way, but there was no need for such theatrics.

He stopped at the river, Westminster Bridge ahead of him. The site of the little melodrama he had recently engineered. Crossing running water was like being exposed to sunlight: irksome, but a vampire as powerful as he could survive it if need be. Fortunately, he had no need to make the crossing today. He turned onto the path that ran along the north bank, past the statue of Boadicea and her daughters – he recalled them well; they'd looked nothing like their statues – and along Victoria Embankment. As he walked, he pulled a pair of black gloves from his pocket. They were thinner than the heavy leather pair he'd used to handle Norskrang in Magor's crypt, but they would suffice for the few moments he would need them. Strong magical wards had been woven into their warp and weft, enough to protect his skin from the touch of the accursed artefact for a short time. He'd been tempted to instruct Bone to do what he was about to do, but the vampire assassin was still busy with his other task, and Charnel rather relished undertaking the job himself.

Hands on. Yes. He had rather missed this.

As he approached the spot he'd arranged to meet, the familiar ache in his leg flared up, burning for a moment. He bared his teeth in a snarl, suppressing the desire to lash out at one of the humans around him. This was the spot, of course. The place he'd been attacked and wounded by the older Shahzan. It was the only significant damage inflicted upon him in his long existence as a vampire, unless you counted the slight inconvenience the living William Bone and his men had caused him a few centuries previously. Returning to this spot for what he was about to do: it satisfied his need for vengeance. It amused him.

It felt like the closing of a circle.

Barely thinking about it, he reached into the minds of the animals milling around, instructing them not to see what was about to happen. It was easier that way.

Tremaine was waiting for him at the appointed spot. The younger vampire barely bothered to conceal the snarl of disdain on his features. With his gloved fingers, Charnel touched the wooden object he carried in the lined pocket of his black overcoat, sending another pulse of discomfort through his leg.

"Why are we meeting here?" Tremaine demanded. "We can't destroy the Office of the Witchfinder General standing by the river. With Earl Grey gone, we need to act now, stamp out the rest of them."

He had lured Tremaine to this spot with stories of the two of them doing this thing together, visibly re-exerting control. The younger vampire seemed to believe that he, Charnel, really did need help in carrying out such a task. Or perhaps Tremaine thought he was being anointed, treated as some sort of equal. He'd imagined, perhaps, the two of them rampaging through the Office, slaughtering each person they encountered, painting the walls with their blood.

It was laughable.

Charnel stood beside Tremaine. The grey, impenetrable waters of the Thames flowed by, long low pleasure-craft chopping through the waves. Charnel recalled when London was little more than a wooden bridge and a cluster of huts on the two shores, long before the arrival of the Romans.

He said, "I have already attended to the matter of the Office. It is destroyed in all but name. It is hollowed out, and I shall be its new leader."

"You? I don't understand."

"No. That is precisely your problem. You are incapable of understanding."

He thought Tremaine would resort to his usual complaints. The whining of the subordinate animal. Instead, to his credit, he said nothing more – and leapt to the attack, seizing Charnel by the neck with his two hands.

There was the briefest moment when Charnel thought he had miscalculated. Tremaine had clearly been preparing for this confrontation; Charnel could feel the raw power thrumming through the younger vampire. His grip upon Charnel's neck was like iron. Tremaine must have fed and fed over the past day or two, preparing himself.

A human would have been unable to breathe. Charnel was obviously at no risk of this – but no vampire, however ancient, however much power he'd drawn from others over long years, was completely invulnerable. Enough brute physical strength could tear his body to pieces, and while even that might not be the end, it would clearly incapacitate him for a time. He couldn't resist searing heat indefinitely and if he were trapped, deprived of sustenance, he would eventually fade into weakness. Then there was the danger posed by artefacts such as Norskrang. Did Tremaine have access to such a weapon?

So far as Charnel knew he did not – but he could never be completely sure. Tremaine was as ruthless as he was ambitious.

The grip on his neck tightened, and an animal snarl of effort and hatred escaped Tremaine's mouth. He intended to rip Charnel's head from his body, perhaps with the intention of working some grim magic on his dismembered body before he could reform. There were stories of vampires whose heads were kept separated from their bodies for centuries, rendering them impotent while the sorcery was performed. The magic certainly existed – although he had spent many centuries tracking down and destroying any reference to it he could find. Was it possible Tremaine had come across some whisper of the foreign magic the Shahzans had brought with them from the subcontinent? Some cruel sorcery Charnel knew nothing of?

Whatever the truth of it, there was only one way this battle was going to go. He allowed himself to appear to weaken the slightest amount, the grip of his left hand on Tremaine's wrist slackening. Tremaine responded by pressing further into his attack.

Of course he did. Charnel let him come. He enjoyed these little moments of intimacy. He allowed Tremaine's body to press hard against his own.

Against the sharp tip of Norskrang, held concealed in his pocket with his other hand. Charnel's mouth close to Tremaine's ear, he whispered the words of the triggering incantation, softly breathing the harsh syllables. The razor-sharp spike of enchanted wood pierced Charnel's clothing, and then Tremaine's own clothes, and then his flesh, burrowing hungrily into him. Charnel felt the heat from it through his gloves as it flared into life. The cursed thing writhed in his hand as if it were alive. It hungered for its victim.

A single gasp of pain escaped Tremaine's pale lips. His eyes went wide, full of malice but fading as Norskrang did its work, devouring all the borrowed life Tremaine had ever consumed. Charnel held him, but after a moment he was only holding a crumbling column of dust. It fell to the floor, a heap that Charnel kicked aside with his booted foot.

A young woman, glimpsing some image of what had taken place, the glamours he habitually wove perhaps slipping for a moment, *saw* him. Saw what he had done and who he was. The look of hunted terror on her features was familiar, primal reactions asserting themselves even as his mesmerisms reasserted themselves and he became effectively invisible once more.

The young woman shivered visibly, pulled her coat tight around herself as she hurried off. Charnel watched her go. He had done well, completed the tasks he had come to London to achieve. Time to celebrate, time to feed. Tremaine hadn't been completely wrong. Part of the attractiveness of London, or any large city, was the sheer dazzling array of tastes available. So much blood from all across the world: the familiar, the exotic, the unexpected and all points in between. Subtle variations and notes of distant lands, different airs. The loyal members of the ridiculous Order of the British Vampire would be appalled, of course, horrified at the nature of his appetites. His underlings didn't matter. They were what they were, and he was what he was. Only he mattered.

Leaving the heap of grey dust on the stone floor, Charnel strode into the crowd like a shopper strolling through a well-appointed luxury emporium, or a wolf ghosting through a flock of sheep.

Early the following morning, back at home in his castle, Charnel lifted Norskrang from its protective case. He wore his heavy gauntlets once again. Always careful not to touch the accursed artefact for fear of the effect that the merest splinter of it might have, Charnel carried it to the fire he had instructed his servants to lay. For all the incantations worked into it, for all its age and power, it was only a spike of wood. It would burn. And when it burned, it would mean there was nothing left in this world that could end him. He would be safe.

For a moment, he hesitated. He had destroyed many of his kind with the artefact over the centuries, obliterating even those who assumed they were immune from harm. There was a chance that he might need the object again, some distant day. But the risk was too great to take. Norskrang was too much of a danger to him. With all known threats eliminated, it was time. He would keep a tighter grip on potential threats in the future. There would be no more need for ultimate weapons such as this.

Charnel dropped the spike of yew into the red flame.

It smouldered for a moment, black smoke curling off it. He watched it char and smoulder, glow orange. Bright blue and green flames licked off it as if all the souls used in its construction were finally escaping. There was a hissing sound and the occasional crackle.

Hours later, he rummaged through the glowing embers of the fire with an iron poker, half-expecting to find the object unscathed, lying there in a bed of ash. There was no sign of it; there was only grey powder.

Norskrang was destroyed.

14 – The Rules of Invitation and Banishment

> I have fled in the semblance of a crow, scarcely finding rest
>
> *– The Mabinogion*

A new shape joined the inky shadows that thronged and thickened in my sight. The vampire's hands crushing my windpipe were still there, but the fact seemed oddly remote, unimportant. The hard world was a distant blur. At the same time, the desperate labouring of my pumping heart was loud in my ears. The sound filled my universe.

I studied the new shape, fascinated by it. It was intricate, a scribble of sharp points and angles rather than a nebulous mass. It moved rapidly around the room, panicky almost, and, as it circled, the blobs it touched faded, as if it were devouring them.

The grip on my throat loosened a little. The huge vampire attacking me was distracted by the new shape, too. Somehow, he could see it. How was that possible? The black clouds were in my eyes, in my head. Not out there. The vampire took one hand off me, flailing at the strange form as it scrabbled at his head. It sprouted a sharp beak and claws as it flew at him. It seemed intent on causing the vampire harm. New sounds came to me as my attacker released his other hand from me: a harsh croaking call. The sound was accompanied by the scuffing and fluttering of something soft.

Feathers.

I slumped to the ground, gulping in air through my tortured windpipe while my brain came back online and began to make sense of the world around me. A bird was in the room. A black bird, but not a blackbird. A crow. Or a rook or a raven, but its black eyes were polished marbles, and it appeared to be fighting the vampire. Some of the black, I saw, had come off it, too, scattering in the air as it flew, and that was soot, strewn about the room in lines. It had come down the chimney, clattered its way down to find me.

I pushed my way up to my feet, using the wall to steady me. The vampire was snarling, lunging at the rapid, flapping bird. I felt the first embers of magical strength rekindling inside me. I had no more wooden stakes, but I had the knowledge and the skills I'd learned. This strange bird emerging from the disused chimney: I could attack the vampire while it was distracted. It probably wouldn't be enough, but I wasn't going to simply give in.

I began the first hand movements, shaping the air into the forms I wanted, the syllables lining themselves up in my brain to begin their dance – when I sensed other magic being wielded in the room. I saw it: silver threads in the air, indistinct like spiderwebs caught in sunlight. They were trailing behind the bird as it drew figure 8's in the air.

The new magic grew stronger and the black shape jerked and warped. It was working some spell. I still wasn't completely sure it was really there or if I were imagining it. The bird convulsed and grew, as if some larger form were trapped inside it and was trying to punch and kick its way out.

The bird warped, bulged … then fell to the floor in a heap. It was no longer a bird. It grew rapidly. Both I and the vampire watched, united for the moment in our puzzlement. Then I realized I knew: this was Stonewall, finally coming to my aid. He'd flown from his deep woods in answer to my summons. My hand went to my throat as I looked on, touching my skin where it burned from the brutal grip of the vampire. I was going to struggle to intone spells, but that wasn't going to stop me.

A figure appeared from the shifting black shape, then, growing upwards from the floor to become the outline of a person.

I was very wrong. It wasn't Stonewall at all.

Sally stood there, dressed in her best goth black and silver jewellery. She was young again; the Sally I'd accompanied to Faebrook Folly. So far as I could tell, she was real and solid, not any kind of projection. As before, I could feel the raw magical power buzzing away in her. I could also see, from the narrowing of her eyes and the way she breathed heavily, that the magic she'd worked had taken their toll on even her.

You wouldn't have known it from her voice, though. Her smile made music play in my heart.

"Oh, hey Danesh. Good to see you again."

I replied with *Good to see you, too* – although what actually came out of my tortured throat was a series of grunts and growls. It hurt to produce even them.

Only then did she turn her attention to the elephant in the room. Or rather, the powerful vampire in the room. The creature stood between us, casting from side to side as it decided which of us posed the greater threat. Pretty rapidly, it came to the obvious conclusion and turned to face Sally. Fair enough, really. I saw it tense as it prepared to fling itself at her.

I was weakened, but I wasn't useless. I had a free shot now, and I was going to make full use of it. I still had my clothcutter knife. It wasn't amped up with any of my grandfather's magic, but it could inflict damage. I reached for the coiling magic inside me, chanting the syllables of a basic attack spell in my head.

Before I could unleash my attack, though, and before the vampire could throw itself at Sally, she spoke. Her voice was loud, her message clear.

"Leave here, parasite. The Invitation is revoked."

The vampire checked its leap as if leashed by an invisible chain. It snarled and took a step towards Sally, then another. The effort of it was in stark contrast to its previous rapidity. It looked like the creature was leaning into the teeth of a howling gale, clawing its way up a steep hill. It refused to relent. If it could reach her and slay her, did that mean it was no longer banished from the building? Because Sally was no longer – technically – the owner? I had no idea how that worked. Somewhere in the library there was probably a book on it that I was supposed to have read.

"Fuck off now!" Sally shouted louder, adding to the effect of the vampire's banishment by pushing at the creature with her outstretched hand, throwing her own magic at it. I circled the room to stand beside her and added my strength to the effort. The vampire howled as it tried to reach us, but the nearest exit from the dwelling – the window that was now behind it – sucked at it as if it were some deep pit the creature was falling into, as if only its sheer will was allowing it to resist that gravity. I could see its muscles rippling, the veins standing out on its skin as it took another step forwards, then another.

It got close to us – a few centimetres away – before the effort of defying its own nature became too much. It suddenly slipped backwards and was blasted away, picked up by a gale only it could feel. It crashed into the window frame, smashing through wood and glass to flail into the air.

The departure of the vampire broke the crackling magical tension in the room. Sally and I strode together to the window. The vampire was on the ground below. It had thumped into the hard floor. From its movement, it was clearly still alive – or at least moving. After a moment, it rose from prone on the ground to standing upright without any effort. I thought it was going to renew its attack, hurl itself at us. Instead, looking up at us only once, then snarling its vulpine snarl, it turned and loped away.

I turned to Sally. There was suddenly something transparent about her, like the blood had drained from her veins. I didn't think she wasn't about to fade away, though. It was obvious as she slumped to the floor that she was solid. But she was clearly exhausted.

Her and me both. I sat down beside her, both of us leaning on the wall, the cold Cardiff air filling the room and making the blinds clatter.

"Going to have to get that repaired," she said.

"Can't you just magic up a new window?" My throat felt maybe a little better.

She grinned. "Oh, sure. But not at this precise moment; that thing was strong. And why go to all the trouble when there are perfectly good builders around?"

"You were there outside," I said. "You were watching. Why did you let me walk into a trap?"

"You don't speak rook?"

"I thought you were a crow."

"Would that have been easier for you to understand?"

"Not really."

"I knew that thing was in here, of course," she said. "I had every faith in you."

"I nearly died. It nearly got me."

"No, you did amazingly," she said. "You hurt it, and it's *really* powerful. You've grown so much as a practitioner. We wondered if you were ready; now we know."

"You let me face that thing as a test?"

She shook her head. "No. A little. We didn't want you to face the Warlock if you weren't ready. I'm sorry, but we needed to know. You've come a long way from that faithful Office operative I first met, denying you were even a magic user."

"Yet I needed you to come to my rescue."

"Oh, it bothers you that you needed help from a woman?"

"It bothers me that I'm not strong enough to survive a fight with a vampire on my own."

She rose to her knees to consider me, brushing a strand of hair behind her ear. She already looked a little more solid, some of her colour returning. The playful smile on her lips sent a thrill through my stomach. It felt like sunlight and magic, both at once. Did she really think she could placate me that easily?

If she did, she was right.

"But you are strong enough," she said. "Better weapons, the *right* weapons, your innate abilities and your heritage. You can do this."

"I'm nowhere near as powerful as my grandfather. Or you."

She shook her head. "You're underestimating yourself. I defeated that thing because this is my abode. I could banish it. In a straight fight, like you had, I don't think I'd have won."

"That's not encouraging."

"Your grandfather didn't work alone, right? He had others, and they worked as a team. Until the Council was disbanded at least."

"Speaking of teamwork, how come Stonewall didn't turn up?"

The sun went in briefly as a shadow passed across her features. "That's a very fair question. He would have come, I'm sure. He's … in the middle of something."

"Well great. Just as well I wasn't depending on him to come to my help and save my life, then. What exactly is he in the middle of? A book that's hard to put down?"

"I'll show you very soon. I promise. We're nearly at the moment."

"You could just tell me, you know. Do you still not trust me, Sally? Even now?"

She was about to speak, but she stopped herself. She put the palm of her hand to my face and held it there, her gaze intent.

She … caressed me, her soft touch gentle. While I was adjusting to this, she moved in suddenly, putting her lips to mine. Her touch was firm and soft and warm, all at the same time. I forgot everything: my bruised throat, the dangers facing me. Everything. Our lips parted as we explored each other, the tips of our tongues meeting. A golden light shone through my body.

Love and death; the afternoon had brought its intoxicating mix of the two. They seemed, in that moment, to be intimately related, almost the same thing. I felt pure joy that I was alive to experience the shared moment. Also, at the same time, a grateful acceptance that I could die happy. That nothing else much mattered anymore. Perhaps it was all the endorphins and dopamine flooding through me. It didn't feel like that. It felt like joy and light and music. Eagerly, I lost myself in it, my arms holding her just as hers pulled me in closer.

After what might have been a lifetime and might have been only a few moments, she pulled back.

"I trust you," she whispered. "I mean, it's more than that. I don't need to say, do I? I ... want you. Why do you think I gave you that other name, put it into your mouth to use. I made you call me *Bella Mine*. And I don't want you to die. I don't want either of us to die. Especially not now."

"When this is over," I started. "If we survive…"

She put her finger to my lips. "We'll talk about it then, if that happens. This isn't the time."

The glow I felt within me was also, unmistakably, woven in with the magical energy that reeled and sparkled within me. I found it was impossible to differentiate between the two; they were the same thing. Falling in love with Sally: was that another reason I'd grown as a user, become more adept? I wondered if magic could take root in other emotions too; if people filled with fear or rage manifested very different powers. Maybe that explained a lot.

"Why?"

She sighed and pulled herself free of my embrace. "There are lots of reasons. Mainly because I have to go."

"We're safe now. There's no one else here. We're alone together literally in your bedroom just after beating the bad guy."

The look of temptation in her wide eyes – of, frankly, unashamed lust – was perhaps the greatest delight of that odd, brief episode. But she shook her head.

"That thing that attacked you – it is known to us. We know its name. It's called Bone. An old enemy. It's powerful, but it isn't the Warlock. It'll come for you again soon enough, most likely – but as soon as our enemy learns *I'm* here, he'll drop everything and come himself. We do not want to be here when that happens."

"Because you know where Stonewall is."

"And the Warlock is powerful enough to overcome any Banishment I can put in its way."

She kissed me again, briefly but urgently. Then she stood.

"I have to go before he comes. You should leave, too. We'll meet again soon, I promise you."

"Where?"

There was her playful smile again. "You already know where. I've left all the clues. I'll text you a time."

I stood too. "Why don't you just tell me? I haven't worked anything out."

She shrugged. "Where's the fun in that? I have every faith in your abilities, clever boy. You'll get there."

She glanced about the room once, as if reliving happy memories of her time there, then stepped back. With a practised hand, she drew a circle in the air around her. I could feel the resonance of the magic she was working. The air around her turned to a faint blue tinge.

As she worked, she said, "Don't come back here; I won't use this place again."

"Wait, I..." But it was too late. The blue light brightened and Sally, standing in the eye of it, shimmered. Became a ghost, an outline, became nothing.

The room fell silent. I looked around at the ring of twelve paintings – with one of them on the floor. At the traces of soot and a few black feathers. At the smashed window and the rucked-up rug. Outside, I could see that the vampire – Bone – was gone, too. I had to hope it had gone off to lick its wounds somewhere.

Still puzzling over Sally's clues, I lifted the rug where the bed had been, expecting to find a magical gateway or at least some words written down. There was nothing.

I touched my cheek where she'd touched me. *We'll meet again soon, I promise.* That was really all I needed to know. I did as Sally had said and got the hell out of there.

I retraced my steps across Cardiff, imagining I was following the run of lost passageways snaking beneath the ground. Nothing attacked me apart from the rain and one or two mad car drivers. At least you knew where you were with them. I was finding it hard to focus; I had the weird sensation that I was floating a few centimetres above the ground. I grabbed a coffee and some food in the city centre, sitting in the window of a café so I could watch everyone hurrying by. There was something relaxing about it, hypnotic. All those people and their busy lives. So far as I could tell, none were vicious vampires intent on slaughtering me.

Olwen emerged from the security doors as I approached the office. I could see she was about to say something flippant – probably, *good of you to finally turn up* – when she took a proper look at me and stopped mid-stride.

"Oh my god. What happened to you?"

For the briefest moment I assumed she could see the glow around me as I basked in the light of Sally's affection. But of course, she didn't mean that. I'd taken a look at my reflection in a window, and I knew I was a mess. I'd seen it in the eye of the young guy who'd served me at the café, too. What she meant was my bruised eye-sockets and the rough red marks on my neck.

"A fight with a vampire. It didn't go well."

She pulled me aside into a corner of the walls, in case any normal members of the Cardiff populace happened to pass by.

"You're still alive; that sounds like a win if you fight one of those bastards. What were you thinking?"

"Mostly I was thinking, *Shit, how do I get out of here*."

"Did you kill it?"

"We banished it."

Not a lot got past Olwen. "Who's *we*?" She obviously knew it wasn't another Office coworker. You could literally count those on the fingers of one hand.

"A … friend."

Olwen glanced around warily, scanning for threats. The standard manner of the Office operative in the field.

"You need to get those wounds looked at. It didn't … break your skin?"

"Just my dignity."

"Still, get checked out."

"Who's inside?" I asked, nodding towards the building. "Are you on a callout?"

"There's no one inside; everyone's up to their elbows in it. I'm investigating a possible Code 8."

Code 8 – interference by the fay. Pretty rare these days, especially in urban areas. Most of the *Tylwyth Teg* stay well out of the way of humans. Some are extremely dangerous: stealing babies, famously, but not opposed to a bit of human sacrifice if the mood takes them. The more playful ones can't resist the opportunity for a bit of trouble-making. Once they'd taken delight in turning milk sour and hiding one of each pair of socks, but these days they loved to glitch out electronic devices and computers. They'd even been known to fiddle with the city's traffic light sequences, seeding chaos and rage as vehicles got gridlocked.

"Be careful," I said. "They can be nasty."

"Yeah, well. So can I, if I have to be." She turned to leave, hurrying off to do battle with the capricious little folk – or not if it turned out to be a hoax.

I called after her. "Hey, Olwen, we're mates, right?"

She turned back with puzzlement on her face. "That's a weird question to ask."

"Sure, sorry, I was just … the vampires after me; the thing is, they might try and get at me through my friends and relatives. I mean, they have already done that. I should have said something to you. You need to be careful. I'm sorry. You maybe need to lie low or go stay somewhere else for a time."

She stepped back toward me so we could have this conversation at a lower level. Again, she missed nothing. "Vampires? Vampires, *plural* are after you?"

"Yeah. Probably, in fact, all of the vampires."

"Fucking hell, Danesh. What are you mixed up in now? There's no record of this anywhere on MORIARTY. You didn't think to even mention it in passing?"

"I should have. Hardknott-Lewis and I decided to keep

it off the books. There have been some ... issues with who we could trust."

"Again, *fucking hell, Danesh*. You need to buy me several rounds of drinks while you explain properly what's been happening. Does this explain Digbeth?"

"It does, yeah. It actually explains a whole lot of things."

She considered that. "Right, well, by my reckoning, that's you buying the drinks all evening while you tell me about it."

"Seems fair. Just, take care for now. Please."

I could see she was about to throw some witticism back at me, but she stopped herself. "I will. You, too, yes? Get those injuries seen to, then don't go getting any more."

"Good advice."

I left her to stride off into the drizzle to battle the fay then returned to my desk. It was weirdly quiet with no one there. Oppressively quiet. I started to become aware of the symphony of little noises that had presumably always been there: the hum of machinery, the rushing of water in the pipes, the muffled calls of gulls. I kicked off some searches on the various leads I'd picked up: the names on the disturbed graves, anything we had on a vampire called *Bone*, anything significant we knew about Blackfriars Priory. While the routines performed text scans on our catalogue of digitized documents, I checked for messages. There was some inconsequential stuff from the Crow, essentially telling everyone that the Office was still in limbo and, for now, to carry on.

There was also a response from Thomas Quirk, the Lord High Witchfinder of the Isles. I'd sent him a request to talk via Hardknott-Lewis, but I knew he'd been badly affected by his experiences on Lindisfarne. He'd seemed unharmed when I rescued him, but the after-effects had hit him later. Couldn't blame him for that. It was so bad that he'd actually taken some time off work – the first recorded incidence of this taking place in Office history according to my contacts in the Isles division. Now, it seemed, Quirk was back in the game.

I requested a call for the following morning, then went down to the library. There wasn't much I could do to tend my wounds, but I did want to quiz the Lady and Gilroy if they knew anything about the vampire that had attacked me. And I also wanted to work on some more wooden stakes. The ones I'd used in Cathedral Road had clearly been effective, and I needed more. I also reckoned I could see a way – *feel* a way might be closer to it – to make them better. Stronger. *Hungrier*. And I needed to run through my combat routines again. They clearly worked, but I'd panicked and lost discipline when facing Bone. I needed the moves and incantations to be second nature.

The Librarian made no mention of my injuries when I spoke to her, but she seemed annoyed that I'd managed to use all my wooden stakes already. After some persuasion, she gave me ten more blanks. I thanked her profusely. Neither she nor Gilroy knew of a vampire called Bone. Gilroy did know that the Warlock used at least one thralled vampiric assassin to do his dirty work – but explained, quite reasonably, that no one knew any names because anyone who met them died soon after. The fact that I hadn't seemed to impress Gilroy.

The main thing that interested the Librarian were the tattoos on Bone's skin. I described as many as I could remember to her, and she even got me to draw out some. My sketches were ... sketchy.

"Are you thinking there's more going on here than vampire fashion?" I asked.

She considered my drawings for a moment. "Maybe. There is magic that uses a drawing or a symbol as a sort of focus. A geas to impel someone operating under a curse to track a target down and slaughter them."

"It said it would take me to the Warlock if I didn't struggle. Without killing me, I mean."

"Well, okay. The hex could probably be used for something like that too."

Gilroy had wandered over to listen in. "A vampire under the influence of something like that would be formidable. It wouldn't stop. It wouldn't be able to stop."

The Lady said, "It's not as simple as drawing a likeness, though. There has to be some essence of the target worked in. Has anyone taken any blood from you recently? Or perhaps some other bodily fluid?"

"I mean, not that I'm aware of."

"The creature – this Bone – it kept attacking you?"

"Yeah. It seemed quite insistent on the matter. It wasn't mindless, though. If it felt there was a greater threat to it, it went for that instead."

"Interesting. Maybe it was impelled; maybe it was just vicious. If the Warlock has used this magic, this Bone creature will track you down again. The only way you can stop it is to kill it."

Something I'd already worked out. It wasn't a particularly comforting thought.

"I'm working on another case, too," I said. "Someone or something is digging up graves and taking bones."

"That could literally be anything," said Gilroy.

I noticed the glance of disapproval at his use of the word *literally* from the Librarian, but she let it pass. "Interfering with bodies is certainly a feature of many forms of malign magic use."

"This is different, though."

"In what way?" she asked.

"For one thing, they're all old bodies as far as I know."

"People dying when they're old isn't unusual."

"No, I mean, people that were buried a long time ago."

Gilroy considered that. "Old graves tend to be less well-tended. Any disturbance is less likely to be noticed."

"Yes, but what's odd is that very specific bones were taken. Like, a femur here, a breastbone there. It's almost like someone is trying to build a skeleton from fragments taken from all over the place. Have you ever heard of anything like that?"

Gilroy shook his head. "Sounds like some crazy to me."

The Lady was equally unhelpful. "It sounds monstrous, some grim necromancy. I'll see if I can find anything in the literature."

I thanked them both – they looked more and more like an old married couple, wiling away their days comfortable in each other's company – and returned to my room. Not only to prepare more weapons: my body was beginning to suffer the after-effects of my battle. My shoulders and legs ached sharply as I moved, and turning my neck from side to side was agony. I'd decided I could take it easy in the safety of the library for a time. I could even – and here was a radical idea – read some of the books in the library to see if I could unearth anything about tunnels or the history of the Priory. I had signal down there; if Sally or my mother texted, I'd know.

I worked long into the night, carving stakes, running through the disciplines described in my grandfather's book. Each time weariness crept upon me and I was tempted to stop, the vision of the Bone vampire throwing itself at me, the cruelty in its eyes, spurred me on again.

15 – An Unholy Trinity

> I believe the presence of three sarcophagi in the ruined chamber on Lindisfarne is highly significant – as is the fact that one is no longer there. Its former presence is clearly evident from the marks left on the ground. Were it possible to track down that missing tomb, my belief is that I might finally learn the whereabouts of the ancient vampire I have spent so long pursuing. The question, also, is *why three?* Who were the creatures slumbering or hiding in the other two tombs? Who were this trinity? My researches suggest there is a single, powerful entity behind much that takes place in these isles; I can only assume that the other two entities were lieutenants or rivals destroyed long ago. Perhaps if we knew how that was achieved, we might be better armed in our pursuit of the third. I shall have one of the sarcophagi removed to my house upon the Isle of Man so that I may study it in more depth.
> – Thomas Quirk, Lord High Witchfinder of the Isles, *private journal*, 2017

The following morning, I was at my desk early – a two-minute commute up a flight of stairs can do that for you – checking my messages and deciding where to go next. The scans on the names on the graves had retrieved nothing useful. There were numerous weak matches, but the names were not rare enough in Wales to give me anything worth pursuing. I spent some time trying to dig up connections between the victims – dying in the same mysterious way, say – but apart from the fact that they were dead and buried near each other, I got nothing.

I did that thing where I kept checking my phone for a message from someone – Sally in this case – and then telling myself not to be so ridiculous. I even turned my phone over so that I couldn't see the screen. It didn't help; I still checked repeatedly.

My conversation with Olwen the previous day was still clear in my mind. I also quickly checked on the other Office members, anxious that the Warlock might be using one of them to get to me. So far as I could tell, no one was facing any unusual danger. Everyone was busy but still alive. Olwen's fae investigation had reported some suspicious coincidences but no actual evidence of an incursion. Apart from the Crow, whose movements I couldn't see, everyone was out in the field.

I messaged my mother to check all was well there – it was – then slipped out to get chocolate croissants and a long black with an extra shot or two.

This time, I carried five of my powered-up stakes with me. I'd rigged up a holder I could wear across my chest by hacking a standard-issue Office gun holster. Fortunately, no vampires leapt to assault me as I walked into the shopping centre past the statue of Aneurin Bevan, his finger pointing down – or perhaps underground, as if indicating to me where my answers lay. Even better, no vampires came at me on the way back when I had my hands full. It would have been doubly insulting to get slaughtered *and* spill my coffee. Frankly, it felt a bit ridiculous carrying five sharpened wooden stakes around with me – although it had been tempting to whip one out to whittle down the queue of people a little as I waited in line to buy breakfast.

I'd managed to resist the temptation, despite my growling stomach.

Back at my desk, the bitter black coffee hosing away the fog in my brain, I turned to the map of sites where bone theft had been reported. There were several locations that didn't fit into my underground tunnel scenario – which meant there were passageways no one knew about, or I needed a new theory. I spent twenty minutes trying to overlay the scatter of reported sites onto the forms of runes from the forbidden alphabets – those I knew about – wondering if someone were maybe trying to form a seriously huge sigil across the entire face of the city to summon something terrifyingly apocalyptic through from a different dimension. It wasn't impossible, so far as I knew. The good news was that I couldn't make anything match.

I also took great care to check against the few vampiric runes I knew about – thinking about the way that Digbeth had fooled me into thinking the sigils used to kill Jamie McTavish had been of that nature. Digbeth had been deliberately confusing my investigation into that case, and I was wary of falling into the same trap with these two investigations – but I needed to be sure that the weird bone-snatching incidents weren't some sort of elaborate trap being laid for me by the Warlock. Again, I could find no significant correlation. I needed to hit the streets and explore the other grave disturbance sites, see if I could work out a pattern to them.

I gave up that line of enquiry for the moment and turned to considering the paintings I'd photographed in Sally's house. I sent them to a big screen and flicked through them in order. There were small trees in the foreground of many of them – little more than a black line against the sky – and I spent some time trying to make each one form a letter. I could persuade myself there were a couple of S's there, and also a Y and a V – but the other trees resembled the symbols of no alphabet I knew.

I was so lost in concentration that I didn't hear Kerrigan come up behind me until he spoke.

"Why are you looking at a series of paintings of May Hill?"

I swivelled in my chair to face him. He loomed over me pretty effectively when we were standing side by side, and the effect was only heightened when I sat. He didn't fool me with his *Just happened to be wandering by* act. My guess was that Olwen had told him about the state I'd been in, and he'd come into the office to check on me. He was supposed to be up in the valleys investigating a report of some *coblynau* making knocking sounds in the dark of an abandoned coal mine, according to MORIARTY.

"What's May Hill?" I asked.

Kerrigan pointed a finger at a line on the horizon in the painting I was studying: a low mound of a hill nippled by a little copse of trees on the top.

"That's May Hill, over by here. Don't you know it?"

I flicked to the next painting, and, just as he'd said, the hill was there again. It was in a different position, but it was unmistakably the same feature. I flicked through all the paintings and found it in each. How had I missed that?

"You know this place?"

"Sure, walked up it many times. Views from the top on a clear day are amazing, like: the Welsh mountains, the winding River Severn shining in the sun. The hills and valleys of Herefordshire and Gloucestershire."

"It's in England?"

"You could be there in an hour or so if the M4 cooperates. It's a strange little hill."

"Why so?"

Kerrigan sat, the chair groaning beneath him. "Partly because it's always there when you're anywhere in the area."

"Hills are always there. They famously don't move."

"Sure, I mean, wherever you are you always seem to be able to see it in the distance. The trees on the top are distinctive. It feels like the hill is sliding around the horizon to get a view of you wherever you go."

"I presume those trees are all that's left of the ancient wild wood?"

"Don't know about that, laddo. There are earthworks up there, a ring ditch, so it must be an ancient site."

"There's a circle marked into the ground around the trees?"

"It's old, but it's there. The whole place feels a bit strange, to be honest."

"How so?"

"Well, it's exposed and windswept, but inside the little

wood up there it suddenly gets very hushed and sort of ... watchful if you know what I mean. Like the world outside dims a little. I took a thaumometer up once but I didn't get any sort of reading."

"You suspected something takes place up there? A summoning or the opening of a portal?"

"Like I say, I couldn't find anything."

I nodded, absorbing this information. The clear message was that this was where I had to go to meet up with Sally again. She was right; the message was more obvious this time. I just didn't know *when* I needed to go. Hopefully, her text would tell me.

I thanked Kerrigan. He still hadn't mentioned my injuries but I could see him glancing at them again and again. He also wasn't dashing off to search for coblynau. There was more he wanted to say.

He circled around the matter some more. "What are you up to today, then?"

I trusted Kerrigan utterly – and I had thought a *lot* about all my work colleagues since Digbeth – but I couldn't bring myself to tell him everything. Perhaps I should have; perhaps it would have been fairer. I loved the man; I think I probably couldn't face his disappointment at his discovering my real nature.

He clearly knew vampires were involved, though. I'd let that slip to Olwen.

"This bodysnatcher case," I said. "It's possible something vampiric in nature is behind it."

"That was what attacked you?"

"A vampire attacked me while I was investigating the case. That's all I know."

Kerrigan pulled on his black beard as he considered that. It had now reached the *pirate* level of bushiness. It made me want to grow my own beard so I could do exactly the same thing.

"I'd like to come along with you when you next go out," he said. "The two operatives rule has become the two operatives general guidance of late – but you shouldn't face something like that on your own."

I couldn't see a good way to deny his request. If the Bone creature came for me again, I could maybe pass the wooden stakes off as some new m/tech, and it would be good to have Kerrigan with me. I doubted I could rely on Sally coming to my help again.

"I have a call with Thomas Quirk first," I said.

Fortunately, he didn't quiz me about my reasons for calling the Witchfinder General of the Isles. He rose and nodded.

"And I need to go and look into that disused mine shaft. They've been thinking about opening it up as another tourist experience, and we can't have the visitors devoured by *coblynau*. Bad for business is that. Can you hold fire until tomorrow morning?"

I assured him I could. He didn't need to know about anything else I investigated in the meantime.

Half an hour later, I sat at a laptop in a quiet meeting room to talk to Quirk. I confess I half-expected him to struggle with the technology, being, as he was, somewhere in his sixties. My bad for the ageism: he was online precisely at the agreed time, without any of the familiar pantomime while I tried to use sign-language to explain that he was on mute. I thought he looked older, though. More weather-worn, the lines on his face deeper. His crazy explosion of hair looked whiter than it had been, on the screen. Maybe it was just the lighting. He'd suffered terribly at the hands of the Warlock.

Despite that, his voice was warm and full of his usual vigour. "Danesh! So good to see you again. I never did thank you properly for rescuing me from my grim incarceration on Lindisfarne."

I recalled the look of madness in his eye as I opened his tomb. That he had recovered at all was remarkable.

"I was happy to help. I was happy to discover you were *you*, too. I have to admit, it had crossed my mind that you might be the Office traitor, secretly working for the Warlock all along."

He barked a laugh at that. "Excellent! Admirable

scepticism. I must thank you for ridding us of the traitor in our midst as well, by the way. We Keyholders utterly failed there. Good to see young operatives using their brains. I imagine Campbell keeps you on your toes."

"He tries. Are you fully recovered from your ordeal?"

Quirk batted the question aside as if it were an annoying fly. "Oh, more or less. Getting better each day. I try hard to avoid getting locked inside cupboards and small rooms" – from what I knew of him, this was a joke – "but aside from that, all is well. Now, I imagine you called to discuss your hunt for the Warlock?"

"You had one of the tombs taken to the Isle of Man to study. I saw it in your house, as you know, the day I went there."

"Which, no doubt, made you think I was one of the Warlock's minions? Or perhaps even the foul creature itself?" The idea seemed to delight Quirk enormously.

"The possibility occurred to me. I wondered if you'd learned anything useful from your investigations."

"They're both here now, you know."

"Sorry, who are?"

"Not *who*, *what*. Both tombs are here. I had the other one shipped over, too, so I could compare. It's right here in this house, down in the basement."

"You have the tomb you were sealed within there in your house?"

"I needed to study it. We can't let former traumas stand in our way on such a vital matter."

"Have you found anything?"

"Tell me, Danesh, are you able to fly over to the island? There are some details I could show you that might prove enlightening."

The invitation was tempting; for one thing, it might throw the creature that was pursuing me off the scent. Crossing so much water might at least slow it down. But I couldn't spare the time.

"I think matters are coming to a head over here. I really need to stay and see them through."

Quirk nodded his explosion of hair. "Understood,

understood. The mainland is inevitably the site of much that takes place in these islands."

"Can you tell me what you've found?" I asked.

"If you'll bear with me, I can show you. The signal is a little weak down in the cellar but it might get through."

There followed a minute's blur of movement, accompanied by Quirk's heavy breathing and the creak and slam of doors as he carried his phone through his house. His footsteps were loud on his hard stone floors. I caught glimpses of wood panels, tiled floors, dark oil paintings, a piano. Then we were descending the wide set of stone steps I recalled. The images froze a couple of times – but then resumed as he showed me the scene in his cellar. Next to the stone tomb I recalled from my previous (illicit) visit, there was another sarcophagus – the one I'd found on Lindisfarne. The one Quirk had been sealed within. Even to my eye, the similarities between the two were clear: they were the same length and height. Both looked old, the carved stone of them weathered, but they looked to be of a similar style.

"The wooden lids are relatively modern," Quirk said. "Perhaps five hundred years old or so. Dating the stone carvings is harder, but from the styles I'd suggest several thousand years. And quite possibly not from the British Isles."

"They were brought over on boats."

"Or they came here a *very* long time ago, hauled on carts when the land bridge to the continent still existed."

"We weren't always an island?"

"Oh no."

"The tombs look like a pair," I said.

"They are, yes." His voice had a hollow quality to it as he spoke. "At least, they match, but *pair* is wrong, my boy. As I think I explained the last time we met, there were originally three of them. Three the same size. The markings on the floor on Lindisfarne were very clear."

"Do you know who the three were?"

"Were or *are*, I should say."

"Yes."

"That's what I wanted to show you. The carvings are worn away almost to nothing, but I've been able to pick out some details, enough to identify letters on both of them."

"Inscriptions?"

"Names, I think. The names of the two vampires who used these tombs as a refuge and a sanctuary when sustenance was scarce or they were travelling long distances. Or when they simply needed physical protection from angry mobs."

"What are the names?"

The video blurred again, and then steadied as Quirk moved his phone to show me the carvings on the tombs. His finger also came into the frame as he pointed out the lines of the symbols.

"This is the tomb I've been studying for a while. It took me a while to decipher the symbols and identify the alphabet being used, but I believe these markings spell out the word *Valian*."

I'd never heard the name. "Do we know who that is?"

"I do not. One of the vampires who travelled to these islands long ago and established a fortress, a sanctuary, upon Lindisfarne, I presume. The ruins you found me in are all that remains of that structure."

The images blurred again – I caught a glimpse of the carved leviathan I recalled from my previous visit – and then another set of faint letters came into view.

"This is the tomb I was held within. This one belonged to a creature called *Magor*. Possibly Magur, but I think Magor."

Again, it meant nothing to me. I knew there was a village in Wales called Magor, not far from Caldicot, but I'd never heard the name applied to a person.

"Any leads on that?"

"I have checked with my colleagues in the supernatural protection authorities across Europe and the wider world. Neither name is known to anyone, certainly not in connection to each other."

"Given that there are no vampires inside these two

sarcophagi, can we assume that Valian and Magor have been destroyed?" I asked.

"Alas, no. A vampire does not need to slumber within a specific tomb, although some soil from the creature's original home generally is needed. We cannot be sure that these two are not still walking the earth."

"And the third name?" I asked.

Now Quirk's face came into view as he addressed me directly. The low angle of the phone chiselled deep shadows into his face, his hair a ghostly halo around it.

"That we don't know. Which I believe is significant of itself. There's a power in names, as you will know. Certain spell components require knowledge of the individual's true identity. The third vampire, I assume, is the entity we refer to as the Warlock. I doubt he would have let his own name be so easily discoverable."

"He took his tomb to some other location."

"I believe so. Long ago, given how worn the grooves are on the stone floor."

"We obviously have no idea where the third tomb was taken."

"We do not. I have spent many years on that particular search. Too many years. It might be anywhere in the world, of course, but given the Warlock's continued influence upon these islands, I assume it is here somewhere."

"You must have unearthed some clue."

He shook his head. "Little of use. We can't search every building in the realm. This creature is cunning, going to great lengths to conceal its location and protect itself from risks. It has been doing so for a very long time. My guess is, these three came here together, long ago, and then the one we call the Warlock slaughtered the other two in order to maintain his authority. For all their aristocratic pretensions, vampires are brutal creatures, pack animals. Any threats are eliminated."

"You keep saying the Warlock is a *he*. Do we even know that?"

"I would argue that they're all *its*. But the scant records we have do suggest a male, yes. This may, of course, simply be the gender bias of the historical record."

I nodded. Both Stonewall and Mormont had referred to the entity as *he* – as had my grandfather's journal. I had to assume it was or had been male in appearance. Which didn't help much.

"Do you know of a vampire called *Bone*? I was pursued by it."

"Bone is hunting you down?"

"Yes."

The shocked look on Quirk's face did little to ease my anxieties.

"Oh, my boy. That's not good. I know about Bone, yes. William Bone to use his full name. Perhaps the most fearsome of the Warlock's lieutenants. It's impressive that you survived his attack. And I'm afraid he won't stop. From what I understand, he *can't* stop. He is impelled to pursue his quarry."

"How do I defeat him?"

The look on Quirk's face gave me my answer before he spoke. "Short of destroying the Warlock, I know of no way. I'm sorry. I don't believe anyone knows of a way."

Not what I wanted to hear.

"Can you tell me, does the word *Norskrang* mean anything to you?"

"Ah, yes! It does. A mythical antivampire weapon. So far as we know, it was destroyed long ago. If it ever existed. It is, no doubt, the source of the ridiculous popular stories whereby any sliver of bit of sharpened wood can despatch a vampire. If only that were true!"

"Would the Norskrang artefact have been powerful enough to destroy the Warlock?"

"Hmm, well, quite possibly, if the stories are to be believed. But they really are just stories, and stories, you know, really aren't to be trusted."

"Can you send me anything you have on William Bone? Perhaps there's something in there that might be useful."

"I've only found a few scraps here and there, but I'll send what I have."

"Are you sure this Bone isn't the third vampire of the trinity?"

"I'm sure. You'll see why."

"And, can I ask if you're planning to continue your investigations into these three vampires?"

"Yes, yes, certainly. But I wouldn't rely on my finding anything useful in your fight, I'm afraid. I assume you learned nothing from Earl Grey at the end?"

"Nothing. He'd grown to hate the Warlock, but I don't think he had any idea where the creature lived. Earl Grey received his orders somehow, but he'd stopped paying much attention to them."

"Earl Grey had stopped paying attention to many things. I'm ashamed to say that I thought of him as a friend."

"Last question, then I must go," I said. "There's a grave in Oblivion with a phantom line or thread running from it to some other plane. Do you know any way of tracing it, finding out where the other end is?"

"You believe the grave in question is of interest to the Warlock?"

"I do."

"Interesting. I have heard of such magics, naturally, but I know of no way to trace them, I'm afraid. Please do tell me if you learn anything, especially if the other end leads you to the Warlock."

I promised him I would and left him to his researches.

A few minutes later, Quirk's notes on William Bone came through via a secure message on MORIARTY. There was still no message from Sally. I descended to my lair in the library, feeling maybe a little safer there, and looked at what Quirk had sent me.

16 – The Brief History of William Bone

We encountered the accursed leech at dawn in the ruined stronghold we had chosen as the place to lie in wait, the shadow creeping back to its lair after its night time foray. If we had hoped it would be exhausted by its work and troubled by the goodly rays of the bright sun, we were sorely disappointed. Its skin was hideously marked with black symbols, the writing of the devil upon it. Although fully six of us were present at the attack, our number proved to be sadly inadequate. The creature moved with a speed I did not think possible, and its strength was that of twenty men. The charms we had brought with us did little to affect it. Five of us were killed, and in truth I was very nearly the sixth. I emerged from a small death of many hours – induced by a very considerable loss of blood – to discover I was the sole survivor. The scene of our battle, of what remained of my sisters, was not one I can bear to set down. Of the beast we had thought to destroy, there was no trace. It has gone to trouble some other benighted corner of the land.

– Sister Agneish Faygold, *Accounts*, 1686

Granted to Gerald Le Bon and his heirs and descendants in perpetuity, the manor of Barnwyck complete with five acres of pasture, three villagers and two smallholders.

– *Royal Decree*, 1088

For the eyes of Father Donahue. My gratitude for your letter received this day. Your letter disturbed me in no small measure, and I assure you I will do all that is within my power to rid the county of the scourge you describe. In these modern days, it is scarcely to be believed that such a fiend should step out of the old stories to torment the living. Know that as knight of this shire I shall take up sword and a goodly troop of local men whom I know to be brave and true, and that we shall, henceforth, proceed to the hilltop lair you mention as the likely domain of this cruel devil, there to destroy it and commit its body to the flames so that it will never trouble these Christian lands again. In the meantime, I have instructed all those who are dear to me, Catherine and our four children most especially, to exercise the utmost care. Please be assured I have greatly fortified the manor house and the servants have been informed of the need for utmost vigilance while this human leech is being dealt with.

– William Le Bon, *Handwritten letter*, 1542, trans. Thomas Quirk

Eight sons of this parish, their remains to be committed to the ground this day of November 12th. In truth, such a calamity has surely never struck the good people of these environs before, and the dire effects on so many families of the loss of their menfolk is scarcely to be imagined. These were fine and true men, giving all they had to protect home and hearth. Their noble leader, William Le Bon, will also be commemorated upon this day, even though, to the lamentation of his good wife and children, his remains were not recovered from the battle that took place but four nights previously. Whatever end he met, we can be sure it was a brave one, and let it be known that the sacrifices made will be marked with a carved stone to be set into the wall of the church, lest eternity forgets the terrible events of these days.

– Register of Births and Deaths (clerical addendum), St Cuthberts, Barnwick, 1542

… beg you, dear brother, to hasten to us, for I do not believe we will survive another night such as the one just gone. My beloved husband, I have to tell you, was not killed in the assault on the demon's lair, hard as this may be to believe. Verily, he is alive and abroad in the world once more, for I have seen him with my own two eyes. There is no mistaking him, for even if I were not his wife I would know him by his stature and his great strength. Oh, but dear brother, he is changed beyond recognition. Some evil spirit now drives him on where once there was kindness and gentility. His noble beauty has been twisted into malevolence. He came to the manor in the depths of last night, screeching and roaring like some beast of the field, and attempted to force his way through our bared [sic] doors. It was all I and the servants – even aided by the children – could do to hold his attacks off. For an hour or more he kept at it before retreating with an agonized howl. I have no doubt that he will return, just as I have no doubt that he intends us harm. Love has frozen to cruelty and malice in his heart, or else that demon we thought destroyed has him in his grasp, driving him on with his whip. I beseech you, again, to hurry to us while we may still greet you…

– Catherine le Bon, Handwritten letter (undelivered), 1543, trans. Thomas Quirk

Calamity upon calamity upon this most terrible of days. The Le Bon family mausoleum, once all but empty, has at a single stroke been filled. I can scarcely conceive of what has befallen this noble clan, although the loss of their good lord, William Le Bon the previous winter appears to have been but the beginning of a series of disasters. Now the whole family is all gone – William, Katherine and their four innocent children, in addition to diverse other members of their household, all rended in the most foul manner as by some brute beast. That such horror should be visited on so fine a family beggars belief. I pray to almighty God that this is an end to the scourge that has bedevilled us.

– *Register of Births and Deaths (clerical addendum),* St Cuthberts, Barnwick, 1543

There was, also, among the conspirators one that was unknown to me: a tall and powerful man, his face mostly in shadows beneath his wide-brimmed hat (as befitted our company). He spoke little, but seemed determined to carry out the destruction of the illegitimate King that sits still upon the throne of England. I recall seeing inked drawings decorating his lower arms, including one that resembled the very crown worn by the false monarch. What became of this conspirator I do not know. He disappeared into the shadows beneath the Houses of Parliament and did not return.

(TQ: It remains unclear whether this creature was Bone. The presence of the tattoos is of interest, but the fact that King James I survived this attempted assassination would not be the usual outcome. If Bone were present under some pseudonym, it is possible that one of the conspirators was his target, not the King.)

– *The Gun Powder Plot – The King's Book (annotated by Thomas Quirk),* 1605

THE ORDER OF THE BRITISH VAMPIRE

Much has been written about the mysterious murder of Sir Paynton Godlove – found dead in a ditch on Primrose Hill – and the considerable agitation against Catholicism the event helped foment throughout England. That Godlove was part of a plot to replace King Charles II and make Britain a republic is clear. The details of the death are less so. We may discount the notion of suicide, for the recent account of one bystander, who stated that Godlove was accosted and slaughtered by *a giant of a man whose skin was pocked and scarred by strange symbols*, certainly suggests that the death was a murder, its intent perhaps to influence wider public sentiments.

– Roger Bedfellowes, *English Civil Wars*, 1787

The suppression of a peaceful if boisterous Manchester crowd – admittedly some 50,000 strong – by cavalry soldiers with drawn sabres, remains one of the gravest crimes in the history of these isles. Eighteen protestors died and several hundred injured as a result of the charge, and at a year's remove we can already see that the massacre was a turning point, encouraging the authorities to further suppress agitation and calls for reform. It remains unclear who, exactly, was responsible for the mounted soldiers' attack on the crowd, although I have read one account that the Hussars – summoned to act merely as a warning – were spurred into action when one of their number, a giant of a man with something like sailor's tattoos upon his neck and arms, led the charge into the crowd. The reports suggest it was he who cut down one of the orators who had come to Manchester to address the crowd. I have been unable to discover who this officer might be.

– Walter Winter, *Observations on the Peterloo Massacre*, 1820

We came across the creature as it stood beside an old stone mausoleum in an abandoned churchyard. The parish of Barnwick is no longer the home to anything human. The creature was surely the one we sought: tall, immensely strong, its skin adorned with hideous tattoos and markings. Yet, as we approached, we saw none of the fury we have come to associate with the creature. It was seemingly in the grip of some overpowering emotion, wailing as it beat its fists against the indifferent stone. Upon hearing our approach, it fixed us briefly with a predatorial stare – enough to chill the blood – but then loped away at incredible speed. The tomb, upon closer inspection, was that of the entire *Le Bon* family, interred some three centuries previously. It is hard to feel anything like sympathy for this monster we seek, but I felt it then, I confess, for it seems the stories are true: that this was once a kind and loving man who was corrupted by the vampire lord and forced to slaughter his own family – and many more besides – as punishment for some crime. This sad history notwithstanding, it remains our duty to attempt to destroy the creature.

– Sister Anna Dottery, *The Pale Sisterhood*, 1886

One vampire in particular continues to cause us considerable difficulty. It is a fearsome creature, powerful, as swift as an eagle, and seemingly impossible to destroy. He – I should say *it* – appears rarely, for which small mercy I am grateful, but when it does emerge from its foul lair it inevitably means the death of one or more serjeants of the Office of the Witchfinder General – and others besides. Its appearance is singular, for although it attempts to conceal itself and to lurk in the shadows and the fogs, its flesh is adorned with numerous markings and runes, giving it a most alarming aspect. It is as if spells have been scored all across its flesh. It is utterly ruthless and brutal, and we would all sleep more safely in our beds were it destroyed.

– Isaac Shackleton, Lord High Witchfinder, *Personal Journal (written in private cipher)*, 1893

…will demonstrate that many key turning points in the history of these islands may be attributed to the interventions of a hidden cabal of powerful figures. One in particular recurs: a supernaturally powerful entity, his skin alarmingly tattooed, who, as I shall show, is the hidden hand behind many unsolved killings or apparent accidents over many years, some of which have profoundly affected our history and…

– Sanderson Thorley, *The Hidden History of Britain (scrap, recovered from flames – rest of manuscript lost in the fire that also killed its author)*, 1958

17 – Earthworks

> Were another of the Undead, like him, to try to do what he has done, perhaps not all the centuries of the world that have been, or that will be, could aid him. With this one, all the forces of nature that are occult and deep and strong must have worked together in some wonderous way. The very place, where he have been alive, Undead for all these centuries, is full of strangeness of the geologic and chemical world. There are deep caverns and fissures that reach none know whither.
> – Bram Stoker, *Dracula*, 1897

My readings of the fragmentary history of William Bone were interrupted by the arrival of a text – but sadly not one from Sally. Instead, it was the vicar of the city church where the graves had been disturbed. It said, in perfectly-formed English, punctuation and everything, *Please come when you can. We received another visitation last night.*

I thought about delaying until the following day so I could take Kerrigan with me – but decided against it. I was already going slightly crazy cooped up in my little room. How Gilroy had stood it for so many years, I couldn't begin to imagine. And a church near the heart of the city during the day – surely that was as safe a place as any. I'd drive, stick to main roads. Even a vampire such as Bone would surely have trouble tracking me down and cornering me. Turning my head to check for traffic was agony after the damage Bone had done to my neck, but I'd manage.

The vicar was waiting for me as I walked from my parked car. She was wearing civilian garb this time, jeans and a jumper. It was already odd not seeing her dressed in clerical vestments, but I guessed she couldn't wear them all the time.

She shook my hand with enthusiasm. "Thank you for coming. Shall I make a cup of tea before we get to it?"

I assured her there was no need. She led me on gravel paths through the little forest of gravestones – it was oddly quiet, as if a long way from the rush of cars on the nearby road – to a remote plot round the back of the church near where the gardeners tipped their grass cuttings and blackbirds eyed us suspiciously from the bushes. It was immediately obvious that the soil on another grave had been recently disturbed. A deep hole had been scooped out towards the foot of the plot. It surely wasn't wide enough to extract a coffin or an entire body if the coffin had decayed – so perhaps the actions of a wild creature burrowing down. It was odd, though, that the soil was not thrown around. Instead, it formed a neat mound beside the grave.

"Was it like this when you found it?" I asked.

"I've touched nothing."

I squatted to study the earthworks more closely. I shone my phone's light down into the hole. A metre or so down, I caught a glimpse of yellowy-white bone in the soil. The neatness of the excavation certainly suggested a human had been responsible – or at least something roughly along those lines. The person responsible had also, clearly, been extremely determined. Why such a narrow hole, though? It was almost surgical in its precision, as if the burrower had sought a very specific bone in the skeleton. I stood to try and read the headstone, whose markings were weathered away almost to nothing. By shining a light at am oblique angle and setting off shadows, I managed to pick out *John Tabernacle* and the date *1811*.

"Do we know if anything was removed?" I asked.

"Impossible to say without disinterring this poor unfortunate. I obviously would like the remains to be complete, but I'm loath to disturb the entire grave."

"Of course," I said. "Is this grave ever visited do you know?"

"I doubt it. That hardly makes any difference, does it? These attacks really have to stop; people come here to grieve and to reflect and a thing like this is hugely upsetting. There must be something you can do."

"The church was open last night?"

"It was. As I told you, sometimes people need a sanctuary in the darkest of hours. I really do not want to turn them away."

I nodded, considering. "For now, let's fill in the hole and put everything back to how it was. No need for anyone else to know. If I am able to recover anything that has been taken from the grave, I will obviously return it to you."

"Thank you."

"Were the other attacks like this? I had the impression whole graves were dug up before."

"The other holes were larger, certainly."

I wondered what the reason was for the change of behaviour. I was sure this was the same person or entity: the taste of the magic around the site felt the same.

"I'd like to check the camera and microphone I left in the crypt, if I may."

"Of course."

"Has anyone been down there since I visited?"

"We left your equipment untouched."

The crypt at the foot of the flight of wooden steps was just as I recalled: damp, musty air; muffled sounds of the waking world from above; shadows cast by the columns upon the old stones as I moved around. I stepped into those shadows warily, conscious that this was an excellent place to be slaughtered should Bone turn up. For all I knew, he knew about the tunnels under the city and I was walking into a trap.

I crouched next to the low opening where I'd left my equipment. I could immediately see from the display on the camera that it had been triggered: two snatches of video had been stored on the memory card. Peering closely at the small screen on the device, I played them through. The video was black-and-white – infra-red in the darkness – and it was difficult to pick out detail at first in the wash of greys. Then I saw a definite flick of movement, the hard lines of something near the camera lens, in front of the iron bars. I paused and rewound until I had the frame clear.

It was a mist, a deeper greyness – but a mist with clear edges to it. In shape it was roughly human in that I could make out arms and legs and a head if I squinted. The mass squeezed through the gap between the iron bars, then seemed to reform itself. It sought around for a moment as if sniffing its way, then drifted off.

The camera picked up sound, too. I'd need to get the recording from the separate microphone I'd left back to the office to extract better audio, but by holding the camera to my ear I could pick up tinny reproductions of the sounds to be heard in the room. There was a low background moaning, which might have been real or might have been an artefact of the equipment. Then, unmistakably, I heard the groan of the hatch being opened. The shape coming out of the ground might be foggy, but it was also material, capable of interacting with the solid world.

I took a note of the time – 4:35 in the morning – then skipped to the next section of video. Here was the weird mass making its return journey, some thirty minutes after entering the crypt. I heard the hatch slamming shut, then saw the shape filtering through the iron bars into its subterranean lair.

It was no longer only a mist, though – I also picked out, unmistakably, the outline of a single long bone, something from the lower leg. The mist had enveloped it and was carrying it within its form. The entity had dug into the grave of John Tabernacle, pulled out one of his tibias or fibulas, then returned with it. A spectral hound fetching bones for some unknown master? It was like nothing I'd encountered or heard of before. The whole thing seemed so oddly precise, very specific bones seemingly being retrieved.

We didn't even have an Office code for such a phenomenon.

There was no more video. I replaced the SD cards in both camera and microphone, checked their batteries were okay, then left them to capture more mysterious goings on. The vicar was hovering in the room above. Not literally. There was an anxious look on her face.

"Did you discover anything? I really can't have this happening."

"There's a creature entering your crypt from tunnels below the surface. For reasons I don't understand it's collecting bones."

"A creature from underground. Are we talking a *demon*?" There was an odd look in her eye at that. Repulsion, fear – but, also, I thought, something like excitement, as if the existence of such a creature was proof for her of something she'd secretly doubted.

"I'm honestly not sure what it is, but I promise you I'll get to the bottom of it."

She stepped a little closer, spoke more quietly. "If you need any sort of, well, exorcism, I can come to your help."

"Thank you," I replied. I wondered what the Crow's response to that would have been. "I'll be sure to let you know if that turns out to be needed."

I left her with assurances that she wouldn't be suffering the attacks for much longer – I had no idea how I was going to achieve that, but it's good to remain optimistic – and left for my car. A quick drive across the city would take me back to the office and the castle where I'd left the other microphone. I wanted to know if that had picked up sounds. If it had, I might be able to work something out about the route of the tunnels beneath our feet (assuming they existed) and maybe even the timings of the movements of the … weird foggy bone collector entity.

I needed a better name for the thing, whatever it was.

I was attacked by Bone zero times as I drove back – which was precisely the number I'd been hoping for. Sam the castle guard – he was probably *technically* a customer services operative or some such, but I definitely preferred castle guard as a job title – admitted me to the locked room. He'd heard nothing unusual and had seen nothing he couldn't explain other than – as he put it – *you know, kids today. I just don't get them. I don't get them at all.* I retrieved that microphone's memory card, making sure to label the bag I put it in to avoid getting it mixed up. Then I congratulated him on his vigilance, assured him I'd be back and left.

At my desk, I listened to the captured audio on headphones. The moaning sound I'd heard was clear on the church microphone footage, unmistakable against the low background hum of the room. It was, to my ears, a voice. Wordless, ebbing and flowing, but a sound produced by a person or some thing human-proximate. I could hear a long, slow sadness in the sound. It might have been the wind moaning through an old doorway, but there'd been no wind down there, and every now and then the sound rose to a little crescendo that sounded, more than anything, like a sob. Then there would be a pause, and a sigh, and then the groaning would begin again.

The time coordinated exactly with the video footage. The creak and wooden thump of the hatch being opened were loud in my ears, and after that the plangent moaning faded into the distance. Twenty-nine minutes later, the sequence repeated itself in reverse. The hatch slammed shut, the low groaning sound grew louder as it approached the grille and the microphone. There was a snuffling quality to it too, I thought: perhaps from the effort of lugging the bone from the graveyard and underground, as if the entity, whatever it was, had become more corporeal, more animal, during its time above ground. Members of the family of beings we call *ghost* and *ghast* and *ghoul* could do that, I knew. They were usually incorporeal, slipping through our world without really being a part of it, but, sometimes, they could manifest, solidify – often because of some powerful emotion burning within them. Anger, sorrow, confusion: a lot of the work the Office did involved finding out what consumed such entities and giving them release. It was quicker and easier and more satisfying than trying to banish them by force or capture them somehow.

There was a brief moment when the sound was very loud in my ears – the creature investigating the equipment perhaps, sniffing at it to work out what it was – then, with a final sob that managed to combine fury and purest misery, the thing was gone.

Next, I tried the microphone left in the castle. It had triggered four times in the day since I'd left it by the drain in the ground. The first one came at 2:35 in the afternoon. Once again, there was a clear sigh. But then, also, the rattle of keys, and a muttered swear word. Something about *Bloody tourists*. Sam on his rounds. The same sequence repeated at 5:45 PM: the guard checking the room one more time before leaving for the evening. I could hear the disappointment in his exhalation when he found nothing untoward in the locked room.

The next two hits were more interesting. The first one came at 4:10 that morning. It was brief and very quiet, but enough for the microphone to decide to grab it. A rising rush of white noise like an approaching wave of water, then a peak when I could just pick out a familiar groaning, then the sound fading. The microphone caught nothing else until an hour and a half later, when the pattern repeated. After that there was nothing, until the sudden cacophony of my own arrival, fumbling with the microphone before I switched it off.

I looked at the timings of the sounds I'd picked up. There was a pattern there. I pulled up a map of Cardiff upon which I'd overlaid the theoretical tunnel stretching from the castle across Bute Park. The pattern seemed clear. Something had followed the route of some underground passageway, reaching the castle at 4:10, then the church 25 minutes later. After it had finished its ghoulish work, it had retraced its steps (if *steps* was the right word), passing back beneath the castle 35 minutes after leaving the church. The return journey had taken ten minutes longer, either because the entity was weakened by its efforts, or because of the burden of the bone it bore.

The question was, where had it come from? Under the castle? That was a possibility. I knew about no tunnel that stretched east or south of the castle, but that didn't mean there wasn't one there.

I wondered how the Blackfriars site fitted into the pattern. The apparent passageway leading from castle to church led through the ruins of that site if the Victorian drawing of a *mediaeval* tunnel was to be believed – and as I studied the map, the thought about friaries drew my finger to the *other* monastic site in the city centre: Greyfriars, a short way east of the castle site.

We'd had numerous dealings with that area before. Although there was nothing left of the ancient site on the surface now – apart from the names of a few roads and a car park – the marks and the memories were still there beneath the ground, and they had a habit of bubbling out every now and then, manifesting as ghostly presences and disturbing sounds. The workers in the modern office block that now sits atop the site had complained of troubling incidents more than once over the years – apparitions passing through walls, deep unearthly chanting coming from … somewhere. I knew there was a locked access hatch in the lower basement of the tower that led down an iron ladder to a small cell of damp soil and piled rubble that were all that remained of the old site. We'd left glimmers there in the past, to attract lost spirits that were wandering the area, presumably confused about what had happened to their nice mediaeval street level.

Was it possible the Blackfriars and Greyfriars sites were connected? That a tunnel extended from the castle that way too? It had to be a possibility. There was nothing on my rough map – but it only needed a quick internet search to reveal that, indeed, there were old tunnels stretching between the castle and Greyfriars. It seemed more and more like there was a whole network down there, even if these workings were closed off. It meant there had to be a chance that the body snatcher entity didn't live beneath the castle, but somewhere further east, towards or beyond Greyfriars.

From Wikipedia, I learned that the black and grey friars

(the Dominican and Franciscan orders respectively) had had different attitudes to the work of going into the community and helping the destitute – but they'd both devoted a lot of time to doing precisely that. These weren't monks locked away in their monasteries. Why they'd needed secret tunnels beneath the city was anyone's guess – although, I supposed the earthworks might have been escape tunnels for both sets of friars should anyone attack the city – as, indeed, had happened more than once in Cardiff's history.

Given that Sam knew of no way into deeper working beneath the castle, I decided to investigate from the Greyfriars end. Once again, there was no one around to join me on the expedition. Once again, I decided to take the risk and venture out alone. There was literally a car park at the site I needed to go to, so the risk from Bone was minimal.

I hoped.

It took me thirty minutes to infiltrate the office tower that now squats on top of the destroyed friary – mainly because the security guard refused to accept the validity of my Witchfinder card when I reached the electronic gates. I couldn't really blame her for that; she was doing her job. In the end it took a text to the Crow and then – presumably – a call from him to some equivalent in the mundane police forces and thence the private security companies – to grant me access. Hardknott-Lewis took a while to respond; he had been more than usually preoccupied of late. I passed the time with a cup of coffee from a machine in the lobby. I knew it was coffee because the machine said it was.

I finally gained access to the lift. There was a button for the *Lower Basement – Staff Only* level, with a keyhole next to it. Fortunately, I had the key, borrowed from our own safe. The tower was one of several buildings that we needed to gain access to from time to time and that we had an arrangement with.

The lift juddered and clanked as it descended into the depths. It was hard not to sense reluctance to its slow progress. A mirror showed me anxious Danesh Shahzan, while a disembodied voice informed me that we were, indeed, descending, and then that we'd reached the lower basement. The doors slid open to reveal a concrete and breeze block room used to house generators and water pumps and the like. Pipes and ducts and swathes of cables fed off around the walls and up to the floors above. It was hard not to think about the great weight of the towering building above me.

In the far corner, around the back of a humming machine in a metal cage, there was an iron door locked with two keys and a combination. Red letters painted onto it said NO ADMITTANCE – AUTHORISED PERSONNEL ONLY, which fortunately didn't apply to me because I was authorised. Again, by prior agreement with the building owners, we had copies of the keys and I had memorized the combination.

I also knew how to defeat the *Wardstone Seal* we'd set upon the door to prevent a member of the public delving into the Stygian gloom. More M/Tech: the devices look like an electronic key for a car, but I knew for a fact that if you opened one up, you'd find that the button made the little LED light up and did absolutely nothing else. It had been designed like that because, of course, the Office couldn't bring itself to admit it used magical devices in its battles. The device, I knew, *also* contained an ensorcelled gemstone that radiated an aura that resonated with the warding runes drawn with invisible paint upon the doorway. You could hear the jewel rattling around if you shook the device. In fact, you only needed to bring the correct device near the door, and it would open.

This it now duly did.

Drawing my gun, I shone the light from my phone into the space behind the door. Smooth concrete was replaced by the rough-hewn stones of old walls. This was the mediaeval street level. It was a small space, empty apart from a few tatty rags. The ground was damp. An iron ladder led further into the ground, to where the tunnel entrance would be – if such a thing existed.

I glanced backwards. There was no sign of Bone, or any pursuit – although that maybe didn't mean much given the vampire's abilities to be at one with the shadows or whatever the hell it had done in Sally's house. I desperately wanted to keep the iron door open so I could get out easily – but I also didn't want to give my pursuer the perfect place to corner me.

I ran through my mantras, my attack spells. They were becoming instinctive; I didn't have to think about the syllables at all. The flow of sounds was calming on my mind. That was part of the point of them, so my grandfather's notes had said: the training of the mind to find a calm space in the chaos of a battle. Perhaps Gilroy had known that when he'd encouraged me to practise them.

I shut the door behind me, conscious that no one in the world knew I was down there – unless they read the MORIARTY logs I'd dutifully made. If I got trapped, I figured, someone would come for me eventually.

Wouldn't they? Yeah. Of course they would. Someone.

Holding my phone in my teeth, I clanged down the ladder. The iron was cold on my fingers, hungrily sucking the heat from them. I'd been down there once before, to investigate a Code 11, a haunting. The room at the bottom was larger than I recalled, the little pool of light from my phone failing to banish the shadows in the far corners. The air tasted of water and stone and age. The walls and floor were rough. I had to stoop slightly at points as the floor rose and fell. It was as if something down there was trying to force its way upwards. Did this look like the lair of a vampire? It didn't seem likely. They favoured the trappings of comfort. Then again, we didn't know everything about the creatures. There would be variations, hybrids. There were thralls and there were masters. What happened if a vampire tried to turn something non-human into a vampire? Damned if I knew. Maybe you got something like that angry wraith I'd glimpsed in the footage.

I walked to the wall – huge old square-cut stones green

with algae – and began to circumnavigate the room. My breathing echoed back to me in the enclosed space. The city was a distant rumble through the stones. I walked around the entire room, hoping to find some grille or opening like the others I'd found – but there was nothing. I tried again with the walls, looking for a loose stone that might be a hidden switch, and then telling myself I was being ridiculous and that I'd watched too many films. There were no hidden switches. This was a sealed stone box: it wouldn't be able to contain or bar an incorporeal entity like a ghost, but whatever I'd seen at the church would not have been able to get out this way.

To double-check, I lay on the ground and put my ear to the cold stone. I swore I could hear the distant rush of water gurgling through some subterranean passageway – but, equally, the sound might simply have been the blood flowing in my ears rather than really there in the Cardiff rock.

It was while I was trying to work this out that I noticed it. My eyes were more-or-less level with the ground, and unmistakably, one of the floor slabs was loose, its lip raised, a line of darkness around its edge. Someone had heaved up – or pushed up – that slab at some point, or else the moving ground beneath it had forced it out of its place.

I levered up the heavy square of stone using the handle of my clothcutter, getting the tips of my fingers under it so I could pull it all the way back. An exhalation of cold damp air on my face told me that there was something other than soil and rock beneath the stone. My light revealed it: a round vertical shaft, lined with more hewed stones. The friars had presumably dug a well into the ground there. The light wasn't bright enough to show me the bottom. A loose pebble dropped in made a watery thud after a second or two. That was good; it wasn't a bottomless pit. It was also far too narrow for me to descend into – plus I didn't have a ladder or a rope that would allow me to climb back out again.

I was about to turn away, thinking that I might be able to make use of some Office or police technology – a remote-controlled robot with a camera say – when I felt the definite tug of magic being worked from down there. It was distant and sort of – this might not make much sense – *cold*, but it was clear.

Light and eyesight might not show me what was down there – but I was learning I had other senses. Without thinking what I was doing, but knowing it might work, I sat cross-legged beside the hole and closed my eyes. With my mind's eye, I reached into the shaft. The magical flame I carried within me burned a little brighter; I was definitely doing something. My grandfather's book had mentioned a similar practise (the *Eye that Wanders the Night*) that he had used to explore the half-collapsed ruins of an abandoned temple in India.

If that was what I was doing, it seemed to be working. I caught glimpses of rough stone walls passing upwards in my sight. The visions were indistinct, as if seen through a haze. I tried not to think about the possibility of someone creeping up to attack me while my focus was elsewhere. I kept my breathing slow and steady, calming myself, and allowed my vision to sink deeper and deeper until I reached the bottom of the shaft.

There was a tunnel, and it was surprisingly large. If I could have reached it, I could have wormed my way through it. Once again, it wasn't natural: masons had lined it with stones, forming straight walls and a curved ceiling. A dribble of water ran through it, but not enough to prevent passage. Pencil-thin, pallid stalactites prickled the ceiling, dropping globs of water to the ground.

I pushed forward, conscious that the farther I travelled from my body, the greater the effort of it became. It was like a stretched elastic band was strung between my body and my phantom eye. The farther away it got, the more energy I needed to expend to keep it there. The visions I was experiencing dimmed a little, as if glimpsed through a thicker fog or reflected in a tarnished mirror, but I could still pick out details.

The tunnel snaked left and right, and then I glimpsed a flight of rough stone steps leading upwards. I couldn't work out where in the living city this might be. The tunnel continued onwards into the darkness, but I flew my wandering gaze up the steps.

I found myself in another small cell. Once again, the walls were of cut stone, finely laid. The roof appeared to be bare rock, as if the space had once been a cellar hewed out of the ground. A rough square cut into the ceiling suggested there had once been a way down from above – but some heavy stone now blocked it completely.

And, unmistakably, there were signs of someone living there. Details were harder and harder to make out. I picked out a low wooden cot upon which an adult might have lain. There was no sheet or any sort of bedding upon it. Sconces had been hacked into the walls to form shelves, and there were books there. None had any letters upon them – but one lay open on top of the others. Its pages were mildewed in the damp, brown rot creeping across it, but I caught a glimpse of some mediaeval illuminated manuscript like the one we'd delved into the library to study. Whatever that meant, it was clear this was no lair for a monster: a thinking being dwelled or had dwelt here. In other sconces, I also saw what appeared to be carvings, tiny sculptures – or they may simply have been interesting stones pulled from the ground.

One other odd little detail caught my eye. Hanging from an iron nail driven into one of the gaps between the stones hung what appeared to be a delicate necklace. Even with my dim vision, I could see it was some untarnished, silvery metal. It was strung with a finely-carved stone in the shape of a crucifix. It seemed an odd thing to find in what had been, presumably, a dungeon cellar of the friary and was now, maybe, the lair of the bone-stealing wraith. In my experience, undead horrors don't feature crosses much when planning their home décor. It's a myth that such symbols are inimical to entities like vampires, but they generally don't go out of their way to look at them, either. The object was odd, also, because it appeared delicate and feminine to my modern eyes – and the friars would, of course, all have been men. Had the dweller found it in some deep underground cavern, taken a fancy to it? Or had they brought it with them?

Then I saw the bones. They were laid out on the floor beside the cot. It was a skeleton, perhaps half-complete: a skull, half a spine, some ribs and most of the four limbs. A few fingers and toes were also laid out, although there were many gaps to be filled.

I peered closer. What was this? Even with my body so remote, I could feel the magic in this room. It coiled in there like poisonous smoke that couldn't find a way to escape. Were these the mortal remains of the entity I'd glimpsed in the church video footage? Some poor unfortunate who'd died down there and who was trying, now, to find their way back to the light? I'd encountered confusion in such presences before. They thought they were still alive and couldn't understand why they couldn't move as they'd once done.

I peered closer. No, that wasn't it. This wasn't all that remained of a body. It was, unmistakably, parts from *different* bodies. The bones had varying levels of discoloration. The two femurs were visibly of a different length. Whatever the thing was that was raiding graves on the surface, this was what it was doing. For reasons I couldn't begin to fathom, it was trying to assemble a human skeleton. Putting together a jigsaw from mismatched pieces taken all over the city.

What the hell was that about? And why was it doing it *now*? I couldn't see how any sort of known vampiric entity would display such behaviour – but that didn't mean this thing wasn't a creature of the Warlock, some other hunter set on my trail. Or was it possible that this was nothing more than a weird puzzle, designed to draw me away from the bright lights and into this dark corner?

Something scraped on the stone behind me at that moment. Not near my vacant body up there in the cellar of the tower; it was in the sealed and remote stone cell with my wandering mind. Something had come through the tunnel and was slithering and skittering up the steps.

I saw it. It was, clearly, the same foggy greyness I'd glimpsed on the camera. It billowed into the room before I could move. It took on a more solid form than I'd glimpsed before – either because this was its lair and it was stronger here, or because it was preparing itself for an attack.

There was no doubt that it saw me, mere spectral presence as I was. The mist became more solid, became a figure wearing something like a black cape with a hood concealing its head. It was like the negative image of your prototypical white spooky ghost. Except, then, its face became clear. I saw it for an instant, appearing from the shadows of the hood. Its face was unexpectedly young-looking. Male or female? It might have been either, or neither, but there was a fine-featured gentleness to those features that were at odds with the entity's behaviour. I also saw fury there – as well as, I thought, confusion. Perhaps, even, fear. It didn't know who or what I was, or why I was there.

It didn't wait any longer to find out. It lashed at me, screaming in an oddly high-pitched keen. It wanted to hurt me. It wanted to kill me.

Panicking, my control slipping, I reeled my mind back in. I saw a blur of movement: stones, that furious face again close to mine, then water and more stones – and then I was back in my own body. I was panting heavily, sweat trickling down my back from the effort of the magic I'd worked. I hadn't realised how much strength I'd put into it. I needed to be careful of that, or I'd return to my body only to find that I'd died from exhaustion.

From down in the ground, I could hear the scuffings and scrapings of the thing in the tunnels sniffing me out. The sounds were getting louder; the creature was only a few yards away, already squirming its way up the well shaft. I didn't need any more prompting. I heaved the slab back into place over the hole, then raced to climb the iron ladder for the Wardstone door and the welcome familiarity of the modern world.

18 – Hooded in Black

> Our lot is to remain forever in the shadows, unknown to the wider public. Our colleagues in the mundane police forces may on occasion be referred to as the *thin blue line*, but we are – we must be – the thin *invisible* line. The thin white line, because it remains always undetectable upon the page. Ours is a thankless task, an unrewarded one – unless it is the reward of knowing that the realm is protected; that people, oblivious to all we do, to the horrors we despatch, may sleep safely in their beds, the monsters kept always at bay.
> – Earl Grey, Witchfinder General, *Office of the Witchfinder General Handbook*, 1999

He waited in the slow silence after the attack, as he'd waited for so long: listening with panic and hope combined that his long incarceration was finally coming to an end. Surely, after all this time. The punishment meted out to him was too much. The word of God was the word of God, but he knew in his heart, also, that he had done nothing wrong. That, perhaps, his elders and betters had misheard the voice of the divine – or listened, instead, to the whisperings of the devil.

The quiet assurances of his saviour were clear to him despite the judgements of the Friar and the cruel, cruel words of his brothers. They'd spat at him, struck him with blunt clubs until his bones broke, then forced him into the underground cell to admit his sins – or to rot. Left him without food or water, cold and broken, while they piled great stones on top of the entranceway, stones he could never hope to lift. The good people he had lived among for three years turning against him in their horror and revulsion, denying him what he was. Didn't they know by then what he was?

A friar. Their brother.

He'd been hounded for so long. His own family had turned him out, turning their backs on him when he'd needed them the most. He knew well the look of distaste on the faces of strangers, their cries following him as he trekked for days and days away from his childhood home in the mountains of the north, calls accusing him of all manner of abomination and devilry. He knew, also, gruelling minutes of horror and pain from the bandits who came across him on the open road. His cries had done nothing to stop them. The way they'd used him had been terrible enough, but they'd also done something almost worse: denying what he was. Using him as a *her*. How could they?

And then, finally, he'd found this unexpected sanctuary in the town of Cardiff. He'd embraced it with a hunger that had surprised him. Here was home. A life of peace and solitude and acceptance – and of helping others – became all he wanted. A shutting-out of the world. A place where he could be himself, because no women were allowed in.

And there were books, too: there'd been no writing in that windswept stone homestead he'd been born into. No one in his family knew how to read much beyond the hymn numbers on display in the chapel. The Brothers had taught him, though. Shown him that simple marks on a page could become thoughts, could become whole new worlds of mystery and wonder. He could have spent the rest of his days lost in such revelations.

Here was where he belonged. He'd left *Lucia* behind – that girl he'd mistakenly been born as, some trick of the Tylwyth Teg perhaps – and become what he'd always been inside: *Lucian*.

Brother Lucian. Again, the power of words: the title and that additional letter *n* made all the difference.

He would not be denied it now. He was aware, dimly glimpsed as through a fog, that a long time had passed since those days. He had slept and then he had awoken, the injustice burning within him. Yet he had lain unmoving for a long time, little more than a cloud of fury – until some chain had been let slip, some bind he wasn't aware of, and he was free. He would be more careful this time, but he would not be denied.

He would walk the Earth as Lucian, and he would let no one stop him.

I made it back to the relative safety of the office without being attacked by a single undead denizen of the nether world. Always a good thing.

I figured the library might shed some light on what was going on at the Blackfriars site. I had to wait an hour or more for the Librarian to turn up. She'd left a note on her desk that said, simply, *Don't touch anything until I return. Seriously.*

I decided it was best to comply. I assumed she was down upon some lower level, but she eventually arrived from above, sweeping in from the stairs with just a nod of recognition. I wondered what she'd been up to but didn't like to ask. She gave me a dismissive look when I asked her where there might be books I could look at. She looked like she wanted to say, *What do you think this is, a library?* Instead, she waved her hand toward one of the tall wooden bookshelves near her desk on Level -1.

"Nothing forbidden was ever retrieved from the site. If it's local history you're after, try over there." The way she said *local history* suggested she thought mundane book categories were beneath her dignity.

"I would have thought you'd have approved of the friars. They did good, right, helping the community?"

She shrugged, her attention already lost in the book she was studying. I thanked her and retreated to the aisle she'd indicated.

A couple of hours spent among archaeological reports and the few contemporary accounts we had revealed nothing of any great interest. The friars had lived ascetic lives, rising early, praying a lot, raising crops, doing what they could for the destitute. No mention anywhere of a good cup of coffee. For sure, the life wasn't for me.

One account caught my eye: a 16th century report from a yeoman commissioner who'd been present at the friary's dissolution – the moment when the crown dismantled the monasteries and other religious foundations throughout the country, taking their wealth and casting out monks and nuns and friars as heretics – or imprisoning and torturing them if they refused to yield. The author was clearly a good soldier, extremely critical of the friars and their godlessness, the supposed luxury they lived in at the expense of the poor. I had no idea if that were true – but the account did describe some underground cells where *the friars betook themselves, or were forced to go, when they wished to suffer some penance or were punished for their sin.*

It seemed possible that might explain the small stone room I'd discovered. It had been sealed up though, heavy stone blocking the way up. Had the friars sealed someone in there for some unforgivable sin, or had that been the work of the men sent to destroy the place, an act of punishment or torture for a friar who'd resisted? I'd probably never know.

The face I'd seen in the foggy entity though: the features had stayed in my mind, returning to me over and over. I'd been confused as to whether they were male or female, which struck me as odd because the accounts I'd read emphasised again and again that, of course, everyone in the friary had been male. No women were allowed. The commissioner's report had claimed that *fallen women were often to be ushered within the walls for the carnal pleasures of the friars*, a statement used to justify the dissolution of the site. Perhaps the face was simply that of someone youthfully male, their features fine enough to appear more feminine. Although there *was* the fact of the delicate little necklace. Nothing in the accounts I was reading said the brothers had adorned themselves with such things. The possession of valuables would have been anathema to them.

Finding the underlying story, pulling on threads of truth and fear and resentment, was often the solution when it came to clearing up a haunting. Being an Office operative sometimes involved a lot of detective work. Inevitably, we never had enough hard information to go on and we had to use our intuition – we had to guess – and now I was wondering about this bodysnatcher. I thought it had been attacking me, coming for me, but had it been? Was that simply my own fear speaking?

The creature hadn't hurt anyone so far as I knew – unless you counted the theft of bones from the long-dead, and I doubted that was something those victims were going to complain about. So much of our work – the work I'd undertaken when I'd been a loyal Office operative – wasn't about guns and blades and grim fights against monsters; it was about shepherding lost entities to a place of peace. It was about getting to the heart of a matter rather than rampaging around attacking creatures because they appeared terrifying. You had to see the world through other eyes, think as others might think, however little sense it might appear to make.

The first inklings of a theory, an idea, were forming in my mind. It could be hard for some people to find a home, a safe place, a tribe, even in the modern world. How much harder would it have been then? Back upstairs, I checked again through all the records provided to us by the police, including those of possibly-related incidents in more remote parts of the city as well as those that had taken place seemingly in isolation months previously.

The pattern was indistinct, but it was there. Bones had been taken, but in a very careful, almost surgical way. Almost, an obsessive way. And, so far as we knew, they were always *male* bones. I thought about that semi-complete skeleton I'd glimpsed. It might have been that of a large and powerful man. Yet the face I'd glimpsed had been quite the opposite. To my modern eye, that necklace seemed like a feminine adornment. Was that just my prejudice talking? And the entity's intonation:

maybe weird haunty wraiths *all* emitted a high-pitched keening. Or maybe they spoke with something like their own voice.

I thought I saw what might really be going on, what the entity's true motivations were. Why this person might have sought refuge in a friary all those years ago – and then been so cruelly punished. Perhaps I was completely wrong, but I thought not. Which meant I maybe wasn't going to get to practise my offensive magical powers on this particular foe after all.

I sipped at a bad coffee. Sometimes, as my doubts had grown about the work we did, I'd wondered who the real monsters were. But you did what you could. And just because we in the Office often did bad things, that didn't mean everything we did had to be bad.

19 – A Final Act of Slaughter

> The thrall is simply a vampire, although it is different enough in its nature to warrant this separate entry. Dominant vampires create thralls to suit their own needs: the creatures have many of the characteristics of what we might call full vampires – incredible strength, invulnerability, a potentially eternal life – save that they lack free-will. The thrall is forever enslaved to the desires of the vampire who raised it. In many ways, this makes the thrall a more terrible foe than a full vampire: when one is compelled to some end, there is nothing it can do to hold back. It cannot choose to withdraw. By its very being, it must persist until its end is achieved or it is torn apart in the effort.
> – Dr Miriam Seacastle, *White Dragon, a Second Bestiary of Modern Britain*, 2003

Kerrigan and I set out to tie up the bodysnatcher case the following morning. If my theories were correct, at least it meant I wouldn't have to reveal my true nature to him in what was to come. Despite everything, it would have felt like a betrayal to do that with Kerrigan. And my new plan meant I'd at least be able to right one wrong before the inevitable showdown with the vampires – with Bone and, if I somehow survived that, with the Warlock himself.

It would, perhaps, be my final act as an operative of the Office of the Witchfinder General. I took Kerrigan through my plans for the operation I wanted to carry out, showed him the new map of the tunnels beneath Cardiff that I'd been working from.

"I got this from Gilroy."

"You were talking to Gilroy?"

I had no idea if Kerrigan knew that Gilroy was roaming free these days. I decided not to mention it.

"He's a useful source on the older records. I guess he doesn't have much else to do."

Kerrigan nodded and let it lie. In fact, our tame necromancer – I had to stop thinking of him as that – had seen me working on the Blackfriars site in the library and had offered me his help. It turned out he had a definitive map of the underground passageways in his personal library, one that the Mystical Council had put together in the 1940s during the failed pursuit of the entity known as the *Lurker Beneath*. The creature (or creatures; no one knew if it was one or many) turned up occasionally in tunnels and passageways, bubbling to the surface to commit apparently random acts of slaughter.

The map was beautiful, finely-detailed, drawn with a draughtsman's skill on a large sheet of rolled paper. Gratifyingly, the tunnels I'd postulated were all there: one leading from Blackfriars to the castle and another leading from the castle out to Greyfriars and then onwards to the church site. I could see the point at which one passed beneath the castle dungeons, just where the locked grid was. There were other passageways, too, down to the docks, following the lines of underground rivers. They didn't all join up so far as we knew – but many did, and it was possible there were deeper shafts down there that the Council hadn't been able to identify.

I'd asked Gilroy how the Council had created the map. "What did they use, some sort of ground-penetrating radar? How did they get round all the buildings in the way?"

Gilroy's response was characteristically scornful, something like his old resentful self. "Fucking Witchfinders! That's science-thinking; the response of an idiot blinkered by antimagical bias. 'Course they didn't use ground penetrating fucking radar. You're better than that. Several of the Council in Cardiff were strong scryers. They could *see* the tunnels from above ground if they worked the right spells and waited for the right phases of the moon. They triangulated their efforts and produced this over a few days. It wasn't difficult."

"Did they track down the Lurker?"

"Nah. Scared it off, though. Seems it was aware of their prying. Buggered off to Swansea as far as I know."

Now, I had the map laid out on my desk, heavy books holding down each corner. I'd marked sites of interest with some fantasy RPG figures I happened to have lying around in my desk. An orc, an elf, a dwarf. If Kerrigan disapproved, he didn't mention it.

I ran my fingers along the tunnels to show him what I'd worked out.

"This is its lair, beneath Blackfriars. I think it died there and, you know, lingered."

Kerrigan ran his fingers through his beard as he considered the map.

"How do you know it's there? That's well away from our access points."

I skimmed over the details. "I'm guessing to a degree. The tunnels go that way and I found an account of friars being put into an underground cell as a penance or a punishment right there."

That seemed to placate him. I wondered why I was going to such an effort to conceal my true nature from him. Did it really matter much at this point? I carried on before he could object any more.

"These are the sites where we have known grave disturbance activity, according to the police reports." I placed the fantasy figures onto the map. The elf was on the church where there'd been multiple attacks. "This one was especially active, but I've been round all of them, making sure they're all sealed up, access to the tunnels blocked."

"With Wardstones?"

"Mostly just with any heavy things I could find."

He nodded, his gaze still on the map. I pointed to the place down on the bay that I wanted to focus upon.

"Because I've blocked the others entrances off, I think the entity is most likely to attack here next. It's more distant, but reachable. There's a clear tunnel, most likely the channel of an underground stream draining into the sea. The modern building on the site is built upon the walls of an old chapel. We know it had a crypt because I've found reference to it in the private journal of Isaac Shackleton."

Kerrigan looked impressed at my thoroughness. "The Victorian Lord High Witchfinder?"

"He investigated a nasty case of possession in the area. Children in an orphanage. In the end, they buried a lot of bones in an unmarked grave, making no attempt to identify individuals. It was all pretty grim. He mentioned a portal beneath the ground in the chapel, one he sealed off with magic and iron chains. I can't tell whether he meant a portal to another dimension or a doorway underground, but I do know there are burials there, related to the chapel. Those and the nearby bone pit created by Shackleton should be enough to lure our entity. This is the only unblocked site on the tunnel network I can find where there are burials nearby."

"You think this creature of yours will know that?"

"I think if it doesn't, it will sniff them out. It seems to be drawn to burial sites."

"Why? Out of familiarity?"

"I think it's trying to build a body for itself. A new body. It's confused, angry, and it wants its old life back. It used to have a body, so it thinks it needs to create another one. This is its twisted logic. It's insane, but it also makes perfect sense. In a way." I didn't tell him what I thought I'd also worked out. That glimpse I'd had of the entity's features with my roving magical eye. The necklace, the high-pitched voice: the more I thought about it, I was sure this was someone who had been female, once.

Kerrigan considered, his eyes scanning the map, looking for flaws.

"How do you hope to defeat this thing?"

"I hope to reason with it. It's confused and maybe violent, but I believe it's intelligent. It's carefully picking one of each type of bone. It knows what it's doing." Again, I didn't mention the semi-complete skeleton I'd glimpsed.

"And it only emerges above ground in the dark?"

"As far as I know. Maybe it would venture out in very foggy conditions during the day, too."

"Okay, but why should it put in an appearance now? Why tonight? Why not last night or in a month's time? Or a year's?"

It was a fair point. "Well, it may have gone to the site last night, but I don't think it would have got all it wanted in one visit. And I think now it will be in a hurry. Like the Council members with their scrying, I believe this entity knows I've been tracking it. The sounds I heard suggested it was, I don't know, angry. It was coming for me. I think it will act quickly, try to complete its work."

Kerrigan's gaze lingered on the map, then he looked up at me. He knew I wasn't telling him everything. I could see only the holes in my plan: how did I know that the entity wouldn't have got everything it wanted? How did I really know it knew I'd been tracking it?

"This doesn't sound like any vampire I've ever encountered," he said eventually.

"I agree. Hopefully we can give this entity the release it craves, and the vicars and priests of Cardiff won't be up in arms because their graveyards keep being dug up. Then I can move on to tackling the vampires."

He nodded thoughtfully, brushing his hand through his bushy beard. After a few moments, he spoke quietly.

"Right you are, then. Tonight, is it?"

"I want to get there during the daylight, get everything ready. Six o'clock say?"

"We'll go together. Come and find me."

"I will. But…"

His eyes narrowed as he waited for me to complete my sentence.

"But?"

"The vampires. There is at least one out there, coming for me. If you join me, you risk being attacked by it, too.

If it comes for us, it's quite possible neither of us will survive. You know that, yes?"

He shrugged. He knew.

"All in a day's work, right?" he said.

As at Blackfriars, the remains of the crypt I'd identified had been worked into the foundations of a more modern building. I got why they did that: preserving as much of the past as possible, finding a new use for old stones. Archaeologically, it made sense. Thaumaturgically, it did not. It just meant that old ghosts and angry spirits found anchors to cling to in the mortal realm. Better to clear the site, give everyone their release, before starting again. But when this particular modern building had been constructed, my forebears in the Office had decided not to risk disturbing the dead in the chapel crypt and had sealed things up as best they could. They'd then kept a watchful eye on the place. Shackleton described the site as an *unholy catacomb* where *grim gods* were worshipped – but he also stated that the site was one *where lines of force cross or the walls between the worlds are unaccountably thin*, which perhaps explained the decision. Or maybe it was simply the fact that, for some reason, town planners rarely pay attention to the objections of the Office of the Witchfinder General.

In any case, Kerrigan and I found ourselves standing at another locked steel door in another modern concrete cellar. Above us was a glass and steel edifice that offered – according to the sign outside – *a range of exciting, multipurpose work and social spaces*. I think they meant that you could put offices and coffee shops there.

Once again, we had the keys. Once we were inside, I made sure to lock the door behind us. I didn't want to be interrupted by some random member of the public wandering down to investigate – and if things went badly sideways, I didn't want anything from below having free access to the outside world.

The crypt was much more cramped than that of the church near Cathedral Road. We both had to duck as we moved around, shambling uncomfortably across the old stones. Most of them had faded letters carved into them, I noted, worn smooth by the passage of many feet – or perhaps by water that had flowed through the cellar. They were grave markers, though, no doubt about it.

The space was divided into lots of little rooms leading off a central aisle. I couldn't tell if these had once been something like cells, or if they'd just needed more walls to support the weight of the chapel above. There was a massive iron grille in the ground, beneath which we could clearly hear the rush and trickle of water. Something to do with drainage, originally, although the former Witchfinders had repurposed it as a Wardstone. We set about levering the grille up with the crowbars our predecessors had left down there. The air we breathed was icy cold, colder than it should have been, and our breaths misted the air as we huffed and grunted with the effort of levering up the grille. Whoever had set it there had wanted to be very, very sure that nothing could push its way up from below.

I doubt either of us could have managed the job on our own and – I'm going to be honest – Kerrigan literally did most of the heavy lifting. Eventually we got it, one of us jamming crowbars into the gap as the other lifted the grate a few centimetres, then using a chain hooked through an eye on the grille to haul it upwards onto its side.

We stood together on the lip of the hole, both of us breathing heavily, staring down into the darkness. We were both, I knew, listening for movement, the scraping and splashing of something approaching.

"So now we wait," said Kerrigan.

"Now we wait."

"You have your weapons ready, in case it doesn't listen to reason?"

"I do. Kerrigan I…"

"What is it, laddo?"

I wasn't sure what I'd been about to say. Perhaps I'd been trying to think of a way to tell him that he might see me using unnatural powers if it came to that. To warn him.

In the end, I said, "I'm glad you're here with me."

He laughed at that, his voice loud in the echoing space. "We haven't worked together enough. You're a damn good Witchfinder."

Hearing him, I felt that I was completely safe, that nothing could possibly harm me. Then our conversation faded away, and the hush returned. We switched off our lights so we didn't scare our quarry, then began our vigil. It was strangely intimate sitting so close together in the darkness, the only sounds our gentle breathing and the water gurgling in its underground tunnel.

An hour or so later, my mind consumed with thoughts of Sally, I became distantly aware of … something. You know how it is when a dissonance, something *wrong*, slowly impinges on your consciousness? Like when there's a distant alarm beeping insistently, or you catch a virus and you become aware you don't feel right? You ignore it at first, refuse to allow it to be real by recognizing it, but after time it gets stronger and you have no choice.

It was like this now. I became fully aware of the cold, dark crypt I was sitting in. I could sense Kerrigan beside me, his breathing, the warmth from his body. The water chortled in the pit we'd opened up. And to my left, unmistakably there was a … deeper shadow in the darkness. Kerrigan wasn't aware of it, judging by his slow breathing, but it was clear to me. Something was in the crypt with us.

Moving very slowly, I reached out to switch on the lamp I'd set on the ground. Light blazed from it when I found the switch: and there he was, the low angle making his features even more threatening, emphasising how massive he was. As at Cathedral Road, he'd moved through the darkness, found his way through locked doors and solid walls.

Bone crouched in the corner watching us, looking more

like some great wolf or bear than anything that had ever been human. His face was a snarl of teeth and malice.

I scrambled to my feet. Kerrigan did the same once he'd caught up with what was happening. He trained his gun on Bone. I could hear the gentle clicks as he selected the anti-vampire round.

Bone ignored Kerrigan. "There's no escape for you, Danesh. Give yourself to me, and your friend can walk out of here unharmed."

"That's not going to happen, vampire," Kerrigan said, his voice taking on the edge of steel I'd heard before when we were in the field. "You want him, you have to come through me first."

Quietly, I withdrew one of the wooden stakes I'd worked on, slipping it out of the chest holster. I glanced aside at Kerrigan.

"No. Don't fight him. He only wants me."

Kerrigan's voice was low, his attention on the vampire. "That is not how we operate and you know it."

I moved first, before Kerrigan could do anything stupid, before Bone could leap across the space in the room and be at my throat. I'd researched his ability to disappear and reappear instantly; my grandfather's notes had described such a phenomenon, and I'd been working on the prescribed mantras to improve my perceptions. At the same time, the attack spell I needed was coiling faster and faster within me, part magic, part adrenaline. I threw myself through the room, the crouch I was in helping me to propel myself forwards. I shouted the base syllables of the *rearing cobra*, but there was no time for the complete incantation, and no room to work the steps and arm movements. The effect would be reduced, but I hoped to hurt him enough to stop him for a second.

Bone, seeing me coming, leapt to one side, but the confined space restricted him. I caught his trailing leg, stabbing the wooden stake into his calf. He screamed pure fury, rolling onto his back to get at the stake, pull it from his flesh. I wasn't going to make the same mistake as last time. Immediately, I pulled out two more stakes and thrust them into him. Behind his knee, his thigh. With each blow I screamed more words of the spell. With each blow, he convulsed as if I were jolting electricity through him.

He scrambled away on all fours. I had him. Two more stakes skewering him and the pain would be enough to cow him for a moment. It had to be. These latest stakes were better, the runes sharper, the incantations woven into them perfected. All I needed was enough time to work the *Wheel of Life Turning* incantation. The killing spell for life-stealing creatures such as him. It took time to enact properly, a full minute to complete all the steps, but if he was writhing in his agony for a few seconds, and weakened enough, I could begin the task of binding him.

I hoped.

Then I caught a glimpse of Kerrigan. He was crouching on one knee, his gun pointing at Bone. But in that moment, it was me he was looking at. He'd seen what I'd done. He'd understood. The stakes, the worked spells. He wasn't stupid. The lamp lit up his features perfectly clearly, and I saw disbelief there. Confusion. The look of someone who'd been betrayed. For the briefest second, we looked at each other, really saw each other.

Then the Witchfinder in him took control. I may have become suddenly one of the enemy in his eyes, but he knew where the imminent threat was. He turned his attention back to the vampire and fired his handgun.

I knew from experience it would be barely a bee sting to Bone – but in the moment, it was the final straw for the vampire, one pinprick too many. He was trying to tear the stake in his thigh from his flesh, smoke rising from his shaking hand as he clutched the spike of wood. As the bullet struck him, he roared in his rage and flung himself at Kerrigan.

The vampire swept across the low room with the speed I'd witnessed at Cathedral Road: one moment there, and one moment there, although his time I could *just* see him moving. He barrelled into Kerrigan. The Witchfinder was a big and powerful man, but he might have been a soft toy in Bone's grip. I watched helplessly as Bone picked up Kerrigan by one foot – and dashed his head into one of the crypt's walls, smashing his skull into the stone. Then he flung Kerrigan across the room, as easily as if the Witchfinder were nothing more than a stick.

Kerrigan thumped sideways into the stone wall. Slid to the ground. Slumped over, legs crumpling beneath him.

Didn't move.

I watched as blood welled from the wound in his head, a black stain on the stone floor. For a moment, the three of us in that damp crypt didn't move: Bone staring at Kerrigan, a weird look of shock on his features, as if he didn't understand what had happened. Me staring at Bone. Kerrigan staring at no one.

Bone broke the spell. I thought he was going to come for me, finish me off, but with a final snarl – a snarl that sounded more like a sob – he twisted and stepped into the darkness around him. I felt the sudden absence of him as a releasing of pressure, as if the air had gone out of the room. He was gone.

I scrambled my way over to Kerrigan. He still hadn't moved. I found the wound on his head, thinking to stem the flow of blood. Then I saw the extent of the damage: glimpses of white that might have been bone and might have been brain. I could feel no pulse, no sense of his presence. He, also, was gone.

I knew it, but I couldn't bring myself to accept it. Protocol kicked in. I raced back upstairs, getting above ground so I could pick up a few shreds of a phone signal. Once I had a bar, I used the Office emergency number, giving my location and specifying Code 0. *Office operative injured or killed*. We would drop anything when that code was used, come running immediately. Perhaps the Crow – or Lady Coldwater if she got pulled in – would be able to do something.

I returned to the crypt to wait with him. I had done this to him, as surely as Bone had. If it hadn't been for me, he'd never have been in the crypt. I placed my hand on his forehead – and I knew with sudden certainty that he wasn't coming back, even if all the Pale Sisters in the land tried to heal him. Some injuries are too terrible. He was gone, and someone would have to tell his family.

Tell his boy.

I sat there with him, my hand on him, and told him over and over how sorry I was. Sorry I hadn't told him the truth about my nature, hadn't trusted him. Sorry he'd died. It was ridiculous, and pointless, but it was all I could do.

Some minutes later, I heard voices from above. Olwen and McLeland. None of us spoke as they entered the crypt and saw the two of us on the ground. One of us crouching, one of us lying unmoving. Between us, we carried Kerrigan upstairs. We called for an ambulance, because there was nothing else to be done. As we waited, the Crow phoned. The shock and hurt in his voice was clear. He said the things people say to you in these circumstances: *It wasn't your fault*; *There was nothing you could have done.* None of it helped.

The Crow said, "What was it that attacked you? Something vampiric?"

"It was the William Bone entity."

"It attacked Kerrigan but left you?"

"It did."

"Why was that? Why did it let you live?"

I didn't know. But I was beginning to think I had an idea why.

Bone ran from the site of the disused chapel, fleeing heedless into the darkness. Sickness roiled in his stomach at what he had done. Another human slaughtered by his hand – but not a target. Not one that he was compelled to kill. In all his centuries of servitude, he had tried to keep that covenant with himself. He would kill only those he had to, never anyone else, however evil or however innocent. He had failed in this more than once – but not for three hundred years. It had become the last thread of his former self that he clung to. He could so easily have slaughtered so many more, all those who'd stood in his way, but he'd refused. And now, suddenly, he'd crossed the line, broken his vow.

This final act of slaughter: it was too much.

Perhaps there was nothing left of his former self, save this sickness at what he'd become. That was what he'd been reduced to; revulsion at his own nature. He stopped at a railing, the chopping water of the sea below him. His stomach clenched and he heaved, vomiting up nothing but a thick black liquid.

He felt the presence of Catherine come to him. He knew it was only his imagination, his need for forgiveness and comfort. He felt her cool hand on his back. Then her gentle fingers touching his cheek. Of course, she was long dead. He had killed her, her and their children. Such had been the Warlock's first orders to him. An act of – what? – entertainment for the vampire who controlled him? A way of showing Bone what he was, how little will he had? Perhaps Bone could have let her live, let the Warlock turn her into one such as him, but he'd spared her that, at least. Spared her the long torment. He only hoped that she knew he wasn't himself when he came to the family home that terrible night. Knew that this wasn't the man she loved, but some demon taking on his form.

He retched again, and it felt like some great fist were clenching his guts. There was no escape for him. He couldn't end himself and he couldn't flee. He could smell his prey nearby where he had left him. Soon, the compulsion to kill would become unbearable, all-consuming.

All he could do was to kill the boy, get the butchery out of the way – and then flee, in the hope that the Warlock left him alone for a time.

Which he never did.

20 – The Deeper Woods

> The month of May was come, when every lusty heart beginneth to blossom, and to bring forth fruit; for like as herbs and trees bring forth fruit and flourish in May, in like wise every lusty heart that is in any manner a lover, springeth and flourisheth in lusty deeds.
> – Sir Thomas Malory, *Le Morte d'Arthur*, c. 1469

The following morning. I'd slept little, reliving the shocks of the previous day over and over. The look on Kerrigan's face. The fact that I was still alive. The terrible wound in Kerrigan's skull. In my troubled dreams, that wound had become a mouth, denouncing me for what I was over and over.

Kerrigan was indestructible. How could he be gone?

Unable to sleep, I'd sat at my desk, trying to decide my course of action. I'd stared at my screen, weighing up what to do about the two cases I was pursuing. They clearly weren't related – unless it was by the Warlock loosening magical bindings to let entities like the bone-taker ghost trouble the world. I needed to resolve both matters quickly. I wasn't going to survive another battle with Bone, and I wasn't close to finding the Warlock. The entity robbing graves of their bones was still out there – and what would happen if it were allowed to complete its work?

The computer wasn't switched on; all I could see was my own reflected face staring back at me. I wondered what *he*, the Danesh in there, looking at everything from the reverse angle, would do. It was nonsense, of course; my mind was exhausted. But then the idea hit me. Two unrelated cases. Two problems I wasn't close to solving.

A possible solution, one arrived at by looking at everything the other way round.

The two cases weren't connected – but what if I made them connected? What if I tried to kill two birds with a single stone? Tried to see both of them the other way round?

I sat for long moments, turning it all over in my mind, trying to decide if it was madness or genius. Quite possibly, it was both.

The text from Sally came as dawn was breaking. I was grateful for it, stirring me into action, giving me a focus from my ruminations. I wanted more than ever to get some revenge. I drove as quickly as the Mini would convey me, following the route I'd taken to reach Jamie Tavish's house in Tintern most of the way, but pressing on into England at Monmouth. Thoughts about Kerrigan remained a raw wound; a thing too big to get my head round. More than anyone in the Office he'd been my friend, always there for me, always looking out for me. I wished he'd known the truth about me before the end – but I also knew that hadn't been possible. Had never been possible. I'd strayed too far from the Office path.

A bright sun lit up the landscape around me, revealing a rolling patchwork of green fields and woods. The shining River Wye sidling away and then popping back up unexpectedly. I tried to focus upon it all, enjoy the brief moments of beauty. I sped around Ross-on-Wye and onto the Gloucester Road. Just as Kerrigan had promised, I began to catch glimpses of May Hill ahead of me and to the side of me and then ahead of me again, peeping out briefly behind folds in the landscape or between hills. The clump of trees on its crown was unmistakable once you noticed it. It reminded me, for some reason, of the last battered vestiges of some defeated army, like a lost Roman legion proudly holding up its banners. Or the outline of some monstrous creature beetling across the horizon.

Surprisingly, for something so large and immobile, the

hill was difficult to track down once I left the main road. The narrow roads twisted sharply, falling and splitting, with no helpful signs anywhere to tell me where I could get to the foot of the climb. I drove for what seemed like far too long, and I was just wondering if some confusion hex had been worked on me, when I saw a little pull-off for the car. A gate opposite led to a path up the slopes of the hill.

There was no one else around, save for one or two seemingly wild ponies, pondering me morosely as they chewed the grass. At least the top of the hill was easy to find. A wide, rolling countryside opened up around me as I climbed towards the familiar clump of trees. A snaking river – the Severn I think – wound between woods to one side of me. To the other, round hills receded into the distance. It was a beautiful crisp morning, the air misty, a few scattered clouds ambling round in the sky. I breathed deeply – partly from the effort of the climb, and partly as an attempt to expel some of the demons from the recent past. Clear my head.

I reached the edge of the hilltop copse without incident. The little wood was larger up close – that's generally how things work, in my experience – and it had a low ring ditch dug all the way around it, as Kerrigan had said. I couldn't fathom the purpose of it; it surely wasn't large enough to be defensive.

Under the boughs, the air became suddenly colder, as if the remains of the night were lingering in there, clinging on. I could cross the copse in maybe a minute. There was no sign of Sally, or anyone else. I stood in the very heart of the little wood, turning around, wondering what it was I was supposed to see or do. Had I missed some vital detail of her clues?

Then I saw the faintest flicker of movement, as of someone hiding behind one of the boughs of the trees, not wanting to be seen, or maybe letting themselves be glimpsed. Was it her? I stepped rapidly to the tree – but found nothing when I peered around it.

Then I saw more movement, the swirl of a black dress or

cape disappearing around another tree. I ran that way. There followed a dance of such movements: she (if it *was* her) leading, me following. We wove a path between the trees, drawing out runes on the ground, perhaps, or at least following some complex pattern that I couldn't follow.

Then I stepped around one of the trees, and Sally was standing there in the open, smiling at me. The woods were different, too: there was bright sunlight, a warm glow to the air, as if her smile had lit up the world.

"You came," she said.

"Of course."

She stepped towards me, looked at me for a moment, a light in her eyes, and then she reached up to kiss me. She put her hand behind my head, holding me there in the embrace. I did the same, hungry for her. We clutched each other, lost in each other.

Then she stepped backwards, her fingers still holding mine.

"Undress me."

I wanted to. I really, really wanted to.

"We don't have time."

Her laugh lit up her features.

"We have time. Time isn't a thing here. This little clearing in this little copse of trees is a bubble. A place outside time. It's my place. Ours. We can spend as long here as we like."

"But..."

She put her finger to my lips, telling me to be quiet.

"Stop talking. Start doing."

I looked around. The trees *were* different. We were in a copse of broadleafs, oaks and beech trees. A different wood. Another part of the wood.

Then her hands were on my body, freeing me of my clothes, and I was doing the same. The sun was warm on our bare skin. We sank to the ground, a soft bed of grass between the trees, and lost ourselves in each other. Our bodies touched, and after a while I could no longer be entirely sure where I stopped and she started.

When the end came, it felt as though golden lights had

been switched on throughout my body; that I'd been turned into a being of purest joy, my blood and tissues transformed into some new substance of simple delight. Light and love and magic filled me, and they were all the same thing.

I fell gratefully into it, and for a time I was lost to the world, all the horror and loss washed away.

The warmth of sunlight upon my face brought me back eventually. I could hear the chatter and chirp of birdsong about me. An insect droned by. I opened my eyes, the light impossibly bright through my flickering eyelashes for a moment. There were trees above me, a scattered palette of leaves describing every conceivable shade of green. The ground was soft beneath my back. My fingers found low vegetation around me: grass or clover. The air was filled with scents of flowers and greenery. The slightest warm breeze breathed upon my skin.

I pulled myself to a sitting position. Sally was there, sitting beside me, watching me. The golden light was still in my eyes, illuminating her face. But there was something else in her gaze, I thought. A hardness. A sadness. It struck an oddly discordant note. She was troubled. Had I done something wrong?

"Where are we exactly?" I managed.

"The woods," she said.

"But which woods?"

She shook her head as if the question made no sense to her.

"I told you. The woods. My own private corner."

"But I don't … I mean, how did we get here?"

"You know that. I led you here. Now we go on; I think you're ready."

That threw me. "Are you saying that making love was nothing more than a *test*?"

There was her smile again, and the sight of it washed away all my doubts.

"Of course not. I did *that* because I wanted to. Wasn't that obvious? But … there was a sense of a balance being struck, too. Sometimes in life things need to be put into equilibrium, that's all. The light and the darkness. The day and the night. I wanted to share those moments with you before ... before the next thing."

"I don't understand."

She stood up, and we dressed. She smoothed down her skirts, brushing stray blades of grass away.

"I will show you. It isn't far."

We headed between the wide boughs of oak trees that stretched out great arms to nearly touch each other. As we stepped into the dappled shade, it seemed to me that the background hum and chatter of the woods quietened, our surroundings taking up a sombre and watchful air. We walked in silence, weaving around the trunks but following no path I could discern.

She stopped at a point where two boughs and their branches formed a sort of archway, if you approached from the right direction. Sally stopped there.

"You used your acorn, but I still have mine."

"I thought we had them to summon Stonewall?"

"They open the ways into his private corner of the woods. To let him out or us inside. All this time, he's had to seal himself away, be sure that they couldn't track him down. Even I couldn't get to him, unless he chose to listen to my call and come to me. Now, though, it is time to step inside on our own.

"Can't you call him?"

There was that troubled look on her features again.

"Come on, I'll show you."

She placed the acorn she carried onto the ground in the archway, setting it on a little stone that might have been placed there for just such a purpose. She crushed the acorn beneath the heel of her boot. I heard a whispering, a wind whistling through the trees, but other than that nothing appeared to change. No glowing doorways opened up; no silver paths lit for us to follow.

"The way will be open for a few minutes," she said. "Through the archway and we'll be in his part of the woods."

She took my hand, and we stepped through. Nothing had changed so far as I could see. Here and there, beams of sunlight picked out glowing patches of bluebells on the ground before us, their buttery tang mixing with the unmistakable scent of wild garlic. Then, a few steps later, as we rounded another tree, I found myself crunching through a deep carpet of fallen leaves, yellow and purple and tan. Then light flurries of snow drifted down from above. I had seen such things before, of course: my trip into the green from the Isle of Man, when Stonewall had first made contact with me, drawing me to his home and the deep pool of cold water I'd immersed myself within. Was that it? Was I to make another descent into those waters? Or were we, perhaps, to do so together, Sally and I?

Then we emerged into the familiar clearing, and I saw this visit was about something else completely. The wide, ancient oak tree was there, looking just as I remembered it. Bright rays of sun lit the scene, picking out the shadows in its rugose bark, but the tree wasn't in leaf. The *black oak* Stonewall had called it on my previous visit. The winter tree. Then, it had been festooned with the corpses of countless woodland creatures: birds and small, scurrying mammals hanging there like grim decorations. They were still there, adorning the wide branches, but now another body was on the tree. Seemingly pinned there on the trunk, hanging upside down from it.

Stonewall himself was on the oak.

He'd been lashed there by a thick rope, tied around his ankles and secured to the tree where it forked a short way above. His arms hung down. Blood dripped from a series of cuts across his bare chest, like a rune carved there, the red rivulets dripping down his neck, his face, through his hair and onto the rough bark. The tree was stained by it. The flow didn't reach the ground, though: it was as if the tree were somehow absorbing the fluid, drinking in the blood. The familiar lurch in my stomach told me what my brain had already guessed: that there was strong magic being worked here. Slow, deep magic.

At the base of the tree, the single exposed root glowed and pulsed with it.

I thought about the Librarian's words when I told her what I'd seen on my previous visit. *So much power. So much death. I wonder if it will be enough.* Stonewall wasn't moving. His flesh was as pale as bone. It was hard not to see the knots in the bark above him as great eyes, as if the tree were some mournful leviathan staring down at me. I glanced at Sally. She met my gaze but didn't speak. I could see how troubled she was by the scene, but it wasn't any sort of surprise to her. The great work of magic being slowly crafted: I now knew what it was. The magic Stonewall had learned from *De Magicae Mortis*. He'd been working on it for decades but had clearly decided – maybe this had been his plan all along – that he needed to add more power to the spell at the end. He'd used the only source available to him, because he refused to use anything else.

I took a step forwards, not sure if there was anything I could do but watch and try to understand. At my footfall, Stonewall's eyes opened suddenly wide, as if he'd simply been asleep and I'd startled him awake.

His mouth moved, his tongue working across his parched lips. After a few moments, he managed to form words.

"You are here. It is good. The weapon is ready. Take it from the tree."

"We have to get you off there," I said. "Get you treatment for your cuts."

He shook his head and something like the faintest smile flickered across his mouth.

"No. No."

He lifted one arm and pointed at Sally. "Tell him. Explain. I am nearly spent. Nearly spent. This artefact and his skills, his wisdom. Between them, they might be enough. I have made you another Norskrang. I have done all I could."

"Norskrang was destroyed long ago," I said.

"He made you another," said Sally. "That isn't the

name of a weapon, it's the name for the magic used to *make* the weapon. The long and gruelling spell. That's what he's been doing all these years, slowly adding to its power. He couldn't bring himself to kill anyone or anything in the process, except for himself. Now it is ready. Now he's giving it to you."

On the tree, Stonewall closed his eyes and nodded. He had no strength for anything else now.

"What will happen to him?" I asked.

Sally's voice was a whisper. "His life's work is done. *The Destroyer*, the vampires and their minions call him. Let's hope they were right. He said to say, before he went on the tree, he said to tell you that he hoped it was enough. That this was all he could do, in the end. He couldn't track down the Warlock and he couldn't tell you how to get close enough to him to wield the weapon. But he could do this. He said, also, that the weapon has only one attack in it. Other such artefacts can be used over and over, slowly weakening. With this, you will get one chance and one chance only. He said to choose your moment carefully."

"But how do I use it? What spells do I need to work to wake it, to wield it?"

"The words he gave me were *Rearing Cobra*. Something he learned from your grandfather. Does that make any sense?"

"It does."

I knelt to the ground to study the root through which all that magical energy had been channelled. I could see there were runes carved into its grain – many, many tiny sigils, intricately worked. I recognized them all. Except, they weren't *worked*, not by a blade: it seemed they had grown there, the fine grains of the wood flowing and curling to form them. When I touched the root, I was lost for a moment as powerful, flaring magic erupted through me, blinding me. Then it seemed to settle into my hand as if it were accepting me.

I pulled the short spike of root free, twisting it from the mother oak, plucking it like a fruit. It came free and sat in my palm: a spiralling, sharpened twist of oak, thrumming with power.

I had a new Norskrang.

Stonewall didn't move. Didn't notice.

"We can't leave him on the tree," I said.

Sally nodded. In the end, the only way to bring him down was to cut the ropes that had lashed him to the trunk. He collapsed into an awkward pile of limbs on the ground. He didn't move. I caught Sally's look, and we both knew the truth of it. I was reminded of Kerrigan's death, the way he'd crumpled to a heap on the ground, too. Too many people had died.

"Let's bury him here," I said. "We should take the time to do that, at least."

She nodded and we set to work, putting him into the ground a little distance from the black oak. He was oddly light to carry, as if he'd been desiccated by his long trial, reduced to a husk.

We buried him deep, in a spot where the roots of the great tree wound through the ground. They would find him. In some way, he would become part of them. When the work was done, and we had the ground covered again, we stood for a moment in silence, hand in hand. Then, Sally took me to the edge of the clearing. The woods were peaceful now. It felt as though some storm had passed by, leaving only dappled sunlight and birdsong.

"Given what I'm planning, I have to go alone," I said. "If you're with me, the Warlock will know."

She nodded. She'd worked that out. We held each other close, not wanting the moment to end but knowing it had to.

"I'll be waiting for you here," she said. "Come into the green. I'll see you."

We both knew that might never happen. I kissed her one more time, then turned to head into the shadows of the trees.

21 – A Bone to Pick

> If ever it may be objected that the creatures I have herein described do not exist – or if they do, that they rarely trouble our modern age so as to be beneath our concern – let it be known that I have several times encountered them walking the Earth that we all share. At some times the fiends congregate openly, dismissive of any power that might attempt to banish them. Lately I have discovered, for example, one such coven in a rough house near the docks in London – a tavern of sorts as it might have been, save that all the clientele were of a most hideous and unnatural form, and I dread to think what refreshments it was that might have been served there. I stayed but for a moment, then fled while I was still able to. The shrieks and calls of that fell establishment followed me into the night.
>
> – The Reverend Jebediah Snow, *A True Study of Imps and Daemons*, 1836

To destroy the Warlock, I had to find out where his lair was, knowledge that had evaded the Office and researchers like Shackleton and Quirk for centuries. But I knew of one person who could tell me – or who might be forced to tell me. And I wasn't going to simply wait for him to attack me again. It was time to take the fight to him.

If I hadn't known, I'd have passed the doorway to the current incarnation of The Shuttered Lantern without giving it a second thought. It looked like it hadn't been opened for years. A derelict Cardiff warehouse outside the centre, awaiting demolition or refurbishment. In its heyday, I knew, the establishment had moved around, popped up here and there. The Lantern wasn't so much a place as a concept. It was here now if the entities inside said it was. Kerrigan had picked up a whisper on the location while investigating a Code 12 (an *Unidentified Troglodyte Species*, so something along the lines of a gnome or a goblin or a troll. For reference, very disparate creatures. Lumping them together in one code said a lot about the Office mindset).

A short flight of stone steps led down from street level. There were weeds growing from the cracks in the masonry. Fly-posters for gigs and festivals from years previously were plastered across the door. It was another emblazoned with NO UNAUTHORIZED ADMITTANCE – and this time, I knew well that I wasn't authorized. If I could get inside, I might not get out again. It was an understatement to say that an Office witchfinder was not going to be welcome in the Lantern.

I knocked anyway. Anyone passing by might have thought I was crazy, rapping on a clearly-abandoned door. They would have been the least of my problems. Nobody replied to my hammering. My guess was there were other entrances to the place, and that the regulars slithered their way inside from below – or, for all I knew, landed on the roof.

I tried again, louder this time. Finally, a little hatch that I hadn't noticed slid back, and a pair of eyes in a bone-white face regarded me.

"I want to come inside," I said (rather unnecessarily, I felt).

A hiss of purest hatred came from the doorman on the other side as a response.

"You are not welcome here, Witchfinder."

"You know who I am?"

"We know you. We know all of you. You are Danesh of the Shahzan line. There will be blood shed if you come in here. Leave now while you still can."

"I give you my word I won't harm anyone. I'm only here to pass on a message."

The eyes blazed red for a moment. "It isn't our blood

that will be shed, Witchfinder. As entertaining as that might be, we know what the response from your friends would be. Walk away now."

I'd faced some scary club bouncers in my time, but nothing like this. But I wasn't going to give in.

"Tell me who you do allow inside."

The speaker hissed again, and this time I caught a glimpse of a mouth filled with teeth. Many tiny sharpened teeth.

"You know who and what is welcome here. No one like you. Nobody – what would you say? – *normal*."

"How do you tell?" I asked.

That seemed to confuse him. "How do we tell what?"

"Who is and isn't normal."

"I make it my duty to know."

"You must have a test if you're not sure if someone qualifies."

Another hiss. "One such as you will never be allowed in here. You cannot possibly pass."

"Then there is a test. You really shouldn't judge people by their appearance, you know. This is the twenty-first century. Give it to me."

There was a snarl from behind the door, followed by a muttering as the doorkeeper conversed with someone within. Then he loomed back into view.

"Round the back, there's another door. You can undergo the trial there. But be warned, I can't guarantee your safety. And before you step inside, tell the scum you work with this was your idea, not ours. We are not responsible for what happens."

At that, the hatchway slammed shut.

It took me a couple of minutes to find the back door, hidden away down a rubbish-strewn alleyway. There was even a flickering neon light attached to the brick wall opposite it, to add to that urban wasteland vibe. The wind picked up for a moment, lifting a few scraps of litter from the ground and whipping them into a micro city tornado. It disappeared as quickly as it had formed. This doorway looked like it hadn't been used in *decades*. It was solid metal, rivetted, green paint flaking off it and a rusted keyhole that looked like it might have seized up before I was even born.

I pounded upon the door, which clanged like a cracked bell.

After a moment, the door was pulled open by no hand that I could see. In its staccato bursts, the flickering streetlight revealed a small square anteroom, devoid of detail or furniture. A heavily-chained door led deeper into the interior.

I stepped inside. There was nothing else to do. The door slammed shut behind me. Of course. I stood in absolute darkness for a moment. It was hard to resist the thought that I'd walked into a clear trap.

A flame flared in the air in front of me, a dancing wraith of yellow and red. I could feel the heat coming off it on my face. There was something sorcerous to it, too, but I couldn't tell what.

A rasping voice spoke from somewhere in the darkness beside me. "Give me your hand. You will be tested."

"What is the test?"

The creature moved a little nearer the flame, and I caught a glimpse of a squat, unhuman creature, some gnome or goblin thing that might dwell in the deep darkness. I, too, was guilty of easy *Code 12* categorizations. To human eyes it was extravagantly ugly, but I tried not to judge.

"Give me your hand," it repeated. "This is the test."

I held out my fingers. A damp, slippery hand gripped my own and thrust it into the flame. I felt the sharp prickle of pain, but the goblin thing held me firm in the fire as I tried to pull away.

There was more to the flame than burning gas. I could feel the magic in it as something alive, like an elemental creature of fire sniffing me out. I felt it pass through my flesh and bone so it could see the real me, taste my thoughts. I fought it, instinctively, trying to banish it from my body.

The flame flared brighter, growing in strength.

The tester's grip was iron-firm. It growled. "Let the fire do its work or fail the test."

With an effort, I took a mental step backwards, channelling my own magic not at the intruder but to my seared flesh, cooling and healing it as best I could. Fighting all my instincts, I let the fire wander the halls of my mind.

After long moments of this, the burning was suddenly extinguished. In the same moment, the creature released its grip upon me. I studied my flesh, expecting to see a blackened, smoking stump, but my skin was unscathed.

"You are one of us," the tester hissed. "You cannot be, and yet you are."

"People can be more than one thing at once. Let me inside."

"You know we cannot guarantee your safety even if you are a magic-wielder."

"So your friend on the front door said. Let me in."

The creature grunted in something like resentment. There was a rattle of chains or keys, and then the inner door was pushed open. Red light glowed out, and I was struck by a wall of heavy, warm air thick with smoke and sulphur and noxious smells that I couldn't identify.

I stepped inside The Shuttered Lantern.

I had the impression of a labyrinth of cramped rooms and corridors connecting randomly, as if a jumble of boxes had been thrown together. The wooden skeleton of the building was visible throughout. Odd little flights of steps led up and down without any obvious pattern or purpose, the passageways twisting and then turning back on themselves. Tables were set in shadowy corners with no apparent order. The whole scene was lit by the flames of yellow candles guttering here and there: on the tables, in brackets attached to the walls. It was light that seemed to bring more shadow than illumination, something I was grateful for. The familiar low hubbub of conversation that might be heard in a normal pub was replaced by a cacophony of growls and squeals and grunts, as if the denizens were rough beasts herded into the place to drink.

I stepped warily forwards, catching glimpses of faces in the flickering light. As I passed through the labyrinth, the conversations – if that was what they were – died away. In the movies, when you step into a country pub, everyone goes quiet to watch you. Just before the slaughtering starts. This was like that, only more so. The locals watched me with a mixture of expressions upon their faces: puzzlement, fury, malice – and other expressions that I couldn't read because many of the faces were not human enough. One shadowy corner wasn't shadowy because it wasn't illuminated; it was shadowy because some creature of shadows sat – or floated – there.

We didn't have an Office code vague enough for what was going on in The Shuttered Lantern. For all I knew, I was seeing *all* the codes, all at once.

One hulking creature – demon or demon-adjacent – stepped into my way. Its face was a twisted mess of teeth and eyes. Silver chains criss-crossed its body. Whether this was some enchantment or fashion, I couldn't tell. The creature sniffed at me, then emitted a low growl from deep in its throat. The sort that dogs make before they attack.

Its voice was rough. "Witchfinder. Your kind isn't welcome here."

I lifted my hand, palm open, and worked a simple flame, letting it dance there for a moment. My control was good, now – although it was a simple enough cantrip. A mere trick.

"You have no idea who I am and what I'm capable of," I said. "Stand aside before I send you back where you came from."

"I come from Aberystwyth."

"Then back to where you came from before that."

This exchange raised a flurry of growls and snarls from the assembled creatures. I could feel them glaring at me, waiting to see how this turned out. The demon didn't budge. If it attacked me, I figured the others would, too.

Another sound bubbled up from the creature's throat. It started out as a growl, but became more of a chuckle.

"You will all be gone, soon. Your time is over, Witchfinder. That won't go well for one such as you. One who has betrayed their own side."

I pushed at him. It was like trying to nudge a wall aside. A rubbery, fleshy wall. With a laugh, he relented and let me pass. Perhaps, in his head, he was letting me into the slaughter ground. I emerged into what appeared to be the Lantern's bar area. I could hear thumping, thundering music from the floor above, accompanied by screeching and growling. Either a death metal gig or somebody was being ritually slaughtered up there. Perhaps it was both. I could feel the booming sound through my feet as it shook the structure of the building.

To my left, a makeshift array of silver and copper pipes of various sizes led from tanks and wheezing steampunk contraptions to feed the taps on the bar with liquids. I was going to take a wild guess and say they weren't all beer. Several drinks were lined up on the bar, served in metal tankards. More than one of them smoked. One was on fire, sulphurous flames licking off it.

A tattooed woman who was probably more succubus than human – her forked tongue flickering as she watched me – stood behind the bar, an amused look on her features.

"What can I get you, Witchfinder?" she asked. "Glass of water maybe? Lemonade?" The chorus behind me bellowed their amusement.

Forcing my voice to be as loud as I could make it, I held up my hands and spoke.

"Listen to me. You all know the Warlock, yes?"

The room stayed quiet, mention of the vampire enough to cow them for a moment. They knew. They knew, and many of them *feared*, too.

I shouted into the silence. "If you know that name, then you'll know the name of his servant, too. His tame killer. The one they call Bone. William Bone."

The silence stretched out. They knew. Quietly, the succubus behind the bar said, "Speak quickly. Get to your point and leave."

I followed her advice. "Twice Bone has come for me. Twice I have beaten him off, sent him scurrying away with his tail between his legs." I didn't need to tell them that Sally's *banishment* and then Bone's odd reaction at the death of Kerrigan were the main reasons. Let them think I had defeated the vampire twice. It might dissuade some of them from attacking me where I stood.

"I will face him one more time," I said. "Third time's the charm. I will face him and finally destroy him, or be destroyed by him. Put the word out. Tell him. I'll be alone. I'm not going to run anymore."

I told them where and when. Would Bone bite? I hoped he would be sufficiently intrigued by my challenge. The location I was giving him was public property, more or less; there could be no possibility of a Banishment, and he'd know it. By now, I figured, his need to capture me, kill me had to be consuming him.

I left The Shuttered Lantern while the locals considered my words. The demon bared impressive teeth but didn't bar my way. A few moments later, I was back on the street, and the doors to The Shuttered Lantern were once again locked against me.

I phoned the Crow as I headed back to the city centre. Again, he took a while to pick up. When he did, the audio was muffled from a bad signal, and he sounded slightly out of breath.

"Danesh. It is very good to hear from you. How is your investigation proceeding?"

I assumed he meant the unofficial vampire one, not the bodysnatcher one.

"I'm nearly ready. If all goes to plan, I'll be ready tomorrow."

"Tomorrow? That is remarkable progress after all this time."

I could just hear a whistling, pumping sound in the background of his call, the labouring of some machine. I'd heard it before, somewhere.

"I do need your help, though," I said.

"Of course. Really, anything I can do. You need only

ask." There was a little pause in his words before he spoke again. "I ... the loss of Kerrigan. It is just terrible. Terrible, terrible. There are so few of us left, now. It feels as though we were being picked off, one after another. I have tried to keep you all safe but I have failed. Failed badly. I am sorry."

I wasn't ready to talk about Kerrigan. I said, "If I succeed, perhaps I can put an end to it."

The sound went muffled for a moment, and I heard him converse briefly with someone else.

"Perhaps," he continued. "But the risks to you, Danesh, they terrify me. We will do all we can here, of course, but I beg you, put yourself in no more danger than you have to."

I wondered who *we* was, and what help they were giving me. No doubt he'd tell me when he was ready.

"There's a locked metal grid in the cellar of the castle," I said. "I believe you hold the keys?"

"I do, yes. There is something going on down there, but it's never been urgent enough to warrant my full attention. You believe the tunnels are relevant to the Warlock investigation?"

"They're relevant to my solution to that investigation. I hope."

He sighed. "Very well. Take the keys, of course. I am elsewhere at the moment, but there's a safe in my office. Inside, there's a brass keyring with three keys upon it, red, blue and green. I'll give you the combination for the safe. Please, I beg you, take nothing else."

I assured him I wouldn't. It was, I felt, a sign of the days we lived in that he was simply giving me access to his private secrets. It would have been inconceivable a few short months previously.

He said, "Whatever it is you are doing, Danesh, are you sure it is, shall we say, the right thing?"

"I am."

"Good, good. I need no more detail, but I beg you to be careful."

"I'll do my best."

Sam the castle guard was more reluctant to help me when I told him what I needed.

"I can't just lock you in overnight. That's against all the rules. Who knows what I'll come back to in the morning?"

"I need to be sure that no one else can reach me while I'm ... working. Can you do that for me please?"

I could see he wanted to know what I'd be up to down in the castle dungeons overnight, but couldn't bring himself to ask.

"I don't like it," he said. "Perhaps if I was to stay with you, but you can't be left down there alone."

In the end, I had to invoke the name of Hardknott-Lewis to persuade him. I returned to the waking world to grab some food and drink, then climbed the stair to the Black Tower to retrieve the three keys, which were precisely where he'd said they would be. I didn't look at anything else in his safe, tempting as that was.

There were a couple more items I needed, and I knew that the Office evidence store – a chamber stacked with shelves off the supply room – would have them. Our repository is nothing as grand as the facility in Aldwych, but we have a wide assortment of objects retrieved from a huge number of investigations over the years.

Everything was carefully bagged and tagged. I thought back to the partially-assembled skeleton I'd glimpsed in my vision, then found the bone I'd need. A perfectly formed upper arm bone, male, identity unknown, retrieved from a summoning ritual that Office operatives had broken up in the 1930s. The skeleton had definitely been lacking a humerus. Dutifully, I wrote in the little log book to explain what I had checked out. Outside, in the supply room, I found the final items I needed: a padlock and a length of iron chain, a little rusty but strong. They were surprisingly heavy, but I didn't have too far to carry them.

Finally, I was ready. Down in the dungeon, I worked the first incantations in the *Wind that Winnows* spell, marking out the containing ring on the ground. I'd complete the ritual only once the circle was occupied. Then I unlocked the little iron door covering the drain. I tasted cold air heavy with water. I could just hear a white noise whisper of rushing air or a running stream.

Wishing I'd brought a cushion, I sat on the floor with my back to the rough stone wall, trying and failing to get my traumatized neck muscles comfortable. I laid my gun, my knife, a lamp, the bone, the padlock, the chain and the five wooden stakes I'd carved on the ground beside me. Norskrang, I kept hidden in its holster. I hoped I wouldn't need it.

Then I waited in silence, alone with my thoughts.

22 – Life and Death

> On murder-bed quickly I minded to bind him,
> With firm-holding fetters, that forced by my grapple
> Low he should lie in life-and-death struggle
> 'Less his body escape
>   – original unknown, trans. Lesslie Hall,
>   *Beowulf*, 1892

As before, I sensed rather than saw the moment when Bone was in the room with me. He stepped through the darkness, the locked doors no barrier to him.

I stood, picking up my wooden stakes. The danger was that he would attack before I had chance to explain what I had planned. Would it work? Was he too far gone to even listen? I couldn't know. I switched on the lamp, illuminating the little stone cell in a pale glow. The shadows seemed only to emphasise Bone's stature and strength.

To my surprise he spoke first, his voice low.

"Who was he?"

"Who was who?"

"The one I killed."

"He was my friend. His name was Thomas Kerrigan. He had a family. He had a child."

An odd silence stretched out at my words.

"I … am sorry."

"Not as sorry as they are."

"I know you won't let me take you alive. I have to kill you now."

"I don't think you do."

"You don't understand. I have no choice."

"There is always a choice."

I thought he was going to ask me what I meant, but instead he chose that moment to charge, throw himself at me. He swept around the room in an arc, no doubt intending to avoid the spellworked wooden stakes I held ready. I was expecting something like it; I knew he wasn't stupid. I'd also grown a little better at seeing him. He wasn't disappearing and reappearing, just moving with huge speed. I ducked the moment I saw him flinch and held out a stake in each hand, one to each side. Bone crashed into me, knocking me to the ground. I bashed the side of my head hard on the stone floor, the pain sickening. From the sharp stab in my ribs, it felt like I'd cracked a bone. The good news was that I'd struck him with the stake – or at least, that he'd impaled himself upon it. I felt it burrowing into his flesh, the glee of it sharp.

I worked my way back to my feet and began to work the *rearing cobra*, performing the basic hand movements while calling out the syllables that would render the remaining stakes more powerful. Bone was upon me before I'd completed the magic, barrelling me backwards against the stone wall. The impact knocked the breath out of me, and the pain in my ribs mounted sharply, joining up with the agonies I already carried in my neck. I couldn't take much more of this beating; in a straight fight I had little chance. Again, I'd hit him, though. I'd felt the second spike go into him, his chest this time. His screech sounded like no sound a human would make. He stepped back, flailing. The lamp got knocked over, but I could still pick out the black smoke rising from his hand as he tried to pluck the stake from his chest, as if the darkness in the room was coming from him.

Not daring to stop, I struck him again, throwing myself at him before he could come for me. This time I caught him in the legs, the third and then the fourth stake finding his flesh. He snarled with the agony of it, writhing, but didn't go down. He'd known what I was capable of. He'd come expecting it – perhaps even welcoming it given what I'd worked out about him. But he'd also calculated that once I'd done my worst, he would still be alive, and we would be trapped together in a stone room. And then the end would come rapidly.

I had one more stake. Bone was briefly occupied with trying to pull the others from his body. I took the opportunity to work a fuller *rearing cobra*, putting as much as I could into the fifth and final stake, making it sing with destructive power. I felt my energies flowing from my gut, down my arm and into the little spike of wood. It seemed to grow hot in my hand, twisting as it hungered for its prey.

I waited for as many moments as I dared, then a beat longer, then threw myself at him. He saw me coming, stepped aside – but not quickly enough. The moves I'd practised and practised had given me speed, too. Speed and grace. Over the gap of years, my grandfather had taught me well. Using both hands, I slammed the wooden stake into Bone's chest. Into his heart, if he still had one.

A small part of me watched what I'd done, and was glad. All that training. All my attempts to uncover the powers and abilities I'd been born with. All my work to uncover my heritage: it had all paid off. I might still not be strong enough to destroy Bone when it came to it – but I was fighting him, and he wasn't winning, for the moment at least. A year previously, that would have been unthinkable.

The vampire staggered backwards into the wall at my blow, howling like an animal with its leg caught in a bear trap, the sound grating shudders through me. He slumped to his knees as he clutched at the fifth stake – but just to touch it with his hands was searing pain. His veins stood out like whip cords as he worked, straining against his own agonies. Perhaps he'd seen there were no more spikes in my hands, and that he had only to extract the ones I'd hit him with for me to be defenceless.

Again, I didn't relent. His body was slumped half within the *Wind that Winnows* circle I'd drawn. I could work with that. I picked up the half-worked incantation, bringing the circle to life with my hand gestures, altering its size and shape to encompass Bone's prone body. The circle didn't have to be a *circle*. It just had to be complete.

I worked quickly, describing the shapes in the air that raised the walls of power I needed: the walls within which the magical wind could spiral and blast, winnowing away the life force of anyone trapped inside.

Too late, he sensed what I was doing. He tried to stand. Either he hadn't thought I was capable of such magic, or he had never seen it before. Now was the moment I needed to hit him hard, take him to the brink of destruction.

I raised the wind, making it rage. Bone was caught within his own personal tornado. It scoured his skin, but went deeper than that, cutting into him, separating his life-force from his body, reducing him to his parts. I put everything I had into it: everything I'd learned, everything I was. I may have screamed from the unrelenting effort of it. Bone writhed and flailed, but couldn't escape the onslaught.

Then, after a battle that lasted long, gruelling moments, the vampire – weakened, agonized, taken by surprise – succumbed.

He fell back to the floor, his eyes closed. For a moment, he looked almost peaceful. I knew it would only be for a moment. The vampire's fierce constitution would bring him round. Perhaps I could have killed him in that moment, attempted to slice his head from his body. Or perhaps he would wake and destroy me before I cut very deep.

That wasn't my plan. With a movement of my hand, I stopped the whirlwind, let the walls containing it drop, then stepped inside. He didn't move. I threaded the iron chain through the eyes cemented into the wall, then wrapped then as tightly around his body as I could, looping them around his tattooed limbs and neck before padlocking the ends together.

He stirred as I did so, expressions of fury flashing across his face. I snapped the last lock into place, stepped back, and raised the containing wall.

Bone stood, the chains preventing him from reaching me. He returned to the task of pulling the stakes from his flesh, the motion awkward with the restrictions of the chains.

He said, "I will kill you in the end. These tricks won't hold me. Chains won't hold me. You know I will destroy you."

I said, "I don't think you will. Because I can offer you the one thing you crave, William Bone."

"What is that?"

"Release."

He laughed a bitter laugh.

"You cannot kill me, Witchfinder. I am too strong. I heal quicker than you can wound me. And if you attack me, even should I try not to, I would defend myself. I would kill you. Don't you think I have tried similar schemes over the years? Don't you think I have longed to put an end to my suffering?"

I circled the creature, held as it was for a moment by the iron chains and the spell I was working. Perhaps his proximity to me lessened his urge to hunt me down. That was my hope.

"You are wrong," I said. "There are ways to achieve this thing. Ways to end your existence."

"The weapon known as Norskrang? That is a myth. There is no such magic. There is no release."

I could have used the Norskgrang artefact I carried with me – but that weapon was reserved for the Warlock. Nor did I want to reveal that I bore such a weapon. The temptation for Bone to rip it from me and end his suffering might be too strong. I carried it with me as a last resort. And there were slow ways to achieve the same thing.

"You say that because you don't know about the magic I wield," I said. "It is too slow for combat, but with a semi-willing victim, and with strong binds of iron and enchantment, it will work. It will leech your life from your body, as surely as any blow from a Norskrang artefact."

A faint light sparked deep in his black eyes. It might have been hope.

"You have done this before?"

I shook my head. "Never. But my grandfather did; he recorded the use of the magic in his journal. A creature not completely like you, but not so different either. Be warned, there is a cost, though."

"What cost?"

"The suffering you will go through as the magic takes hold. It will be gruelling."

The look on his face might have been a grin. "Suffering is nothing."

I knew it wasn't as simple as that. Even if he wished to cooperate, the agonies he would suffer would bring out the animal in him. He might try to kill me even if it meant his survival. I didn't know if he would be able to contain himself – or if I would be able to contain him.

"There is more," I said. "If it works, after you are gone, I want your body."

He hadn't expected that. "What do you want with it, Witchfinder?"

"I want to give it to another."

"Who?"

"You'll see."

"You said you were coming alone."

"I did come alone. But I hope a third will be arriving soon."

"What will this *third* do with my physical form?"

"That will be up to them. But if you need any more persuasion, my hope is to destroy the Warlock."

I saw the hunger in him for that outcome very clearly.

"How long until this other comes?"

"I don't know."

"Pull these cursed stakes from me and we will wait."

"They stay where they are, weakening you."

He consented with an animal snarl. We sat on opposite sides of the room, Bone contained by magic and chains and his own hopes, me watching him warily for signs of betrayal.

In the end, we didn't have to wait long. Less than an hour

passed by before I sensed the approach of the tunnel-dweller. A tendril of faint mist curled from the grating into the room, sniffing the air, feeling the ground. Bone watched it with narrowed eyes. I didn't move. The newcomer was wary. If I scared it away, it might never return.

The sliver of mist found the arm bone I'd brought, curling itself around it as if tasting. The object appeared to be to its liking. The mist solidified and features began to appear. There was the black-cloaked form, the gentle face I'd glimpsed before.

Finally, keeping my voice low, I spoke.

"Take it if you wish. It is a gift."

The mist thinned for a moment, pulling itself back to the grid.

"Wait," I said. "I can offer you something much better. I can give you what you really want."

The mist paused. It didn't vanish, but it didn't solidify either.

"Let me tell you what I believe I know about you," I said. I didn't know anything for sure, but I needed to engage with this strange, shadowy entity. "You were born female. I mean, you were born with a female body. But it was never *you*; it never felt right. You wanted the world to see you as a *he*, or perhaps as neither of those things. You didn't want to be defined by that. You found a home with the black friars; they treated you as a brother. You were happy for a time. But then they found out about you and locked you away. It was a cruel punishment, terrible."

The foggy presence solidified again. I could see the clear outline of its black cloak now, that face watching me from within. There was sadness there, but also fury. Bone looked on from the corner, not speaking.

I continued. "The necklace in your cell. It had been yours as a girl, a memory of your former self. Or perhaps a gift from someone dear, your mother. Perhaps that anchored you, though. You were confused and lost for a long time. Then something changed, and you found your way back into the world. Perhaps you didn't know you were dead at first. You decided to build yourself a new body, construct one that you could possess. Finally walk the earth as the person you wanted to be. That was why every bone you stole was from a male. And you took great care to take only one from each place, to minimize the harm done. You took only old bones, hoping there would be no one left to feel the loss."

The shadowy form finally spoke, a voice that sounded like the distant whistling of the wind. "I didn't wish to cause harm."

"I know. And now I can help you."

"Why would you help me?"

"We can help each other. I can give you a body to possess. Own. *Become.*"

"Who?"

"He is there, chained in the corner."

The mist crept over Bone's body, tasting, touching. Bone suffered the intrusion with a growl.

"Is the form to your liking?" I asked.

"I don't understand what you are saying."

"This body can be yours. It is strong. Powerful. This can be you."

"Why would this one give me his body? Is he your prisoner?"

"He seeks oblivion. You both get what you want."

"You can do this thing?"

"I believe I can."

"Why would you?"

"Because it's the right thing to do. But also because I need you. As with him, there is a cost to you, if you are willing to pay it."

The ghost's suspicion was clear from the way it twisted and writhed. It had been betrayed too often. I explained my plan to both of them: the deception I planned to use to trick my way into the Warlock's presence. The risks they would face. What I was suggesting was so far outside of the bounds of acceptable Office behaviour that I didn't like to consider what the Crow's reaction would be if he learned the truth. I could see no other way, though, weakened and broken as the Office was.

Both were silent for a time after I finished talking. The misty form spoke first. It was brighter, now, its lines drawn more clearly. It longed for this but almost didn't dare hope.

"Will this sorcery work? You say this Warlock has given Bone an invitation into his house. But it won't be Bone returning there; it will just be his body with me inside it."

"In truth, I don't know if it will work. This is all I have. Are you willing to try? I can't guarantee your safety if it goes wrong. Or mine, come to that."

"What will I be if we do this thing? A ghost animating a dead revenant's body. Is such a thing possible? What manner of creature would that make me?"

"I have no idea. I hope that what it makes you is *you*. Perhaps you get to decide what sort of person you become."

"I may become something you fear and despise. You may turn me into a monster, a thing you pursue and try to kill."

"Perhaps. I think it's unlikely, given what I know of the two of you, but if it happens, I will deal with it then."

"You said he is a drinker of human blood."

"Yes."

"Then I would have to be that, too?"

"Yes. I think so."

"The idea repels me."

I ignored the low growl from Bone. "I understand," I said. "I believe we can help you, find ethical sources of sustenance. The recently dead for instance, or willing donors. Then again, we can grow whole body parts from cells these days; perhaps we can do the same with blood."

The light from the ghost dimmed. It said, "Will that work? I don't understand your words."

I turned to Bone. "Well?"

"It might; feeding off carrion can suffice for a time. Or

else the lust for blood may become so overwhelming that you cannot resist it. I have done much that I regret."

To the ghost I said, "I can't say for sure what you will become, or how it will affect you. If we both survive, we may become bitter foes. I am willing to take the risk, but it has to be up to you."

"I will try," the misty form said eventually. "This collecting of bones ... I think I may have strayed from the path of wisdom."

"You were desperate."

"Yes."

"And you don't mind the tattoos?"

"I don't know what they are."

"The markings on his skin."

"I think they're beautiful. They remind me of the pages of the books the Brothers made."

"Bone?" I asked. "Are you willing?"

"I am, human. Give me an end."

"Good. Let us begin."

The magic took long hours to perform. Gradually, I winnowed away Bone's soul, detached it, leaving his body unharmed. The effort of it was gruelling, for Bone and for me, but I refused to relent.

At one point, the agonies of it too much, Bone howled aloud.

"Act quick, human. Do it now or I will tear these chains open and slaughter you where you stand!"

I continued to chant, working the spell, powering it from my own body. But I also kept one hand on Norskrang, in case I needed it. The ghostly form wandered the room, fading in and out, waiting.

There came a moment when Bone, writhing from the agonies, barely human, screamed in his torment.

"End this, human! Enough!"

The pain of the winnowing was too much even for him. I drew Norskrang, ready to use it when Bone tore open his chains and leapt at me.

But Bone, howling, held on. Every muscle in his body was tensed, straining, as if electricity were pulsing through him – and then he stopped. He went suddenly limp.

I placed my hand on his forehead, and I could feel: he was there but not there, his tether to his body, to this world, a mere gossamer thread ready to snap. Bone whispered through gritted teeth to the presence, now hovering nearby.

"What is your name, ghost?"

"Lucian. I was baptised something else, but Lucian."

Bone nodded, absorbing that. "Know that I was good and noble once, before I was changed and killed so many, many people. I had a wife and children who loved me. Please … try and be like that. Use this body well. There has been no joy in my existence for many years."

"I will," said Lucian.

"And you, Witchfinder, destroy the Warlock for what he has done to me."

"I will try," I said.

Bone nodded and closed his eyes for a final time. I felt the moment he was gone. I worked quickly, setting aside my own exhaustion. I dropped the magical wind and began the possession magic that would let Lucian fill the void left by Bone's departing soul.

For a moment, I thought it wasn't going to work, that I wasn't skilled enough, wasn't powerful enough. I persisted. If this failed, everything was lost. Then, gloriously, the mist that was Lucian began to flow into Bone's mouth, like an exhaled breath in reverse. It siphoned into the body and, in a few brief moments, the ghostly presence in the room was gone.

I watched, stepping back, utterly spent. Had I done it? Nothing happened. I was alone with William Bone's dead body.

Then the body twitched and writhed, its limbs moving at random, clenching and relaxing. Moving awkwardly, it heaved itself to a sitting position. Opened its eyes. And I saw: it wasn't Bone in there anymore. It was Lucian.

"Welcome," I said.

Lucian took a while to work out how to move his throat

and mouth muscles, but he got there in the end. There were tears in his eyes as he spoke.

"Hello."

When the dawn came, and Sam unlocked the door to the cell, he watched in surprise as the two of us walked out. Only one had been locked in, and for a time there had been three of us, but now there were two.

"Thank you," I said to Sam. "I did what I had to do. You won't be troubled anymore."

Sam opened his mouth at the sight of us but couldn't find the words to speak.

23 – An Ancient Vampire

> Our battles against the curse of vampirism that has spread throughout the British realm in latter years are, perhaps, our most pressing and serious matter. I did today explain our latest actions in this regard with Mr Gladstone, who went to considerable lengths to express his dismay at the lack of progress in rooting out the scourge. It was his fixed view that the meddling by these troublesome parasites in our national political procedures can no longer be tolerated – and, indeed, that Her Majesty, having been kept apprised of the situation, was of the same view. I assured Mr Gladstone that we would leave no gravestone unturned in our efforts, and that I was sure we would be successful in our effort most certainly within the decade, if not within the very year.
>
> – Isaac Shackleton, Lord High Witchfinder,
> *Personal Journal (written in private cipher),* 1892

Once again, Charnel gazed down from a high window in the Eastern Tower of his castle. He could feel Bone nearby, loping through the woods, bringing with him the despised Shahzan. The boy was alive, but being carried. That was good. He could have his sport with him, make him pay for all the pain and trouble his brood had caused. There was no question about the outcome; the Shahzan boy would die tonight.

And then this would be the end of their vicious foreign folk magic. He would see this Danesh destroyed and he would see the twin killed too, and that would be an end to it. There were no more in the country. The mother was too old and withered to litter any more. He would ensure that no others who might be a threat were allowed in. Once this little difficulty was finally resolved, with Magor gone, Tremaine gone and the Office and Norskrang destroyed, his long life at the heart of events in the country could continue unthreatened. He was safe. The world turned, but he stayed at its centre. A fixed point. As the new Witchfinder General, he would be in the perfect position to ensure his own primacy. There was nothing else that could endanger him.

He descended the stairs. The nagging agony in his leg flared up unexpectedly. Some memory of former fights returning to him. He put the discomfort out of his mind as he strode into the grave bell chamber. This was the place for this confrontation – or, as it had turned out, this torment to be inflicted. The stone slab where Danesh would be laid for the work to be done had been set up in the centre of the room. In the boy's torments, he might even be compelled to sever the bell rope himself, kill his own brother before meeting his own end.

The neatness of it brought the snarl of a smile to Charnel's lips.

A few hours before, slumbering in his catacomb, he thought he'd heard the bell ring, as it had never rung before. Alarmed – an unfamiliar sensation these days – he'd raced to the room to find that all was well. The line and the bell and the statuette were intact, unmoved. The whisper from the spirit possessing the boy at the other end was unaltered. Were vampires capable of dreaming? He never had, so far as he knew, but perhaps this had happened now. In his concern about the danger Shahzan posed, he'd dreamt up the ringing of the bell. Of course, he need not have been concerned. His protections, his trap, were unaffected.

He watched and waited. Within the hour, he would be secure in his position. He would be unassailable.

From the edge of the trees, the castle walls were only a short distance away. We were at the endpoint of so much now. The turning point, one way or another. The Warlock had blighted my life and the lives of my family for so many years, going back before I was even born. The vampire Lord had learned of the dangers posed by my grandfather and had sought to control and limit that power ever since. He'd killed Bi Bi, and then my father. He'd incarcerated Az then controlled me, arranging it so that Earl Grey admitted me into the Office to find out what I was capable of – and to give me dangers to face if it turned out I was too powerful.

I'd survived them all, and now I was here. Now it would end.

Lucian-as-Bone set me down beneath the eaves of the last line of oaks and pines that made up the forest. My phone chose that moment to vibrate. The screen said, simply, *The Crow*. He was lucky; it was the first time I'd had a few dribbles of signal for the past half hour, our trek through the forest. We could have driven up the single-track road, but Lucian had explained that we should approach through the trees, that this was more in keeping with Bone's normal behaviour. How he had known this, I didn't like to think about. Some essence of the vampire's behaviour or muscle-memory seeping through into Lucian's mind.

I picked up the call and spoke in a low voice, my mouth next to the device's microphone.

"Whatever it is, I don't have time. I'm about to…"

The Crow's voice was fuzzy from the poor signal as he interrupted me. "Do you trust me, Danesh?"

"What?"

"Do you trust me?"

Despite the bad reception, there was some iron in his voice that wasn't to be denied.

"I … yeah. Sure."

"Then, in what you are about to do, please trust what I am about to tell you. If you get chance to destroy that monster, despite any words he uses to persuade you or any threats he makes, do it. Do not hesitate. Put an end to it. Do not let anything stop you. Do you promise?"

The grey stone castle loomed against the iron sky ahead

of us. It looked utterly powerful, utterly impenetrable. I could say anything I wanted. It wasn't going to matter whichever way this went.

"I ... sure," I said. "I promise."

There was a fuzz of white noise before his voice came through again. "Dorothy Coldwater is here with me. She is of the same mind. Do not let anything stay your hand. Do you understand? This is very important. If you get close to him, let nothing stay your hand."

"I won't hold back," I said. "You have my word."

"Excellent. And, good luck. Please, I beg you, be as careful as you can."

He rang off. Lucian looked at me questioningly. I shrugged. Was the Crow trying to convey a cryptic message, tell me something he dared not say out loud? Like he was worried I'd be overheard or the message intercepted? Maybe it was just guilt because I was doing this thing and he wasn't.

"No idea," I said. "Come on, let's see if the terms of Bone's Invitation will let you inside. Remember, I'm your prisoner. You don't have to treat me well. You've brought me here so the Warlock can butcher me. Carry me again so it looks like I'm out of it. Remember to plead for your release, show all your impotent fury at the Warlock's control of you. He must suspect nothing."

"And if he realises and attacks us?"

"Then, I'm sorry. At least we'll have tried. We'll do what we can, but it probably won't be enough. It's up to you whether you want to do this. You can just walk away."

Lucian gazed up at the castle, then back to me. In Bone's powerful body, he towered over me. He looked terrifying, but his voice was quiet.

"Let's go. One way or another, let's put an end to this."

He picked me up without any apparent effort – his control of Bone's body was complete now – and strode across the open space towards the walls. I let myself flop as if unconscious. I held Norskrang ready in a little holster I'd rigged up on my wrist. I could bring it to hand in an instant. I also had my usual Office paraphernalia with me, but I knew it would be useless. They were there for show, to say that I'd come armed only with my usual impotent weapons. That I was powerless. I did also have three more stakes from the Lady, carefully carved and ensorcelled. They were my finest work yet. Again, I knew they weren't going to do more than irritate the Warlock. But I quite liked the idea of irritating the Warlock.

Bone hammered upon the great wooden doors, holding me aloft in only one of his powerful arms. Here was the first moment. If Lucian-as-Bone couldn't cross the threshold, I would have to fight the Warlock here, and there would be no element of surprise. I would have very little chance. He wasn't going to let me get close to him once he saw the weapon I wielded. Aware that we were surely being observed, I began to writhe and moan, as if returning to a dim consciousness.

The door was pulled open. A tattered wretch stood there, bent over, his lined skin sallow, his body little more than rags stretched across his bones. A thralled slave, no doubt, a vampire given barely enough power to serve his master. I wondered how many centuries he had been opening the door.

The thrall studied us, despite his milky eyes, then stepped backwards into the gloom of the castle to allow us entry. Lucian played his part well. He didn't step warily across the threshold, wary of being barred or hurled backwards. He strode on through.

For a second, I felt the barriers resisting us, invisible walls of magic pushing us back. They were powerful, stronger than stone, and for a second I thought we weren't going to make it. Then we pierced the veil, and Lucian placed a foot onto the tiles of the Warlock's castle. Then another. We were in.

The thrall led us into the exterior, walking awkwardly as if his bones were no longer properly connected to each other. I glimpsed my surroundings through half-open eyes. The castle was what I would have hoped for in the lair of a powerful vampire: stone walls and oak panels and gold-framed paintings, the fine home of an ancient English aristocrat. We climbed a set of wooden stairs that creaked under Lucian's weight, then turned down a long corridor, past many doors. Finally, the thrall stopped outside a large, arched door, indicating to us that we should go inside.

I could feel in my gut that the ancient vampire we called the Warlock was nearby. Was in that room.

Lucian, still playing his part well, walked in, holding me sideways so I fitted through the doorway. I took in the scene. A raised stone slab stood in the middle of the room, its top flat. It might have been a sarcophagus or the altar of some fallen church – but it looked in that instant more like an operating table. I saw, also, a silvery line descending from a patch of purple fog, hard to focus upon, high up in the vaulted space. I had seen one like that before, of course. Indeed, I had seen the other end of it, leading into Az's grave in Oblivion. This was how the Warlock watched over my brother. A bronze bell hung on this end of it. Next to it on a wooden plinth stood a little statue: a goblin or a demon, its red features twisted and melted as if by fire, its mouth open as if it were talking into the bell.

At first the Warlock was nothing more than a growl echoing from the shadows of the room.

"Set him down on the slab, Bone."

Lucian did as he was told, dropping me hard onto the stone slab. I didn't have to pretend to groan; my back and neck had barely recovered from my battles with Bone.

To my surprise, Lucian spoke.

"This is the last time, vampire. I will help you no more. I will kill no more."

For a second, I though Lucian had betrayed himself, revealed his true nature. Then the Warlock made a sound that might have been an attempt at a laugh.

"This again? I grow weary of your protestations. Leave now. When I have need of you again, I will summon you, and you will obey."

Lucian, his hand still on my shoulder where he had set me down, squeezed me once. The only outward sign he dared make, a gesture of farewell. Then the tattooed figure strode out. I wondered if I would ever see him again.

I wondered if I would ever see anyone else again.

The Warlock emerged from the shadows to stand over me. I had seen the creature before, of course. That day in Downing Street: the tall, hairless figure I'd glimpsed in conversation with Earl Grey. It had been him, relaying his instructions to the Witchfinder General. I couldn't resist flickering my eyes open to study him. There was the same white – almost translucent – skin that I recalled, and the same black robes. I could see his eyes now, though. They were deepest black, just as Bone's had been. It was like staring into two deep wells. The pendant hanging around his neck was a five-pointed star. It was all I could do to remain so close to him without reacting. This creature was an anathema; it screamed wrongness.

He spoke quietly – almost, I thought, warily. He didn't know for sure what I was capable of.

"Ah, excellent, you are awake. If you are conscious, you'll be able to experience everything I am about to do to you. Your brood has given me a great deal of trouble."

He thought I was half-dead, that I'd fought Bone and lost badly. That all my strength and fight was gone. My bruises were real enough. Hoping Lucian was making good his escape, fleeing the castle, I rose to a sitting position, looking around me as if in befuddlement – then slid from the slab to stand shakily, the bulk of the stone table between us. I pulled out two wooden stakes – but not Norskrang, not yet. I needed to be sure that my final strike was true.

I shook off my supposed wooziness, standing tall and straight, then dropping into an attack stance, the stakes held ready. I began to run through the syllables of *Rearing Cobra* in my mind, mouthing them silently. Briefly, I saw alarm on the Warlock's sallow features. He actually took a step backwards.

Then he recovered himself. "It seems you are not quite the broken wretch I had been led to believe. I'm impressed that you managed to trick Bone."

"I did not trick Bone. I gave him what he wanted."

Again, it took the Warlock a second to understand my words.

"And what was that?"

"He must have told you often enough. The end to his suffering. His death."

"Ah, that. Then that was merely Bone's body, animated by magic?"

"Something like that. Enough for me to find your lair and cross your threshold."

I rubbed my thumbs over the stakes in my hands, feeling the grooves of the runes. They would do him some harm. I wanted him to think they were all I had.

The Warlock walked across the room, seemingly deep in thought. Heading, I saw, for the bell and the statue.

The Warlock turned to consider me again. "Well, if I am honest, I had grown tired of Bone. His constant mewling was tiresome. And now you have presented me with another opportunity. I made Bone what he was because he caused me some difficulty many years ago. And now there is you, causing me difficulty. I think I won't end your existence in this room after all. You will make an excellent replacement for Bone. I will mark your skin, call upon you to carry out the killings I wish to see carried out. As with Bone, I will, of course, ensure that you cannot resist my commands, and also that you are fully aware of what you are doing and what you have become. Who shall we start with? Your mother perhaps? This Sally Spender? It will be amusing to make you kill them, look on as your own hand deals the fatal blows. After them, there will be others. Many, many others."

"Why have your pursued us?" I asked. "My family."

"Oh, because I feared you were a threat to me, obviously. I had everything neatly arranged in these islands, then your ilk appeared with your strange and dangerous magic, sorcery I knew nothing about. I needed to understand you. Failing that, control you. Failing that, destroy you. We have now reached the latter of those. You have some power, but you are no real threat. You are disappointing, really; I thought you might be capable of so much more. I shouldn't have waited so long. Now I will finish your line off. Your little wooden sticks cannot harm me."

I threw myself at him, vaulting the stone slab where, no doubt he planned to butcher me, chanting aloud the syllables that would give the stakes their magical edge. If I could time my strike correctly, I could harm him at least. Cause him some pain.

I didn't get close. The Warlock raised a hand, and I was stopped as surely as if I'd run into a wall. Then he plucked me from the ground, thrusting me backwards to punch into the far wall, knocking the wind out of me. I writhed there, pinned to the wall, feet off the ground, unable to do anything.

I still held the stake. The Warlock made a hand movement that did something to the bones in my right hand. Something cracked, and there was an agonizing spike of pain in my wrist. I dropped the stake to the floor.

A joyless smile crossed the Warlock's features.

"Is this it? Is this what I've been afraid of all this time. You are nothing."

Another movement of his fingers, and the stake flew to his hand. A few faint wisps of black smoke rose from him as he gripped it, but he appeared to suffer no discomfort. He clenched his fist and shattered the stake, turning it to splinters, then, turning his hand over, spilling dust to the floor.

He clenched his other hand – the one that had been pinning me to the wall – into a fist, and I fell, crumpling to a heap on the ground.

My own magical power thrummed through me, rising up in revulsion at this creature. I lunged again, spinning into an attack that led with my second stake. The steps and syllables of *Rearing Cobra*.

Again, I didn't get close. This time, the Warlock pinned

me to the ceiling after stopping me, holding me there as if fascinated by the sight of me. A collector studying a pinned butterfly or an interesting bird in the sky.

"You must know you can't defeat me," he said. "Your Office toys have no effect. Your stakes and spells have no effect."

It was hard to speak with my chest pressed to the ceiling. I knew the drop to the distant stone floor would be enough to break a few bones.

"My grandfather harmed you once," I managed, "and I have learned from him."

Again, he twisted my fingers from afar, making me cry in agony and drop the second stake. Again, he drew it to himself and turned it to ash.

"As I say, there is some power in you," he said. "But not enough. You were never enough. I should have destroyed you all years ago."

He let me drop. I flailed in the air, plummeting to the hard ground. I tried but failed to cushion my fall, crunching into the ground. Agonies spiked in my pelvis and chest where I hit, and my right wrist, caught under me, raged with pain.

I refused to relent, forcing myself to stand. If he thought I was no threat, he might allow me to power up the *Rearing Cobra* strike fully. I pulled out another stake – still not Norskrang – and intoned the syllables more slowly, stepping and moving my hand in the required manner. My right hand refused to obey my commands, hanging limply. I switched the stake to my left hand and did what I could.

Spiralling closer to the Warlock, I stabbed hard at the right instant, on the required word. This time the Warlock didn't even bother to bat me away. He held out his hand, palm flat, and let the spike slice through him.

He wrenched the stake free of my grip, then studied it, fascinated as black smoke curled off his hand. After a few seconds, he pulled it from his flesh and crushed it as he'd crushed the others.

"Enough of this," he said. "Now you will die. Die and

be reborn as my slave. But first, there is one other death to take care of. One that concerns you. It amuses me to know that this will be your last act as a free human. You do so value your supposed freedom, don't you?"

I stepped back, panting, spent. He was right; I couldn't come close to defeating him. But there was no one else.

"This silver line," he said. "I assume you know what lies at the other end?"

"My brother."

"Very good. And this statuette. Are you familiar with it?"

I shook my head.

"Let me enlighten you. Your brother is possessed by a spirit that longs to destroy him, eat away his soul. But this statuette houses another soul, the spirit of a sorcerer trapped in there long ago. You should be grateful of this artefact. It has been keeping your brother alive all this time. Whispering the spells that subdue your brother's possessing spirit. Listening to its replies."

The Warlock placed his white hand on top of the statuette.

"You see, even if you could harm me, I am protected. Even if there is some trick that your Hardknott-Lewis has taught you, or that you learned from your grandfather, I am protected. I have only to smash this statuette, dash it to the floor, and your poor little brother dies instantly. And you would never dare risk such a thing, would you? If it came to it, this would stop you. Would stop any of you. The *compassion* you feel, the *love*: how it weakens you. You are so attached to your twin, you would probably die rather than see him killed."

"My brother would gladly see you killed," I said.

The Warlock waved that away. "It doesn't matter. Here is what is going to happen. Entertainment is so hard to come by for one my age. *You* will smash this statuette. *You* will kill your brother. This shall be the first killing you will carry out at my command. The first of many."

"No." I said.

"Yes," said the Warlock.

He held up his hand to work his magic, his palm facing me and his fingers splayed as if I were his puppet and he were pulling invisible strings. And I felt his mind overwhelm mine, seize it, devour it. There was nothing I could do to resist his terrible strength. I cowered, terrified, destroyed, my hind brain screaming with primordial visions. The demons that lurk in the darkness beyond the campfire. I was utterly powerless to resist. I took a step forward. And then another.

Except: the faintest flame flickered in the darkness of my consumed mind. I hadn't only learned the movements of combat magic; I had learned to be myself. Everything I was; all that I had laboured over; all my powers and strength and determination; the people I loved: they all amounted to that faint flame; the tiniest space within the darkness where my will could live. Such a small, weak, thing. A candle in the vast night. I was reduced to that, but I was not destroyed.

Here was the second moment. I had promised the Crow I wouldn't hold back if I could get close enough to the Warlock. Here was how I could do it – but the risks were terrible. Did I trust the Crow? I'd told him I did, but I also knew what succumbing meant. Knew I might lose myself in the storm of the Warlock's mind control. And if I let that happen, one way or another, there was going to be death. The question was, whose?

I chose. I let myself be pulled along, pulled closer to the Warlock. I could feel Norskrang in its holster on my forearm, even as I stepped again and I was one stride away.

"Now you will smash the statuette," the vampire said. His willpower flared up, and the hunger of it controlled me. The flicker of light within me dimmed. I thought about my brother and my mother. My father and grandfather. Sally. The Crow and Kerrigan and the Lady. Zubrasky and Stonewall and all the rest of them. I thought about the things they'd told me and the things they'd done for me, and I tried to hold on.

The Warlock, seeing me resist, exerted his will even

more, and there was finally nothing I could do. The inner light was snuffed out. I tried to speak the mantras I'd learned into the darkness of my mind, the quiet words of power that kept my will my own, but my voice was silent.

My mutinous limbs, meanwhile, obeyed the commands of the ancient vampire. I lifted the statue from its plinth. It was a hideous thing, twisted goblin features leering at me. I held it above the stone ground, hearing the endless babble of whispers coming from it.

"Let go," the Warlock said. "Smash it. Be assured your brother will feel it. The possession will run rampant, but he'll be aware of it. He'll die alone and lost, confused and terrified, and you'll have done it to him. Smash it."

Do you trust me?

I ... yeah. Sure.

The Warlock's willpower was a clenched fist around my mind. And all I could do was to let the statue slip through my fingers, dashed to the hard floor, smashed to a thousand shards. The faint whispering sound became louder, louder, became something like the beat of the wings of a thousand butterflies, then a thousand birds thronging the air around us. From somewhere I heard a cry of anguish – that of a young boy – and the silver thread fell from the ceiling to land in a coil upon the ground, a mere length of rope, all light from it gone.

The Warlock laughed. I had killed my brother, and I was utterly in his control, and he laughed.

The tiny flame within me rekindled. For this instant the Warlock was so sure of himself, so sure I was beaten, so triumphant, that he let his control slip that tiny amount.

Here was the brief, final moment we had bought.

I pulled Norskrang from its holster and buried it deep into the Warlock's chest.

The vampire's laughter stopped. Amazement entered his eyes as he studied me, intimately close as we were. He clutched at his chest. Thick coils of black smoke were roiling off him, the stench like old, old bones burning.

He spoke one more word, putting all his confusion and fear and fury into the one syllable.

"But..."

"A gift from Stonewall," I said.

And then The Warlock was writhing and shaking, and his iron grip on my will fell away. I stepped back to watch in silence as he flailed and sank to his knees. He gripped the end of the stake to pull it from him, but his hands burned where he touched the wood. His flesh became fire, raging through him. Consuming him.

He screamed once, a strangled, agonized cry – and died. In a few moments, all that was left of him was a long pile of ancient dust, neatly cradling the spike of wood that had destroyed him. The remains of a person who had died a long, long time ago but that had only just stopped moving.

I collapsed to sit on the altar, panting, waiting and watching to see if anything else would happen, if others would come running. But all was quiet in the ancient castle.

Four of us filed into Oblivion in our *Inimical Dimension Exploration Suits*. Beware the march of IDES. The Crow went first, followed by the Lady, then Olwen and then me. I moved slowly, each step a chorus of agonies from my injuries. Olwen and I carried the magically-charged iron spikes we would need. The Crow carried a simple linen sheet. Four people to remove two others from the life-stopping ice of that terrible domain. One of them still living, the other gone.

No one spoke over the crackly intercom. The rush of my breathing was loud in my ears. The words the Crow had uttered outside ran around in my head; we'd been alone for a moment as we'd pulled on our clumsy suits.

"I have to thank you, Danesh, for everything you have done. Your methods have allowed you to succeed where anyone else, myself included, would not. Defeating the Warlock is a remarkable achievement."

I'd seen by the wary look in his eye that he knew precisely what I'd done with the magic I'd learned from my grandfather, despite my efforts at concealment. He knew that I'd allowed Lucian-as-Bone to walk free. His words were, what, an admission that his beloved Office was inadequate? It was no time to cause him further pain – but he carried on, determined to say what he wanted to say. Perhaps he was trying to distract himself from what we were about to do.

"I told you I might be the last Witchfinder General. I think that is right. The Office as we know it surely cannot survive for much longer, but I thank you for showing me there is another way. That something more effective can perhaps emerge from our ruins. It is a notion that I have resisted for too long."

I chose not to say that I thought he was correct.

Now, we stopped at the plot where the silvery line dropped out of the sky to pass through the ice into the ears of the torpid boy inside. His red jumper and blue jeans. His eyes were shut now, though. That was a change. Even in Oblivion, his final death had had its effect. The Crow severed the line with a pair of silver scissors, then set about driving the iron spikes into the ice, marking out the small, small rectangle we would need to excavate the lifeless form out of Oblivion. Olwen joined in. I did the same, as best as I could. Some enchantment in the spikes – or maybe it was just because they were iron – allowed us to push them down without too much effort. We drove them in at an angle to form a V-shaped wedge. Then, labouring in our clumsy suits, the four of us levered it out onto the surface.

The ice surrounding him was already beginning to melt, fall away from his small form. That didn't make a lot of sense, but of course it was a mistake to expect Oblivion to follow the more usual laws of physics. The melting accelerated as the Crow knelt to place his hands on the body.

His voice came over the suit intercom, then, his words husky. Whether he meant us all to hear, I didn't know.

"I should have given you this release a long time ago. I let you linger, but I was doing it for my benefit, not yours. I see that now. I hope you can forgive me. You were always a kind boy, always thoughtful. I think you'd have liked the idea that your final death saved the life of another. I hope so. I hope so."

I put my gauntleted hand onto the Crow's shoulder. He didn't respond. When Gregory's blue skin began to emerge from the ice, the Crow covered his form in the sheet.

The second grave was nearby. Once again, we drove in the spikes to form a wedge of Oblivion ice. We soon had another small form lifted from the ground. This time, I held him as the ice sloughed away, watching as my brother's features appeared.

"Quickly now." The Crow said. "He's exposed to the atmosphere. We have to get him out."

Moving frustratingly slowly in our bulky suits, we headed to the glowing purple blue gateway, me carrying Az, the Crow carrying Gregory, Olwen the spikes and the Lady the watchpiece she'd retrieved from Gregory's grave. The one she and Hardknott-Lewis had switched just as they'd switched the grave rope, transferring the possession from Az to Gregory in the hope that the Warlock wouldn't notice the brief disruption. She'd told me it was dangerous and difficult magic, but that the watchpiece I'd embedded in Az's grave had allowed her to work out the nature of the long magic the Warlock had been using, listen in to the whispered syllables that had kept the possession in check. That was what they'd been working on when I'd called the Crow to retrieve the three keys, as Bone had died, as Lucian and I had made our way north. The Crow hadn't explained what it was they were attempting: at that point, they hadn't known if it was going to succeed. There'd been a good chance that none of them was going to return from Oblivion.

Three women waited for us on the other side of the portal: my mother and two I didn't know. Members of the local chapter of the Pale Sisters, I assumed. They kneeled over Az as we worked our way out of our suits. My brother still hadn't moved. I watched as they worked magic, weaving complicated patterns in the air over his body, half-speaking and half-singing a flowing sequence of syllables.

Olwen and the Crow, Gregory still in his arms, left us. The Crow glanced at me but didn't see me, his eyes glass. We had destroyed the Warlock, destroyed the Order of the British Vampire just as we'd destroyed English Wizardry. In the moment, none of it seemed important. My mother gripped my hand while we looked on, helpless to do anything else.

The moments stretched out. I caught nervous glances passing between the two women. The Lady knelt to join them once she was free of her suit, working spells of her own, a frown of concentration on her features. I could feel the repeated rush of the magic being worked, jolting again and again through my brother.

The Lady stopped working her spells, kneeling up, leaving one hand on Az's forehead.

"Will he make it?" I asked. "Will he wake up?"

She took a long moment to reply. "He's been in there for a long time, the possession gnawing away at him. I think, in the end, it depends on how much spirit he has."

He was too far gone. His little lifeless form would remain forever frozen. The room was silent. A look passed between my mother and I. She was thinking the same thing, all her luxurious, terrible hope fading.

Then, movements began to play across Az's features, like he was practising unfamiliar expressions: fear, surprise, delight.

Finally, with a flicker of his lids, he opened his eyes. He looked to our mother, then to me. Confusion clouded his features for a moment, then his amusement swept it away. He laughed, as if I were the funniest thing he'd ever seen.

He reached out a wobbly hand to me. "But you're so old! What's happened to you, Danesh?"

END

Acknowledgements

As ever, my thanks to my wonderful wife and our two daughters. All of this is for you. My eternal gratitude also to Elsewhen Press for believing in these books, and for producing them with such care and good humour despite all the threats of the Office of the Witchfinder General. Thanks also to Andrew and Anthony Walton for the many gigs – including the one whose location inspired The Shuttered Lantern.

A special mention, also, to my mother, who we lost during the writing of this book, and who would not have enjoyed it at all – but who gave me a love of books and reading. When I was a young boy, she would take me on the bus to the local public library, and to her exasperation I would have them all read before we got home. Happy days.

As with the previous three volumes in this history, I'd like to extend a special thank you to "The Whisperer", my contact in the Welsh Division of the Office of the Witchfinder General, without whom details of the Office's inner workings couldn't have been brought to light. The continued co-operation of "Danesh" is appreciated, and I very much hope that he survives the Office's current difficulties.

Elsewhen Press
delivering outstanding new talents in speculative fiction

Visit the Elsewhen Press website at elsewhen.press for the latest information on all of our titles, authors and events; to read our blog; find out where to buy our books and ebooks; or to place an order.

Sign up for the Elsewhen Press InFlight Newsletter at elsewhen.press/newsletter

Also by Simon Kewin

SIMON KEWIN'S WITCHFINDER SERIES
"Think *Dirk Gently* meets *Good Omens*!"

THE EYE COLLECTORS
A STORY OF
HER MAJESTY'S OFFICE OF THE WITCHFINDER GENERAL
PROTECTING THE PUBLIC FROM THE UNNATURAL SINCE 1645

When Danesh Shahzan gets called to a crime scene, it's usually because the police suspect not just foul play but unnatural forces at play.

Danesh Shahzan, an Acolyte in Her Majesty's Office of the Witchfinder General – a shadowy arm of the British government fighting supernatural threats to the realm – is called in to investigate a murder in Cardiff. The victim had been placed inside a runic circle and their eyes carefully removed from their head. But there are wider implications…
ISBN: 9781911409748 (epub, kindle) / 9781911409649 (288pp paperback)

THE SEVEN SUCCUBI
THE SECOND STORY OF
HER MAJESTY'S OFFICE OF THE WITCHFINDER GENERAL

Of all the denizens of the circles of Hell, perhaps none is more feared among those of a high-minded sensibility than the succubi.

The Office of the Witchfinder General may employ 'demonic powers' so long as their use is 'reasonable' and 'to defeat some greater supernatural threat'. After recent events Acolyte Danesh Shahzan had been struggling to define 'reasonable'. Then an unexpected evening visit from his boss to discuss his succubi thesis presaged another investigation.
ISBN: 9781915304117 (epub, kindle) / 9781915304018 (334pp paperback)

HEAD FULL OF DARK
THE THIRD STORY OF
HIS MAJESTY'S OFFICE OF THE WITCHFINDER GENERAL

Quis custodiet ipsos custodes?

There is clearly someone in the Office of the Witchfinder General who is working for or with English Wizardry, and Danesh and the Crow are determined to track them down. It might even be one of the Lord High Witchfinders. Who can they trust? Can Danesh even trust the Crow?

To ensure the traitor is not alerted, Danesh conducts an off-the-books investigation under cover of an inquiry into a cold case. But not all cold cases stay cold; not all dead witches stay dead; and not all traitors stay hidden…

… and what is the significance of the goat's skull?
ISBN: 9781915304384 (epub, kindle) / 9781915304285 (338pp paperback)
Visit bit.ly/WitchfinderSeries

ALSO BY SIMON KEWIN

Red Dragon
A Bestiary of Modern Britain
Dr Miriam Seacastle
2022 FACSIMILE EDITION

Elsewhen Press are pleased to be able to produce this facsimile of the 1999 illustrated, limited edition privately published by the author but since unobtainable.

"Dr Seacastle's … Bestiary was the product of a great deal of solid research and investigation. It is a short volume … but there is much in the book that is precise. Not only that, she makes several rather inciteful remarks about actions taken by Her Majesty's Office of the Witchfinder General over the decades."
– **Simon Kewin**, author and OWG scholar

The original edition has all but disappeared, but we temporarily gained access to a copy from the library of the Cardiff Office of the Witchfinder General, from which we have been able to create this facsimile edition.

"A must-have for historians, students, and those interested in the OWG or indeed protecting modern Britain." – **Sally Spender**

An invaluable collector's item.
ISBN: 9781915304155 (epub, kindle) / 9781915304056 (72pp paperback)
Visit bit.ly/RedDragon-Seacastle

YOU MIGHT ALSO LIKE

King Street Run

V. R. Ling

To Thomas, archaeology was time travel... little did he know how literal that would turn out to be.

King Street Run is a satirical fantasy thriller set among the iconic buildings of contemporary Cambridge.

Thomas Wharton, an archaeology graduate, becomes drawn into the problems of a series of anachronistic characters who exist in the fractions of a second behind our own time. These characters turn out to be personifications of the Cambridge Colleges; they have the amalgamated foibles, history, and temperament of their Fellows and students and, together with Thomas, must enter into a race against time to prevent their world being destroyed by an unknown assailant.

At the age of six V.R. Ling (Victoria) watched the TV adaptation of *The Hitchhiker's Guide To The Galaxy* and it sparked a life-long love for science fiction and fantasy (she therefore considers the first five years of her life to have been a waste). Science and fiction have separately shaped her life; the science part came in the form of a degree in archaeology, a Masters in biological anthropology, and then a PhD in biological anthropology from King's College, Cambridge. On the fiction front, Victoria is influenced by the likes of H.G Wells, Jules Verne, M.R James, Charles Dickens, Wilkie Collins, and many others. Victoria by name, Victorian by nature. She is a huge animal lover, vegan, loves sixties music, adores classic *Doctor Who*, and has an antique book collection that smells as good as it looks.

ISBN: 9781915304513 (epub, kindle) / 97819153041414 (304pp paperback)

Visit bit.ly/KingStreetRun

YOU MIGHT ALSO LIKE

The Vanished Mage

Penelope Hill and J. A. Mortimore

A vanished mage…
  A missing diamond…
    The game is afoot.

"From Broderick, Prince of Asconar, Earl of Carlshore and Thorn, Duke of Wicksborough, Baron of Highbury and Warden of Dershanmoor, to My Lady Parisan, King's Investigator, greetings. It has been brought to my attention that a certain Reinwald, Master Historian, noted Archmagus and tutor to our court in this city of Nemithia, has this day failed to report to the duties awaiting him. I do ask you, as my father's most loyal servant, to seek the cause of this laxity and bring word of the mage to me, so that my concerns as to his safety be allayed."

The herald delivered the message word-perfect to The Lady Parisan, Baroness of Orandy, Knight of the Diamond Circle and Sworn Paladin to Our Lady of the Sighs. Parisan's companion, Foorourow Miar Raar Ramoura, Prince of Ilsfacar, (Foo to his friends) thought it a rather mundane assignment, but nevertheless together they ventured to the Archmagus' imposing home to seek him. It turned out to be the start of an adventure to solve a mystery wrapped in an enigma bound by a conundrum and secured by a puzzle. All because of a missing diamond with a solar system at its core.

Authors Penelope Hill and J. A. Mortimore have effortlessly melded a Holmesian investigative duo, a richly detailed city where they encounter both nobility and seedier denizens, swashbuckling action, and magic that is palpable and, at times, awesome.

ISBN: 9781915304186 (epub, kindle) / 9781915304087 (212pp paperback)

Visit bit.ly/TheVanishedMage

YOU MIGHT ALSO LIKE

Galata

Ben Gribbin

'Seven days.
Seven deaths.
Seven brides for seven rivers…'

It is New Year's Day. The city of Galata, with its ancient river-streets, is slowly sinking into the sea. But for one week its citizens want to forget this, and celebrate the city's thousand-year anniversary.

For Joseph, a jaded ex-detective, the day brings a glimmer of hope. Last night he met and kissed Celice, a free-spirited artist. Tonight he is meeting her again. But Celice never turns up.

Then her body is pulled out of the canal.

There are papers on her; charred at the edges, with mysterious writing on them. As Joseph teams up with his former police colleague J. D, they discover this may be just the first in a series of eerily similar crimes that took place on exactly the same week, 100 years ago.

Is history about to repeat itself? And can they stop it happening again?

ISBN: 9781915304391 (epub, kindle) / 9781915304292 (162pp paperback)

Visit bit.ly/Galata-Ben-Gribbin

YOU MIGHT ALSO LIKE

LACUNA
CHIMERA
Part One

Erin Hosfield

**You can abandon your past…
but your secrets won't abandon you.**

As a tattooist, it's easy keeping people at arm's length. Distract them with questions, and when they inevitably ask their own, reply vaguely. Lie. When the lies pile up, disappear.

It's a cycle Lynna's all too familiar with. Staying guarded is a necessity, but what keeps her safe is also what keeps her lonely. It's an empty existence, hiding behind lies, and she wishes she was someone else. Someone not burdened with a secret.

A year into her most recent move, the loneliness bleeds into her work, and she admits a few truths. At the insistence of a client, she explores the city's night scene, where she meets the enigmatic Rhys. As the months progress, so do her feelings for him, despite the risks of getting too close. When a dangerous encounter leads her straight into his arms, she abandons her past in exchange for a new beginning, only her secret refuses to be abandoned. With her life hanging by a thread, she's forced to confess, but the secret that will change everything isn't hers.

Set in an alternate present, *LACUNA* opens with Lynna's transition to an atmospheric northwestern city. Derailed from what she's built, she finds herself immersed in the lush world of medicinal horticulture, enveloped in the kind of close-knit relationships she always craved. Her fantasy has become reality, but not without caveat. As she plunges further into this new life, she begins to expose the conflicting threads holding it together, and what she discovers will bring more questions than answers.

ISBN: 9781915304537 (epub, kindle) / 97819153041438 (386pp paperback)

Visit bit.ly/Chimera-Lacuna

About Simon Kewin

Simon Kewin is a pseudonym used by an infinite number of monkeys who operate from a secret location deep in the English countryside. Every now and then they produce a manuscript that reads as a complete novel with a beginning, a middle and an end. Sometimes even in that order.

The Simon Kewin persona devised by the monkeys was born on the misty Isle of Man in the middle of the Irish Sea, at around the time The Beatles were twisting and shouting. He moved to the UK as a teenager, where he still resides. He is the author of over a hundred published short stories and poems, as well as a growing number of novels. In addition to fiction, he also writes computer software. The key thing, he finds, is not to get the two mixed up.

He has a first class honours degree in English Literature and an MA in Creative Writing (distinction). He's married and has two daughters.